A Man, a Dog and a Ball

In July of 2010, during a visit with my family I had an opportunity to have a discussion of an unpleasant nature with my father. I have been a disappointment to him in my years on this world. I'll not forget how my frustration grew as he told me my writing was garbage, all while he held a copy of *To Kill a Mockingbird*. He mentioned that the book he held was a classic and my writing was not even comparable.

The gathering was a birthday celebration for family members and for a strange reason I chose not to engage his taunts. My pal and loyal friend, Coda was by my side so I disengaged the discourse, took the tennis ball he loves to chase and tossed it with him. I settled my rising frustration while tossing the ball to the black lab who loved me, regardless of my past. After a while it was time to eat and that is just what we did.

Soon after eating we got into the car and left, offering our goodbyes. We weren't on the road but a few moments as I wrestled over my father's instigating ways. The words he spoke became a challenge. I looked to Tracy and the words *Man, Dog, Ball* passed my lips and the idea for a classic piece was born.

Coda and his ball was my avenue of keeping the peace. I thought about the storyline on the four hour drive home. Since that time the story has evolved into what you are about to read. My father's disparaging comments inspired this bit of scribing. My God gave me my particular gifts in weaving stories. My dog, Coda and his fondness of chasing tennis balls became a therapy for me and a lost anger. My partner and Love, Tracy supported my efforts in all ways imaginable.

It is our hope that we can help animal causes through the appreciation of the story.

MH. Petry

A Man, a Dog and a Ball

by Martin H. Petry

A Man, a Dog and a Ball

Henry Peters woke to the first day of spring. The cool of the morning's air lacked the harsh cruelty as Old Man Winter's grip faded with the lengthening of light each coming day. Henry remembered as a boy the joy which came with the warming of spring. In his younger years the anticipation of summer adventures and discoveries in nature had always been a hopeful time. Henry wondered if he'd ever know that anticipation again. Days like today made that wonder the more painful for him because the anticipation of adventure and discovery motivated him to jump out of bed and prepare himself for the day. During the winter, the biting cold made comfort of the body reason enough to dress as quickly as he did when he sought adventures and discoveries of boyhood. In his thirtieth year he missed those days of boyhood. Getting out of bed had become an empty chore.

Henry sat up and swung his legs to the floor. He stretched his arms and shook his head, beginning his morning ritual. His house was familiar to him. He knew every piece of furniture and every piece of décor. He chose his liking of all except those things given to him by his community for appreciation. He had plaques on the walls for community service of one type or another. Other items were tributes of thanks for his generosity in donations of money or time. The truth of Henry's belongings demonstrated an inverse to most others. He had less of his own chosen furniture than those things given to him by the community.

Henry made his way to the kitchen after a visit to the bathroom and began making a simple breakfast for himself. His manners were frugal and his nature was simplistically complex. Henry fulfilled his need for the morning as he did any other day. He did so without the need of a clock. It had been quite some time since he needed a clock to manage his days. His doings of the years offered him freedom over any need to earn a living, his time was his own.

After his breakfast of some favorite fruit and toast washed down by carrot juice, he took his one cup of coffee into his office. His office was more of a functioning library. The shelves he built after he bought his home some years ago were deep inserted structures that stood on the floor and reached to the ceiling. His skill as a master carpenter was depicted along the crown molding of the casing by a hand carved timeline of the Earth's seasons. Each season displayed upon the specific wall of direction. North was winter, East was spring, South was summer and West was autumn. Those who visited his home and took council in his house considered it to be a masterpiece and work of art. The sculpture was his recollection as a boy, seeking adventure and discovery throughout the seasons. Many times he was asked to reproduce the work, but he had no such desire.

Today was the day that Mr. Smith would come by and collect books that Henry donated to the Library. Mr. Smith came once a month. Typically, in a day Henry would read two books, if not three. He really didn't have a favorite type of book to read. His enjoyment of reading only resulted in a greater amount of knowledge he could draw from in helping people through issues they faced in attaining a better type of life. And that was Henry's vocation of these days.

Henry would spend the first part of the morning reading. Most folks weren't yet to their jobs of the day. He'd take the time to process information he thought people would need, based upon a system he used of his own design to let folks seek his advice. They would submit a request and depending on the request Henry would begin working on it within the week. Sometimes those requests would require Henry to leave his house so as to determine a course of action. Other times Henry could listen to the request over the phone and stay in his office working on the details as they were revealed to him. The mornings allowed him quiet time to absorb the knowledge he'd need to facilitate his vocation.

After the rest of the world became busy; Henry's day was fulfilled by reviewing requests folks submitted. He typically chose one request out of every five he got. Henry chose the one need that he could respond to which would provide solutions to at least three of the four he denied. Plainly what Henry did was to consider all the issues at hand and show those with their need how through cooperation they could all realize satisfaction in assisting others for their own benefit. Henry was indeed a problem solver possessing great wisdom.

æ

The people in his community watched Henry grow from a young man to one of the youngest town fathers anyone ever knew. Henry's place in the community was as deeply rooted as any other; it was that way because those in town raised him from an early adolescent after his parents had died in a terribly freakish accident.

During a town festival on a beautiful summer day all appeared to be well for the localities celebration of the day, tragedy struck. A young and well liked couple, recent to the community met with unlikely and unforeseen disaster for participating. Henry Peters and his wife Kimberly-Lee took up some grass in the common under the majestic oak tree on the town green. Henry was a carpenter by trade and Kimberly-Lee had been a college professor at a prestigious University close to town. She retired when they came to be in a family way, so as to raise Henry Junior. They were a model family in a working class community of good integrity.

Most who recalled the disaster remembered it to happen just after the noon hour. The weather was perfect for a summer afternoon and all hopes for the day were abundant. There was a slight breeze as most remember, and while the Peter's family was enjoying a picnic a strange gust of wind blew across the green. By all accounts of recollection the gust offered the nuisance of blowing unsecured items around that required folks to chase down what the gust dislodged. Without warning, the mighty oak which offered the Peter's family shade from the sun yielded a large portion of the tree's top. Henry senior only had enough time to pick up his son and use his strength as a carpenter to toss the boy from harm's way. Henry Junior was tossed away from the crushing injury far enough to survive the collapse, but he did endure injuries that left him comatose as the great branches of the top remained longer than his father's ability to toss him. The celebration of the day came to a sudden end while a community mourned the loss of two fine parents, leaving behind an orphaned son.

Both Henry and Kimberly-Lee had no other family so there was no next of kin to notify. Moreover, the condition of Henry Junior lingered and in the memory of his well respected parents the town decided that Henry junior would be a town son as he recovered. Henry Junior recovered, but he had no recollection of the event. Doctors couldn't explain his complete amnesia. For his loss, he never knew any loss. It was as though nothing had ever happened. He was just simply Henry Peter and from those days of recovery the community marveled at his ability to learn.

As Henry's parents were diligent in their affairs, they had seen to the business of the worst. There was a life insurance policy and they had named custodians for Henry Junior. As Henry was placed into their care it was only a short time that they could see to the duty of caring for him. Henry Senior and Kimberly-Lee took confidence in a couple who Henry knew through business dealings. Henry had been contracted by the town's younger bank officer to do some work on the home he and his wife wanted as the house they'd raise their family in after they had children. It was to be their dream house. Thomas and Jennifer Carlson were the named custodians of Henry Junior as they were very close friends to Henry and Kimberly-Lee Peters. The custodianship seemed to be a perfect match and a town's mourning was met with the best possible outcome.

It was only a few years after Henry was living with the Carlson's when another tragedy fell to the community. Thomas and Jennifer Carlson were still trying to have their family when that came to an end during a trip to a ground-breaking ceremony of a building complex that Thomas' bank was funding. He and his wife were both expected at the 3PM ceremony in the adjacent town. During their journey to the ceremony they met with disaster when the brakes on a truck failed. They happened to be at the wrong place at the wrong time when the out of control truck flipped over and slid down the roadway they were on. There would be no Carlson family in the town's future, just a ceremony of burial with urns of these deceased as the departed.

Thomas and Jennifer could have never imagined that they'd be victim of such a hapless ending, but because they were as diligent as the Peters in business, they, as diligent custodians invested Henry's life insurance policy. At the age of sixteen Henry once again faced life alone, but did so with a town's compassion.   Henry wasn't a liability to anyone. The money invested from the life insurance policy became an annuity after the Carlson's deaths. As Henry was a well liked young man, the probate magistrate of the county who knew Henry and his parents asked if he had a preference of the remaining two year of his age of minority. Henry was an exceptionally bright and gifted young man and the probate magistrate saw no need of employing the inner wheels of the bureaucracy used to determine a foster parent function.

The greater surprise for the magistrate was Henry's answer. Henry chose to remain to his years of age of majority with an elderly couple he seemed to favor, who had recently come to some difficult times. He indicated to the magistrate that he liked the thought of being able to help run the business of their farm as a young man wanting to know more of the mysteries of growing crops. After the magistrate heard Henry's choice he took council with the town fathers, sharing the request. During the time it took to make the calls Henry sat in the magistrate's office and read a book completely on state law written for agriculture affairs.

After the unanimous support from the town fathers the magistrate spoke to the Clemson couple, requesting their audience. After the time it took for the elderly couple to arrive, the magistrate informed them of Henry's choice, to which to they agreed. Henry's special qualities of living within the community were born on that day and his contributions to the community had just begun.

Œ

After the morning read, Henry made ready for Mr. Smith's arrival. Mr. Smith was a long time friend of Henry's and he looked forward to the monthly visits of gathering up Henry's donations. Usually Henry would speak to his latest project, while they loaded up Mr. Smith's trunk with the boxes of books.

It was a bit of a surprise to Mr. Smith when Henry told him it would be likely that for some time there wouldn't be any more need to pick up books. After the men were done with the effort Mr. Smith accepted the news of halting the pick-ups. He wondered why Henry was making such a change but he didn't ask about it, he figured Henry was thinking of something else. Mr. Smith knew Henry as a thoughtfully forthright man. He felt as though maybe Henry was thinking of doing something for himself, something like a vacation. Mr. Smith was a man of simplicity and his business of the day was to serve function. He saw to the needs of the library as it required maintenance and quite honestly a large part of the books Henry donated were still stacked up waiting to be categorized. He'd miss the monthly visits, but he was comfortable in thinking that he'd see Henry about in town over the missed appointments. Mr. Smith got in his car and left, carrying the last load of donated books he'd ever pick up from Henry's house.

Once Mr. Smith was gone Henry decided that instead of his usual business he'd spend the day taking a walk, like he did as a boy trying to find adventure and discovery. The winter departed gave him great longing for the innocence of his boyhood. Henry's motivation to his vocation became more difficult to summon each day. He took his coffee cup back to the kitchen and tidied up before he left for the stroll.

Leaving his house, Henry's mood followed along with him. He walked, feeling a chill to his usual nature. The chill wasn't a physical sensation, rather like a sense of losing himself. The friends he saw along his walk he met cordially and greeted. Some of those he went to school with were busy with their young families. The ladies who were interested in finding husbands who knew Henry as a bachelor had long since given up on him. The truth of the ladies in his town was that they'd given up having interest in him. What they wanted out of life he truly had no interest in pursuing. Henry was a man who served adventure and discovery and honestly friends of his, male or female were pursuing paths in life which were average in his eyes.

Along his walk Henry thought of all the places he'd been. In his vocation he traveled extensively, helping folks out. His potential from living with the Clemson couple had extended to places that many in his town would never visit. His expertise of reading took him to foreign lands.

Usually the need was for things such as problem solving construction issues that engineers were stymied by. They'd arrive at a place to begin a project unaware that they would suffer a cultural gap. As Henry was fluent in so many languages he could bridge conveyance of differences between those hired to oversee the work as well as those employed to do the work from the area. Sometimes Henry would bring his own innovation to the issue so as to marry the distinction of difference. Henry walked beyond his neighborhood's distribution of structure and road surface to the fields of nature he loved as a boy. His town wasn't large and his own home was in the outskirts of the planned area. Henry was a very fit man and his pace of walking was as unusual as his tendency to deliver solutions that would take others eternities to arrive at.

As the sun rose in the sky and the ground warmed the softness his steps found on the path of his journey did little to comfort him. He continued the trek seeking some clue of innocence yearned. He thought of those things he had a hand in over the years to which he dedicated himself. In each step he took there was reflection of deeds to be counted. The satisfaction for his past only amounted to a half empty glass of water. He pressed on, examining his life and all he accomplished. He wondered what it all meant to his own purpose. It came to be noontime and Henry found himself to be at a place that was magical to him in his younger years. It was there where the trees draped themselves, whispering secrets to him while he sat upon the altar of nature, perched above a mountain stream. He remembered spending time as a young boy listening to the trees' ancient stories. He heard them explain the mysteries of winter's imprisonment yielding to the liberation of the spring setting in all things alive. It was then that the anticipated adventure and discovery he waited for became his to conquer. Yet, on that day no mystery was revealed. What he found the day to be was just another day of passing, pointing to a future of subliminal existence.

Henry departed his once enchanted location. He began his way back to his home wondering what he could do to revive his love of interest in life. He thought of those he met in his days and realized that as good of character they were, none of them could fulfill his core need. For all of his days, he'd lived to help them with his wisdom, yet as much as they wanted or needed for him, none could do for him as he did for them. The steps he took lost the potential of his capacity and he realized the walk home wouldn't be as expedient as the journey there.

Œ

Before Old Man Winter had become his greatest Tyrant for the season, a mutt bitch was in the agonies of delivering her litter in an outdoor shed. Her owners were folks who could barely see to their own needs. She was swollen with pups, bordering on malnutrition and she felt death in her litter. She was lucky to get a bowl of kibble a day and even luckier to have spoiled food from her owners dropped into the kibble. At the very least the shed offered her some protection from the furies of the cold hearted tyrant known as Old Man Winter.

Her time to birth came and the passing of pups exhausted her. She began in the afternoon on a day when Old Man Winter raged in his glory. The wind howled and the snow flew. The biting cold stole the new life from the weakest of her litter. When her task was done four of six remained and their tiny yelps of need were no match for the thunder of the ensuing tyranny. The pups living nuzzled mercilessly on the desperate bitch's teats. She had to consume stillborn pups to see to those that remained alive. Such were the choices of being a pet to irresponsible people.

On the morning of cold calm after the tyrant slept and the sun rose upon the powdery ice the puppies whimpered in a chorus of hunger. The people who were so poorly prepared for the new life and its need became ashamed in their negligence. They dug the powdery ice away from the shed and revealed urgency unknown if not forgotten to collect the puppies and their exhausted mother to bring inside for warmth. The people smelled bad, not mean but bad. The pups lie frightened as their mother breathed weakly. No milk from her teat could be nuzzled and life left her shortly after they knew the place of bad smelling people.

The bad smell of people became the puppies' reality. The pups barely lived as they could nuzzle something that tasted poorly and felt nothing like the teat they knew and expected. The only warmth they knew that was familiar to them was when they huddled closely. One of the pups began not to nuzzle the poor tasting food from the bad smelling people. He had life leave him. The remainder of pups numbering three faced an uncertain future. After a time their eyes opened and movement changed. They figured out the secret of mobility, even only slight to start. They came to learn things by discovering possibilities. That never happened when the bad smell of the people was close. When the bad smell from the people was present it was time to nuzzle the poor tasting nourishment.

After more time of discovery, another of the pups began to nuzzle less, until life left her. So it came down to two pups; one smelled like the mutt bitch life came from, while the other smelled different. The two kept warm together by lying on or next to each other. As they grew, they played. All they could do was discover this uncertain life together as they started from the same place.

A day came when there was a great noise that the pups heard. The noise was as bad as the smell of the people who fed them. It scared the pups as they huddled together. The noise became louder. One of the bad smelling people came and instead of giving them bad tasting food each of them were put inside something they had forgotten since being birthed. All of the movement they learned in their young lives seemed useless. They tried desperately to use the new mobility, but it didn't matter. The suddenness of movement scared them. Weightlessness in the air came to both of them, holding them together and lifting them away from the place they learned how to move on.

A great thrust came; they felt a sense of quick movement. The motion was violent and for seconds they tumbled without knowing where the place they learned to move on was. After the tumbling stopped, the place they settled at was very cold and it became wet. The one pup employed the skills of movement, but the other didn't. The pup could only fight his way free from the sack they were both in to find himself at a place he had no knowledge of in the shortness of his life. He turned to the thing he escaped and waited for the one he knew. He sniffed at the sack. It had a scent he couldn't resist. He was frightened to be sure but the scent drove him to seek out his other. He discovered the scent to be warm as he lapped at a wound his other received from the toss. It was a bitter taste and very salty. He lapped at the other as he became last of the litter.

The times of light got longer as the times of darkness grew shorter. He discovered many ways to eat and earned the wisdom of not being eaten. His nose followed the smells that came to him. His nose told him which could be eaten and which would eat him. As the days grew he noticed differences of places. His ease of going to and from became greater as he grew. Movement became easier as well as faster. He learned how to come to food quietly and gently and he knew how to explode in movement so as to avoid danger.

His greatest curiosity was of those he knew to smell badly. He had come across those who he thought would smell badly but didn't. Sometimes they might toss him a bit of what he could eat. Other time they threw things at him that brought him pain. He always approached them with doubt and hesitance. He never knew what they would do or how his curiosity would affect them. What he did know was that his hunger became great as the light grew. When the cold smells went away, there were more smells than he could imagine. It seemed that every day there were new smells. He came to realize that the things that smelled like food moved quickly. They weren't easy to eat. Sometimes he'd tire himself from and the chasing would only leave him hungrier. Days came to pass when he moved between places where the ones who smelled bad seemed to have food that was easier to get than chasing.

He went to those places when it was dark, because that was when he didn't see them as much. His nose led him straight to where it was that the food was at and most times he ate well.

One thing he loved to do was chase things where the bad smelling people weren't. He could chase things for hours. He felt like chasing things was the thing he was meant to do. Some times in the light he'd chase things well passed being hungry, but too tired to find food. He'd find a place to sleep until he was rested and then he'd go to places he knew where to eat.

His curiosity of those who he thought to smell bad waned. It seemed the more he'd come close to them the more he got hurt by them. It even got to be difficult at the easier places to eat; they just always seemed to be around when he was hungry. One time he ventured to where the easy food was; his nose didn't work for him as it had in the past. He moved gently and slowly like he did and came to a wonderful smell. The smell was so good that he stopped and wondered if he had ever smelled anything that good. He looked around and all seemed as it usually appeared. He tried to smell for anything that might bring him harm but that smell which caught his attention was irresistible. He moved very slowly and the smell grew greater. Then he could see the source; as he looked upon this food he moved closer. He was weary. There was nothing near it to hide by. He went to it exposed to those who threw things at him. The smell was wonderful. He moved more slowly than he ever had and he figured to get what he could and run away with his explosive movement. He was so close, so, so close and then he heard a noise. His ability to explode almost got him away, but this thing he never knew seemed to drop on him. He couldn't escape. It was just like before he knew what wandering alone meant, but it wasn't cold or wet. It held him back. It was almost a thing that pulled at him. He could move but he couldn't escape. The thing seemed to grab him, drawing him closer to what smelled so good. Then the pain began. He heard the noise he remembered from the bad smelling people. More pain!

He rolled and wiggled as he clawed to get away. More pain! He felt a different kind of pain. It wasn't like this grabbing thing. It was sudden. He turned to bite at that thing and it was in his mouth. He chewed as though it were something to be eaten, something he chased for food. There was more loud noise, noise like he heard when he suckled off the teat of his mutt bitch when he first knew hunger. The thing that grabbed at him was gone; he released the thing he bit. The speed he knew to use to avoid being eaten came to him, but it hurt. He ran to a safe place and then the pain took his speed away from him. And then he smelled what he smelled when he knew his days of wandering alone. He smelled it on himself and licked at it. There wasn't as much of it on him as when he first knew it in the cold, it was much less. He smelled more and discovered it on him elsewhere. But again it was less than what he knew at first. He limped to where he drank and sat in the stuff he drank. The pain eased but it would remain.

After he slept in cover of dark the day came again. The pain was troubling as he couldn't move like before. The coolness of what he drank gave him less pain. And there he stayed for the cycles of day and night. He did manage to get some food as he waited on the pain to leave, enough to keep from having life leave. For a time he thought about the smell he wanted so badly and realized that there were things that weren't worth smelling. He hated those that smelled badly. He knew to never be near those that could hurt him in such a way. He didn't know what it was that grabbed him, either. In places he loved to chase things, nothing like that grabbing thing ever revealed itself. He did know those things in the ground that grabbed but none that he couldn't get away from. He discovered them and simply moved around them when he smelled them. Why didn't that grabbing thing have a smell? Why didn't he smell the bad person?

He wasn't likely to go back to the places to eat that would have such good smelling things. Now he knew bad smelling people... and that those people who smelled bad were usually near such good smelling things... It was a lesson he wouldn't soon forget.

After a time the pain went away. No more of the smell he knew coming to wander alone came from him. He stuck to the place where he chased his food. He was hungry, but not so hungry to go back to where he could get easy food. He learned how to wait for things to move. He lay in wait and pounced on them. He'd eat them after he caught them. He tasted what it was as he came to wander alone. Other times the things coming from the thing he moved on had good smells to eat. But those never had the taste of what he knew when he wandered alone.

One day when the light was out and all the cold was gone he began his day chasing things, he wasn't hungry he was celebrating the lack of feeling the pain he knew from that grabbing thing. After a while during the light he was surprised by a sound he never knew to be where he chased things. He moved gently to the noise and to his surprise he saw what he knew to be one of those who smelled bad. He crouched and watched the person. He smelled, but didn't smell anything bad. The person walked in his place to chase things in a confusing way. He seemed to know everything but pay attention to nothing. His walk was surprisingly fast. He followed him but did so quietly and slowly.

After a time he noticed that the person stopped. What was more surprising was that he stopped right where he had lost his pain. The person that didn't smell bad stayed there for a while. It seemed as though the person with no bad smell was losing pain, he couldn't tell. Suddenly the person got up and began to move. What confused him was that the person moved more slowly than he had, but he moved in the same way, like he knew everything, but paid attention to none of it.

He sensed that the person with no bad smell didn't get rid of his pain. The speed of the person seemed to be like his own speed when he had his own pain. His curiosity of this person with no bad smell became intense. Not so intense as to reveal himself, but enough to allow him a closeness that proved out he was a person that had no bad smell. His excitement grew along the slow walk as the daylight shined. He watched the person with no bad smell stop to bend over and pick something up off the thing he moved on. To his amazement, the person with no smell launched what he held. He watched it fly into the place where things flew. He lost sight of the thing, but heard it fall to the thing he moved on. He almost ran to where it landed. He could sense it. As the day seemed to grow shorter the pain seemed to increase for the person with no bad smell. He hated that as much as he hated the grabbing thing with no smell that brought him to so much pain. He followed the person with no bad smell right up until he realized he was going back to the place where he found all the pain.

The person with no bad smell stopped in a very strange place. He would have not stopped there. Flying things that moved in the place where light came from always lurked where the person with no smell stopped. That thing was what you moved across to go to find the easy food. It wasn't where the things he chased lived. Nothing lived on it, the span wasn't natural.

He watched the person with no bad smell looking over the edge of the place where things moved from where the light came. He wondered what the person of no bad smell was thinking. Why did he stop there?! He sensed that this person with no bad smell was about to have life leave him. He liked how the person with no bad smell seemed to make him want to chase things.

He decided that chasing things was more important than anything. In that decision he showed himself to the person with no bad smell. The person with no bad smell walked towards him and bent over while keeping an eye on him. The person with no bad smell was as leery as he was. And when the person with no bad smell stood straight he held something in his hand. He wondered what he would do with it. He hoped he would let him chase it. He crouched on his front quickly and suddenly as to ask him to throw the thing he picked up off of that which he moved on. The person with no bad smell did. It flew, he saw and he chased after it. He brought it back to the person with no bad smell and they spent the day moving into the night tossing the thing in his hand. The person with no bad smell said something to him... The person said, "Get the stick!"

While he chased the stick he got more tired, then he chewed the stick. The person began walking. He was moving to where that grabbing thing was, along with the pain. His love for chasing the stick diminished his fear of the grabbing thing. He sensed the person's pain had also diminished. When the person with no bad smell was on the other side where he could move he heard him say something else. It was, "Come, Adoc. Come!"

He needed to trust the man in following him because the man moved towards the place where the grabbing thing was along with the bad smelling people. The very place he didn't want to be.

Henry and Adoc walked along the sidewalks to Henry's home. Henry tossed the stick ahead of them a few times and Adoc faithfully got the stick and brought it back. Henry didn't say much at all. He watched how Adoc fetched the stick and marveled with curiosity. Henry never had a dog, he knew of dogs but he didn't know what being a friend to a dog was or meant. As they walked Henry gave thought to the possibility of whether or not Adoc would stay with him. His mind began processing questions that arose. Adoc watched the person he walked with lose pain that seemed to be with him walking earlier.

When Henry finally arrived at his house he walked to his door. Adoc remained behind. Henry looked back to let Adoc into the house and noticed he was sitting some ten feet behind him like he had some type of invisible barrier in front of him. Henry didn't understand why Adoc was hesitant to come into the house, but Henry didn't become upset, he reasoned through why a dog might be hesitant about entering a house. After rationalizing some possibilities Henry decided to throw Adoc his stick. He tossed it beyond where Adoc sat and Adoc fetched the stick and approached Henry to return it to him. This time the threshold of an invisible barrier was closer than the last time. That was curious to Henry; there was something about the stick which meant something to Adoc. Adoc sat and chewed at the stick. Henry watched as little pieces of the stick fell away while he chewed it. Henry thought he'd go inside and see if there wasn't something Adoc might like to eat. Henry wasn't long. He went to the refrigerator and grabbed up some cheese and leftovers with some meat in them. He put them in a bowl and thought that for chewing on the stick Adoc might be thirsty. So he took some milk out and poured that into another bowl. Once he had his bowls in hand he returned to the door and went to where Adoc sat. He bent down to present the bowls to Adoc and watched the dog.

Adoc watched the person put the things in front of him. He could smell the good smells coming from what the person put in front of him, but he remembered the pain for the last time he tried to eat the smells. Adoc dropped the stick and moved closer. He watched the person and he only came close enough to better smell the good smells. He wouldn't go any closer.

Adoc's actions gave Henry concern. He wondered, *Why wouldn't a dog want food?* Henry pondered the reality facing him and in all his thinking he didn't have an answer. That frustrated him and when he got frustrated he internalized reasoning. He thought to himself again, *Why wouldn't a dog want food? Was it food he didn't like?* He saw the dog move towards it so he doubted it was that he didn't like the food. Henry sat down on the stoop leading into the house.

To his amazement Adoc became more curious towards the food. Henry began to think of external factors. It wasn't that the dog didn't like the food, nor did he not want it. He gleaned wisdom by casual effect. Apparently, it was something about the dog and approaching food. Henry watched some more and Adoc moved closer to the food. He lowered his head to the bowls, but didn't take his eyes off of him sitting there. Henry decided that the issue at hand was a trust thing. He thought that to be the likelihood, but he wasn't positive. The more he watched Adoc, the more he felt a need to learn about dogs and owning them. Eventually, Adoc did eat the food that Henry put out for him. Without knowing it, Henry began a new adventure and was on to more discoveries.

When Adoc had consumed all that Henry put out, Adoc looked at the person. He wasn't sure what to make of the person. He liked chasing the stick and he even liked the food. He wondered why this person didn't smell bad. He watched the person at his own eyelevel and wondered if he was gonna be able to chase the stick more. He decided to give the stick to the person where he sat. Once close enough to the person, he dropped it, hopeful that he could chase it.

Henry was surprised once again by the dog. He looked at the stick and then back at Adoc. "Want me to throw the stick?"

Adoc didn't know what any of that meant. The person was making noises that seemed to be towards him. They were strange noises, none like any he ever heard before. None of the other creatures he knew sounded like that. The person did the same thing again.

"Want me to throw the stick?"

Adoc became excited, wondering, *Why is that stick was still there, why isn't the person letting me chase it?* Adoc did what he did before in lowering himself to the ground, he figured the person let him chase it after he did that, he'd try it again.

When Henry saw Adoc drop, along with his building energy he reached for the stick and held it up. The dog's eyes followed it. Henry shook it slightly. Then he spoke, matching the shaking of it. "Get the stick!"

Adoc wagged his tale waiting to chase it. Henry tossed the stick onto the lawn. Adoc summarily went to the stick and returned with it. Henry had moved the bowls to the side and began time throwing the stick back and forth with Adoc. The only trouble Henry saw was that Adoc chewed the sticks into smaller pieces until there was nothing left to throw. At the very last throw he could possibly toss Adoc retrieved nothing but what he chewed into pieces of wood. Adoc looked at the person wanting to chase more but the person made some more noise. "There is no more stick. You ate it."

Henry noticed Adoc's head tilt to the side when he talked to him. That also struck him with a curiosity. He repeated what he said. "There is no stick you ate it." Just as he said it the dog tilted his head again.

Henry was fixated on the dog. He reached for the dog so as to pet him and the dog retracted. That too surprised Henry. The day had turned to darkness and Henry was beginning to realize that he needed to read up on dogs. He looked at Adoc and his condition. He was scruffy and dirty and he looked thin. Henry turned around and picked up the bowls to head in. When he got to the door he turned back Adoc was sitting at his invisible barrier. Henry figured to offer the dog some more food and see if he could coax him in the house. When he returned the dog was waiting. Henry put the food to the side of the steps for Adoc. Again he didn't come right to the food. Only after Henry stepped in the door did the dog move toward the food to eat it. Henry concluded that even though the dog liked the food there WAS some type of trust issue that went along with the food. He watched Adoc eat the food and when he was finished he sat back down behind the invisible barrier. The barrier was closer than it had been earlier so Henry reasoned that if the dog chose to move the barrier then it had to be a trust thing. He went to pick up the bowls and the dog moved back. He took the bowls inside the house and returned once more with a bowl of milk. This time he left it inside the door and turned moving inside the house. Henry grabbed a chair and placed it to the middle of the hallway halfway to the kitchen and sat down. He waited to see if his thinking was right.

Adoc saw the person leave the thing that had the good smelling food in it at a place he wasn't sure about going into. He wondered what kind of good smelling stuff was left in that thing.

He still wasn't too keen on pain for the eating, but two times he ate without any of it. He wondered if would see the person again. Adoc's temptation to have some more of the good smelling stuff eventually led him to begin moving closer towards where it was. As he got closer he smelled the stuff that he licked up. He remembered the mutt bitch teat and how that tasted. That was about as close as he got to remembering anything he'd eaten since then and he liked it a lot. It tasted good. He put his head just inside the door. He was very frightened thinking that the grabbing thing would catch him and then the pain would follow. He looked at this thing the person went into and nothing of danger was present to smell. He moved even closer to the good smelling stuff he wanted to lick. The taste of it was familiar; before so many he remembered had life leave them.

Henry noticed Adoc's interest he held his breath quietly while remaining hopeful of his new friend's curiosity. He was quite sure now that it must be trust. In coming to know his discovery he was happier than he'd been all day long and for that matter for quite some time. Once he saw Adoc drink the milk his surprise overflowed in releasing the words, "Good boy, Adoc!"

Adoc spooked at seeing him sitting in the chair in the hallway and rushed out of the door. His elation was slightly dampened but as he figured out that it was a trust issue, his good feelings remained even though a bit disappointed. Henry stood up and almost moved towards the bowl. He caught himself. The dog also liked a stick. That was what stopped his motion towards the door. Henry thought about if he had anything laying about that might be like a stick. He went to his fireplace and he found a piece of wood that might have been a bit thicker than a stick, but Adoc had a propensity to chew sticks to nothing. He held it and thought about tossing it. It seemed like a good match. Once armed with his stick, he went to the door expecting to see Adoc at his invisible barrier. His heart sunk when Adoc wasn't there.

The surprise of the person making noise when he was in the place where the person left the food was more than Adoc wanted to know. He liked the food, he even liked the chasing of that thing, but being frightened like that gave him reason to get away. Adoc had stayed in the area where the person threw the thing he liked to chase, but he hid in the darkness. And when he saw the person holding another thing he wanted to go back to him. The good things the person gave him to eat made him a bit tired. So he laid there watching the person realizing that some of that pain found its way back to him. He had that same look when he walked in the other place. Adoc decided that when the light came back maybe he'd have another chance to chase that thing he held... But for now he'd rest; it had been a fun day even if the person scared him at the end. There were no smells of danger and he was comfortable where he lay. He fell asleep thinking of that person and the noise he made. It was very strange... two of the noises kept coming to his mind... *stick* and *Adoc*.

Henry went back in the house and put the bowls out again with more food and water. He took one last look around before he went in and shut the door. He hoped Adoc would be back, but until that time he was thinking about any books he might have had that had anything to do with dogs.

Once he realized he had none he decided that in his day tomorrow he'd do some investigating of his own. He knew bunches of folks who knew about dogs and then he thought to call some of them.

He sat down to put on his thinking cap. Did he want to talk with those who owned dogs or did he want to talk with folks who worked with dogs? Who did he know who knew dogs instead of having a pet? Henry seemed to be lost in his thinking. He knew lots of folks who had dogs; he was sorting through those he knew who knew dogs. It was clear to him that having a pet wasn't the same as knowing different types of dogs. Finally he arrived at a pretty good thought. He'd give the animal control officer a call and seek information from her.

Henry did everything by a process and he wouldn't make a call without making a checklist of those answers he sought. Henry dealt efficiently in all things he did. While he made his list he thought about how many times he sought primary information from those he helped. He never lost his temperament around folks who hadn't seemed to know simple solutions that were within their grasp, but would have if they gave the issue some proper consideration. Most of the things he helped people to see were unrealized opportunities at their disposal. He grew weary for their lack of focus on what he considered to be primary tools for problem identifying and resolution.

What gave him greater discomfort came when he helped them once and demonstrated resolution of their problem, only to have them find another problem and an inability to duplicate what he already taught them. They sought him out without effort to apply what they learned, or at least what he thought he taught to them. Those were the mounting frustrations he faced, which led him back to wanting earlier days of adventure and discovery.

Henry reviewed his list. He wasn't sure that it was complete and he realized that he was hungry. He looked at the clock and was satisfied to call the animal control officer the next day. He could fix some dinner and think about what might be missing from his list. After he set the list aside he rose up to make his way to the kitchen. A thought came to him so as to have a peek out the back door. He didn't expect to see Adoc, but he thought to check on the bowls anyways. When he looked out the window of the door he saw that the food remained. He wasn't disappointed, but he seemed stuck on something for being at the door. He went to the kitchen and began making his food. When he put food to hand there was an evolution of thought in Henry's mind. Hand, food and door. He stayed with the opening of understanding he lived by. Things came to him as he did the mundane.

Adoc ate the food when Adoc wanted to eat. Adoc came inside the house to eat but his limitation was that confounded invisible barrier. Henry put trust in the middle of hand, food, and door thinking. As he finished up his preparation and brought the food to where he sat and ate, his thinking of evolution expanded in its gathering.

Hand delivered the food and the door was the limit of trust? Henry felt as though he arrived at the cusp of understanding. He could taste the wisdom on his tongue while he ate, but he couldn't put a flavor to understanding. Henry thought as he chewed, *What was it about the door and trust?*

Henry internalized trust and then he thought about obstacles. Trust was easy, he didn't trust much more than his own capability. He trusted less in others' capabilities. Trusting in others would have meant that they would have taken his wisdom and had no need for him again. As his frustration of the days was, trust for others couldn't be counted on as normal. The simple figuring was set aside as he pondered obstacles or things that needed figuring to solve. For the most part of problem solving his trouble was to unlock the ability for others to see a course of action in resolving their problems.

Henry finished his food and brought his dishes to the sink. He washed up his dishes and implements of cooking and set them to dry. *Unlocked Door.*

Henry tried to bring himself to what Adoc might feel. He didn't know dogs so well. There was a bit of infancy in his manipulations. *Trust and unlocked door.* Adoc had entered the house and no doubt he only entered because he could leave. After Adoc realized his surprise for venturing into the house, he left. Did Adoc have a need to know he could come and go so as to make a place his favorite?

Henry went back to the door for one last look. He stood at the door for some minutes. The food bowls remained full as he peered through the glass. Even if he left the food in the house, Adoc wouldn't be able to get it. The door had to be open. It was warming up in the days as winter fell away, but he wasn't interested in walking into a kitchen of cold floors. It was the door. If Adoc could come through the door to get food, he'd begin to gain trust, but he couldn't very well open and close the door. Henry turned after peeking one more time at the food bowls. As he walked away he felt strongly that Adoc would be back. He enjoyed eating the food and chasing the stick.

Henry realized that he needed to provide a dog door in his own door to welcome Adoc in gaining trust. Henry smiled to himself... One revelation of evolutionary thinking resolved in having hope that when he saw Adoc... he could let Adoc know that he could come and go. Henry reasoned if the dog had no fear of entrapment, he'd have no fear of visiting. Henry took hold of his list for inquiry and reviewed it. The night was early, but Henry usually went to bed early. He thought his list was a good one, but he thought it would be better if he slept on it. Maybe in the morning he'd even expand it. He already figured out the hand, food and unlocked door thing could be resolved. Now it was just more discovery not knowing adventure.

Œ

Adoc woke before the light would reveal him, or where he might be for the danger that came with the light. Condensation of the evening's settle to cool gave him sweet smell off the ground he laid on. His tongue licked out as he stretched, catching the tastes of moisture that his nose smelled. He knew enough to lay flat when he stretched, even in the dark just before the light there were unfriendly critters still looking for food on their way back to their own spots of hiding from the light. After his stretch he smelled beyond the moisture he just licked. Something that smelled good was close. That made him think about the food that person gave him before he lay down.

Slowly he rolled up on his belly so he could sniff more. He a looked around while sniffing, taking notice of what might lurk in the dark. That hint of good smell was strong. He began hoping that the person he ate with and played with as the dark came before his sleep had done what he did before the sleep.

After his certainty of knowing there were no other critters of danger lurking, he slowly pushed himself off his belly. He followed the good smell. His hopes were met with realization as he saw the things that contained the good stuff he ate. He walked like a thief in the night hoping the grabbing thing wouldn't notice him. Adoc didn't hurry through the eating or the lapping. He savored it. It didn't mean that he didn't keep an ear to the darkness, he did. When he was done he smelled around again. There was no smell of danger.

Adoc decided to sniff around. He was free to smell here as his nose revealed. Those things that lurked elsewhere didn't seem to be around. He proceeded in the area. It was limited for what he was used to, but he began to know the boundary. He was determined to find the place where danger lived… but there was none present. Not in all his sniffing along edges, not sniffing in the middle of where he was and where he ate the good stuff. Adoc went back to the place he slept and snoozed through the night's turning into day. He listened to the noise that came with the day begin. The noise was different to listen to here. It was more quiet.

Henry woke early as usual. Before he did anything he checked on the food he left out for Adoc. He noticed it was gone and that gave him hope that he'd see Adoc again. He rushed through getting dressed. He decided that today he'd call the animal control officer at the opening time of her office. Then he'd begin on building a doggie door. The sun was just beginning to rise and so was Henry's spirit. He liked the feeling as it hadn't been so familiar lately. Before he could get to the door he noticed the work he had in process. He realized it was no longer important to him so he evaluated what it meant to those who were waiting. After some thought, only one project struck him as very important. He made a mental note to see to following up on that at some point in the day. All others could wait. Anxious as he was to get the bowls up he almost forgot going to the door with the stick. If Adoc was close he figured he'd toss the stick with him for a time.

Henry opened the door to the coolness of the morning; he stepped out to gather up the bowls, turning to put them inside the door. After putting the bowls up he looked around to see if Adoc was close by. He walked to the corner of the house and scanned around the corner. Seeing nothing he continued his visual seeking. The more he didn't see Adoc the less hopeful he became. He figured that maybe a walk along the path he took yesterday might have better results. When he turned to prepare for that trek he was joyously startled!

Adoc was behind him, staring at the stick in his hand. Henry got the dog's attention even more focused by raising the stick and shaking it. "You want the stick?!" He could see Adoc's eyes flash back and forth between the stick and his own eyes. Adoc's mouth was open loosely and his tongue hung out of the side.

Henry threw the stick with Adoc well beyond the sun's rising Henry's heart swelled with delight watching his new friend's enjoyment. After a time of running, Adoc began chewing on the stick in between panting. Henry realized that Adoc might be thirsty. As he went towards the door to get some water, Adoc followed him. He stopped at his boundary and waited for Henry's return.

Henry wasn't long for getting water. He was out of milk so he filled a bigger bowl than he used earlier for food and milk with water. He made sure it was cool. When he returned to Adoc with the water he could see anticipation or curiosity from Adoc as to what was in the bowl. Henry stepped close to Adoc and he didn't move away. He let Adoc move his nose toward the bowl to sniff it. Then he held the bowl single handedly and reached to pet the pup. Henry stroked Adoc a few times, gently. There was a second between them which occurred during the stroking of Adoc's head that both knew to be bonding without acknowledgment. Henry lowered the bowl to the steps and Adoc lapped the water.

Henry sat next to Adoc while he lapped at the bowl. He stole a few more strokes from Adoc as he consumed the water. Henry felt good about that petting because he hadn't been successful earlier in his attempt to touch him.

When Adoc had his fill he looked to the person who'd thrown the stick and who had just given him what he needed after the exercise. The adoration both came to know for sharing the time with each other was likely the greatest mutual satisfaction either had known. Henry and Adoc's eyes met and they stared deeply into each other's souls. Adoc could see the happiness on Henry's face and Henry could see that Adoc was ready again to chase the stick. When Henry picked up the stick, he noticed just how much chewing Adoc had done to the stick. He was surprised by the diminishing of the stick for Adoc's chewing.

Henry didn't make Adoc wait after his hydration. He tossed the stick and Adoc chased it. Adoc chased it and chased it until he went back to the water bowl. The two sat silently while Adoc lapped at the bowl. He emptied it and let Henry pet him more frequently.

Adoc liked the feeling of the person touching him. It felt good. It felt so good that Adoc didn't think about the grabbing thing or the pain. He thought that avoiding pain was good, until he discovered what this touching was like. Adoc sniffed to take note of difference in smells. The difference he came to know was how the person smelled. Adoc decided that the smell of the person was good. Not like the bad smell of those he remembered when he first remembered. For the stick chasing of the day's beginning, Adoc thought to lie down would be nice. If the person would continue to pet him that would even be nicer. This was all very strange to Adoc. He, in his short life didn't recall anything of the feelings he had at that moment. He chased the stick, he didn't thirst and this person touching him smelled good. Better, the touching was like nothing he ever knew.

After a while the touching stopped. The person reached for the thing he lapped the water out of and stood up. The person's movements surprised Adoc and in that surprise he leapt up. He watched the person and heard some more noise. He didn't understand it, but it sounded okay. The noise the person made seemed like he was saying it to him, but nothing he heard made sense. The person was standing, holding that thing that he lapped the water out of, making more noise. Adoc's head tilted. It sounded like nothing he had ever heard. *Bowl, water??*

The person turned to go back to where he went, taking the bowl with him. Adoc wasn't sure what to do. The touching stopped and the noise was made and then gone. Adoc's curiosity gave him the courage to go beyond his comfort line. He stepped up to see what the person was doing. He stepped slowly into the door that he was startled by last night. When he stepped as far as his gut would let him he saw that person leave his view. Then he heard more noise, not like the noise of the person. Some other kind of noise, almost how water trickled along the thing he moved on where he used to lay away from the other critters. The noise stopped and the person was coming back with the bowl in his hand. Adoc backed out of the place he wasn't sure he wanted to be in while the person came closer to him. He sat where he felt comfortable and when the person reached down with the bowl Adoc took a smell of the bowl. It was more water. He lapped at it a bit and then looked again at the person.

Then the noise began. Henry watched Adoc have more to drink. He voiced approval for Adoc's actions. "Good boy, Adoc! Adoc likes the water?"

Once again Adoc tilted his head looking at the person. Adoc saw his hand extend to touch him and he welcomed the touch. Henry stroked Adoc in boyhood wonderment. His wonderment of innocence came to an end when his hands came to the scars Adoc had on his skin under his fur. The discovery shocked Henry. Adoc took notice of Henry when he discovered the scars. When Henry focused on the scars he was gentle for his study, but Adoc was less relaxed. Henry sensed it and ceased his examination. Henry looked into Adoc's eyes and searched for the causes of these cuts. Adoc couldn't very well tell Henry what happened which resulted in gaining the scars, but Henry knew that it had to do with trust. Here he was finding the scars but only because Adoc let him pet him.

Henry reached towards Adoc's head being very sure to be gentle. Adoc welcomed the strokes on his head.

Henry knew then that he would never raise a hand to this dog, nor would he tolerate any such kind of behavior toward the dog. Between the two a level of bonding occurred somewhere neither knew to name. It was an understanding. That is all it needed to be. Henry realized that if Adoc was going to be his companion, he'd have to see to the business of being a dog person.

Henry began thinking through his mental contact lists wondering if he knew any vets. He knew that there were vets in town, but he didn't know them personally. It was time to make that call to the animal control officer. Henry left Adoc at the bowl of water. He went inside and got the phone. He flipped through the town offices brochure until he came to the number he sought. He dialed the number of the office realizing it was earlier than opening hours; he figured he'd leave a message. To his surprise the call connected.

"Hi, this is the Animal Shelter. Kristina speaking, how can I help you?"

Henry began his story after he and Kristina had shared greetings. When he concluded Kristina mentioned the name of a mobile vet she knew. Henry took down the number. Kristina also mentioned that she'd like to see Adoc as he might be a missing dog, or a stray. Henry said that they'd both likely be there that was unless Adoc had other ideas. Kristina said she'd be over within an hour or two. They hung up and Henry made the call to the vet Kristina referred him to.

He left a message as there was no answer and hung up the phone. He turned back to the door and went to where Adoc was sitting. Adoc lie comfortably. The early chasing of the stick was a likely cause for the rest. Henry took up his seat next to him as Adoc raised his head to see him sit. Once seated, Henry carefully began stroking Adoc again. He watched Adoc's responses to the touching and petting. Adoc seemed to be relaxing and enjoying the petting by Henry's observation. He noticed that when he drew his fingers across Adoc's back just towards his hip his leg began moving. Like a motion that Adoc might employ for trying to scratch himself. Henry scratched in the area for Adoc's foot movement and located the exact position. The scratching Henry used to manipulate Adoc's leg made him smile. It made Adoc look back at Henry with a look that made Henry feel as though he was very useful to Adoc. Henry thought he saw the look as a tell for Adoc conveying the words... *you don't know how good that feels!* Henry didn't stay at the spot too long but he revisited it through the petting. After the scratching movement of Adoc's leg Henry rubbed Adoc's belly and the touch produced a tail wag each time. It wasn't a whole tail wag; it was just the tip of the tail that wagged.

After a while Henry thought Adoc would enjoy more chasing of the stick. Henry wasn't wrong. They tossed the stick until there was no stick left to chew. Henry once again produced another stick from the burn pile in the house. Henry's enthusiasm and wonder over Adoc consumed him. Watching the dog run after the stick and bring it back to him for another toss mesmerized him. He imagined Adoc's motivation to chase the stick, much like he felt when he was having adventures and making discoveries as a young man. The repetition was only interrupted by petting and Adoc's visit to the water bowl.

When Henry noticed the animal control vehicle pull up to his property he couldn't imagine that a couple of hours had passed. He stood up and spoke to Adoc, "Adoc, ready to meet a friend?"

Adoc brought him the stick wondering about the noise he made. It sounded to him like the person wanted something. After the person took the stick Adoc noticed another person. He didn't know what to make of the extra person. Henry felt Adoc's apprehension and kneeled to him pet him gently, calming him. Adoc allowed Henry to pet him while the other person approached them. There was a difference about the other person.

Kristina and Henry made gestures that Adoc watched. Adoc saw a size difference between them. There was also a smell difference and the other person had many smells. Many more smells than the person who threw the stick. Adoc's curiosity went well beyond his caution. The smells made Adoc very excited, but calmly so. Adoc approached Kristina with a wagging of the tail Henry hadn't seen. Adoc didn't even know of such a motion within his capability. It was like the smells on this person made his belly feel like it was being petted with as many hands as could pet it. His motion sideways seemed to be irresistibly uncontainable. The closer he got to Kristina, the more he wagged.

The two people spoke and made noises that sounded wonderfully inviting, somehow Adoc knew they spoke about him. He kept hearing *Adoc*. Then, *good boy* along with petting of hands he could smell and lick. Kristina loved dogs and she didn't mind that Adoc took advantage of putting his nose all over her, wherever he could reach. Henry watched Adoc's surprise and thought his antics were beautiful. Henry also took notice of how Kristina examined the dog while she greeted him.

Henry figured she'd discuss her thoughts on the dog with him, but for the moment she enjoyed just getting to know Adoc. Henry watched Kristina and the way Adoc responded to her. He was amazed at how quickly they became friends. She seemed to know Adoc with every pet or any exchange. She calmed his excitement in a manner he thought to be mystical. Kristina seemed to know this dog better than he did and in just a few moments. After she broke contact with Adoc she looked to Henry.

She plainly said, "The dog is a stray!" She looked at Adoc once again as to reference a thought. "Just a puppy, too. But a big tough puppy!" She pet Adoc's head. "If I had to guess, maybe he is only three to four months."

Henry wouldn't have known any of her insights; quite honestly the comments didn't matter to him. He was just amazed by the dog himself. Henry gave Kristina's discussion some thinking. He tried to make sense of what it was she might have been trying to say. He looked at Adoc and patted his back while she pet his head.

Adoc never knew such pleasure. He never thought he could feel so good. The warmth that came from these hands by these people was a sensation he never wanted to stop. In the middle of the stroking he heard them making noises. He didn't hear the word *Adoc* but the noises seemed to sound as though they were about him.

Kristina inquired as to whether or not Henry called the vet. He answered that he left a message. Kristina nodded her head and produced a cell phone. "This dog is loveable and as loveable as he is needs some attention, and he needs it immediately."

Henry's heart felt broken. He would have never known. Henry's body language changed, he became more tense. Adoc felt the change by Henry's touch. Kristina also felt it and she made another comment to Henry. "There is nothing to worry about. No need to worry!" Before she could continue she connected her call and pled her case.

While she talked Henry's attention focused on looking to Adoc. He gave the dog a look trying to see what it was that Kristina saw about him. He looked a bit thin, but other than that Henry thought he was okay. That scared him. Adoc seemed to worry about what he felt in Henry's hands. When Adoc looked up at him with his tongue hanging out of his mouth, Henry saw a look of pacification. The look seemed to convey to Henry that everything was going to be all right. Adoc just wanted the person to know that he felt great and he loved the petting. Henry was caught between things he never experienced. Not as a helper, not as a solver of problems. The thought of not being able to see a dog's need in the presence of another who did know dogs shook his sense of what was right. He felt inept.

Kristina broke the focus. If she saw the pain of learning between a person and a pet once she saw it a hundred times. Adoc was obviously a stray looking for someone and Henry was a fulfilled person who never gave himself a time to love anything, including himself. Her wisdom tickled her compassion bone earlier and she saw what needed to be accomplished. She asked Henry if he was going to be keeping Adoc's company as it was an investment, but she did so already knowing the answer. Regardless she needed to ask.

Henry sat stroking Adoc, thinking about her question. "If Adoc wants to be with me, then I guess I will be caring for him."

When Kristina heard those words she was exposed to all she ever wanted to be sure of in considering animal care. She had known Henry as a warrior for human dignity for all the time she was engaged as an animal control officer. Henry was a pillar of the community and he was cute. Now that he gave her the truest testimony of the thing she dedicated herself to in life, she was willing to see to his needs and those needs met Adoc's. She couldn't have fulfilled herself any more than where she drove to that day.

Kristina gave the whole situation thought. She paused in the beauty of the moment and made a mental note of the day. She had thought that her job would be fulfilling but lately the job just became an everyday dealing with stupid people and she accepted it. She loved working with animals and hated the days when the killings happened. Seeing Henry and Adoc become friends gave her reason to have hope. She asked Henry a question. "So, you are thinking of keeping the dog, right? Well, when are you gonna shop for the dog?"

Henry looked at Kristina. He knew her, but he realized what he knew wasn't at all adequate. He hadn't thought about shopping for Adoc. But as she asked he knew... Adoc needed some things. "I was really just thinking about what I needed to know when considering having a dog as a friend. Never did think about the pragmatism of it all."

When Kristina heard his response she laughed. She saw the confusion on his face but his love for the dog was constant. "Why don't we take a ride and go get some things for Adoc? I'm sure he'll be a neighborhood favorite in no time."

Henry looked at her and then he looked at Adoc. She immediately saw his concern. She reached over to pet Adoc. "Good boy!" She gave him a last petting and turned to Henry. "Henry, I think Adoc will be all right for some time, why don't we take a ride and get some essentials?"

Henry listened to Kristina and took a doubtful look at Adoc. She giggled a bit seeing the doubts of a puppy father paralyze Henry.

"Henry, the vet won't be here until later, we have plenty of time and I don't think Adoc has any interest in leaving." Kristina watched Henry respond to her comment; his pause was worthy of a smile. She watched him as though he was a father being asked to leave a doctor stitching up the knee of a child learning to manage the skill of walking. "Come along, if you want to keep this dog as family, you are going to need things to keep him. After all, he doesn't need you... he chose you."

When Henry heard what Kristina said he broke from his trance of being worried. He patted Adoc and then refilled his water bowl and replenished his food, then he and Kristina got into her truck and drove off for Adoc's goods.

Henry knew a lot of things; he knew how to offer folks answers they would have never thought of on their own. He never knew the responsibility of a dog. The drive to get Adoc things was something he didn't understand. He figured food, and maybe things he'd need to bring

Adoc into social settings, but in all of his doubt he was thankful for Kristina's mentoring. In his whole life he couldn't remember not having a plan and for it he was very unsure and unsettled. Kristina felt his anguish on the ride to the feed store. It was where they bought all the food for the shelter animals and all business in her mind, went to a good cause. The city got a discount from the owner because he too was a pet lover, more than that he loved animals. Kristina thought that Henry and Francis might be able to work out difficulties Francis was having staying in business. The big stores sold everything he sold for less than he could and his business was declining. Moreover the community itself was catching up to modernization and agriculture in the area was disappearing as fast as the farmers were selling out to developers for prime land.

Kristina had a way about her mannerisms that made Henry comfortable. During the ride he couldn't help but think about how Adoc loved to chase the stick. He thought it to be the most beautiful thing he ever put his eyes upon. The wonders of the world were relics to Henry; they withstood life and even time. Adoc was abundance in living, even if it was such a simple thing. Henry was addicted and the only one seeming to know it was Kristina.

The trip to the feed store didn't take long and for Henry it was twice a new experience. He met someone he didn't know and he purchased things he never had a need to buy. After Francis and Kristina had greeted one another, Francis asked Henry what he was interested in as far as purchases.

When Henry heard the question he really didn't know what to say except, "Well, I'm just a beginner."

Kristina took control of the banter and inquiry. "Francis, why don't we start with say, fifty pounds of puppy food and all of the new dog owner fare?"

Francis needed no other direction. While Francis saw to the order he had a feeling that Kristina's recommendation would be just what he needed for his future. He heard about Henry's abilities and he had long hoped for an occasion to ask him for help. He thought that his own condition as a feed store owner was part of the way of the day. Times changed and he couldn't compete. He didn't need to pay overhead, he owned everything in the store, but he just couldn't sell his goods to compete. Heck, he couldn't get the prices the big stores bought their inventory for and he couldn't lose his livelihood to do business for a loss. He had prayed many times about how to realize the reality of things as they were. Fulfilling the order for Henry... well that let him think of days past and being the best feed man around.

When Francis was done with the order he didn't tally it up right away. Instead he asked a question of Henry. "You say ya met this dog and now ya want to keep him... And if Kristina is here putting your order in for the dog, I need to ask you... what makes you think that you know enough to keep the dog as a pet?"

Henry responded honestly, "I don't know that he will be my pet. I guess I just hope he wants to be that pet."

When Francis heard Henry's answer he laughed loudly. Then he winked at Kristina and spoke to her. "I owe ya extra food on the next order. You bring those of such hope to me that pay bills. I gotta keep the finder's fee alive!" He looked at Henry. "You will be a great friend of this dog and when it gets crazy all ya need to do is get a hold of Kristina here... she'll do the translating."

Henry listened to those he spoke with as though he believed what they said completely for the hearing of it. Henry always knew that his contemplation of the conversation later would expose contradictions or a conflict in the speaker's reasoning. The suggestion that Francis offered was new for him to hear, because for the most part Henry had little need of others in living his life. Francis made a declaration of wisdom Henry couldn't know about himself. Once the provisions were loaded into the truck Henry shook Francis's hand.

"I'd sure like to have him as a pet and I thank you for offering me your wisdom."

Francis nodded in affirmation. "When you get things sorted out you bring that pup of yours on over for a visit. I may have a few treats or things I haven't just thought about to load up in the truck, but I reckon I'll know when I see that pup of yours." Both men released their grasps and Francis made a parting similarly to Kristina.

Kristina smiled as they drove away and Henry thought her humor was interesting. His experience with folks didn't usually convey such a greeting. Most of the time, they came with concern or worry on their faces. In fact the kindness he knew or happiness they revealed only came after they accepted his wisdom for resolving their problem. Other times his advice wasn't accepted well and there was very little happiness or generosity for the dynamic of interaction. He wondered how it was she could be so bubbly in nature. Kristina giggled and that gave Henry a surprise.

"What's the giggle for?"

She didn't give a look while she drove and it took a moment to compose herself. "Well, in my business one of the highlights is to see a pairing of a pet and a human. You see, so many times I have to deal with the lacking of such a partnership and truthfully it is heartbreaking. So my giggle was a celebration of seeing you become a pet person."

Henry heard her reasoning and accepted it, but it did nothing for his curiosity about her bubbly nature. In fact it gave him a greater curiosity as to the dichotomy in her job. *Why would anyone take a job that gave so much heartache in the first place?* While Henry thought about Kristina's motivations they pulled up to his house. He didn't see Adoc immediately but by the time both of them began unloading the supplies the pup presented himself.

Adoc saw the people and that they were doing something. He saw them going inside the house and he waited where he ate the good stuff.

When Kristina and Henry put up the goods she gave Henry the appropriate toys for Adoc. She explained to Henry that even a stray puppy would need to chew. She also said that he should try different fetch toys rather than a stick. Even as she spoke Henry began taking her explanations as gospel. Indeed Adoc would be chewing as he did with the sticks. She also said that he'd need a pocket full of treats. She gave him a handful of doggy biscuits. "These will help you with training him to behaviors you need him to demonstrate."

Henry put them in his pocket as she gave them to him. He had a confused look on his face. She smiled at him as they turned to go be with Adoc.

"Henry, don't worry this will be a wonderful time. Both of you have to discover just what you'll both need to be friends. And to be honest, the dog's job is far more difficult than yours. You see, if he is to be a pet, he'll have to trust you to take care of all his needs."

As Henry heard Kristina his panic seemed to ease. She had a way of making his doubts less than what they were. He'd never thought to be responsible for another life, but she made it sound like it would be all right.

Adoc saw the people come back to the door. The one with many smells he liked was first and then the other one who gave him the good stuff to eat was there. He had some things in his hands, but he wasn't holding a stick. Adoc wagged because the one with many smells was giving him pets and scratches. She kept making noises at him and he liked the sounds she made. She said *Adoc* many times and he began to think that what she was calling him.

Henry watched her and tried to remember how she worked with him. It all seemed as though he played with Adoc similarly, but she seemed to have more sincerity than he did. She turned to him and told him she had to get back to work. She watched Henry as he knew she did have to leave. She smiled at him before she leaned down to pet Adoc one last time.

"My shift ends at 3PM, if you'd like I'll stop on back and help you along with other things."

Henry watched her put her love on Adoc before she turned to leave. After she gave Adoc more of a reason to wag she left for her truck.

Henry called after her, "I'd appreciate that if you could find the time."

She waved and left the Man and the Dog behind. Before she got into her truck she hollered back at Henry, "I'll be back to see the Man and the Dog after work. Besides, you need to get ready for that vet!"

She was gone. Henry thought about what she said. Something about the Man and the Dog made him feel good. He didn't over think it but he did repeat it to Adoc as he introduced him to the toys.

"Adoc, what do you think, boy? Kristina thinks we will be fine as a Man and a Dog?"

Adoc sniffed the toys Henry had, showing very little interest in any of them. He wondered what the person was doing; he wanted to know where a stick was. Adoc checked out the toys as Henry presented them... none were like the stick. Henry even tossed a few of them but Adoc wasn't interested. As Henry watched the pup's displeasure, he realized a large part of the toys he bought retained none of Adoc's interest. His heart sank as he was hoping for a better response from Adoc. Adoc exhausted the supply of toys Henry presented. Henry considered his doubt and thought of what Kristina mentioned... something about enjoying the process of getting to know each other. How it would be more difficult for Adoc than he. Henry took heart in Adoc's tail-wagging. That lifted his spirits even if Adoc rejected the chew toys. He was standing at Henry's feet, sniffing at his pocket. Henry remembered that Kristina told him about the cookies, or whatever she called them. Snacks to get him to be the dog he needed, or something like that. Henry decided he was going to forget his doubt... he stroked Adoc on the head and neck.

"Adoc, do you smell something good? You want what the Man has?"

Adoc heard the noise and tried to pay attention, but the smell was too enticing. When the person kneeled down the smell was removed. Adoc lost the scent as Henry's pocket folded. After Adoc lost the scent he let the person pet him repeating, hearing the word *Man* amidst other noise. Adoc's smelling didn't retire, it just stole smells seeking the good thing on the... Man's body?

Once Henry stood up Adoc noticed the smell again and he saw his hand go to the source. He wondered what the Man was doing and as he watched his hand removed the good smelling thing; Adoc's eyes brightened to focus. The smell of the good thing was right in his nose. Adoc's excitement became very visible to Henry and his heart swelled with happiness.

Henry asked, "Adoc, are you hungry? Do you want a snack?"

The Man's noise spoke *Adoc,* he showed a want for the stick he dropped his head to the ground with his hind quarters up, and then he barked. The Man's noise changed and it sounded more like the other person with smells. The Man held the snack close to where Adoc could sit sniffing as high as he could reach without jumping. Adoc sensed the Man's gesture as a gentle and nibbled for the good stuff. The Man relinquished it. It fell into Adoc's mouth and it was good. It wasn't like the food that the Man brought him earlier, it was better than that. Adoc wondered after he chewed it down if there would be any more. He could still smell the good smell in the pocket. He focused on the Man. He listened to the noise he made. In all his hope for more good things he'd go to the Man hearing *Adoc*... after some more jumping low and barking Adoc got another good thing. After a while another person came to where they were. The Man and the other person grasped each thing that gave the good stuff. He smelled no bad smells and his time was better than he ever knew or recalled!

After the man and the other person finished making their noise the other person looked at Adoc and came towards him. Adoc smelled that this person also had many smells on him. He wagged, welcoming the touch of the other person. His touch was different. It wasn't a bad touch and it didn't make Adoc less excited, he just knew that this touch was different somehow, like it knew him. Adoc sniffed the abundant smells on the person as he was touched. When the other person made noise he kept hearing *Adoc,* always while being rubbed.

After a while the person did different things to Adoc. He felt a couple of pinches that would have made him flinch, but the touch was why he didn't. Soon Adoc was being touched by the Man and the other person. The other person stopped touching him and stood away. After a few more touches; the man also stood up and away. The Man and the other person made that noise that they made then the person with other smells left.

Henry walked over to the toys again and tried once more with Adoc to see if he would play with them. Adoc sniffed each of them but had no interest. Henry collected them up and put them back into a bag. He brought the bag back into the house and Adoc waited on him outside. Henry didn't much like things scattered about so if Adoc wasn't going to be entertained he didn't want the mess. Henry went to the fireplace area and grabbed another stick. When he brought it out to where Adoc was waiting, he found the pup happy to see him with the stick. Henry showed Adoc the stick and asked him, "Chase the stick, Adoc? Chase the stick?"

Adoc did his usual bow and a bark and for it Henry began the tossing of the stick. After some time of chasing, Adoc came to drink out of the bowl and when he drank his share they were back at the stick chasing. Henry watched Adoc's pure joy of chewing on the stick as it disintegrated. Henry marveled at Adoc's energy. He was amazed at the focus Adoc gave to chasing the stick.

Henry realized that he was becoming hungry; he hadn't really followed his morning routine and with all the business of the day he thought to fix something for himself. He imagined Adoc might like some of the food he bought earlier so he went into the house and Adoc waited at the door again. Henry went about preparing some food for himself and realized he hadn't brought in Adoc's bowl. He finished up his food and went back out to get Adoc's bowl. Adoc was lying on the ground near his bowls looking toward the door. When Henry saw him he reached in his pocket and held a treat in his hand. Adoc lifted his head up looking at the Man's hand. Adoc liked those good tasting things the man gave earlier. He sat up and waited to see what the man would do. The man made noise again and Adoc heard his name.

Henry looked at Adoc respond and he figured from in the house he'd toss Adoc the treat. Henry gave it a gentle flip towards Adoc and Adoc caught the treat before it could fall. Henry stepped out of the house and got Adoc's bowl. Adoc looked at his hands to see if there was more, but there wasn't. The Man turned and went back into the house with the bowl. Adoc waited patiently. He heard a strange noise and wanted to know what it was, but the memory of the grabbing thing was still haunting him. When he heard the steps of the Man he became very hopeful and when he saw him, his wagging was uncontrollable.

The Man's hands were full and when he approached Adoc the Man made more noise. "Good boy, Adoc! Are you hungry like me?" Adoc sat waiting to taste the good stuff in the bowl. He heard more noise. "Ah, what a good boy, Adoc!"

The man came close to Adoc and lowered the bowl to him. Even though Adoc liked what was in the bowl from before his sniffs told him that this was better than the good stuff. Once the bowl was lowered the man stepped back and sat on the entry that Adoc didn't like. Adoc began eating. He didn't need to eat his food quickly; he sensed the Man would always have food for him. When he was done he sat by his bowl watching the Man. The Man was eating and Adoc watched politely.

Henry never really made much more than he could eat for himself, but from what Kristina and the vet told him, Adoc was in no danger of being fat. Henry decided when he made his food, he'd make extra. He wanted Adoc to be benefited for being there; his hope was to call him his friend. When Henry had his fill he looked at Adoc watching him.

"Adoc, come here, boy."

Adoc tilted his head for hearing the Man. The Man made the same noise. Adoc remembered the words.

"Adoc, come here, boy!" Then he saw the Man pat on his leg. Adoc stood up and moved closer to the man and the place he thought where the grabbing thing might be. Adoc was closer to the Man but he slowed moving to where he sat. He heard the Man make more noise.

"That's a good boy, Adoc." Adoc didn't stop moving, he was cautious as he padded slowly to the Man.

"That's a good boy, Adoc." When Adoc reached the Man, the Man patted his head. "Good boy." Then the Man reached to him with the food he was eating himself. Adoc sniffed it, looking into the Man's eyes. Then he nibbled out of the Man's hand. Once the Man stopped giving him food he sat back down near the place where he was unsure.

Henry felt better for eating, but his happiness was in the sharing Adoc and he came to trust. Henry saw that Adoc had some type of concern about the entry to the house and figured he had good enough reason to worry. Henry imagined that maybe his young life wasn't so easy. The vet voiced concern about the scars Adoc had. He also said that they had begun healing enough so as not to need attention unless there was infection. He gave him a dose of antibiotic and told Henry to bring him to his office regardless of any infection developing. There were other things needing to be done after he was six months old. The vet told him he'd need heartworm tests that came after six months. Henry would see to visiting him within the month. While Henry thought about what needed to be seen to he stroked Adoc. Henry reckoned that the day was past the noon hour. He hadn't noticed the time when he was inside. He thought he'd see if Adoc would wear the collar he bought him.

"Adoc, I'll be right back. Gonna come back with a present for you."

Adoc looked at the Man with his head tilted.

Henry stood up and petted his head. "Be right back."

He turned and left to get the collar he and Kristina bought earlier from Francis. While he went for the bag that held the collar he gave thought to Francis. Something in the meeting with him earlier gave him a concern… nothing bad, but he thought that Francis and he would be getting to know each other more than just as customer and shop keeper. Henry grabbed the collar. He inspected it and wondered what Adoc might think of it. Today Henry had been involved with some folks not as an expert and that was what his usual role would be. He was the student and dependent on the expertise of others. Kristina was expert because of her vocation. Henry had no doubt of that.

He could only assume Francis knew his business, why else would an expert do her business with anyone lesser? As Henry approached Adoc he took his seat where they ate. He looked into Adoc's eyes and offered up the collar. Adoc sniffed at it and began wagging.

The Man was holding something that had a good smell. It wasn't anything he could eat, but it smelled familiar. Adoc began to want to know what the Man had in his hand more than his concern for the grabbing thing mattered. His curiosity seemed to increase as he wondered what the smell was. The Man made more noises.

"Okay, good boy, okay. Can you sit, Adoc?"

Adoc calmed down and sat as he had watching the Man eat. The Man did something to the thing in his hand and it got bigger. Then the man reached around Adoc's neck and began to fasten it so that he felt the familiar smell on him. The sensation was very strange. Adoc shook freely. It almost felt like the grabbing thing but he could move. When the Man lowered his hands Adoc stood up and walked in a circle once. The sensation was different but the smell made the sensation not scary like the grabbing thing.

Henry watched Adoc's reaction for wearing the collar. He saw Adoc deciding a willingness to wear the new thing. Henry picked up the stick once again and tossed it. Just like that, Adoc was running after it. He returned the stick to Henry and the tossing resumed. Henry reflected on his thoughts of Francis. Kristina's expertise led him to another expert and Henry felt fortunate to be in such company.

More time went by and Adoc seemed to be enjoying the tossing even while wearing the collar. The tossing was interrupted by Kristina's return. The day was flying by and Henry and Adoc weren't paying one bit of attention to time. Time for them mattered little while chasing the stick and bonding as friends.

Kristina showed up greeting Adoc. Adoc dropped his stick and ran to meet her directly. Henry watched Adoc's explosion towards her as he went to where Adoc left the stick.

"What a handsome boy Adoc is with his collar on!" Kristina leaned down to greet Adoc with petting and scratches. "Yes, you are a handsome boy, Adoc!" Adoc took all the petting and scratching Kristina offered. She rose up to greet Henry.

"It looks like you two have been working out some understanding. It isn't an easy thing to put a collar on a stray." Adoc turned to Henry and Henry threw the stick. Adoc was back into the routine of chasing the stick.

"Well, I'm not so sure that it was all my own doing to put that collar on. Sure, I did the job, but Adoc seemed to invite it and I think that you and Francis may have had something to do with that."

She listened to Henry's response and watched Adoc with a huge smile. Henry could feel the happiness radiate from her body. The energy she let flow was a marvel to him.

"If I may ask you, what is the story with Francis?"

Kristina seemed to be surprised by the question, but not for long. "Well, it should be evident; he's a store owner who supplies animal people with all their needs. Unfortunately, like most other things of these days, he is having trouble competing with new corporate chain stores. They can buy product for bulk he can't carry. Money is what it is all about these days for folks and folks like Francis can't afford to stay in business."

Henry listened to her explanation. He processed the information for a time later, which was coming. "Yes, the days are coming to forget the importance of wisdom for the savings of a few bucks. I see it all the time and it seems like a snowball rolling down hill. Trouble is that it is one long hill."

Kristina thought about Henry's metaphor. She watched the stick tossing and Henry sensed she was about to dispense some more wisdom.

"Downhill isn't a bad way to live, it sure beats an uphill climb. What I notice is how many folks don't think things through. The result is evident all over the place. Take Adoc for instance... it used to be that folks considered the responsibility of having a dog. Sometimes the dog's purpose was to work, other times it was for guarding or just companionship. Today folks get dogs to create an image for themselves, or they just don't consider what the burden of responsibility is. The victims of that thinking are left to the mercy of nature or the cruelty of mankind and it isn't pretty. But not all of us choose the steepest part downhill; some of us enjoy the ride using the force of gravity to ease our journey. As you say, most get right on the expert slope only to get caught up in the craziness of being unprepared."

Henry didn't expect to hear such a manner of her understanding. He was in awe of who Kristina was for her revealing. Henry felt as though something deep in his core was fighting to escape with urgency. His elation of coming to know Adoc was an emotion he never thought to have, but he did when he was standing on the bridge. This awe that he felt was built upon that elation and the only thing he could attribute it to was a sense of feeling grateful. "I know we don't know each other well, but there is something I want to let you know about because I think it is important."

Kristina gazed at Henry without saying a word. Henry took it as an acceptance and continued with his thinking. "When I first met Adoc, I met him over on the walking bridge over the river. I was thinking at the time that there was nothing in this world I cared about and I guess I was thinking about the value of life." Henry thought about what to say next and before he could bring forth the words he threw the stick to Adoc. The stick was being reduced like before but he figured as long as he could throw it... he would continue.

Kristina spoke up to his last utterance. "So, you are telling me that you had a perch to look from and make a decision about taking the double expert slope that would have required a parachute that you didn't have... That is what you are telling me right?"

Once again Henry felt humbled and he welcomed it in complete acceptance, grateful that another understood. "Yes, something like that, I suppose."

She smiled and stepped closer to him while they both kept a focus on the dog, Adoc who didn't know fatigue. "So, you made a pal who showed you another, easier way down the hill of life?"

Henry laughed. "Well, I think maybe three pals and this was the point of what I meant to say. You know me, I guess, as a problem solver to a degree. So what I want to do is offer you help that you made have a need for, as well as some help for Francis."

Kristina heard what Henry said and gave his offer some thought. "Well, we can always use a hand down at the Animal Shelter. There's always something to do there. And a far as what Francis may need, I couldn't really tell you other than what I already have told you. You'd need to discuss that with him."

Henry's need was satisfied by her answer. "Very well, then. I imagine Adoc and I will be down at the shelter contributing time and whatever else we can do to help. I'll also make a point of talking with Francis forthwith."

"That will be fine Henry, we can always use help at the shelter. The town's budget isn't one that considers more than having Animal Control Officers for problem animals. We don't press the issue of needing more funding; we just submit our budget and keep our fingers crossed."

Henry listened to her explanation. The town council had their work cut out for them; everyone was feeling the pinch of economic change. "It isn't just the town council. They represent the town folk and the policy they embrace isn't perfect, but they keep the town moving forward." Henry thought about what he said and realized how pathetic it sounded.

Kristina wasn't one to make an issue of the council policy. She never had been of that mind. Her focus was always on the animals she tended. "As I said, we just submit the budget and keep our fingers crossed. A lot of generous people make up the difference. Love for animals usually affords humane conditions for our needs."

Henry listened carefully to her analysis. His mind was already designing options for her particular problem, but his thinking didn't stop there. Henry was considering the possibility of how he could make his influence applicable to both her condition and Francis', simultaneously.

He did so through enjoyment of Adoc's endless chasing. Eventually Adoc took pause from the chasing for a drink of water. The bowl needed a refill and Henry grabbed up the bowl and used the exterior hose to replenish the water for Adoc. As he did the filling he thought about the issue of Adoc's hesitance to enter the house.

"Kristina, let me ask you about Adoc's unwillingness to enter the house? He seems to be very frightened of coming inside. My thoughts were on how to change his behavior. I might do that by installing a dog door within the door. How does that sound?"

She thought about Henry's logic and truly was impressed. She had an idea that Henry was likely more of an animal person than he knew himself. "Well, providing a way in which Adoc can come and go freely is a fine bit of thinking. I'm not sure it directly addresses his doubt or whatever is bothering him, but it sure does give him a option... That is what you need to do when involved in behavior modification."

Henry was satisfied by the affirmation of his thinking. He watched Adoc lap up the water, taking time from tossing the stick that he had reduced to almost nothing. "Oh, by the way, those chew things we bought aren't of any interest to this dog so I figured you may as well take them along with you. Maybe they'll be of use down at the shelter?"

Kristina nodded. "Sure, I'll take them for the shelter. Good thing for other dogs that Adoc only seems to like sticks!"

Henry told her they were inside and that he'd get them for her. Adoc finished up his lapping of the water and stayed with Kristina, accepting her petting. Henry was direct in gathering up the toys Adoc had no interest in so it wasn't but a few seconds before he was back.

The sun was falling to the horizon and the chill of the evening began to settle over the grass. For Henry, time seemed to be going faster than he ever recalled. The only time that came close to such a sensation was during his boyhood years when he sought adventure and discovery. "So, I'm thinking that I could build this door for Adoc while I try to lure him inside the house."

Kristina heard this in a sort of surprise. Before he could espouse his thought she interrupted him. "You want to build a door?"

He looked at her, hearing her doubt. "Yes, that is what I was thinking. You see, I could cut a hole in the lower panels and-"

Kristina interrupted him again. "Well, if you are dead set on building it I suppose you could but I'm quite sure that Francis might have a doggie door in his store. That way it would simply be an install."

She seemed to think that was the way to go and Henry hadn't considered purchasing a door, he just figured to build it. When Henry thought about it, he wondered if Francis was still at his shop. "Do you think Francis is still at his store? I mean, I would really like to do that bit of work as soon as possible."

Kristina knew that Francis kept late hours. His business was his life. As a matter of fact she and Francis did a lot of business during times others businesses closed. That was one reason why Francis and the Shelter had such a great relationship. "Yes, I'm sure he is open. It may just be that he is having some dinner about now."

Henry wondered if he'd be able to convince her to take a return trip to see Francis. To his delight she offered to take him back. She was a person who lived by herself to and she had no responsibility to anything except her work. Now that she was off duty, her time was her own. They all three moved to her truck and entered it intending to drive off. Henry was excited by the prospect of seeing Francis again. He realized suddenly that with Adoc included in his life, he'd have to do the unthinkable before that time and go buy a car... or some kind of vehicle.

Adoc sat in the truck on the bench between both the Man and the other person with good smells. Being in the truck was something new to Adoc and it was an enjoyable experience. He saw blurs as though he was running and there was the feeling of moving he loved without chasing the stick. He knew that in this place there was no grabbing thing. It was the furthest thing from his mind. The Man pet him along the ride and that was even more pleasurable than the sensation of not having to chase the stick. Adoc never felt anything so secure. He hoped that this feeling between the man and this person with so many smells would be forever...

Henry Kristina and Adoc arrived at Francis' place. Adoc exited the truck after Henry, on his side. Adoc began smelling more wonderful smells and followed his nose. He smelled the

Man there and he smelled the other person with many smells whom he had just came with, in that no-chasing-stick moving-thing as he followed his nose. His excitement didn't give him time to wonder how it was that he smelled them there, but he did. And as he followed his nose the aroma of the Man and the other person with many smells became lost. There were many more smells! Adoc couldn't help but to run about and lift his leg. He wanted to be sure to let the whole world know that he had visited such a wondrous place.

Adoc was so lost in his focus he didn't hear the Man or the other person with good smells make their noises. What did get Adoc's attention however was a noise he hadn't heard from either the Man or the other person with the good smells. Adoc took notice of the Man and the other person making noise with another person. He looked at them looking at him. He heard the Man making noise. "Adoc, come boy." Adoc had no reason to hurry. There was plenty of smelling to do while moving towards the Man and the other people.

Adoc moved towards the Man and the other two people and what he discovered moving closer to them was that there was another person with good smells, but different than before… He began to hurry towards them and he discovered that the third person had smells as good as the first other person and that the third person had a very sure hand when it came to feeling his pets. Adoc was wagging uncontrollably; the joy in his being was more than he felt on the ride over. He liked this third person so much he couldn't help but to rise up on his back legs to lick along with the excessive wagging.

Francis demonstrated unconditional love even when he stepped away from Adoc to avoid his jumping. "You must be Adoc! Oh, my. You are a handsome boy!"

Once Adoc was down on all his legs Francis bent over and began greeting Adoc so that Adoc responded properly. Adoc let the third person rub him and pet him. He had no bad smells. His touch calmed Adoc's excitement, for Adoc it felt so good. The third person made some noises to the Man and the other person with good smells, then they all made noises. After a while the touching ended and Adoc seemed to know that he had experienced enough of the praise and good feelings. When the third person stopped the petting Adoc wanted to rise up again, but his want didn't let him rise. Adoc rather sniffed the third person at his nose level.

Adoc didn't notice the Man until the Man made noise. "Adoc! Want a stick?"

Unlike wanting to rise on the third person and not being able to, Adoc couldn't resist the temptation of the stick. When the Man tossed the stick Adoc chased it. It was dark but he left his hearing guide him to the stick as it fell. When he got close to where the stick fell, he let his nose guide him to the Man's scent. Once he had the stick in his mouth he began chewing it carrying it back to the Man.

Francis was glad to see Henry, Kristina and Adoc, but he wondered why they visited as late as they did. He reckoned there must be some purpose. "So, to what do I owe the late visit?"

Henry was still tossing the stick with Adoc and before he could respond Kristina answered. "Well, it is apparent that Adoc and Henry are taking to each, but Adoc isn't of the mind to enter Henry's house, so Henry thought to build a doggy door for him. I told him that was fine thinking except the part of building it from scratch and that is why we are here."

The explanation that Kristina offered gave Francis even more of a reason to be happy. Doggy doors were an item Francis had purchased some time ago thinking they'd sell well. They didn't and he still carried an inventory. Parting with one gave him relief from lost expense, but more than that it gave him a sense of value to the community. That sense of value had been eroding as the bigger stores drew his former customers for lower prices.

"I'm sure we have a door for Adoc to trust in for ability to come and go as he pleases, and I'd have to agree that is some fine thinking." Francis began leading the way to where the doors were and they all followed. While they did Henry looked around as Francis turned on lights to get to the inventory. Henry soaked in the history of past when Francis ran this business as a greater service to the community. He felt as though he were an archeologist passing into the ruins of a lost empire. Ultimately they ended up at storage shelves that contained the doggy doors. They lay on their sides in packaging with the size of the doors facing out for quicker retrieval.

Henry looked at the dusty packages along with cobwebs draping them. The doors were sorted small to large from left to right on the shelving. Francis reached for the large package and Henry intervened. "Let me get that, Francis."

Francis stepped aside and allowed Henry to remove the box from the shelf. Francis took note of Henry's diligence in managing need and he was reminded of his younger days watching the other man remove the door from the shelving. Henry grasped the door and carried it to the truck, putting it into the back only to return for another. Henry's actions surprised both Francis and Kristina, even Adoc seemed interested. Henry felt the notice of their curiosity and paused after removing the second door. He put the door on the ground and looked at them.

"Well, I do have two doors on the first level. If one door is meant to gain Adoc's trust, then two doors ought to only earn the trust faster."

Upon hearing Henry's reasoning Francis let a belly laugh loose. Kristina stood in a happy reality. "Kristina, I think the appearance of these two as being a likely match has a bit more behind it. It almost sounds as though it was meant to be."

Adoc followed the Man on the second trip. He watched the Man load the second door into the truck. When Henry was done securing the rear door of the truck he turned to Adoc and told him, "Tomorrow you'll be able to come and go as you please in our house. You can help me out with the carpentry and then we'll throw sticks."

Adoc heard the Man make noises towards him. The words sounded good and his excitement offered wagging for the word *sticks*. They returned to Francis and Kristina shutting off the lights and exiting the store. Henry felt like a pillager entering the ruins of a lost empire with a couple of trinkets for the passage. When they met with each other Henry spoke directly to the cost.

Francis stopped him directly. "Henry, why don't you all come on in for a bite to eat? I made some food and it is more than I'll eat myself, besides I'd appreciate your company."

Henry looked to Kristina and she offered no objections. He replied, "Sure, there are some things I wanted to discuss with you anyway. I guess we can do it over breaking bread."

After the offer was accepted they all moved towards Francis' house. They entered to some good smelling food that was cooking. Henry noticed Adoc's willingness to enter into Francis' home without any of the hesitation which he offered at his home. It was a curiosity to Henry, but it wasn't a consideration of resentment, it was more of another clue as to why Adoc had such an unwillingness to go into the house. Henry realized that Adoc warmed up to all of them and that might have made him feel more comfort towards entering Francis' home. At Henry's house it was only he and Adoc.

Francis' house was much like his store. Henry felt as though he entered a time capsule of the past. Francis was a type of hoarder but in a very organized way. Henry concluded that Francis found value in the way he kept his home and he also felt as though Francis knew where each and every treasure of his life was placed. Henry watched the older man manage his kitchen, his steps in providing hospitality of he, Adoc and Kristina was flawless. Before long they were sitting around the dinner table enjoying the bounty of a man who claimed to prepare food for himself, when it was clear that somehow he knew he'd have unexpected visitors. Even Adoc shared a bowl of food Francis prepared.

When all were full Francis began clearing the table, returning with a dessert drink. Francis called it an after dinner wash down. They sat again at the table enjoying the beverage. Henry inquired about the drink and Francis told him it was a portion of his homemade wine. Francis swore that it made digestion so much easier. Henry didn't know about such things but he took Francis' word as he said it, enjoying the sweetness of the drink.

"So, Henry, you mentioned that you wanted to discuss some things. I guess now is a time to listen."

Henry put his drink glass down after finishing it and began to think of his statements. He was glad for only having to say the words once as both of those he wanted to hear them were there.

"Well, I have been giving some thought to how much you and Kristina have been helping me along with Adoc, and I wanted to suggest that along with buying the food and doors from you that I would also like to pay for supplies that Kristina may have a need for even if her budget doesn't cover it. More than that I'd like to help you out in whatever way I can so as to negotiate better prices for you to remain competitive."

After Henry was done speaking Kristina decided to wait to comment on Henry's generosity. She decided then Francis might have something to say since it was he would ultimately gain the most for Henry's offer.

Francis stood up and poured another glass of wine for the group as a gesture of appreciation for Henry's offer. When they all held the glasses Francis toasted the gathering.

"Here is to knowing lovers of stray dogs. In my estimation the most generous two-legged creatures around." They all sipped the drink and relaxed.

After a few seconds Kristina made a comment. "Henry, that is mighty generous of you and I know that the community will appreciate your offer."

Henry looked to Kristina. He wanted to let her know that it wasn't necessary. "Kristina, I'd rather you not say anything of the contribution to the community. Because of the work I want to do with Francis here it is better to keep it close to the vest."

Kristina nodded, accepting his logic and acknowledged his wishes. Francis took delight in Henry's offer, but he also wanted to mention a few things to Henry. "I'll accept anything you will help with Henry, but of course I'll want to compensate you for any help given."

Henry wasn't going to hear of any compensation. "I have no need for any monetary gain. As a matter of fact I have already made more money than I'll need for a few lifetimes. You see your wisdom, well both of you have shown me happiness with my new pal Adoc and it is likely I'll never be able to explain what that means to me."

Francis looked at Adoc and Henry with a great admiration. "That may be true, but I'm pretty sure I know what it means to Adoc." Francis looked to Kristina "Would you agree with that, young lady?"

Kristina wasn't much for words; she just nodded and smiled at both of them.

Adoc enjoyed the Man stroking him. Somehow he knew that the Man and these people who smelled good, with kind and old hands would be around a lot and Adoc couldn't be happier about having that sense. It was new for him and seemed like such a long way from where he used to stay. He liked the food he was eating recently; it filled his belly enough for him to sleep easily.

He liked being able to sleep. When he had food in his belly he wasn't so driven to hunt down what might smell good to eat or what might not smell so good. He remembered that type of eating too, anything to eat so as to stop the belly from growling. Now it seemed like chasing the stick was all he wanted to do. Besides, he loved chewing on the wood. Bits of it fell out of his mouth until there was nothing left to chew while running. Adoc's life seemed to be more fun than he remembered being alone. He did like the Man. He trusted the Man; it wasn't like he remembered with loud noises and bad smells in the beginning of his awareness.

The three finished their last bit of drink and Henry decided it was time to go home. "I have a lot to do tomorrow with installing these doors and I need to buy a vehicle as well. It figures, I never needed a car until I got a dog."

Francis thought about Henry's need. He had a spare car he wasn't using. He never got rid of his wife's car after she passed away. "Henry, I have a car I don't use. It was my wife's car and I never thought to get rid of it. If you want, I'll let ya buy that car, I'm sure it will do for you and Adoc just fine."

Henry thought that Francis' offer was a good one, if nothing else it would save him the aggravation of having to deal with people he might otherwise not want to deal with. Henry was still protective of his privacy even though he welcomed the present company. "I guess tomorrow we can have a look at the car you have. Maybe you could drive on over to my house with it and we'll see if Adoc likes the ride."

Francis smiled widely, "That will be fine. Let's say mid morning?"

Henry nodded. "Sure, sounds good. It is likely Adoc will be chasing the stick I'll be tossin' him."

They all rose up after shaking hands in closing the evening. Francis stood in the doorway of his ancient dwelling while Adoc, Henry and Kristina got into her truck. Francis thought that they made a nice looking family, even though they weren't. As they drove away Francis took time to talk to his departed wife as he did at the close of each and every evening. It was his way of demonstrating his own sort of spirituality. He turned back into the house after watching them drive away.

"Well, Mildred, I guess my time here won't be so lonely after all. Even as I want to be with you, my old love, I haven't yet been called home, so that must mean I have more work to do. I reckon that Henry and Adoc need some guidance towards our Kristina. I think she has an interest that she is unaware of with this fellow Henry."

He began picking up the dishes from dinner to bring them to the sink. "Yes, Mildred. I think so, too. Yes, dear, I think after some time they will be a happy family too, but right now they are just coming to know themselves and their own value."

He began washing off the plates, continuing his conversation with his dearest Mildred. Adoc would have known who he talked to, but the others would just think he was an old man muttering to himself. "Yes, yes, Adoc is quite the dog and I know he reminds you of Huntzy... Huntzy was a very good dog, but Adoc is very young, just still a pup and we'll watch how Henry gets along with him. I think both with teach each other equally." He began rinsing the plates to put them in the dish rack. "Yes, Adoc had a tragic start, but then again so did Henry and yes, my beautiful wife, I'll keep an eye on all three of them for as long as I can... Well, I don't know if Henry will want the old place, let's just wait and see. But I have a feeling he will, he offered to help out with what he thought he could do to keep it alive."

He began putting up the food that was left over. "Oh, Mildred, you must have faith. You were never too good at having faith and don't you hush me up, you know I'm right. Like I always said, everything in its own season." Francis finished up the last of his chores. "Yes, my dear wife, I will be there as soon as I can, but everything in its own season." Francis shut the lights off and began his walk to the bedroom. He got himself prepared for bed thinking of the next day and just where the day would bring him. He slept as well as he had in a long time. He once again had a purpose that made life matter. He was thankful his life could be full once again in his last days. Before he took his last waking breaths he spoke again. "Nope, it won't be much longer now, just wait a bit longer, hun. Then we'll be back together yet again."

Francis took his rest. A big day was coming and there was plenty to do.

On the ride home Kristina remained quiet. Henry didn't have anything to say, but both were filled with thoughts that might be better expressed rather than withheld. Neither felt comfort in either of their thinking. Somehow both thought what they wanted to share just needed another time for sharing. When they arrived at Henry's house she got out of the truck with him to help as she could with the doors Henry needed for Adoc. Adoc never seemed to be too far away from Henry and that was fine, but he didn't get so close as to be in Henry's way, either. Henry grabbed one of the doors. It was bulky more than what it weighed and after he removed one Kristina reached for the other. She followed Henry, managing her load with ease. Henry was surprised as he thought he'd get the second door, but he hadn't seen her removing the second box. If had seen her he would have said something to her, but there was no need now. He put the doggy door by the back porch door and took the second door from Kristina then walked it to the front door of the house. After he put the door down where he wanted it he turned back to Kristina. The words he wanted to say wouldn't come from his tongue.

"I guess after Francis and I do business tomorrow I won't need any rides, so at least you are off the hook on that measure of helping me."

She smiled. "Well, we wouldn't want people thinking the wrong thing now would we, Henry? I mean the most eligible bachelor in town driving around with the animal control officer, it would be scandalous."

When Henry had heard what she said he felt a great embarrassment. He didn't expect her to say such a thing, but she had. After she said it she sensed Henry's discomfort. She wished she hadn't said it, but her spontaneity often got the best of her. She frowned a bit and Henry saw her self disapproval. He quickly tried to make her feel better. "No worries, Kristina. I know it sounds kind of stupid coming from me, but here it is... I've never been with a girl to be scandalous."

Kristina looked at Henry with a very surprised look.

"I know it doesn't sound right, but I never had an urge to be with a woman for the obvious desires of human beings, it just never was a need of mine, so I never sought out a woman's companionship."

Kristina hadn't been without knowing a man. She did have an old flame when she lost her virginity, but ever since then she had no desire either. Men, to her, were aggravating; their needs always required her offering herself in manners she really didn't like. Even the time she lost her virginity she wasn't thrilled by the whole experience. Her love came from the eyes of dogs and other pets, but her favorite passion was dogs.

Both stood there spending the last moments of being together watching Adoc. She thought Adoc to be a great pup and her admiration for Henry only seemed to grow by getting to know him by the moment. She thought about the time and realized that she was up later than her usual hour. She figured that she'd take her leave from Adoc and Henry to make herself ready for work in the morning.

"Okay, you two have fun tonight and keep getting to know each other; personally I think you two were made for each other." She turned and started back to her truck.

Henry thought her comments to be supportive. He spoke to her as she walked away. "Okay, I suppose after first things tomorrow you should be expecting to see me over at the shelter, I still want to give you some volunteer time. I'm sure Adoc will love seeing other animals."

She waved at him and started the truck. Henry watched her drive away. After she was out of sight he turned and saw Adoc sitting there with his stick. Henry noticed Adoc wasn't chewing on the stick while sitting and waiting for him to throw it. That seemed strange but Henry thought it could be that he was just focused on having the stick tossed.

"So you want more stick toss?" Henry took the stick from Adoc and tossed it. Sure enough when Adoc returned he was chewing on it. Henry was wondering if there was a difference that made his consideration important or just over focused. He took up the stick again and played with Adoc for quite a few more tosses.

Adoc loved chasing the stick. He felt like he could do it forever and each time he ran after the stick he stretched his gait for the run. His smelling ability seemed to zero him into where the stick landed and every toss he thought to find it faster and bring it back to the Man more quickly. If Adoc knew how to speak or think as the Man thought, he'd tell the Man the things he felt. When he chewed on the stick he thought about the noises the Man made. The chewing seemed to help him focus on noises the Man made. Adoc knew that he'd begin to understand the Man's noises just as he felt his abilities get stronger for chasing the stick. He wanted to please the Man because of how he smelled and for the good tasting food the Man gave him.

Henry was tired from the day and Adoc was working up a thirst. When Adoc gave him the stick Henry took it up and moved towards the bowl to get Adoc water. Adoc followed him, hoping for more tossing, but glad to see the Man was grabbing the bowl for licking on to quench his thirst. Henry went to the hose he used to put water in the bowl and filled the bowl then he placed it down for Adoc to drink. Adoc didn't need any coaxing. As soon as the bowl was on the ground he had his tongue lapping it up. While Adoc lapped the water Henry's thoughts led him to wonder if the pup might like to sleep in the house with him tonight. When Adoc had his fill of water Henry began petting him and speaking to him.

"Adoc, it has been a long day, buddy. Yep, and I'm ready to get some bed." He sat petting Adoc, giving him scratches otherwise. "Do you want to try out the pillow I got for you and see about sleeping in the house tonight?"

Adoc tilted his head at the Man. He thought the noises the Man made sounded different. He knew that the noises were important, but he couldn't figure why they were. Even as it mattered the petting and scratching diminished the importance. Adoc was happy for not chasing the stick if he was going to be pet or scratched. After a bit of time the Man stopped the petting and scratching and made more noises.

"So what do you say, Adoc? Do you want to check out the new pillow we got for you?" Henry stood up and stepped towards the door, but stopped. He turned and looked at Adoc, thinking through what might be a bother for him.

Adoc looked at him with a bit of confusion, tilting his head. Henry found confidence in trying to coax Adoc into the house not through the back door but he decided to try the front. Instead of walking towards the back he turned and walked along the side of the house towards the front door. It was just the door and no type of hallway. Henry turned back to look at Adoc. "Come on, Adoc." Adoc began to follow him to the door. To Henry's surprise Adoc didn't show the same hesitance in approaching the front door. When Henry opened the door and walked in Adoc peered in the house and took steps on the stoop to enter the house. Once Adoc entered the house Henry was overjoyed and showed Adoc great appreciation.

"Oh, that's a good boy, Adoc! That is a GOOD BOY!" Henry leaned over to pet Adoc and praise him. Adoc didn't know that by coming in the house he had made the Man very happy, but he sure did like the praise coming his way. He licked the Man's face and wagged his tail. After quite a bit of praise Henry gave Adoc the house tour. Henry noticed that Adoc had a great interest in his library. Henry watched Adoc sniffing intently at the book stacks and the shelves working his way to the desk where Henry sat for so many hours. While Adoc sniffed to his delight Henry snuck off and got him a treat. Henry returned to the doorway to the library taking notice of Adoc's curiosity. He didn't enter the room but decided to surprise Adoc with the treat.

"Adoc want a cookie?" Adoc ceased the sniffing and looked at the Man. "Adoc want a cookie?" Henry held his hand up towards Adoc. "Come here, Adoc."

Adoc gave a thought to the noise the Man made and decided to know what he had. Adoc padded over to the Man with his nose high and sniffing.

"Adoc, can you sit?"

Adoc tilted his head. Henry held the treat out to Adoc's nose to let him sniff it, then lifted the treat up just enough to let Adoc want it. "Adoc, sit."

Adoc looked up at the good smelling thing in the Man's hand, wanting it. He thought about when he wanted the Man to throw the stick and sat as he did when the Man did throw the stick.

"Good boy, Adoc sits."

The cookie was lowered to the reach of Adoc and then given to him. Adoc enjoyed it immensely. He even looked for more once he was done. Henry reached down and petted him.

"That is a good boy, Adoc." Henry turned and continued the tour. They went towards the back door where the kitchen was and as Henry watched Adoc he didn't seem to have an issue as he did outside. That gave Henry a good feeling. He understood now that something about the outside was what troubled Adoc. He was surer about how to manage that fear with Adoc because it was only one sided fear for the pup. Henry grabbed another couple of treats along with Adoc's pillow. Then he turned to Adoc and walked passed him towards the stairs. Adoc followed along, he knew the Man had more of those good tasting things. Adoc also wondered about the other thing the Man carried. There was a smell about it Adoc knew and that was something he remembered smelling while he ran in the place he met the Man. Henry kept walking towards the stairs going up to the bedroom. He looked at Adoc examining the steps. Henry kept moving to the top. When he reached the top he turned and waited on Adoc.

Adoc had been on steps before, there were plenty where he used to run, the trouble giving Adoc concern was the slippery floor. The Man was making noise he thought sounded like before.

"Come on up, Adoc!"

Adoc thought about the good tasting thing and slowly began to negotiate the stairs. His grip wasn't as it was in the place he used to run, but if he stepped carefully he seemed to be okay. He moved with more confidence as he stepped and when he got to the top the Man made noises that were familiar.

"That's a good boy, Adoc!"

Adoc wagged his tail, sniffing about the Man's hand. Sure enough the Man gave him another good tasting thing. After he did he turned and walked some more. Adoc followed him. Henry turned into his bedroom and Adoc followed. Henry took the pillow and placed it on the floor next to the bed. "Check that out, Adoc. See what you think of hopefully what will be your new bed."

Adoc sniffed at the pillow and moved closer to it. Henry watched Adoc smelling with curiosity. He marveled at Adoc and what appeared as the dog's sense of caution and it seemed that his caution worked well for him. Like a father watching a young child attempt to take his first steps Henry doted on Adoc's acceptance of adventure. When Adoc finally stood on the pillow he couldn't help but to keep smelling the cloth. The pillow was made from cedar wood pellets, kind of like a bean bag. Francis and Kristina mentioned that the cedar chips would be a big help in keeping fleas from Adoc's fur. Henry needed no other convincing as he wanted no flea infestations. Henry reached to Adoc and began stroking him. Adoc responded to the stroking by relaxing.

"That's a good boy. You like that pillow Adoc, is that comfortable?"

Adoc heard the Man and the noise he made gave Adoc a wonderful sense of awareness, nothing like when he began knowing things. Adoc wagged his tail for his feeling good. Henry thought that he'd give Adoc another treat. He reached into his pocket and removed the remaining treats to place under Adoc's nose. While Adoc gobbled them up Henry started to get ready for bed. Adoc watched him as he undressed and then followed him to the bath. He watched the man standing in front of something to do something that Adoc would have just raised his leg to do. The sound of the water gave Adoc a need to tilt his head and when the Man finished up he saw him reach and a strange whooshing noise happened for the reach.

The man moved to another thing and began doing something to the things he chewed with. Adoc watched all of the Man's actions because he never saw any such a thing. It was strange but it was okay. When the Man was done he moved back over to the place where Adoc just discovered and he sat on the higher thing next to it. Adoc walked back onto that sweet smelling thing that felt so comfortable the Man had put down. Then he watched the Man move to cover himself with things where he sat. Then after a reach and more noise the Man made, "Good night, Adoc." There was no more light.

Adoc settled down onto the thing that smelled so good and found a place of comfort to close his eyes and sleep. The place was quiet, not like where he used to lie. That place had all kinds of noises. The only noise he could hear now was the Man breathing. Adoc slowly fell off to sleep.

Henry could only think of how thankful he was. Thankful for a dog who was willing to trust him as Adoc had come to trust him and thankful for his new friendships with Kristina and Francis.

The night came easily to Henry. He fell off to sleep dreaming of his youth seeking adventure and wanting to find discovery. That first night with Adoc at the foot of his bed Henry wasn't alone in his dreams; he had a companion that would make any best friends jealous. He and Adoc were the team he always wanted but never had... until that night.

Œ

The morning came to Henry early. Adoc yelped while asleep. Henry rose to a concern for Adoc as he never heard a dog dream until that morning. The sounds Adoc made startled him from slumber. It was almost as though his partner was reminding him of something he wasn't aware of or something he just didn't see coming. After Henry realized what was happening he relaxed but the impact of the noise left no ability to return to a comfortable or peaceful sleep. The hour of the day was nothing new for Henry. Most of his waking came to him preparing for the coming sunrises. Henry had seen to accomplishing more work during those hours than most would accomplish in a day.

Once Henry stirred from his bed Adoc woke and decided that he'd had enough sleep to accompany Henry on his visiting the newness of the day. Adoc watched the Man with curiosity, wondering what came next. The morning wake for Adoc was like none he ever knew.

The night was quiet aside from the Man's breathing and a full belly of food gave him serenity that he never knew. Before, in the other place the noises of the night would keep him semi focused on his proximity. The flying things would give him a need to be partially awake if for no other reason to be assured they wouldn't carry him away. Other things lived in the night, things he only knew by smell and noise, but those things were not worth investigating, they all seemed very troublesome to Adoc.

The Man did strange things when he rose from the place he slept. He visited that thing where he stood the night before making the water noises and after that Adoc had to decide if he could make his way down the slippery stairs. Adoc watched the Man walk down them with awe.

He trusted the floor which was not what Adoc was ready to do. Adoc's footing wasn't as sure as it was in the place he used to live. The Man's place was tricky. There was no smell of danger as Adoc knew from smelling deep waters. There was just the smell of the Man and the ancient wood in the place he woke at to meet the new day. Once Adoc negotiated the slippery stairs... he followed the Man to the place where the good smells came from. He watched the Man and listened to the noises the Man made.

"Adoc, come on. Let's go outside so you can water the plants." Henry entered the back hall and opened the door leading outside. He called Adoc to leave the house and have himself a leg lifting.

Henry remembered the evening prior and kept notice of Adoc not demonstrating the fear of the inside as he did from the outside. He coaxed Adoc out the door easily. Adoc left the house with no issues and did his business of leg lifting. The re-entry was not anything Adoc was interested in or having anything to do with as Henry tried to coax him. Adoc sat outside the door.

Henry saw the unwillingness of the dog in the darkness of the pre dawn and decided to shut the door so as leave Adoc where he sat. He proceeded through the house to the front door. When Henry opened the door and called to Adoc the dog responded positively. Adoc came to the door and re-entered the house. After the re-entry Henry figured that reinforcement of feeding would continue to leave Adoc feeling good about coming into the house. He put away Adoc's hesitance at the back door and focused on what did work. Adoc had a bowl of the food as well as a bowl of water to drink. He made a mental note to get milk at some point in the day coming. While Henry watched him eat, he fixed his own breakfast. When he had his plate ready Adoc had already finished the Man's morning offerings. He waited at Henry's side completely fixated on what Henry ate. Henry was excited. His cooking habits changed, portions weren't important. He could leave the last bites on the plate for Adoc. When he lowered the plate to Adoc his reaction didn't let his change in behavior go to waste.

Henry thought about how dinner at Francis'. Adoc had his own bowl. He wasn't sure he liked that so much. The wantonness of the companionship he had for Adoc gave him the hesitation. He figured that Adoc would always eat in their house with proper food and then Adoc would get a treat as he just did. Henry felt that to be the correct way to do things with his pal. Henry leaned over to pet Adoc. While he petted him he wondered what might be the reason Adoc avoided entering the back door. Henry didn't like circumstances without explanation. He did however settle on the reality as Adoc wouldn't ever be able to explain why he disliked the back entry from the outside. As much as Henry didn't like the mystery he wouldn't allow himself to dwell on it for long.

"Adoc, are you ready for a busy day?"

Adoc's focus turned to Henry as his tail wagged at hearing the Man speak to him.

"Oh yes, we do have a very busy day right here installing the doors you'll need. Afterwards we'll look at the car Francis has to sell."

Adoc's excitement grew. He stood wagging his whole body while Henry spoke to him. The words came while the Man's hands scratched and petted his body.

"After that we'll be going to visit Kristina and see other dogs and cats and I'm sure you'll really like that."

Adoc's happiness became even greater than it had been. He couldn't help himself when he jumped up to lick Henry's face. The move was sudden and the result of the lurch upwards ended in a contact between the top of Adoc's head and Henry's chin. There was a hollow thud for the contact that surprised both Adoc and Henry. Henry's petting ended as he recoiled up, reaching for his chin. There was also an impressive pain felt at least by Henry. After realizing the pain Henry shook it off, wondering if Adoc felt similarly. Rubbing his chin Henry looked to Adoc.

"Adoc, how did that feel?" When Henry looked at Adoc there was no way to be sure about Adoc's pain. All Henry could see was what seemed to be a dissatisfied look in Adoc's eyes, a type of look that said Adoc was worried. After a second or two Henry lowered his hands to Adoc and said, "Come here, buddy." Adoc moved with less excitement than he just had, there was no wagging as he moved closer, his tail curled between his legs. When Henry's hands met Adoc the touch was gentle and assuring. "That's a good boy, yes but that jumping up isn't a good thing, Adoc. If I were a little boy I might have been hurt much worse than just a knock on the chin."

Adoc heard the noises the Man made. The noises were very different as the Man made them. Adoc heard the differences of tone in the Man's noises. That gave him a better way to understand the noises. As the Man scratched Adoc he began to feel better than he had for jumping up. His tail was still curled up between his legs.

Henry's chin would hurt for the day and maybe two, but he understood that it was just an unfortunate condition of bonding. After he calmed Adoc, he went to the room where Adoc was reminded of ancient wood smells and sat at his work station.

Henry thought of the one item he had to see to finishing up as promised and gave it the consideration he committed to. Adoc found a place close to Henry and sat while Henry managed his work. Adoc relaxed and smelled the room. He didn't sniff; it seemed that the Man was focused and he would rather avoid the tone of the noise the Man made after the collision. The top of his head stung a bit from the bumping into the Man, but it was nothing like the pain he knew when the grabbing thing got a hold of him. Adoc didn't like how he felt for bumping into the Man. He didn't expect to be petted after the bump, but the Man did pet him and he enjoyed that feeling. Adoc began realizing the difference of the place he was in right now compared to the place he lived before. Outside was when he could run and jump and chase smells or even sticks, but here Adoc realized that in this place he had to control his nature to be excited.

The light of dawn spread into the windows of Henry's house. He was just finishing up with what would be the last assistance he'd offer in the capacity the community came to know him for. He put his thoughts into the envelope and would deliver them through the day's errands. Henry gave thought to having another coffee while he tossed the stick with Adoc for a bit, then he'd get the tools up so as to install the doggy doors. He wanted to let Adoc have a bit of fun before he began the work of the day. Henry stood up from the chair at his work station and began walking to the kitchen area. Adoc followed the Man wondering what he was up to and sat while Henry began preparing another cup of coffee. Henry loved the fact that Adoc followed him. In the process of fixing his second cup he spoke to Adoc. "Adoc, do you want to chase a stick?!"

Adoc's head tilted as he heard *stick*, his tail began sweeping the floor. Even if he didn't understand the other words he knew what stick meant, but the Man wasn't holding a stick, his hands were busy doing something else. "Adoc, do you want to chase a stick?!"

Adoc became excited, but not so as excited as he was when he jumped up to meet Henry. He stood up and his wagging began. After Henry finished his coffee Adoc began sniffing at it wondering if it was the stick the Man mentioned. Henry decided to go out the back door again and as he did Adoc followed him to the outside.

"Adoc, go get your stick!"

Adoc heard *stick* and began running around with his nose sniffing at the damp grass. He was thrilled to be outside in the cool morning, he was ecstatic searching for the stick. Adoc sniffed through the grass. Henry watched his tail wag and his erratic pace. Henry was amazed at Adoc's explosive speed and immediate agility changes for the speed. Henry realized why that bump hurt so much. He wasn't sure that Adoc knew his own strength. The dog was fast and energetic.

Adoc's nose led him to where Henry had put it the night before and when he found the stick he sat. Henry saw that Adoc was satisfied in finding the stick; he took a sip of his coffee and moved towards where Adoc sat.

"Good boy, Adoc, you found the stick. Good boy!" Henry reached for the stick and moved it about getting ready to toss it. Henry watched Adoc's eyes as he moved the stick. There was no break in his focus as Henry moved the stick. Adoc's tongue hung out of the side of his opened mouth, waiting to fetch the stick. Henry launched the stick and Adoc sprung after it demonstrating a greedy need to expel his energy. The chasing and returning began. When he fake tossed the stick Adoc wasn't moving for the fake. His focus was too intent. This surprised Henry and it became clear to him that Adoc had an innate purpose to chase and return. He didn't look like a retriever, but Henry figured Adoc was no dog to judge for his cover.

The tossing went on for quite a time. As usual the stick was reduced to nothing more than a twig that couldn't be tossed. Henry showed his hands to Adoc saying, "No more stick, Adoc. You ate it!"

Adoc panted waiting for another stick and Henry held his hands out as he walked to fill the bowl with water. Adoc lapped up the water while Henry decided that work needed to begin. Henry walked to the garage where his tools were stored. He began collecting what he'd need for the job of installing the doors. Adoc lapped until he was done, and lay at the bowl catching his breath. He knew where the Man went, but he'd remain patient to see what the Man brought back. He hoped it would be a stick. He heard noises coming from where the Man went but none of the noises interested him.

Henry managed to collect his gear and carried it all out in a gear bag. He looked at Adoc waiting to see him appear and said, "Nope pal, no stick, the work has begun." Henry walked towards the back door and put his gear bag down. Adoc stayed at the foot of the step and watched Henry's motions. His interest remained high as the Man dug through his bag, he hoped there would be a stick, but the Man began working on the door and offered no sticks. Adoc laid his head down continuing to watch the Man. The things he did were strange. Adoc watched ever so hopeful that the Man would have a stick. Adoc saw the Man hold and use something that looked like a stick, but he didn't throw it. He was doing something to the wall that Adoc left the house by this morning. It wasn't there when they came out to chase the stick but it was now and it was where Adoc remembered the grabbing thing. Adoc sighed, he would have loved to get close to the Man doing whatever he was doing, but the fear of the grabbing thing was greater than his curiosity.

After a time, the Man put the stick thing away and managed something else. The noise made by the almost stick thing sounded like what he heard below the ground. It was a constant low growl that he heard from previous investigations of sniffing.

The next thing the Man made was a noise he never heard before. The noise was loud and the Man moved a lot. To Adoc it sounded like big wind blowing across the ground releasing the ancient smells in the woods. Almost like the back and forth of the sky in the place he used to sleep. Adoc heard phuuuf- pheeewf and the Man made that noise for a long time. Adoc lost himself in the noise. He remembered seeing a critter he'd love to know and play with being in his view and then a blur and it was gone. The noise the Man made now sounded like the flying things that left a silence where once was what used to be alive; his hopeful friendship for play, just gone. He never wanted to sniff those things out to eat, he just wanted to chase them and bite on them and growl. But before he could... they were gone. He thought about the time when he met the Man. The place where the flying things took his happiness of hope away; hoping they wouldn't show up there. Something about this Man gave him an understanding that the flying things wouldn't be around. He seemed to be waiting on them when he met the Man. He thought that the Man was crazy because he looked like he wanted to have the flying things take him away leaving the silence he heard as they squawked going away into the distance. Adoc didn't want to think that all he knew could happen again, and that he'd never know the chasing of sticks with the Man. The noise was pounding on his hearing, but the Man didn't look back at him.

Adoc didn't like the noise. Then the phuuuf- pheeewf stopped. The Man stood up and left what was in his hand at the place while he moved suddenly. Adoc saw the hole in the wall that he came through that morning. Adoc forgot the bad things... He watched the Man intently. Adoc could see the Man lower and take his hand to rub the new edges of the hole in the wall that wasn't there earlier. Adoc sat with a tilted head. He wondered why the Man would do that. The Man turned to Adoc and looked at him. Adoc smelled a good feeling from the Man.

"Adoc, do you like your new door?!" Adoc heard the noises and wanted to go see the Man to feel a pet, but he couldn't let go of the grabbing thing in his memory. Adoc watched the Man while sweeping the grass with his tail... The Man made more noises. "Okay, suit your scaredy cat self!"

Henry got up again, retrieving the doggy door. He brought it back to the new entry and fitted the unit into the hole made for accepting it. The doggy door was fitted perfectly. Henry's thinking affirmed satisfaction for the install. He held the door where it belonged in its new home and turned to Adoc. "What do you think, pal?!" He took his hand and pushed through the door showing Adoc how it worked.

Adoc tilted his head. The thing the Man did was interesting to Adoc to be sure, but that grabbing thing was still to close in Adoc's mind.

Henry pulled the door back out of the hole and began to prepare the hole with all the insulation and caulking. Once it was prepped for the final installation Henry applied the necessary fasteners to make the project permanent. When that was finished Henry picked up the tools and moved to the front door. Adoc followed him and sat right next to Henry to be a shoulder tapper.

When the Man began the same work at the new place, there was no danger of the grabbing thing. Adoc sniffed at everything but he didn't sense any grabbing thing like at the other door. Henry's productivity went from professional installer to teacher of a student. The difficulty of the job became the frequency of Adoc's interruptions. Outside Adoc didn't worry about the bumping. Adoc licked the Man as much as he could and surrounded him. On a back pull of the hand saw the Man's elbow clocked Adoc in the head. Adoc let off a yelp. Henry stopped his work and turned to him. "How did that feel?!"

Adoc heard the noise the Man made and back-pedaled away. The Man reached for Adoc's belly. He pet him and then stroked him. "Look, pal, we are going to have to become aware of each... it seems like we enjoy being close, but neither of us can ever see impending sudden moves." The Man laughed while Adoc listened to his noises, shaking off the pain.

Adoc wasn't so energetic and he kept a distance as the Man worked. Henry capitalized on Adoc's change of proximity. When he finished cutting the hole he repeated his actions for the installing of the doggy door panel. When he completed the job Henry began cleaning up the work areas, it didn't take long as he worked in a very orderly and professional manner. Adoc followed him as he put up his tools but he didn't go in the garage. Henry wondered more about what Adoc's hesitancy was for not coming into the garage. Henry thought little of it as he grabbed a short scrap piece of wood. He left the garage carrying the wood and when Adoc saw the man holding the stick he became excited again and wagged his tail and body.

"Is this what ya want, Adoc? More stick time?"

Like before Adoc's eyes focused on the stick until Henry tossed it. Henry wondered about Adoc's focus on the stick. He tried to imagine such a dedication to something so simple. Henry was grateful to share in such an enjoyment. Watching Adoc run and return the stick to him was what Adoc seemed to need and even want. Henry liked the simplicity of the exercise. It occurred to him that as he wanted to participate, it could replace the things he used to do. After a time of tossing the stick Henry realized the day to be passing mid morning. Francis would be showing up any time as he mentioned and since Henry was a bit dusty for the morning he thought he might have a shower.

On the last toss Henry went to the hose and filled Adoc's bowl. Henry watched Adoc carry the stick to the bowl and hold it for the Man to grasp. Henry didn't offer to take the stick and Adoc, sensing the tossing was over dropped the stick at Henry's feet. Adoc looked at the Man while he panted. Henry bent down to pet Adoc and noticed the wood splinters in and around Adoc's mouth.

"Good boy, Adoc! Now you drink up some water and I'll get you some more food." Henry turned and went in the back door. Adoc watched the Man go inside the house. He lay down and began lapping at the water. In between pants Adoc thought about the Man while he lapped. Adoc hadn't finished half the water in the bowl and the Man reappeared with his other bowl.

Adoc pushed himself up off the ground holding his nose up to sniff out what the Man brought him. When the Man put the bowl down next to the water Adoc sat and ate up some of the good smelling stuff. Then he returned to the water. Adoc's happiness was shown in his tail, he couldn't help sweeping the ground as he lapped the water and ate some of the good smelling stuff. The Man lowered himself to begin petting Adoc. Adoc lifted his head to allow the petting. He licked gently at the Man's face. He didn't want to bump his head again on the Man's chin.

"Adoc, you hang here while I go have a shower. I won't be long. Okay, boy?"

Adoc heard the Man making noises but it sounded to Adoc that he didn't have to be frightened. Adoc watched the Man go back into the house after he put more water in his bowl. The Man went to the door where Adoc felt the grabbing thing might be and went into the house. Adoc lay back down in front of the bowls eating and drinking. The morning sun beamed on his fur and gave him warmth that made him think about the coldness of his younger days. He finished up the good smelling stuff the Man left in his bowl and washed it down with some more water. When Adoc was through he put his head down on the ground. The lawn under him was flat and soft. The sun climbed and lured Adoc into a snooze. He remembered the coldness he couldn't seem to escape before and he was very happy to be here. There were no scary things around, no noises of the forest to be heard here. Adoc began to think that his life changed and he had a place that was far better than he ever found trying to get out of the cold. There was something else different that Adoc was thinking about and it wasn't easy to know, but there was difference. He thought about laying in the dark cold place and what he did during the light. He sure didn't lay like he laid now, he always seemed to be moving sniffing, listening... and then it came to him. It was his belly! It was in the dark that he usually laid down trying to avoid the many things that came out when it was dark. It wasn't just the cold he tried to get away from; it was the emptiness in his belly that drove him when the light came back. He chased things that made noises trying to catch them and fill his belly that ached so much. Then Adoc knew why he liked chasing the stick and even better why he liked this place and the Man.

Adoc came out of his snooze, he smelled the air and it smelled different. He stood up and followed his nose to the edges of Henry's yard. He remembered the smells from the first time he walked this route, but this time as he walked the route he lifted his leg and put his scent at the appropriate places. As Adoc was making his mark on this place he heard a strange noise and ran back to where the noise came. He reached the place where he left the bowls and his stick. He saw the noise, it was one of those things he saw come here before and one he got into with the Man and the other who had so many smells. He sat attentively waiting. The door behind him opened and he saw the Man come out of the house. The Man walked quickly towards Adoc and he stood up. He kept watching the thing that arrived, waiting on the Man. Adoc's excitement was revealed by his tail. It wasn't just wagging, it was flicking quickly. Adoc smelled the Man's approval and expectation.

"Are you being a good boy, Adoc? Are you keeping an eye on the place?" The Man scratched Adoc's back and then finally patted the top of his head. He stood up and moved towards the thing in the yard that made the noise that attracted him there. After a second or two a door opened and the other person from yesterday appeared. Both the Man and he made noises that sounded familiar. Then the other person with the good smells said his name.

"Adoc, you are going to be a very good watch dog!" The other person with good smells leaned down and pet Adoc, he scratched him, too. This was the person with the wise hands and the smells of him made Adoc even more excited. His flickering tail seemed to wag his body so that his head swayed from side to side. The other person lowered himself to Adoc's nose so that Adoc could lick him and taste him.

Henry welcomed Francis. Francis took notice of the doors. "My gosh, Henry, we all heard that you had skills as a carpenter, but it is quite another thing to actually see the result of the hearsay." Francis examined the doors with awe on his face. Francis looked at Henry asking him, "Has Adoc tried out the doors yet?"

Henry smiled and shook his head. "Nope. Adoc here was more interested in chasing the stick."

Francis saw Adoc's stick next to the bowls. He shook his head as he examined the stick. "That dog sure loves to chew, eh?" He reached down to pet Adoc.

Henry affirmed Francis' question. "Believe it or not, that stick is the second of the morning. The chewing on that one is the chewing done after I finished the install."

Francis whistled. "Holy smokes! He chews like you work." Francis let out a big belly laugh after his comment.

Henry heard the simple reasoning of Francis' comment and it struck him truthfully. A truth he didn't consider. Henry nodded and took up petting on Adoc. Henry's hands clasped Adoc's head and he turned Adoc's face to his own. "Did you hear that, Adoc? You chew just like

I work!" He took a lick from Adoc and released his head. Henry stood up and asked, "So, that is the car?"

Francis nodded, turning to the vehicle. "Indeed it is the car. This is the car my Mildred drove."

The men walked towards the car and Adoc seemed to know that it was the focus; he sniffed around it as it was parked. Francis began the seller testimonial and even though Henry didn't need to hear it, he listened. Henry figured it was the proper and respectful thing to do. He listened to Francis speaking about the vehicle sensing nostalgia wrapped in the words Francis spoke.

Henry really didn't care about having a car. Before he came to know Adoc his transportation needs were met by those seeking his help. For him owning a car wasn't important and without need of a car he saw no economic sense to owning one. Now that Adoc was going to be part of his life the need to own a vehicle seemed to make sense, at least enough to own a car for transportation. When Francis finished up his declaration of the car's condition Henry gave it a respectable focus. He kicked the tires, looked at the interior and surveyed under the hood.

Truth be told the transaction wasn't important to either man. If Adoc wasn't a mutual interest the car would never have had a need to be sold. Francis would have been happy to leave it in the estate of his Will.

Francis finished up his pitch. Henry asked, "Why don't we take a ride to the bank? Besides the car we have to settle other business."

Francis held his hand out, offering the keys to Henry. "I reckon that will make for a good test drive; you can see if it suits you and Adoc."

Henry took the keys from Francis. He put them in his pocket and gave Francis an explanation of having a need to go into the house to sort some things out. "Why don't you come on into the house? I'll have to collect some things before we take this ride."

The men walked towards the rear door trying to coax Adoc along. He sat at the back door when the men went into the house. When they disappeared inside Adoc ran over to the front door and went into the house through the newly installed doggy door. He joined up with the Man who tossed the stick and the other person with old hands in the place with the ancient smells of wood. Adoc's excitement was abundant. He wagged his whole body, driving his head into hands and legs, into whoever accepted him. Adoc heard both the Man and the other person with the old hands make noises that only left him wanting to wag more. Shortly after that he was only petted by the Man. The person with older hands must have decided that he too appreciated the ancient wood smells Adoc did.

"So, Henry this is the carpentry I have heard of being crafted. I'll be honest with you, the stories do the work no justice. This is truly amazing craftsmanship. It is clear to me how easily those doggy doors were installed."

Henry heard Francis and continued to pet Adoc. He let the comments be the last said. Henry didn't think of himself as a great carpenter, he just did the carpentry like he did everything else; he simply applied perfection to refinement as he learned. He thought to point out the errors he knew of in his own work, but he had an urge to stay on course with business of the day. He and Adoc were expected at the animal shelter and he didn't want to explain tardiness to Kristina. Francis didn't seem to have urgency of time to this day and Henry figured Francis could argue with him about whether or not his errs of carpentry were ingeniously disguised as intentional aspects rather than what Henry knew as mistakes.

"Well, Francis, I'm glad you find the work to be better than you heard, but I have a need today and I'm not even on the other side of seeing to that need. Shall we see to that bank business?"

Francis realized a young man's desire and humbly apologized for carrying on. "Yes, of course we shall see to that need of the second half. Don't mind me, Henry. I'm an old man and it isn't every day that old men are so impressed. Let's see if you enjoy the ride."

Henry felt something of a thief towards being impatient. He wished he could read folks better for simple need of appreciation, but he never learned such nuances of being with people. He decided to make amends. "If you look at the top right side of that case you might see the evidence of not measuring twice before cutting."

Francis made an inspection of the pointed out area. After some focusing he did see the difference of continuity. "Well, I have seen some things in my life and I can tell you the experts... nine out of ten wouldn't even see what you are talking about. I think it is about time to take that ride, Henry. After all you are still on the short side of the day."

The men left the room and Adoc followed. Henry saw to securing his home and then as they approached the car Henry invited Adoc into the back seat. "Come on, Adoc. Want to take a ride?"

Adoc remembered driving in the thing that moved them along and he really liked what the other times felt like. He jumped on in even though the jump was easier than in the other thing that moved fast. Adoc sniffed around and seemed to be keenly interested in the smell of the car. Somewhere in that car, the pair of old hands the other person had didn't belong here, even though they did. Adoc smelled another essence, but it was part of the other person with old hands. What Adoc smelled was something so familiar he just couldn't reckon what it was. It was something gone... like before.

Henry started the car and began driving it out of the drive way. He made the turns to the bank and while he did it seemed as though folks in town couldn't help but to look at Francis and Henry along with Adoc drive to town. The attention made Henry uncomfortable but it didn't seem to have any effect on Francis. Francis did however sense Henry's discomfort for the attention. Francis knew a time would come when he could offer Henry a few thoughts to set him to ease, but it wasn't then and more importantly Adoc was enjoying himself thoroughly. Francis decided to focus on Adoc's condition so as to give Henry enjoyment of his new pal while being observed.

"Adoc, you young fellow, you seem to be a likely partner for a road dog... maybe I'll let your Man know what that means."

Henry heard Francis and wondered what he meant. Francis felt the distraction and kept up the ploy.

"Yes, Adoc, that is right, but you can't expect the Man to know all of your needs right away. He isn't quite sure of his own yet, even though he is expert at all he puts his hands to; oh yes I know he knows all about ancient wood, just as you do and that is why both of you are so important to each other." Francis reached back to pet Adoc. "Good boy!"

Henry was very well distracted. He didn't even know if he was more uncomfortable for hearing Francis' comments rather than being watched. Francis had zeroed in on who he was and what he was like nothing he ever encountered. It truly was the first time in his life. Henry took to Abe Lincoln's quotes and remained quiet, rather than giving Francis more of an insight to make him foolish. They arrived at the bank and Henry parked the car. Immediately he became worried about leaving Adoc in the car. It came to him as panic. He didn't think through this ride and now he was going to leave his buddy in the car. Once again Francis surprised him.

Francis reached over to the rear door on his side and invited Adoc out of the car. The directness of Francis' actions set Henry off his panic. When Adoc showed up from the passenger side of the car he was wagging and once Henry saw him he didn't feel like he was becoming unglued.

Francis took a moment to coax Adoc to sit. Henry hadn't thought to bring a leash. Francis had one in his pocket. After Adoc sat, he put the leash upon the collar Henry gave him and then dropped the leash. "Go to your Man, Adoc. Let him walk you."

Adoc didn't need to understand the noise from the person with the old hands. He didn't hear noise all he could do was think that the Man was ready to throw a stick. He didn't have a stick so he investigated with sniffing. He let the Man grab the newly attached leash. The Man took it lightly but he possessed it. He looked at the Man to produce a stick but none came. For a second Adoc was confused, but then the other person with the old hands was back to making noises he didn't understand. The Man and the other with old hands made noises and Adoc didn't want a stick anymore, he wanted to know what was next. In Adoc's eyes and thinking, these two, the Man and the other person with old hands would provide something better than the stick. At least that was what he expected.

Francis saw Henry's doubt. He knew Henry thought taking Adoc into the bank was about as bad as being watched by the town for driving in his passed wife's car with him and a dog. Francis moved towards the bank saying, "Henry, you are still short on this side of the day. We can keep you on pace, but we must move along."

Henry wasn't sure of anything, but he felt as though Francis might have been gleaning him wisdom he could never gain from all the books he read. Francis seemed like a father he never knew, and that was very powerful to Henry. Francis offered his being freely. Henry wondered if it might have been like that between a son and dad learning to trust each other. A son might have to just do as he was told rather than to figure what the old man was saying. He followed Francis into the bank holding Adoc's leash. Once they passed in through the doors Henry felt worse than he had driving the car with the town's eyes upon him. He thought that the bank staff might decide that bringing a dog into the place was worthy of notifying the authorities that the bank was being robbed. Henry and Adoc followed Francis, both stepped as though they were debuting on a stage. Fear of stage fright kept both moving forward. Francis was congenial and greeted everyone, as they did him. When Henry heard the tellers greet him he began feeling relief. When he heard others fawning over Adoc he felt gratitude towards Francis.

After the three of them entered the commotion got the bank manager's attention and while in the middle of other business, he asked for pardon with his customer to go see the men and the dog. When he arrived to greet them he apologized for having a need to delay them until he could finish up with the business at hand. The manager asked his assistant to see to them as they waited.

Francis shook Zachary's hand and thanked him. Zachary left and once they all sat in the waiting area a free teller came with a dog bone for Adoc. She asked the men if they'd like anything for the wait. Both men declined the offer but enjoyed watching Adoc chew on the treat.

Henry had some questions for Francis. The ride and the leash thing as well as walking into the bank with a dog left him more doubtful than everything he'd ever known. Francis knew Henry's doubt but he also knew his patience that was applied to seething curiosity. For the welcome Henry seemed to be better eased, but still he was not on center. Francis was glad that Adoc was helping him keep calm.

"Henry, when we set this business aside you can ask me all you want. Here we have business and it will soon be over. After that we'll converse."

Henry simply nodded. The words had a calming effect on him. He wasn't used to being spoken to for companionship. He couldn't remember anyone second guessing his thinking. He never knew anyone who gave him a reason to second guess until he met Francis. That was unsettling. Henry wasn't sure of his reality. He had Adoc and now Francis and Kristina were his mentors. His life was full instead of peering into the depths of a river. It was a scary proposition, life always was scary. Henry decided he was sick of being afraid and it was clear to him these folks he needed were going to teach him on how to not be afraid.

Zachary gave them an apology for the wait as he returned. "Francis and Henry, so sorry you had to wait. And who is this fine looking friend of yours?"

Francis answered Zachary. "Zachary, allow me to introduce you to Adoc. Adoc is deciding whether or not Henry is going to be his choice of a master, but I wouldn't be taking any bets against it; you do have bank stockholders to protect."

The comment gave Henry a reason to laugh even if surprised. Zachary gave a shallow laugh and the men began business. Henry informed Zachary of his intent and the deal was done on both accounts of Francis' business as well as Kristina's needs at the shelter.

Zachary escorted the men and Adoc on their way. Henry owned the car. The walk to the car focused on Adoc and once they were in the car Henry asked, "Do you need to get home right away or do you want to come over to the shelter?"

Francis expected Henry to be less than much of a conversationalist. "Oh, I expect dropping me at home would be fine… our business is done and you are now even with the day. An old man like me might keep you from seeing to getting through the second half."

After Henry heard what Francis said he felt badly. He didn't want to push Francis away. He just didn't know what to make of his insights. Henry didn't want to converse while driving. They drove along the town green with ample parking for his new car. Henry diverted his travel to a parking spot and stopped the car.

"Francis, I appreciate you selling me the car and I really have a want to be your friend. When you say things, I hear them. It seems like I always wanted to hear, but never did hear them. Hearing them now…" He took a breath to continue.

Francis interrupted him. "Don't worry about what it is you fear, don't give fear another thought. My friend, life is too short and now you have a life. It is two responsibilities that you didn't know just a few days ago."

Henry thought to be more confused than he was leaving the bank. Henry never thought of responsibility except to those who depended on his wisdom of getting around a problem. Adoc noticed the stop and took full advantage of it. He licked Henry's neck and ear, Henry flinched and Francis laughed out loud.

"That, my friend, is the number one responsibility."

Henry realized that to be true enough. He gazed at Francis and Francis had an even bigger laugh. "Your second responsibility is the person you seek for the second half of this day!"

Henry was stoic. He felt as though he wanted to be upset, but he also felt like his own frustration was the thing withholding him from a truth he needed to know. Henry sat in the car with Francis and he wondered what he was doing. Adoc licked him again and for it he smiled and flinched again. It was time for Francis to reveal some wisdom; he could see that Henry was undone or soon to be as such.

"Henry, start the car and begin driving to life you never expected, I'll explain as we drive."

Henry followed the instructions and the car began moving. Adoc enjoyed the focus of motion. Francis gave wisdom so that Henry could get through the second half of his day. "When you were young and this town came to know you as an orphan; nobody quite knew what to do with you. Nobody could have ever expected the misfortune that you faced as a young man." Francis laughed a bit under his breath. "Lord, have mercy, when the town fathers asked you what you wanted I thought they were more relieved than anything when you gave them a sensible answer." Francis paused a moment. Then after a thought he continued. "Henry, my Mildred and I spoke about your fate for many nights. Well, she did more talking than I did. Anyways, after I exhausted her talking for listening all I could say was that life for this young man is no more than a piece of paper to a sketch artist wondering what to draw."

Henry heard his metaphor and was intrigued. Francis looked at Henry. "That is right, son. Your life is nothing more than a sketch on paper undone in an artist's mind. He may have given you a form, but when you realize that you are the sketch artist, you'll know the satisfaction of the world. You see all that you have done in your life is just the beginning of your life. What you do from here... well that is your revealed identity. Now let me tell you, Henry, you have no idea about the quality of drawing you have already put to paper. You, my son, have already become a renowned master at life's struggles."

For all that Francis hinted at Henry was more than stupefied for what he just heard. The heat in Henry's chest made him want to drop off Francis and return home. The whole conversation he had with Francis gave him even more reason to be afraid.

Francis felt his discomfort. "Henry, you should try having faith in yourself like this dog does and I say that because you are too insulated from knowing your potential as a carpenter of great skill or as a great problem solver. But you will. Adoc here is going to show you the things about you that you don't yet see. I have a hunch that Kristina will as well. Then of course I'll be here for a time. Henry, it is okay to be frightened. We all know what it is to be frightened and it always usually happens about the time we truly become responsible for our own living."

Henry was approaching Francis' house and Francis hadn't yet to think of much more to say since his last statement. Henry heard enough for the morning and he'd take time to process all he heard Francis mention. Henry negotiated the turn onto Francis' driveway and drove up to his house. After they stopped Francis left Henry with one last thought.

"Henry, when you are ready to get the paperwork done with the transaction of the car, you can drop Adoc off here or I suppose Kristina wouldn't mind watching him either. I also want you to keep this in mind; if it is helpful you can think of me as an uncle or even an older brother and you are welcome here any time."

Henry took his comments with more comfort than at any time of the previous conversation. "Okay, I'll be mindful of that Francis, and thanks for everything." The men shook hands.

Francis turned to Adoc and gave him his goodbyes before he got out of the car.

Henry watched Francis until he made it into the door, then he asked Adoc if he wanted to come up to the front seat. "Come on, boy. Want to sit in the front?"

Adoc eagerly jumped into the front seat, taking up the other person with old hands place. "Good boy!" Henry petted Adoc. He turned the car around and began the drive to the animal shelter.

Œ

Henry noticed that when the car was moving Adoc seemed to be too involved in noticing the motion to make himself any trouble. That was good as Henry saw it because he never did much driving; he sure didn't need Adoc distracting him. The ride from Francis' place to the Animal Shelter wasn't a long ride and Henry was glad for that, he wasn't interested in processing the conversation he had with Francis. Now he was simply living up to his promises. He hoped that arriving at this hour of the day would be advantageous to Kristina in helping at the shelter. After today he could help her any other time if it were more beneficial for her needs. All he could do would be to wait and see.

Adoc's focus on the motion of the car changed as Henry's trip came closer to the shelter. His anticipation became more intense. Adoc began to smell other dogs close by. Henry noticed that his back hairs started to stand up as Adoc smelled the shelter not too far in the distance. As Adoc smelled the source growing he raised his ears up to listen to the loudening noise of noises he understood. These were noises that gave Adoc a type of reflex he didn't know how to manage. He heard hatred in some of the barks and he heard sadness in others. Adoc tilted his head. He wondered how so many different voices could be coming from one place. The smells made him think about the time he became aware of things. There were lots of smells then, but this place had so many more. When he thought to be aware of things the smells of his litter were of him or he was part of them. He couldn't imagine a litter like this, but that was what his nose told him.

After Henry pulled into the shelter's parking lot, Adoc's excitement gave him the shivers, he was literally shaking. Henry figured that Adoc might be a bit scared. All of the noise was his focus and Henry knew his doubt. He petted Adoc to sooth him a bit. "It's okay, Adoc. This is where Kristina works."

Adoc heard the Man making noises and in his excitement he could only turn to him and give him a quick lick. Henry saw that Adoc wanted out of the car. He grabbed a hold of Adoc's leash and exited the car. "Come on, boy. Get on out of the car."

Adoc saw the opportunity and followed Henry. Once out he darted to follow smells. The jerk on the leash was unexpected to Henry as it pulled him to the ground. Henry didn't let go of the leash and Adoc stopped in his tracks. His anticipation knew nothing of a leash's purpose.

"Adoc, easy, boy. Take it easy." Henry stayed on the ground and waited for Adoc to come back to him. Adoc looked to Henry and forgot his need to follow smells briefly. He went to Henry and gave him licks. "Good boy, Adoc!" Henry patted him and stood up. Once Adoc saw the Man on his feet his distraction was gone as he went back to reaching the end of the leash. Henry talked to him gently. "Adoc, here. Come here, boy."

Adoc looked at the Man and did his best to stay close. He tried with great difficulty to resist his urges. It was easy as long as Henry moved and only a few times was Adoc denied a direction he would have rather gone. Adoc wasn't sure about the leash, he didn't know why he needed it, but it was on him and the Man was who he chose to be with so he wore it. Even as

Adoc wanted to lose himself in following the smells he knew that the Man was going to the source of the smell. Adoc's truthful desire became easier to ignore.

As Henry and Adoc walked up to the door Henry decided to have another word with Adoc. He stopped and knelt down to speak to him. "Adoc, do you want to go see Kristina? You know Kristina."

Adoc listened to the Man but it was noise compared to all the voices he understood coming from the place they were going into. Adoc's urge to go into the shelter seemed like a temptation he wasn't sure about. Henry's willingness to go in was like a promise he might have wanted another chance to offer. Both were fixated on what came next but neither could move forward without each other. Henry's courage to overcome the morning's discussions led them forward. "Come on, Adoc. Time we own up to what we promised friends."

Henry stood up and called Adoc to follow. Adoc's temptation was coaxed by Henry's dedication to unfamiliar notions. Together they walked through the door of the shelter to find a desk assistant.

The young man's name tag indicated his name was William. He said, "His how are you both today?" He peered over the counter with brilliant happiness to see Adoc in attendance. "Are you Henry and Adoc?" Henry was a bit taken back for being recognized but responded.

"Yes I am Henry and this is Adoc." He leaned over and petted Adoc as he introduced him. William's countenance gave Henry a sense of the unexpected but he was soothed by Adoc's willingness to consider William as a friend. Once William began the interaction Adoc sensed he was pure of intention and Henry followed Adoc's instinct.

"I guess Kristina mentioned us coming, I hope we aren't late." William shook his head and simply said, "Volunteers offering help are never late. It is only when you miss your schedule that you are late and as a volunteer it isn't like it is a paycheck is getting lessened." William held up a rawhide stick for Adoc and offered it to Henry. Henry accepted it and gave it to Adoc... He gobbled it down. Adoc was too concerned with all the talking going on somewhere else. William told Henry that he'd let Kristina know they were there and that he'd only be a minute.

Henry watched Adoc with a keen eye; he didn't want to be cleaning up an accident stain of excitement. Adoc seemed to be wagging uncontrollably sniffing himself into hyper-ventilation. Henry noticed he must have been at all edges of the room twice smelling smells. As William promised he came back and it wasn't but a few seconds before Kristina joined them. When she entered the lobby she immediately greeted Adoc.

Adoc knew immediately the other person with so many smells and then he understood why she had so many other smells... She was at a place where there were so many voices he heard and wanted to know. Adoc couldn't help but to act as though he met Jesus Christ in the flesh. He danced in circles to show her appreciation. And all the while he listened to her noise as he heard the noises elsewhere in the place.

"Adoc, such a good boy. Oh, yes, you are such a good boy!" She pet him and scratched him and Adoc felt as though she had hands that brought a greatness of warmth. A warmth like she was connected to his first good thoughts in being aware. After a certain greeting Kristina stood up and welcomed Henry.

"I'm glad you found time to get over here, how was the visit with Francis?" Henry had to compose himself. When he saw her greet Adoc he became mesmerized with wonder.

"Well the visit with Francis was fine, ahhh Adoc even met Zachary at the bank and got a dog treat there... I think he was the guest of honor for the day." Kristina was still praising Adoc while paying attention to Henry's recanting. She turned her focus back to Adoc and praised him more which gave him another round of wagging and jumping in circles. "Adoc! You were the guest of honor at the bank today? What a good boy and a smart one too!" Henry watched Kristina's way with Adoc. He watched like a student learning the truth of gravity while seeing his friend as the example falling on his face for allowing the lesson. Henry laughed and smiled about Adoc's antics.

Kristina asked Adoc if he wanted to make new friends. She looked at Henry and asked, "While we are at it, I'll give you options for helping out around here.... How's that sound?" Henry said, "Sure, I'm sure Adoc wants to make new friends and I am here for the volunteering." He turned and winked at William. William gave a smile back and said,

"That is great, 'cause we need the help." Kristina, Henry and Adoc made their way into the rear of the building. The first area they came to was where all the procedures were done for health care of the animals. There were all kinds of tables big and small and above them hung lamps for illumination. They were the procedure lamps as they weren't on. They'd be used if one of the residents would need some type of attention. The room was very clinical by nature and somewhat close quartered. The machinery available didn't look new, but it seemed like it functioned well enough. Kristina gave a brief summation of the room's purpose. She described the different functions that the room served. Henry listened and he was surprised how well Adoc was managing. The dogs within the shelter were still barking and howling and somewhere in between the barks and howls cats made their own noises.

"Right now we are full to the limit. This morning the room was very busy. That part of the day is over so the time after is spent making it ready again. Depending on when you'll be here Henry, we may ask you to help in here." Henry listened to what Kristina was saying, but he didn't feel like this was a place he'd want to be a part of, something about the room gave him trouble. Instead of nodding he shrugged. "We'll see when I'll be getting here to help... mornings may not work out." Kristina led them through more doors into the kennel area. The area was a long narrow corridor with two sides made up of ten pens on each side. The floor and walls were concrete and the only wood in the area was used in the panels making up the ceiling. Fluorescent lamps ran down the center of the ceiling giving the area sufficient light. Kristina said this was the dog kennel and the work needed happened twice a day. She explained that the first portion of work occurred in the morning. It involved feeding, then exercise and cleaning of the pens. The second portion happened before they closed up the evening. She told him that all these guys are candidates for placement into homes.

A Man, a Dog and a Ball

Henry felt easier in this part of the facility and he didn't know why. In the procedure room he felt as though something he didn't want to know about would greet him there. It was a strange feeling to be sure. Henry walked by all the pens with Adoc looking at the residents. Adoc was excited by them all as he was still a puppy. Henry was surprised by the amount of dogs. Some of the pens had more than one occupant and of different breeds. Henry wondered about such a circumstance and Kristina took notice of his curiosity.

"I did say we were full up at occupancy and when different dogs friend up we can bunk them, it isn't perfect but sometimes it works out." Henry listened to what Kristina said and processed thinking.

"Is this ordinary, having to pair up dogs?" Kristina took a moment to answer.

"Well, it never was but lately it seems to be a more frequent thing and not just here. There are a lot of people who breed dogs that just don't understand the ramifications. Or they just don't fix the pups and nature runs her course." Henry continued his tour of the pens. He was obviously taking in the larger picture of the shelter. It wasn't like anything he'd ever imagined.

Adoc examined each pen with first time in delight. He wanted to make friends with all of them and none of them showed violent aggression towards his curiosity. They all seemed to know that Adoc came from a worse place than they were at for the time. They could see Adoc's innocence of life even as though he had more experience in survival than most there. There was an elder dog that seemed very interested in Adoc. Both sniffed at each other through the pen screen door. Adoc sensed that this old timer could easily be a friend if not a pal and the older dog did as well. The older Dog sniffed at Adoc with much less exhibited curiosity than Adoc presented, but it was clear to Henry and Kristina that a solid interest existed between the two, more so than any other dog in the shelter.

"It seems as though Adoc has picked Old Ben as a new favorite pal." Henry looked at Kristina and asked, "Old Ben, that is his name?" Kristina nodded, "Yep, we added Old to Ben. That is what his tag said and he seems to respond to Ben." Henry figured if he had a name tag he'd have to have an owner tag.

"That was the only tag he had on him, one that said Ben. Wasn't there an owner tag or a license number?" Kristina shook her head.

"The only tag on him said Ben and I figure he became a stray who just went his own way, maybe his owner left, there really is no telling. I never saw him in these parts and nobody around seems to know where he came from." Henry knelt next to Adoc while the two dogs sniffed each other. He gazed into Old Ben's eyes as the dogs introduced themselves. He didn't interrupt the two he just watched; after a time he stood up.

"What is it about these two that makes you think Adoc found a best new friend Kristina?" Kristina didn't expect the question; she figured an observation of both made it clear. She tried to understand Henry's question and what would motivate him to ask it, but he offered nothing else.

"Well, Henry, I guess I see it in the body language of both dogs. I mean, neither dog has their back hairs raised up, and Adoc seems to know his place with Old Ben I don't know, I guess just a hunch." Henry heard her explanation and seemed to be satisfied with it.

"I'd guess you'd be a good judge of such a relationship." He looked back at both dogs and asked her another question. "So what is the story with Old Ben?" He looked at her after he asked and he didn't like what he saw looking in her face. She wasn't any too happy to have to tell Henry what lie ahead for Old Ben, but she gave him the low down.

"Well Henry, Old Ben has been here the longest of any dog we have. He is a gentle giant as far as I am concerned but folks looking for dogs just don't want to adopt an older dog like Old Ben. It is breaking my heart, but the next round of euthanasia includes Old Ben. It's no good for him to live in a cage."

Henry felt as what he just heard seemed to be the most impossible news he ever heard. He wondered how such a reality could upon fall a dog like Old Ben. He stood there horrified for what he heard. He thought that there must be something that could be done to prevent Old Ben's certain end. Henry knew that Kristen hated the facts as she presented them to him. He held his verbal thinking out loud to himself. The last thing he wanted to do was give her more of a reason to feel badly. In fact he wanted to let her know that Old Ben would enjoy the rest of his days being loved and looked after. He didn't want to make an absurd offer by suggesting that he'd take the dog, but he knew that Old Ben was going to be put down. He was sure of it because Adoc took such a liking to him.

"Well Kristina when is that date, the next time to put dogs down?" She told him simply,

"Three days." She winced and dropped her head. "Henry, believe me when I tell you that time is the worst part of the job, I absolutely hate it." Henry nodded to what she said.

"Yeah I can't imagine looking into the eyes of Old Ben having to deliver him to such a place. Must make you sick."

"It is worse than that Henry... It makes me very upset with people. It is just another reason to truly dislike them. I mean what kind of person wants something without realizing the responsibility of that want? I mean, how these people even arrive at a place where they can make such decisions, it seems like they escaped natural law. It is like Darwinism doesn't apply to humans." Henry gazed at Kristina understanding her trouble.

"You know I have arrived at the same thinking. All the times before now I wondered how it was that so many people just couldn't figure out what I consider to be simple. It is a rarity when I deal with someone who had a truly difficult problem, or one that truly needed some study to solve." Henry looked back at Adoc and Old Ben. "Can we let them out so they can visit or play with each?" Kristina thought that was a good idea.

"Sure, we can." She walked to the end of the corridor and opened the door that lead to the exterior. "While we are at it I'll give you the rest of the tour." When she moved towards the door Henry and Adoc followed. They came around to the rear entry of Old Ben's pen and opened it. Old Ben came outside meeting Adoc. They sniffed each other more completely; Adoc was more animated in his happiness. He jumped around Old Ben mindful of newness between both of them. Old Ben let Adoc play on him without any hostility, somehow Henry knew the way these two carried on would be Old Ben's salvation. He just didn't know how that would happen yet. Old Ben began loping around the fenced in area, Adoc followed him sometimes running circles around him or just lunging at him. Adoc offered Old Ben a few growls but they were playful growls and Old Ben offered no such return. Henry and Kristina watched them play and Henry told her that she had a good eye. They turned back to the gate and finished up the tour with directions as to how things got done.

"Generally speaking we let the dogs out by quarters of the pen area unless we have aggressive dogs, then it is pen by pen. We don't want to create a need for an unwanted vet visit to fix wounds from dog fights. When we let them out we clean waste and then hose down the pen, we don't want any diseases from unclean conditions." Henry followed her directions without comment. She spoke clearly enough for his understanding. After a while Kristina stopped and listened for something.

"What is it Kristina?" Henry asked. She looked at the dogs in the pen with surprise. Henry's curiosity grew. "Henry the dogs are quiet; that never happens!" When they walked down the outside corridor all the pups on either side were paying attention to Old Ben and Adoc frolic.

Kristina acted as those she was a child discovering something brand new. Henry made the connection and offered a suggestion.

"Why don't we let them all out?" Kristina looked at Henry like he was crazy. But after she thought about it she wondered how crazy was the idea? She had never heard the entire unit quiet such as it was and both of them could keep an eye on the dogs in case there was trouble.

"Well Henry that isn't usual policy, but I've never had a usual time of quiet like this... so why don't we open pens and see how they all get along? If everyone is happy then I suppose that would be fine, but first sign of trouble and well you know." Henry nodded in deference. They began with the first pen. The dogs communed and there was good energy everywhere. As the pens opened and the growing pack of dogs played and ran Kristina's surprise was evident. She couldn't believe what she was seeing. She didn't know how it was happening but there was cooperation she never thought she'd see. After the first half of the pens was open Henry looked to her with a surprise.

"What do you think, boss?" Kristina looked at the other dogs; they were quiet and focused.

"Hold on a second, Henry. I want William to see this." She went into the shelter and reappeared with William. He stood in amazement shaking his head. She smiled in wonder; the dogs seemed to know that Adoc and Old Ben were magic or just belonged together.

"William, go to the other side and open the gates, we're interested in seeing what happens."

William froze up in disbelief. He never knew Kristina to be so reckless. "Are you sure about that Kristina? I mean there will be an awful lot of dogs out. What if-"

"Yes, William. I'm sure… listen to them, none of them are barking… let's see what happens."

William did as she said but did so with trepidation. He really didn't want to be the guy who let them all out so as to have real trouble. But he followed through. Gate by gate the dogs joined the pack and the pack followed Old Ben and Adoc. Everyone behaved and that was truly surprising to both Kristina and William. For Henry it was simply amazing. He couldn't help but think Adoc was the key to it. All three of them watched the dogs play and get along. They did so for at least fifteen minutes. While they watched the dogs Henry stole glances at Kristina. He thought that at this time if anyone asked her of the most dreadful times of working there she wouldn't know an answer, which pleased him. William spoke up and reminded Kristina that his time of volunteering was just about over, he hated to do so, but he had responsibilities of his own.

"William, that is fine, I'm just glad you had a chance to see this. It is unbelievable isn't it?"

William nodded with an agreeable smile. "Indeed it is." He looked at his watch and asked her if she wanted him to stay longer, but she shook her head.

"No, that is fine. We should be all set. It is Leanna's day to come late, so we should be all set."

Henry decided that he'd clean out the pens and let Kristina watch the pups. She seemed so happy. It was a distraction from considering the fate of Old Ben. He figured he could manage the work and the other volunteer could join her in the merriment. He walked with William to the structure.

"I guess I'll start my volunteering today, William."

William smiled and held out his hand to shake Henry's. The men clasped hands. William said, "Welcome aboard." Henry got the tools he needed from the earlier directions Kristina gave him and began his work. He tackled the job as he did any other work and it went quickly. He disposed of the waste and began the rinse down of the pens. He was surprised by Leanna showing up and both greeted each other with friendliness.

Leanna seemed confused to see the pens empty, but became mesmerized with wonder in seeing the cause of it. Henry finished up his work by stowing the hose where he found it. The work was done in record time. That provided more time to enjoy watching the pack of dogs run about playing in harmony. Leanna's wonder became her obsession. After her shift when she left the shelter, her tales of that day would reverberate around town. When it was a half hour to Kristina's end of the day she mentioned it was time to get the dogs back in and feed them, then close up shop. Nobody wanted it but the day was coming to an end. Somehow the dogs knew it. Leanna saw to the cats in the other wing. It usually took her longer to finish up with the cats so she closed up the shelter.

Kristina clapped her hands indicating the time to return to the pens. In smaller groups the dogs responded with minor unwillingness to return, but this day her clap summoned the dogs attention. They all stopped to look at Kristina. After a strange and long focus upon the people Adoc darted back to Henry. Old Ben began the trotting to his pen and all the other dogs made their way back to their individual pens. Kristina and Leanna were speechless. They never saw such an occurrence. Kristina was spellbound while Leanna was running excitedly to secure the pens. It was like St Francis of Assisi was calling the dogs for blessings. Kristina said nothing. She couldn't do much except shake her head and walk around with this crazy look on her face… Henry appeared as a child might have at first experience of a magician. They began feeding the dogs once they were in the pens. Henry watched Kristina in the feeding. It appeared to him that she might have had the radiance of a new mother feeding her infant. Kristina didn't even take notice of Leanna's departure to the cat area of the shelter. Henry did take notice out of politeness.

Leanna had no concern for Kristina's amazement; Henry thought that her amazement was great enough. After the dogs were fed, Kristina did her rounds saying goodnight to all of them. That night she took extra time with Old Ben and instead of dread she demonstrated hope. While she looked at him tears of joy broke from her eyes and Adoc licked each off of her. She let him do so but tried to convince him that he was more trouble than anything. Adoc wasn't hearing anything but noise she made and Henry thought he saw in Old Ben's eyes a pride only a father could have of a son… and in that second of a glance it became clear to Henry just how Old Ben was going to be spending his last days as a free dog.

The three of them left the corridor of the shelter and made their way out through the building. Henry reminded Kristina that Leanna was doing her chores and Kristina thanked him in her forgetful way. She peeked in on Leanna and mentioned that they were leaving. Leanna stepped away from her duties and went to Kristina. She was jubilant.

"Don't you worry about a thing Kristina… I'll do as usual and close up…" She paused, pregnant to speak needing to say something, but all she could do was hug Kristina. More tears fell and Adoc forced his way between the two wanting to be in the hug… Henry laughed silently while a tear got loose from his eye. Henry quickly wiped it away and then commented.

"Sure, I see how you are Adoc. A regular ladies' man."

Leanna turned to Henry. "Oh you! Stop being jealous…!"

Henry didn't know what to do or even what to say; he let her comment ride. The ladies spoke about details and then the three of them walked out. Once outside the building Henry said that they needed to go see Francis. Kristina didn't disagree and Adoc heard Francis with a tail wag.

"After we see Francis I'll drop you off and then I'll pick you up tomorrow and get you to work… we'll finish up the tour, how's that sound?"

Kristina smiled and said, "Sounds good, let's go!" It was clear to Kristina that Henry's option for Old Ben was a placement with Francis, and she didn't know why she didn't think of the thought. They were in Henry's new car going to see Francis.

On the ride Kristina realized that only a few moments ago she'd likely go home this evening in a very depressed mood and now that just wasn't going to be the case. The realization was something she never really experienced. She liked the change and she could only attribute it to knowing Henry. During the ride she watched Henry driving the new ride. She didn't want to give him a distraction by letting him notice that she was staring at him so she stole glances. She tried to process all she knew about Henry while she was getting to know him. It never made sense to her why she stole glances. It was one of those things she wished she could change in herself.

Henry didn't think that Francis would mind the unexpected visit. He was excited to meet with him as his focus became more of a certainty. Henry's anticipation got away from him a lot. It was almost obsessive. He knew it to leave him distracted and even isolated to others. It remained difficult for him to avoid getting lost in his focus. Henry's focus and Kristina's self recriminations were interrupted by Adoc. He sensed that the Man and the other person with so many smells were missing the fun of the ride. He considered that to be a strange thing, he wondered what might have been wrong with them and knew that each of them needed to be licked.

He did lick both of them and they seemed to pay attention to the fun of the ride. After the licking he sensed the Man and the other person with so many smells were now right for the ride, he couldn't understand them when they got that way. He kept them in line if only to enjoy the ride himself.

Both of them began talking to each other about Adoc as they came to the last part of the drive to Francis' house. They laughed at Adoc for his licking, but each knew the dog's motivation. Henry's laughter became laughing at himself. His fondness for Adoc just kept growing. He was amazed at the dog's instincts for making him feel better about things. For Henry Adoc was almost too good to be true. As they drove to the end of Francis' driveway Adoc became animated in his excitement. It was clear to both Kristina and Henry that Adoc knew where he was at and could hardly wait to exit the car.

When Henry parked the car and opened the door Adoc jumped out to begin his wonderful need to smell. His nose led him in a frenzied seeking of something unmentioned running in circles. Henry and Kristina watched him in amazement. They both moved towards the front of the car keeping a focus on him like they were two parents watching their child chasing blown bubbles.

Francis heard the car, just as he had so many times when his wife returned from one errand or another. When Adoc became aware of the other person with the old hands he was more surprised than his need to smell all the wonderful things. Adoc darted for Francis desiring the touch of the old hands. Adoc wasn't a leaper by nature and his trust of people wasn't big enough to let him expose his vulnerable side to them. Adoc wagged on his legs in front of the person with old hands smelling a lot of smells. Adoc sensed smells about the person with old hands. They weren't like the Man had or the other person with a lot of smells had. The smells of the other person with old hands confused Adoc because the smells of the person with old hands told him that there was another he couldn't see. The old hands that pet him eased his confusion because it distracted Adoc's curiosity. The Man and the other people made noises that Adoc didn't recognize so he enjoyed the pets until they ended. After they ended he heard his name. It piqued his interest and he chased his name to each who said it looking for more pets. Then they all began to walk towards the house that he remembered eating at before the dark came. They followed the light that was disappearing today. He remembered how good that food tasted and was hoping there would be more.

"I'm glad to see you young folks and that silly dog. I hadn't expected you and that is what makes it even more wonderful. Will ya being staying for long or is this just a *'Hi how are you?'* sort of visit?" The question hung out there for a long pause until Henry answered.

"Well it is definitely more than a *'Hi how are you?'* sort of visit. It is actually a visit of inquiry."

Kristina listened to Henry converse with Francis and she liked the way Henry conveyed information. She thought he was quite good at it so she felt comfortable letting him speak first. It was after all his idea.

"I see… so an inquiry eh? Well you might as well come on into the house and have a seat. I'll get us a glass of wine to help consider this inquiry properly."

They entered the house. Once again Francis certainly had some dinner working on the stove top. The smell was heavenly. They took their seats as they had the night before. Francis went through the steps to make both Kristina and Henry comfortable. He also produced a treat for Adoc.

"Yes, my friend I hadn't forgotten your presence either." Francis gave Adoc a large piece of rawhide to chew on while they enjoyed the homemade wine over the inquiry. After Francis set the drinks up he went to the stove and stirred on some of the food. He checked in the oven and even fresher warmth came from his inspection. He then took a seat next to his guests. Francis held up his wine and toasted.

"To unknown inquiries!" They all raised their glasses and drank. "So the inquiry, may I hear it?"

Henry liked Francis' forthright nature. "Certainly you may hear it. When I was at the shelter today Kristina pointed out a dog slated for destruction and I thought you'd be the perfect match. His name is Old Ben and he has taken a real liking to Adoc. I'd take him but Adoc and I are still working out the newness of our own relationship."

Francis kept a straight face for the request he didn't reveal any inkling of a positive response or a negative response. Both Henry and Kristina waited on a response that didn't seem like it would come. "Just a moment." Francis finished off his wine and then excused himself from the table. He walked back to the oven and opened one of the pots on the surface. He added a spice to it and then stirred the contents. Henry and Kristina looked at each other in a quizzical way hoping for a positive response to the request and then Francis seemed to have a conversation... it sounded like he was talking to his wife. Even though they couldn't hear her Francis was clearly having a conversation. Adoc stopped his chewing and focused on Francis with great curiosity. It was an interest to both Henry and Kristina.

Adoc heard the person with old hands making noise, but he also heard a different noise that seemed to go along with the noise the person with old hands was having. He had a little whine as he listened and that gave both Henry and Kristina even a greater curiosity. Francis returned to the table with the jug of homemade wine.

"I hope you don't mind if I have more wine, but when I get into considering living arrangements it is best to be lubricated for the thinking... Besides the wife is having some concerns about fostering an old dog, she thinks it will keep me here longer than I'm supposed to be here."

Henry finished his drink as did Kristina. Both were surprised in a loving sort of way at hearing Francis' comment.

"You mean your passed wife, right?" Henry couldn't help but to ask for clarification.

When Francis heard the question he seemed like he couldn't really believe the question, but it had been asked. Francis poured more drinks after he noticed them finishing their drinks. "I'll take it that everyone is agreeable to having more libations. And yes, I speak of my wife."

Once the drinks were poured Francis noticed the shock on both Kristina's and Henry's faces. Before he toasted he thought to ease them with a *'Didn't you see that?'* type of question. "I'm surprised that you didn't notice Adoc's awareness because he knows she is here." They looked even more shocked at his statement. "Didn't you hear him whine when I was over tending the food?"

They both nodded at hearing his question. After their nods he held his wine up and began his answer after a quick toast. "To the unseen." He sipped on his wine and both Kristina and Henry did the same. They waited to hear his words as though he might be a judge rendering a criminal verdict at the accused.

"Dinner won't be much longer. Mildred is unsettled about this Old Ben addition. She is very impatient." He sipped some more on his glass. His words left both Kristina and Henry mystified. Neither could formulate words and that was okay... He wasn't done.

"What I am going to say to both of you doesn't need an answer immediately, it can wait. Henry I'll keep Old Ben with me, he'll enjoy the old place until the last of his days. There is something else though that goes with the bargain and it just has to be."

Henry heard he had conditions and waited to consider them. Kristina just listened, as she heard it Francis was speaking to Henry thus far, and she intently listened when Francis said he was talking to both of them. She wondered how her part of this whole thing was going to be told. Francis took a smell out of the air with a movement of his head towards the dinner cooking.

"Excuse me while I tend to dinner serving, it won't be but a minute." He rose from the table and began putting the portions on plates. While he was busy he looked at Adoc and smiled...

"Oh yes, Adoc, don't you worry I got something for you too." Adoc watched Francis' moves with an unbreakable gaze and when Francis made noise he seemed to understand the noise. Adoc knew that one of those servings was going to be his by the noise Francis made. For that noise, Adoc could only lick his nose. Francis spoke to him again.

"Adoc, there are very important things in life... Very important! And when you see a person at the oven as you do now... that is the most important thing you'll ever know... that's right, The Man is cooking and nothing else matters."

Adoc rose up on all his legs and moved towards Francis. His nose was on overtime, his nostrils flared as he pre digested the smells of the food. His tail involuntarily wagged as he began to drool.

Henry watched the interaction of Adoc and Francis and soaked it up. It seemed to Henry that Francis was a pro at dealing with dogs. He wanted to see the nuances so as to try and employ them later while he and Adoc would be with each other. Kristina took notice of the dynamic that was happening between Adoc and Francis with Henry watching. She was on the outside looking in to a magical little scenario and she was thinking it was beautiful. Her face involuntarily smiled and she couldn't have been happier. Francis brought two plates to the table and spoke again to Adoc.

"Don't worry, the last plate is the best one and you get the last one and maybe even you get to lick the plates... That is up to your dad."

Adoc remained fixated on Francis. Henry and Kristina were silent, watching Francis interact with the dog. It was almost as though they were in a Twilight Zone TV Show. Nothing they watched seemed real. Francis was highly animated at delivering his portion to the table while holding Adoc's. After he put his plate on the table Francis had a word with Adoc before giving him his share.

"Adoc, you aren't going to know enough to give thanks for your food and that is okay. But when your dad does this for you in days ahead just know that he'll do all the thanking to cover you. And when he lays his head down on the pillow at night he'll give thanks to Adam for calling you a dog, because Adoc couldn't be your name if you weren't a dog. He'll also thank the Creator for having you as a buddy, because only a buddy like you is given by the Creator."

Francis lowered the plate at the side of the table. Adoc watched him place the plate down. He could smell the food. He wanted it so badly but without Francis telling him to eat he waited. It was the most difficult wait of his life, but that person with old hands held his focus and until he gave him the command to eat, he'd wait.

"Dig in, you youngsters; the food is best when it is hot." He looked at Adoc and nodded, Adoc began eating. He gobbled it up as fast as he could grab it up with his mouth. All tasted the food and both Henry and Kristina were amazed of the taste delivered to them by Francis' cooking. The flavor of his handy-work was as good as the enticing aroma that seemed to live within the house.

Francis might have known animals and what they liked to eat, but his true passion above all other things was his cooking. He also knew how to converse over a meal and did so in between savoring of his efforts.

"Lordy, ever since Mildred passed I finally get to cook as I always wanted to. Oh, she was a much better cook than I am and it was a rarity when she'd let me have my way in the kitchen. Even now she keeps nagging me when I am cooking about this or that. How much spice to use or the order of preparation... That woman cooked to feed the world but none of the hungry would dare step into her kitchen, heck even the mice skidaddled when she turned on the heat." Henry was amazed at Francis' stories.

Kristina felt as though she might be reading a romance novel dining on food that gave her a sense of home. "So are you telling us that your cooking was second to Mildred's? Is that what I am to believe?"

Francis laughed aloud. "Oh, my cooking amounts to preparing a peanut butter sammitch for lunch, compared to Mildred's doing; it seemed that anything digestible in her hands was straight off the Menu God eats from." He looked at both of them finishing off his wine and winked at Kristina.

Henry picked his wine glass up and made a toast to Mildred. "Here is to the second place cooking skills of your wife, Francis. If I ever tasted her food I might have thought I died and went to Heaven."

Kristina raised her glass and Francis rose up to get more wine from his jug. As he poured himself another to join in the toast he sat back at the table. "To Mildred's cooking!" They all sipped their wine and returned to eating. While they ate Henry gave thought to the mention that Francis gave earlier. He wasn't done with his conveyance and Henry's curiosity was keen. Francis checked on Adoc's doings and noticed he was done with his portion.

"You have quite the dog here in Adoc. You are aware of that?"

Henry's curiosity was sidetracked. "Francis, Adoc came to me when I thought I was done with this life. I reckon he saved me from doing something that would have ended it all."

Francis heard his response as did Kristina. Francis continued eating while Henry responded and then spoke back to him. "You might have thought your life was over, but that just shows you what your own thinking for yourself is worth, doesn't it?" Adoc's focus remained on Francis. Henry simply said, "Not so much I guess." Francis resumed eating while Kristina was feeling as though she was waiting on some unknown cue. She didn't know if she might have a part in the drama unfolding. Adoc broke his focus from the Man with Old Hands and sat next to the Man; the Man pet him gently.

Henry felt a bit uncomfortable at that point but he sweat it out because he knew Francis had more to say. He decided to enjoy more of the food in front of him fully aware that Adoc watched his every bite patiently. Kristina didn't say anything, she continued to eat she figured when Francis was going to speak to her he would. The food was delicious and because it was she remained polite by eating the food as doing so was easy. Francis decided to continue more of what he needed to them both. For the immediate time he'd be talking to Henry, but Kristina also needed to hear what was meant for both of them.

"Henry, there are a few things you need to understand and I'm gonna try my best to get you understanding plainly; it will probably be best to let me finish even if questions come to mind. When I do we'll deal with them afterwards." Henry nodded and continued to eat. After Francis swallowed his bite he began. "Now, that dog of yours is a very special gift and I reckon he was meant for you since before you were born. All you have done up to meeting Adoc had to happen. I don't know why other than to say that is how it all works out. You'll also need everything you came to know for all that is coming your way." He took another bite of food and another sip of his wine. He looked at Kristina before he continued.

"As for you, young lady, just as Adoc was meant for Henry, so are you meant for him and what you two need to come to realize going forward is what will be. You both have a partnership and it is the business of your work Kristina. That being said it will be up to Henry to take his gifts of knowledge in helping you do more than you are right now." Francis began to shake his head then he looked up at the ceiling. It was strange for Henry and Kristina to see him make such gesticulations. What was even stranger was Adoc offering a light whimper just as Francis gave his displays.

"Yes, Mildred, I know you think I am long winded, but my dear love; these kids can't hear you and if you keep nagging me it will only be more long winded, now hush, my love." Francis looked at both of them while Adoc hunkered down on the floor as though he had wanted to avoid scolding.

"Mildred was never one to parse words. She is nagging at me to hurry it up." Henry and Kristina were very interested in hearing about this unknown partnership; it wasn't that they disbelieved hearing it, but it sure did make the partnership thing more of an interesting proposition. Adoc let another groan out. Francis laughed aloud and explained for the benefit of both Henry and Kristina.

"Oh, Mildred has a bee in her bonnet now and that woman of mine and I had some doozies of battles, but we never went to sleep upset with each other, we always kissed and said how much we loved each other before going to bed. But right now I am just going to offer her selective hearing and that always gave her reason to carry on. Adoc is hearing her right now." Henry found what Francis to say as truly funny and he began to laugh, but Kristina wasn't laughing. She knew better.

Francis made a face that offered a surprised look as though the laugh was inappropriate. "Oh, laughing now probably isn't such a good idea... as a matter of fact trust me; it isn't."

Once again Adoc let a heavy sigh loose. Quickly Henry tried to compose himself with great difficulty.

Francis took notice of his anguish and told him, "In my experience, it isn't easy to laugh with a mouthful of food, so enjoy the vittles."

Henry began eating and composed himself for doing so. Kristina ate as well but she was a bit more serious in considering what Francis spoke to before the outburst.

"Back to it then. Now I don't know what your partnership is supposed to be, that is for both of you to work out. In a time coming and I don't know when, but I'll be departing this world and it will be up to both of you to do what your partnership needs at this old house." When Francis paused to have another bite and a drink of his wine they could have heard a pin drop. Both Henry and Kristina were stunned as though they had the air taken out of them. Francis saw their displeasure for his last conveyance.

"Now don't either of you fret. It won't be tomorrow but it is inevitable and there is no way around that fact." Francis looked at both of them with a serious glare. "We are born to die in this life. Now Mildred always told me if we lived with integrity after we died, we'd live again." He got back to his food and drink and his comment somehow settled them a bit. After a pause Adoc interrupted the dinner nudging at the Man. When Henry looked at Adoc he didn't know what the dog wanted. Adoc tilted his head at the Man with a wonder. Francis and Kristina laughed out loud together and that made Henry even more confused. Adoc wagged his tail for the noise the others made. They had many smells and old hands because they knew what he wanted unlike the Man.

Adoc figured to put his head in the Man's lap just under the table. The motion gave both Kristina and Francis even more of a reason to laugh.

Francis finally gave Henry a clue. "There are two sure things about a dog and one of them is that he is always hungry, now because Adoc is special he isn't being rude, but I'll bet he is wishing he could tell you to know the one thing of his need." Henry shook his own head for hearing Francis' explanation and felt a bit ridiculous for his short-sightedness. He pet Adoc's head and then lowered his plate in front of him.

For the short time it took Adoc to finish the remains on Henry's plate the trio delighted in his appreciation. Adoc's feasting went on as after he finished cleaning off Henry's plate; Kristina lowered hers to his level. Adoc cleaned hers as well and after he went to thank her she gave him a long pet and a kiss on the nose.

"You liked that did you, Adoc?"

Adoc let his tail wag realizing that this other person with many smells wasn't as dense as the Man. And after he smelled on her again it clicked from long memories. It was a she! She was like the bitch he knew in the place of bad smells. The one who tried to sustain his life, but couldn't. So now he knew the Man and he knew this other as his mother type. He licked her while she doted on him. Adoc was no fool, he also kept in the back of his thinking that the other with the old hands and many smells had a plate too. And when he came to realize the mother type's place he turned his attention to the other with old hands and many smells.

He also had a plate. Adoc wasn't given the plate right away; rather the old hand hands gave him long slow pets. And in the pets Adoc found a familiarity of the old hands to the Man's hand. It was as though they were from the same source, but just different by the touch. Adoc treasured the old hand's as he was stroked and waited patiently for the plate. After a time, the old hands yielded to his want and he received the plate. After he was done he went to the middle of the Man and the mother type and lay down.

Francis poured one last round of the wine as they sat around the table. The home made wine already had its affect on Henry and on Kristina. He saw their hesitation towards the drink and told them not to worry, but to enjoy.

"Mildred told me to make up two rooms for you to relax in and that is just what I did. So enjoy the wine and feel as though you are test driving your future this evening." Francis held his wine up as did Henry and Kristina. It was a time for sipping wine and enjoying digestion of a great meal. Both Henry and Kristina shared a notion that Francis always had a solution and as they both observed Adoc... He seemed to be just fine where he lay. Francis rose up from the table and began clearing the dishes away. Kristina thought to help and even tried to intervene, but Francis wouldn't hear of it.

"No, I won't hear of it. What I want you to do is take this partner of yours out to the porch with that dog and enjoy the evening air. I won't be long and you need to let him know about all your years knowing Mildred and myself. Now go do as I say and I won't be long at all."

Kristina stood up after Francis finished and looked at Henry, "You heard the man, partner. Let's go. Come on, Adoc. Maybe you'll find a stick?" Henry rose up as she said it and Adoc was up the instant he heard stick. They thanked Francis for dinner and took their wine out to the porch. Sure as anything Adoc found his stick and over the tossing and chasing Kristina revealed her part in knowing Francis and his bride Mildred. Neither of them heard Francis speaking to Mildred, but he heard the laughter between both while they played with the dog waiting on his return.

"Yes, Mildred. I know you get frustrated with my manner, but it is MY manner and I did get to your points." Francis laughed while he finished up his chores and continued his one way conversation. "No my darling I didn't forget, but it can wait till tomorrow." He laughed again. "Oh stop your fussing tomorrow will be soon enough and that is all there is to it." He put the last of the plates away and cleaned the work area counters off around the sink. When he was done he went to is humidor and grabbed cigars of his favorite liking. He grabbed three. Then he grabbed the jug of wine and made his way out to the porch. When he arrived, Adoc stayed put after Henry threw the stick. He let off another groan. Francis assured Adoc that everything was fine. Then he explained to Henry and Kristina.

"Mildred is all worked up about a gift she wanted me to give you. Then when she saw me reaching for the wine and these; well she got to raising her own type of Cain. Mildred never did like my fondness for the fruits of the vine, nor did she like me partaking in an evening smoke. She always told me it was an insult to God and it was like spitting in His face." Henry was astounded and Kristina just knew that what Francis said was absolutely true. She just didn't know that he was still talking to her.

"So Francis, let me get this straight… you are still busy at giving your wife passed aggravation and on purpose?" Francis handed out the smokes and set down with the jug pouring another. He thought on Henry's question and handed him the jug after he poured his own.

Henry took the jug up and poured another for himself and gave the jug to Kristina. She did the same and then the lighting of the cigars began. After all were set with drink taking draws from the cigars and after Henry got through his first choking episode for the inhalation Francis addressed Henry's last question.

"Henry all while you were growing up, the Mrs.'s and I were doing our business; we heard stories about your abilities. Word came to us from people all over that we had business with, they couldn't speak enough praise in the way you got to seeing things. It occurs to me that's why Mildred had such a fondness of you." Francis looked at Kristina first and winked then looked at Henry.

"You see Henry you and Mildred had that one thing in common. Just like you saw something for what it was, so did My Mildred. She differed in the manner she let folks know just what she knew." Francis took a sip of wine and another puff on his cigar. Henry watched the puff on the cigar and did the same.

After he expelled it without coughing Henry realized the pleasure in the ritual. Francis laughed and looked to Kristina. "He sure is a quick study, isn't he?"

Kristina gave a smile back to Francis and then a comment. "Well, I know he cleaned out those stalls today like nobody has since I did it, but I got to be honest. Adoc stole the show today and I'm sure happy that Henry came up with the thinking on asking you about Old Ben. That is a big relief to me."

He looked into Kristina's eyes and leaned towards her. "Child, Mildred tells me to let you know that more is coming and that you are finally at the steps of your true path."

Kristina's countenance revealed to Henry something he couldn't recall seeing. It lasted only a second before it left, but in that second Henry reflected on all things he recalled as beautiful. None of his recollections or any of his likely imaginative considerations had any measure to that second. Henry felt as though his thought for the glimpse wasn't something he wanted any to know about, his shyness was that way.

"So what is your reasoning on why you still talk with Mildred?"

Francis realized he hadn't completed his thought. "Well, she is still here talking with me because in as much as she knew and loved God, she thinks he is wrong and she'll go when she is good and ready… I guess when we go to see him together."

Henry had some more of his smoke and some more wine. Francis finished his off and poured another. His smoke was burning nicely and while they sat he continued his smoke and finished the last bit of his wine. He then told them he'd take his leave for the evening.

A Man, a Dog and a Ball

"Kristina, you know the rooms upstairs that I fixed up for you both. I'll let you figure out the arrangements as I am off to bed. I set out some nights clothes for both of you and of course Adoc is welcome to stay with you Henry in which ever room you find yourself in. But as for me... I am off to bed." Francis looked at Adoc. Adoc rose up and gave the other with old hands licks.

"That's a good boy, Adoc, and when tomorrow comes I'm gonna give something to you so you can share it with Henry." Francis left telling them, "Enjoy the evening." He was gone. After Francis left Henry looked at his smoke and then looked at Kristina smoking her cigar. That was a sight he'd not likely forget. He hadn't ever drank much in his life nor did he think it would be any kind of habit he wanted, but on that night he considered all that Francis told him and decided to have another. After he poured his he held the jug out to Kristina. After hesitation she took the jug and poured herself a last drink. They sat in the darkness of the evening wanting to say things, but the words weren't yet ready to be said. Henry needed to say something he had an itch.

"Do you think all that conversation is really happening?" Kristina looked at Henry and nodded. He smoked his cigar wishing she responded with words, but he took the nod as a positive response. His itch hadn't yet been scratched. "Well that was the first time I ever heard anything like that, it is still something I'm trying to get my mind around." Kristina shrugged, and sipped on her wine.

"I've heard of such things and honestly it doesn't surprise me, but then again I knew them as they both lived together." Henry was relieved for the intercourse she offered. It was better than a nod. He smoked on his cigar and finally decided on finishing off his wine. After he did he looked at Adoc and gave him a pet.

I guess boy in between stick throwing I am going to be researching this talking to the dead subject and see what it is all about. Adoc tilted his head. Henry gave him more pets. Kristina laughed. Henry turned his attention to her for the laugh wondering why she loosed it.

"It's nothing." She giggled some more and continued, "It's just that Adoc doesn't seem to have any problem hearing their conversation."

That sounded funny to Henry and he too laughed. After he was finished with the laughing he asked Adoc a question. "Are you gonna teach me how to hear those words Adoc? Well are you?"

Adoc's tail wagged even though all the Man said was noise. He knew they were speaking about him but none of it mattered. He was happy. He knew he liked being with the Man and the mother type that was there. More he liked that they were at the place where the person with many smells and old hands lived. Above that there was another here he couldn't see. He could hear her plain as day but he couldn't see her and he knew that the other person with old hands knew she was there too. He figured it would be like when the Man took so long to figure out that he wanted to share his food from the plate. The Man had trouble knowing what he should know and he would need help to seeing things that seemed so obvious. It was almost like when the Man was looking over the edge of the place where the things that fly come to get you from.

Adoc knew that even though he had an irresistible urge to be with the Man, the Man needed some learning.

Kristina sipped the last of her wine and extinguished her cigar. She was ready to get some sleep and mentioned as much to Henry. When Henry heard her intentions he too extinguished his cigar.

"Why don't you boys follow me upstairs and pick a room you think you'll be comfortable in for sleeping?"

Henry followed her into the house as they took their glasses inside to leave at the sink counter. Henry waited on Adoc to follow them and indicated to Kristina that he'd let Adoc pick the room.

"Seeing as Adoc hears Mildred I'm sure he'll know what her thinking is regarding the room choice." Kristina liked what Henry said and smiled with a nod. What she heard for the words Henry spoke gave her insight to who Henry was and the more she considered the details she was coming to know, the more respect she had for Henry. After the conversation she listened to from Francis she thought that whatever partnership he spoke to would depend on a great deal of respect for her partner. Henry was gleaning great quality of characteristics for the words he mentioned.

At the top of the stairs Kristina pointed out the rooms Francis made the invitations to earlier. Just as Henry mentioned he followed Adoc to the room he chose. "I guess this is where we'll be sleeping." Kristina was fine with Adoc's choice and a little surprised because the dog chose the room that she new Mildred would have picked. Both took the appropriate night clothes Francis left out for them and said their good nights to each other.

Behind the closed door Kristina changed into Mildred's former nightgown thinking about the day. She didn't think she'd be getting to sleep anytime soon as she slipped into bed, but to her surprise the wine coaxed her to an early relaxation that brought sleep to her shortly after she slipped under the covers. She'd wake later having enjoyed a night of sleep she hadn't had in quite some time and the day following would be one of the best she'd live through in quite some time too.

In the other room Henry dressed into his clothes for sleeping. Adoc quietly sat at the foot of the bed. After Henry turned to the bed he saw Adoc waiting for him on the floor at the foot of the bed. Henry felt badly for Adoc. The pillow he liked was still at his house. Henry took one of the pillows and a quilt off the bed and placed them at the side of the bed on the floor. Adoc investigated Henry's activity, after sniffing the pillow and blanket he put on the floor Adoc's tail wagged. Henry just shook his head. "Good night, buddy."

Henry got under the covers Adoc took his place. He wasn't used to consuming wine, but he enjoyed the effects of it, or he thought he did. He knew of others in town that seemed to have trouble with the drink to the point of losing all control in managing their lives. The manner that they drank consumed everything and he didn't want that to be his result for drinking the wine. Henry figured Francis seemed to do alright with it so it didn't give him more than a concern. After he gave all the points of the day consideration, he listened to the rhythm of Adoc's breathing. It lulled him closer to sleep and it wasn't long before Henry fell off sleeping. The morning would come to both of them offering Henry a reason to feel grateful. Adoc's deciding to choose the Man at the bridge would be enough reason for Henry to remain grateful until his last days.

Francis heard all of them as they made their way to bed. He lay in bed awake for sometime as he rested his body much like he did throughout his life not sleeping. Francis wasn't much of a sleeper he learned how to replenish his body without sleep in the days of his service through the wars he battled in before either Henry or Kristina were children. He shared his nightly conversation with Mildred. She was impatient as always but she seemed a bit more relaxed for having Henry and Kristina where they would be before Francis could come home. He tolerated her banter and even ignored parts of it knowing fully that for ignoring it he'd have to listen more. Then when he had enough just as he always did he ended it by telling Mildred "Yes they are here and that is a start, you'll just have to wait a bit more. I love you Mildred. Good night."

When Francis said good night the banter ended. It is just how it was when Mildred was alive because she understood that she was afforded her venting by the man she loved and for his patience she honored his departure after he said he loved her and good night. She didn't compare her own condition to other marriages, but she did know that her man unlike other men worshipped her as his wife. She also knew she exploited that worship to be who she was and she enjoyed making life difficult for him. For her it was the cost of her devotion and both were mutually accepting of the relationship as it was. It was unique love because even departure from life hadn't changed it. In fact Francis might have been more dedicated to her after her passing because he still spoke to her even though she no longer walked the earth.

Francis loved the mornings. In those hours before the sun's rising he owned his time. Mildred wasn't one for sleeping in but because of his service and his limited need for sleep he was always first to rise. He rose even before Henry did. He always woke at 3:00 AM and he spent his time getting ready to prepare breakfast. In the duties of making coffee and preparing whatever delight he thought to make for morning sustenance he considered the day. Francis was a humble man and without fail in his ritual of the day, he offered thanks to his creator for meeting another.

He wasn't a fan of scriptural study or even going to church. He in fact knew the Scriptures and maybe better than those preaching the words on Sunday Sermons. Upon returning from the Wars he experienced a very difficult time wondering what to do, so he lost his confusion in reading the word of God.

Francis was a principled man and kept his politics and religious leaning to himself. It was better that way for his business in serving the general public. For all of his public life he kept a very private and personal life upon his own convictions. Mildred was about the only one who had any idea about the torments in his life and she had no clue as to the depth of his reality. He shared none of his considerations with any save Mildred and he only gave up to her that which she endlessly nagged him over. Francis was a man who held to his own truth and from that place he was steadfast and considered a righteous and good man by all that knew him. Francis knew many types of folks. He'd heard many things from people and even if he thought they were crazy, he listened to them as though they were his best customers. Early on Francis knew that in order to avoid getting sucked into the drama he only had to avoid in the drama. When folks wanted to talk to him, they had to come to him. He wasn't one for passing the day mindlessly doing anything, nor did he hang with buddies that would deliver him to a place where the absurd dwelled.

Francis liked waking at the 3:00 AM hour because once he heard at that particular hour the hour opposite to holiness of Jesus came alive. In fact he heard it from lots of people. They spoke to strange occurrences at the particular time of day he woke. For all the hearing of the tales Francis never knew any of it that he could witness. He thought with a great amount of humor at what those folks claimed. As far as Francis was concerned it was off by four hours to his figuring. The strangeness always occurred after Mildred rose, which was 3-4 hours after the time they spoke to when the strangeness happened.

While Francis was having a cup of coffee and preparing the flapjack dough there was a rustling from the upstairs and he knew it to be Henry and Adoc. He expected them and actually was looking forward to sharing the morning with both of them. As far as he was concerned two men and a dog needed time before the ladies of the house woke. When he heard them coming down the stairs he realized that he felt younger than he had since Mildred passed. And he also knew that the feeling was the beginning of a short amount of time remaining in which he needed to convey to both of them some very important details. When both of them entered the kitchen Adoc was obviously the first to be greeted.

Adoc was excited about seeing the other with old hands for a greeting and as he walked into the kitchen. The smells were as good as the night before. Adoc began to wagging abundantly for seeing the other with old hands... he walked straight up to him and allowed the scratching and petting to begin. Adoc felt wonderful for the touch of the other with old hands. His need to go outside and empty the marking of the day was put off. There was something strange to the old hands though... something mysterious. It wasn't bad there was no bad smells around. In fact Adoc developed a curiosity as to what it might be. Then the other with old hands stopped the petting and scratching and turned to the door opening it to let him mark his day. As he left he heard the Man making noise to the one with old hands. The cool air of the morning filled his nose as he hunted down the spots to leave his mark. As he made his rounds he thought that His presence there would be the rest of his knowing smells and running after the stick with the Man. After making his marks, he made room for the next eating he'd be doing. He went to the limit of his comfort. He hadn't been there in the light to know the place well enough. Adoc felt to go any further would be like going to the grabbing thing. There is where he made room for the next food. He sniffed his emptying before he left to go back to where the Man was making noise with the other with the old hands. After the sniff he looked upon the great expanse of the tall things in the ground. He felt a danger from that place, like there might be a lot of grabbing things there. In the light he'd look more but only while smelling for the grabbing things. The rest of the time he'd being chasing sticks or chasing smells where he marked his place. He padded back to the door which was left open for him returning to the Man and the other with old hands and wonderful smells.

Adoc came through the door rejoining both Francis and Henry. Henry watched Francis welcome the dog. Francis talked to him softly. "Ah, there is that good boy, Adoc. I'll bet you are pretty hungry, eh?" Francis accepted the wagging Adoc put in front of him, but he didn't touch him. Henry noticed that Adoc didn't take his eyes off Francis. Henry watched the interaction closely. He knew it was a lesson. Francis held up a bowl of milk with a bit of honey in it. Adoc smelled the sweetness of what was in the bowl and waited patiently. He looked at Henry before he set the bowl down.

"Henry, this is milk with a tease of honey." He set the bowl down before Adoc and after a sniff he began lapping at it. Once Adoc was busy lapping Francis turned to Henry. "Don't be afraid to let the pup have a bit of honey in milk or on some food. Don't listen to the quacks who call themselves docs saying that honey is no good for him." Francis looked at Adoc lapping and spoke to Henry watching Adoc. "You are going to be responsible for not just him, but for old Ben in a time coming and I have a good feeling that the number of four-legged critters will be expansive that you are overseeing." He looked at Henry then he said something that Henry never heard.

"Henry, the way it works with animals goes something like this: When you can understand what the animal is trying to tell you, the animal will hear your words. That goes with any animal. Dogs are easier for most people to figure and that is because Adam thought the Dog was the mirror of his understanding God. The dog, like God offers unconditional love. But the dog has no voice. The dog is a creature that will take a beating but still remain loyal to he who beats him. No other animal will do that and that is something to reckon for what comes your way."

When Henry heard the words Francis spoke he reflected on wisdom of all his reading to understand. Once Henry was finished with all of the grappling of an idea he came to know it as nothing than less than truth. What he heard in Francis' words was truth. He knew it for hearing it. Henry heard many claim truths, but he usually ended up finding out that they were versions of truth. In Henry's experience people who held on to their own distorted truths always had something to lose or gain for holding onto it. Francis had neither. Nothing in what Francis said presented a complaint or even a supplication. What Francis revealed to him was unabashedly a truth. Henry sipped on his coffee.

Francis saw that Henry had grasped his conveyance. He also knew that for the acceptance it was time to lighten the conversation. "Henry do you cook food much?" Henry heard the question and wanted to respond flippantly, but reserved himself. "I'm not much of a cook, Francis. I manage to stay alive, but for me alone... I never really put any effort into it." Francis turned to his batter preparation.

"In this life there are all kinds of experts to tell you what you want to know. In your case it came by the written word. There is value to being your own expert in the details of living." After some mixing of ingredients Francis turned to Henry. "You just saw how Adoc lapped up that milk with the honey right?"

Henry nodded.

"You see, the thing that makes that milk taste like it came from the teat of the bitch when he was first born was the honey... If you'd listen to the experts you'll miss the best life you can ever know." Francis looked to Henry to see that he was with him. After Francis knew he was he continued at the batter prep. "Cooking is a thing a man does to define how he lives. The better you are at cooking the better you are at life. The more you put into your meals the more you take with you in this life. And those smart enough to know what good living is will never miss a meal with you. Look at that dog right now... go ahead. Look at him... That milk with the honey will hold him over long enough to wait on the slab of bacon I'll cut off that pig gut in a minute and he'll stay sleeping until the bacon is ready to be served." Henry stood up and walked over to Francis' counter. He examined the pig gut to slice off the bacon. Francis saw his desire to begin learning.

"Slicing bacon off a pig gut is worth watching before attempting, but I do like your hands on ability. What ya can do is go over to the knife block and pick a knife that you think will do the job. That'd be a good place to start." Henry took Francis' advice and studied the knife block. On the move towards the block he saw the beginning of the rise of the sun. Blackness was receding and the brilliance of the heavens began to dim. Henry began examining the several knives in the block. It was the first time he ever thought to notice the different collection of a cook who used knives. He himself only had a couple of knives he thought of a knife as generic. To his surprise a cook had many. He imagined each had a specific function as he examined the sizes and differences of all that Francis owned. They were all very well used and very good quality knives.

Henry finally settled on one of the larger knives. He held it up to Francis. Francis gave him a shrug but Henry picked his weapon. Once Francis was done with his efforts he approached Henry holding his choice. Francis held out his extended hand as a gesture for take the knife. Henry handed it properly to him. He began cutting the gut producing a slice of bacon. Once he produced the slice he extended the knife to Henry and allowed him to do the same. After some effort Henry managed to cut off a lesser looking slice than what Francis produced. Francis nodded his head and said, "Not too bad." Then he went to the block and produced another knife, the proper knife and gave it to Henry. "Try this one." Henry took the knife from Francis and repeated the butchering. The difference of the knife made the job easier and it also produced a much better slice. Henry was surprised by the difference.

"You see, every choice you make in this life doing anything beats what experts will tell you because you learn from the doing. No cook is worth his salt if he doesn't know the purpose and function of his tools." Henry nodded and began cutting off bacon slices for the breakfast. While the men worked at breakfast Kristina woke to the morning and stopped in the bathroom and made her way down the stairs. When she entered Francis got busy making her a cup of coffee.

She took up her seat at the table looking at Henry slicing at the counter and Adoc lying on the floor below the work area. When Francis brought her the coffee he whispered to her, "Don't mind Adoc, he just had some milk and honey and now he is waiting on a slice or two of bacon. Good morning, did you sleep well?" She held up her finger to her lips and made a shhhh sign then she nodded with a smile. Both Henry and Adoc never noticed Kristina's arrival; she might have as well been a ghost. Adoc was feeling like the time when he first remembered and Henry was focused on butchering the bacon. Francis had managed to serve up a coffee to her and greet her without either of them knowing. When Henry finished cutting off a proper amount of bacon for the breakfast he turned to notice that Kristina had joined them, he smiled and said, "Good morning. How was your sleep?"

Adoc heard his greeting and also took notice of the mother type and rose up off the floor with an animated excitement his tailed wagged as he made his way to her for a morning greeting. Francis took notice of Adoc's greeting.

"Well, I reckon that milk and honey would keep him under bacon slicing until it was cooking, but a better *slice* was introduced."

They all laughed and the morning came alive. It was too early for Mildred's appearance and Adoc fussed with the mother-type. Kristina spent a good amount of time doting on Adoc and he loved every second of it. Henry cleaned the knife he used and replaced it to the knife block then he took up a seat at the table along side of Kristina and Adoc. After the morning greeting with Adoc Kristina finally had an opportunity to enjoy her coffee. As she did, Adoc made his way over to the Man for more petting and scratching. Henry gave Adoc the attention he sought. During the quiet at the table Francs spoke to what their motivation of the day was.

"So, when do you think Old Ben will be arriving?"

The question surprised both of them because they hadn't really discussed it other than to hear what Francis said about Mildred's discomfort for taking the dog. Henry obviously couldn't answer so he let Kristina respond to the question.

After having a sip of her coffee she put her cup down swallowing the gulp and offered her thinking. "First of all I want to thank you for doing this. As far as when, well it would be helpful if we did it first thing. I was thinking when Henry dropped me off we might just get Old Ben right into the car and have him return Old Ben to you immediately."

Francis didn't stop his preparation. He put a large frying pan on one end of the six burner stove and set the heat to low. Then he placed the bacon Henry cut off in the pan. He looked at Henry and gave him instructions. "Henry any time you want to make a breakfast with meat it is always good to cook the meat first and fry it on low heat that is when bacon tastes best. A slow fry, and if you start with the meat then your timing will all work out to serve all the food hot at the same time." He worked through his response to Kristina while placing a large cast iron griddle on the stove surface on the other side of the frying bacon. He set the heat to a level proper for making flap jacks and said, "That will be fine and it is then likely better to leave Adoc here while you return with Old Ben in the car Henry. I doubt you'll want to deal with two dogs in that car while they are romping around bonding with each other." Henry became part of the conversation for Francis' response and he affirmed Francis' reasoning.

"Yeah, that sounds about right; I can bring Old Ben back here and at some point get back to the shelter to do my volunteering." Francis held his hand over the griddle testing the heat. He took a scoop of shortening and dropped it on the griddle. The shortening began to liquefy slowly and expanded on the surface. Once it was completely liquefied Francis used a rag to coat the entire griddle. Then he lowered the heat a bit more.

"How's everyone for coffee? Are we ready for more?" Kristina sipped more off her coffee and mentioned she could use a warmer as did Henry. Francis grabbed up the pot of coffee and moved to refill their cups. It was apparent to Francis that Adoc had a new focus. After he filled the cups he poured some more into his own cup and turned to look at Adoc. He wasn't interested in anymore pets or scratches. The bacon was beginning to sizzle and Francis knew Adoc was on smell overload.

"Remember all you are seeing here today Henry for this cooking. Remember it because of those who are about to receive the blessings of your effort." He continued gazing at Adoc. Henry looked at Adoc and found amazement at Adoc's attention.

"Henry, when you take up with a being in life such as a dog it is important how you manage that relationship. It is important because in a relationship such as the one you and Adoc are building it won't be like other interactions with just any dogs. This is something to be mindful of especially as the relationship between you and Adoc has to be understood by other dogs.

Remember what I told you about understanding animals." Francis grabbed a spatula and began flipping the bacon. After he flipped the bacon he turned again towards Kristina and Henry. "Unfortunately when you have a love for animals such as Kristina does, you have to realize that as much as you want to help there is only a certain amount that you can help and it can be heartbreaking, I'm sure you'll see more and more of that as you volunteer over at the shelter."

"Well, I have come to see a bit of that already and I am doing some figuring on that heart break." Francis heard Henry's comment. He checked the heat on the griddle once again. Then he stirred the batter. He flipped the bacon again and then poured off some of the grease in the pan into a large coffee cup.

"You always want to save your bacon grease. It is a great base for making suet and you'll want that for birds in the winter." Kristina witnessed the interaction going on between Francis and Henry. As much as she felt happiness for the interaction, she knew that Francis wasn't explaining these things for nothing. He was prepping Henry for what was ahead which was a time coming when he wouldn't be here. She knew what it meant and tried to enjoy the moment rather than get lost in the pain of the inevitable. She looked at Henry wondering if he was aware of the same thing.

"Henry, come on over here I'm gonna show you how to make a flap jack. Henry went to Francis and watched him use the ladle to drop the batter on the griddle. Francis made six cakes on the griddle. All were uniform in size and thickness. "I like to keep them about the same size that makes for good stacking. Now you don't want the cake to be too hard or get too brown so your heat is really important. You keep an eye on the bubbles because that tells you when to flip them." Francis gave the first flip with the spatula and the cakes were golden but not brown. "That is the color you are looking for. Also the cake is cooked now so it won't take as much time to get the same color on this side." Francis looked at Henry. "It isn't difficult to ruin a cake for waiting too long." Francis scooped up the first batch and stacked them on the plate, and then he handed the utensils to Henry. He stepped to the side and managed the bacon. After flipping the bacon Francis removed a brown shopping sack from a drawer under the counter. He placed it on the counter open and unfolded. He looked at Henry's progress making the flapjacks. Henry demonstrated a great ability at cooking and he made some excellent looking cakes.

"Those are fine looking flapjacks. I'm sure Adoc won't know the difference between your hand and mine."

Henry smiled at Francis, imagining Adoc eating flapjacks; the thought was funny to him. It wasn't difficult for Henry to imagine Adoc eating human food breakfast. Francis began scooping the bacon out of the frying pan. He let the extra grease run of the slice before he put them in the brown sack. That was a new one for Henry he would have never considered drying the bacon in that manner, but when he saw how the sack was closed up and then shaken it made all the sense to him in the world. Francis dumped the bacon onto a plate and moved to the pancake stacks and placed the plate next to the stack Henry was building. He went to the cupboard and produced plates and silverware for serving the breakfast. He turned and asked Kristina if she wanted juice she nodded and Henry did as well. He produced 3 glasses and filled them with some orange juice. He placed the orange juice on the table along with the silverware. After that he produced an older clay jug that contained homemade maple syrup. He placed that on the table as well.

Henry worked on the last batch of cakes as Francis made enough batter for twenty four cakes for the portions; six cakes each and two pounds of bacon for four. When Henry finished the cooking he thought that he overcooked. He grabbed up the plates and brought them to the table. He took a seat and waited on Francis. Francis joined them with some butter and didn't take a seat immediately.

"Henry, the flapjacks look great you did a fine job, just one thing; unlike us, Adoc doesn't have thumbs." He took up one of the plates and looked at Adoc. "I know, Adoc, he is a likeable guy but we still have to teach him some things."

Adoc's head tilted listening to the other with the old hands. His tail was wagging while he remained sitting next to Kristina. Francis began putting bacon slices between the cakes with syrup on each layer. When he was done with the stack he turned his attention to Adoc once again. "Don't worry, Adoc. Henry is a quick study so he'll be in shape very soon." Francis stole a glance at Henry and said, "When there is a lack of thumbs like with Adoc here, you have to consider how the food needs to be prepared so as to taste heavenly instead of just putting it down as cooked."

Francis lowered the plate to Adoc and told him he was a good boy. Adoc began eating Francis' preparation. It was so good that he ate it slowly instead of the way he ate his kibble. It seemed that each bite of the food had hidden flavors Adoc never tasted before. Adoc even paused to look at the other with old hands as to marvel at what he gave to him. When Francis saw Adoc's satisfaction he took up his seat and prepared his stack the exact same way as he made Adoc's. Both Kristina and Henry decided that they'd make their stacks as Francis made his and Adoc's. Once done with constructing the stacks they began eating.

Francis knew what to expect for the first bites of both, but they didn't, he watched the eyes of both of them and when he saw the reaction he expected he smiled. "Making the food taste heavenly comes by how you serve it. You see, most folks just know that they are hungry, but very few know how to prepare it for the best way it can taste. So when you cook the food, you also need to then present it, unless of course you are making a burger on a grill."

Henry couldn't believe how good the food in front of him tasted. Kristina had her first bite and had to compliment Francis. "I remember Mildred's cooking and even though it is food to sorely be missed, this is excellent." She resumed eating, as did Henry. For the moments of the eating there wasn't much conversation at all. Any noise was the silverware being used or maybe Adoc licking his chops for the breakfast, then there was the licking of an empty bowl. Adoc sat up and watched the rest eating their portions. It wasn't long before they were done. Unfortunately for Adoc there were no table scraps. That fact alone surprised Henry as he thought he over cooked.

"I would have never thought I'd eat the portion in front of me, it just seemed like it was way too much food." Kristina nodded in agreement. Francis laughed and shrugged.

"I'm sure Adoc was hoping you'd think it was too much food too." Francis looked to the day. The sun had risen and the sky was clear. Francis knew that Kristina would have to depart soon; she kept a tight work schedule. When Henry stood up to clear the table Francis stopped him.

"You don't have time for that silly business. Kristina needs to get to work and you need to bring our new pal back here. I'll see to the kitchen with Adoc's company while you get that part of your day started."

Henry shrugged. He looked to Kristina, waiting on her plans. She excused herself from the table, thanking Francis for the delightful breakfast. "I'll be right back down, Henry. Then we can go."

Henry nodded while he remained with Francis and Adoc. He was glad he dressed before coming down to breakfast. During the wait for Kristina, Francis spoke again to Henry. "When you get back with Old Ben we'll introduce both dogs here. I know they met at the shelter but it will be different to both of them outside of the shelter. We'll also need to speak to things coming."

Henry heard Francis and was agreeable to his conveyance. Henry was satisfied as things were developing; there was mystery in all of it, but he didn't lack any sureness or have any doubts. Francis was taking the time to reveal things to him and he understood that the revelations would only benefit him. When Kristina returned they made their departing comments and once again Kristina thanked Francis for breakfast. Adoc watched them as they left, if it weren't for the other with the old hands he might have been more confused, but as the other with old hands and many smells just fed him food he never tasted before the departure of the Man didn't concern him too much.

Œ

Henry's newness to the car was still getting worked out. As they drove to the shelter Henry's skills provided a decent amount of laughter between him and Kristina. Even though it was an automatic he managed to drive it as though he was a student driving with an instructor. Kristina thought it was cute and cut him a lot of slack. Between the laughter Henry wanted to speak about Francis. He thought there was a history Kristina hadn't mentioned to him about her and Francis.

He wasn't wrong for thinking there was a history, but he was wrong as to the subject... Kristina only knew Francis because Mildred had taken a liking to her in another lifetime. All she could tell him is that they were like foster parents to her. She wanted to avoid the past and she had her reasons. She answered Henry's questions as they talked and Henry seemed to accept her answers even though they were told with omission. Henry didn't know that she was withholding her past. He thought she was being candid. When they arrived at the shelter they both exited the car with anticipation for the day. Kristina was thankful for not having to put down Old Ben as well as being reunited with Francis. Her connection was with Mildred and when she met Francis they only engaged over business. It was a loss to her that now was half returned. Henry had just begun life anew. He was like a kid at school figuring out that he had every answer for the teacher and that he'd be getting straight A's for the semester. Both were inexorably attached to a future neither was aware of and Adoc was the reason. If they had been as Adam and Eve, God decided that Old Ben would give them a reminder as to why not to screw it up as the former did.

The animals in the shelter knew when Kristina arrived. It was a result for her consistency. When Old Ben heard the door open he knew that this day was different. He knew that yesterday would never be his case again and he liked that. The other dogs felt Old Ben's change and the entirety of the shelter was relatively quiet. Old Ben knew he'd be leaving this place and very soon. He knew it because of his interaction with that wild pup Adoc. He knew Adoc needed him and today was different. Before he knew Adoc he thought it was the end. He saw the pain in her eyes and he knew that she felt for him. But when she left yesterday before the dark came her tears seemed to be tears of joy and happy thankfulness. Old Ben felt that, no he smelled that on her.

After entering the office they made their way to the kennel. When they entered Kristina gave a general greeting. "Hello, dogs!"

The dogs were still experiencing Old Ben's energy jumped up on their gates and did so with tails wagging. There was some yelping but the kennel remained very quiet. Kristina wasted no time with her greetings. She moved along until she reached Old Ben's pen. She looked at him with a sense of the greatest appreciation she could ever imagine and she didn't know why. Old Ben knew why. Old Ben had seen many things and known many people. His life was ending before he arrived there and as it was still ending it wouldn't end there and then. There was one thing he knew he needed to do and it was to take the wild out of that Adoc. There were many things that pup needed to know and it was because that pup was chosen. Old Ben's time had been extended for his wisdom, but he'd pass living freely, teaching that pup he met. He also knew the Man that brought the pup was also chosen, and if he could he would have explained it to the one who was the mother type. All he could do was sit proudly with soft eyes of generosity so she could see his presence.

Henry and Kristina doted on Old Ben when they arrived. Old Ben just remained calm and proud. After the greeting was over Henry invited Old Ben to follow him. Old Ben calmly left the pen and walked with Henry along the corridor to the office. The other dogs remained quiet. Not so much as though they thought Old Ben was going to the end, but because he was escaping it. There wasn't one dog there who wished anything else for themselves. And by everyone's thinking... Old Ben would come to know the end for being there at that place. When Henry Kristina and Old Ben left the kennel there was just a slight pause until the usual barking began. Both Kristina and Henry looked at each other with a smile.

Henry made a comment. "Everything is back to usual."

The statement made Kristina smile and giggle but that wasn't enough to show her delight. A tear broke loose from each eye. When Henry saw that he assured her again. "It is going to be a good day my friend... a very good day."

She looked at Henry and said bye to Old Ben. Henry and Old Ben left and she began her day. She did so with a wondrous happiness she didn't think she knew. If she did ever know such peace in her heart she couldn't remember it. That day was when her life began anew, when Old Ben was returned to his days walking free. Kristina's new day began watching Henry take Old Ben to his new and last destination. She knew from vet reports and her own eye that Old Ben was coming to his end. It surprised her that he was still alive. None of that mattered now because even though he was an old dog she could see in his eyes that he wasn't supposed to be put down. He was a dog that was supposed to live until his natural end. She could see that in the dogs she cared for. Old Ben had a purpose and it wasn't to be lived under humane auspices.

When Henry managed to drive his car away with Old Ben Kristina returned to her day, thankful for the reprieve. The rest of her day would be one of the best she ever knew.

While Henry drove Old Ben sat like it was a day at the park after a bowl of food. He gazed out of the window without moving too much or slobbering. Henry was amazed at his manners. He was sure that Francis and Old Ben would become great friends. He thought about the way he acted with Adoc... he was intrigued at Francis' ability to know what dogs seemed to need or want. Henry wondered what old Ben would have thought of a flapjack and bacon breakfast and then laughed at himself... Old Ben would love a flapjack and bacon breakfast, heck Old Ben was gonna love his new home. He and Francis could aggravate Mildred. They drove on until they arrived at Francis' home. Old Ben seemed to know that the ride was over and that this was the place he'd know as home.

Henry got out of the car and then he opened the door for Old Ben. Old Ben moved slowly out of the car with a deliberate manner. His days of needless bounding and jumping had long since left him.

When he stood on the property out of the car, sniffing the air became his priority. It was a brief sensation as Adoc came to the Man and Old Ben. Adoc's speed wasn't clumsy and in his hurry to greet the Man and Old Ben he was able to stop without a typical puppy collision. He approached the Man, wagging his tail furiously. Henry pet him briefly because his focus shifted to Old Ben with a type of veneration. Old Ben knew that Adoc was excited and for it he was patient. He tolerated Adoc's greeting for a short time, but he was greatly curious to know where the ancient smells came from.

Francis remained at the entry to the house, waiting on Henry and Adoc to return with Old Ben. Henry watched the interaction between Adoc and Old Ben with a familiar curiosity. He had already seen the dogs interact at the shelter so he wasn't sure why he had the curiosity, but he knew that the next seconds coming there would be gift of wisdom revealed. After tolerating Adoc's hello, Old Ben began moving towards Francis. Henry noticed Adoc taking paces alongside Old Ben, a head behind him. Henry walked with them two lengths behind the dogs towards Francis. The gift of wisdom revealed to Henry came to him by each step he took until he saw how Old Ben finally met Francis. Henry watched Old Ben sit at Francis' feet, lifting his head to present himself. He remained sitting pretty for seconds before Francis reached low to greet him by hand. Once the introduction was made and after Old Ben smelled Francis' hand Francis bent down so his face was level to Old Ben's. When both took gazes in each other's eyes they shared a silent conversation that was deafening to Henry. That was the instant when Henry understood what Francis meant about understanding the language shared between man and dog. Henry watched Old Ben lift his paw up to Francis. Francis revealed to Old Ben what it was that he was going to call the motion.

"Old Ben, you want to shake my hand?" Francis emphasized the end of the question then grabbed Old Ben's paw. "Shake my hand, Old Ben. Shake my hand!" Francis released Old Ben's paw and Henry believed that from that moment going forward Old Ben would shake Francis' hand whenever Francis commanded it. Francis stood up and reached in his pocket removing two bits of jerky. He extended one to Old Ben and then turned to Adoc. Adoc went to Francis and sat just as Old Ben sat. Then Henry witnessed the awesome authority of Francis' dog whispering ability.

Francis presented the jerky to Adoc out of his reach. "Adoc, shake my hand!" He said it the same way he said it to Old Ben and just after he gave the command Adoc raised his paw to shake Francis' hand. Francis took Adoc's paw in his hand and said, "Shake my hand!" Then he released Adoc's paw and offered him the jerky. Henry was further amazed by the gentle way each dog responded to Francis' offering. When both dogs were chewing on the jerky Francis looked up at Henry with a smile.

"Well, Henry, I'll give you this, you know dogs. Old Ben seems to be a fine dog just as you claimed."

Henry didn't know that he had instincts about dogs; he just knew what he observed commonly. He thought about what Francis said with a reflection of doubt and Francis saw it. "You are going to have to learn how to listen without skepticism pertaining to yourself. These things I tell you are true. You may not know them as you have come to study other things you have discovered. What you need to do is figure out how to discover these truths about yourself without so much study."

When Francis saw Henry's consideration of his last remarks all he could do was laugh. Henry tried to follow Francis, but it seemed like the more he explained the more he became confused by what he heard. Francis' laughter ended and he tried to explain it with more simplicity. "Okay, look at it like this: You are a master carpenter and you took no formal education for carpentry. Other people could take all the formal education there was to be studied for being a carpenter and their skills wouldn't come close to matching yours." Francis saw that his confusion lessened and that he had a foundation to work with in what he tried to convey.

"Your natural abilities, Henry, are special and uncommon to most others, in fact I believe, no wait, I know I have never met another person like you."

Henry knew he was unique in many ways, but he couldn't get his head around why Francis was mentioning his qualities. He continued to listen.

"Henry, some folks are built to be good at one thing; call it a vocation. They also have abilities to be good in other areas of their lives with things like relationships or hobbies. But you, Henry, have a vocation and that vocation is to be expert at anything you chose to do. That is your advantage."

Henry looked at the dogs. They were sitting and waiting intently on some attention while they kept each other company in a friendly sort of way. "Francis, nothing you have told me is anything new to me and as you have said it, nothing I have heard removes doubts I have, nor does it convince me that my vocation of being an expert isn't a curse. I mean to say that it seems as though being good at one thing and then being good at relationships or even a simple hobby wouldn't make for a happier life."

Francis turned from the dogs and Henry. "Let's walk. Come on, dogs!" Francis began walking away from the house as Henry followed. When he began the walk the dogs hurried along past Francis but not too far ahead. After a few paces Francis spoke more to Henry.

"Henry you are a learned man so tell me who it is that you know of that you consider being exceptional?"

Henry thought about Francis' question and the first response that came to his mind was what he mentioned. "I'd say that Abraham Lincoln comes to mind as an exceptional man."

Francis nodded. "Sure. Lincoln was an exceptional man. Do you think he didn't have doubts or feel as though his reality wasn't cursed?"

Henry saw where Francis was going and he gave it some thought before he responded. Old Ben was sizing up the land he walked upon. His nose smelled the history of the place. The soil and the calm breezes told him that there life was abundant, death was present and the gate between both places loomed. He knew he was home and that this pup Adoc needed his wisdom so he wouldn't go to stumble into the gate. He turned to Adoc and invited his play. Adoc barked from a dip and then leapt at Old Ben, he nibbled at Old Ben's ears and neck. Old Ben could have easily dispatched Adoc any time he wanted, but that wasn't his job. His job was to teach Adoc how to play for now and as he grew, he'd teach him how to fight. Old Ben knew that this place was home and as the gate between life and death loomed here, there was nothing but difficult living and death beyond the tree lines past the meadow. When Adoc got exuberant in his biting Old Ben opened his mouth and nibbled gently around Adoc's mouth. Later he'd bite on his neck and the teaching would evolve as the play continued.

Adoc was in heaven. He romped and barked, lunging at Old Ben taking bites at different accessible parts of the older dog. He growled ferociously before he became subdued by Old Ben's gentle reminders of who was boss. Adoc's energy was unending as he ran in circles around Old Ben. He tried to outsmart Old Ben with faking a lunge that might have lured him to commit to vulnerability. Old Ben wasn't fooled. Adoc began to wonder how it was he could fool others he knew but not Old Ben. Adoc's wonder of Old Ben's inability to be fooled couldn't satisfy his desire to run and he lost interest in continuing his trickery. Adoc figured the Man might be more interesting. He lowered a last time towards Old Ben and growled then barked at him. He darted away towards the Man in a charge running well past him to turn and charge again. Henry lowered himself to meet Adoc but he wasn't coming slowly enough to allow him a pet.

Adoc was loving life unlike before he knew the Man.   Old Ben watched Adoc running towards him. He waited for Adoc to commit to a lunge and as soon as he did, he took one step backwards. Adoc flew right past him, landing unexpectedly and with no footing. He rolled head over paws like a tumble weed in a gust. He jumped up shaking himself wildly and when he focused on Old Ben he just sat down tempting him to try it again. Francis prompted Henry again.

"So, do you think Lincoln had doubts?"

Henry looked down at the ground interrupted from watching the dogs for the question.

"I suppose he had his doubts, but he was President, I don't even have a name for what I do."

Francis expected his response and tried to lead him along the journey of wisdom. "That's right. He did have his doubts. It isn't important that he was President, what is important is that he was exceptional. You see, because he was exceptional he influenced many lives. You have also done so in your years. Now imagine this world if exceptional people didn't exist…"

Henry saw his logic and he gave him a glance. "It wasn't so long ago that I didn't want to exist. I almost ended it when Adoc interrupted."

Francis wasn't surprised and he didn't let it shock him as Henry might have thought the comment would have. "If you didn't know, Adoc is an exceptional dog and it is likely he doesn't know it yet, or maybe he does know and just doesn't care. It doesn't much matter; he is an exceptional dog." Francis began his walking towards the dogs. The dogs took notice of his movement and waited for the men to get closer to them. Francis changed the discussion as they walked.

"This property deeded to me is about a thousand acres. It runs to the west and has an international border with Canada. It spans two counties. That timber at the end of the meadow is virgin wood as I have been told. It has been in my family since the days of settlement. Now Mildred and I wanted heirs, but we have none. I want you to take the property over and you'll need Kristina to help you manage it."

Henry heard all that Francis said and it shocked him to ponder the totality of his desire. "Why in the world would you want to do something like that? I mean where did you come to think that is a good idea?"

Francis laughed at his questions. After his laughter ended he answered Henry. "I didn't think it was a good idea and I didn't want to do it, I wanted to gift it to a conservancy." He laughed again and began looking at the expanse around him. Old Ben came over to Francis and sat next to him quietly with a calming nature. Adoc did similarly to Henry's side. Henry wondered why he made the offer if he thought to do otherwise.

"It isn't worth thinking about too much and I don't need an answer directly, you have plenty of time to talk it over with Kristina and see what she thinks. Truthfully, what I have told you isn't my idea." He waited on Henry to hear any type of skepticism but none came. "Do you remember when I told you of Mildred and my conversations about you when you were younger?" Henry remembered the telling of them and nodded. As soon as Henry did Francis continued.

"Okay, believe it or not even before Mildred passed she mentioned that if there was ever a time when you needed a family that we'd offer to be your adoptive parents. The idea seemed to be a long shot to me; somehow I knew that you'd do well for yourself. And since she has passed she has hounded me in having this conversation with you."

Henry looked at the dogs. They focused on Francis intently. Henry had a thought. "Francis, is Mildred talking to you now?"

Francis shook his head. "Nope, she isn't here with us like in the kitchen. Mildred was a homebody, she did some work in the garden but she never came out into the fields... I swear these fields were the only escapin' her wrath when she was alive."

Henry laughed when he heard Francis answer. "So why do you think she felt the way she did?" Henry waited on his answer.

Francis ran his hands through his hair and then sighed. "Mildred always claimed that she heard God speaking to her. If you want to know what I think about God don't concern yourself too much. I don't think about God much at all, I never had to; it seemed my Mildred did all the interpretation; hell she still does..." He chuckled at himself. "I used to tell her that God was the best practical joker in the world and that use to get her more riled up than anything else I did to get under her skin. She used to say to me, *well now Francis, if you think God is a practical joker then He must have made you stupid and I am His way of smartening you up.*"

Henry laughed for Francis' telling the anecdote. "Tell me, did you believe her when she made those claims?"

The question gave Francis a look of confusion at first but it faded into a smile after. "I never had a need or a reason to disbelieve anything she said. We were one and that would be like not trusting yourself. Now that doesn't mean I didn't think she wasn't crazier than a rabid dog at times, but that wasn't hard to accept. I sure know I have had my craziness in this lifetime. So living with her craze wasn't anything to reject." He laughed, as did Henry.

After a bit more of walking, Francis continued in his thinking of his Mildred. "You know, when I told her I thought she was crazy about her being an oracle she used to speak to the Old Testament. She used to look at me like he thought I needed smartening up and she'd paraphrase the scripture of those old books. She said, *Francis, what you think of me being crazy matters little because old Noah was belittled and chastised and ridiculed for wanting to build an Ark on the hills in the desert and it just so happens his craziness is the reason why you have a life.* I swear my Mildred used to rebut everything I said to her and the darned thing of it was... she always had a biblical scripture to back her thinking up." Francis looked at Henry and tilted his head. "I think God exists, but unlike others who seem to have a faith in him, well, wait a minute... others had to have faith in him... well I was never one of those types. Nope, about the only thing Mildred and I came up short on was having a child. Everything else in this life seemed to go our way so I can't say I ever had a reason to have a relationship with God."

Henry took in Francis' ruminations with great consideration. After a few more steps Francis turned in another direction to walk. "I've known a lot of folks who seemed to bring on their own troubles for believing in God. They seemed to do nothing while praying for a miracle. When they were waiting on that miracle their world's evaporated." He thought some more in the strides. "I remember one guy during the war. He was in our unit and he was the most likely to get dead. I mean this guy didn't take the business of killing seriously and for the life of me I have no idea why he was even in a combat unit. But one night on patrol we got bushwhacked. We were out manned and out gunned. The bullets were whizzing through the air like mosquitoes gathering for fish dinner on a hot summer's eve . Somewhere else they were launching mortar shells at us. We held down in fox holes while guys were getting picked off by the minute. The line of command all got killed. We were left to our own surviving and a couple of us decided to retreat in perfect military fashion. We told him to get ready to leave cause we were going and all that silly guy did was get to praying. It was like he was in a trance... we couldn't get him to move... We left and not fifteen paces out of the foxhole, one of those mortar shells landed right on top of his praying. Pieces of him rained on us as we broke loose from the dying." Francis shook his head. "Then there are times when it seems like bad folks in the world get good life's, while others who live right just get sick and suffer."

They continued walking while Henry considered the paradox presented by Francis. He never knew too much about religion or the God thing, but it sure sounded interesting. After some more walking Henry asked another question.

"How did she explain that contradiction?" Francis stopped his paces. He looked at Henry and asked him, "You really want to hear how she explained it?" Henry nodded. "Okay we'll want to head back to the house. By the time I'm finished it will take that long to get back there." They turned towards the house and the dogs kept pace with them.

"Mildred use to say that once Eve took the bite of the apple, men knew the meaning of knowledge and God sent them out of paradise into the world of evil. She said it wasn't God's idea for men to choose evil, but he did give them a choice. Then she said that God never promised that life would be fair and even God's son said there would always be suffering. There would always be those that chose evil over living righteously and Jesus' promise was to live as he did and in living as he did we would die to live again in eternity with him when the time of counting came." Henry was trying to follow what Francis was saying, but the time of counting was something Henry needed explanation on.

"Time of counting? What is that?" Francis shrugged for the question hoping he could explain what he wasn't sure of. "Well the time of counting comes in the book of Revelation and that is when Armageddon is supposed to happen. Then Jesus comes as the judge of God; that's when he will do the counting of souls who want to go to his house in Heaven." Henry followed, "Oh okay all that stuff about heaven and hell and the end times with fire and brimstone, I got ya." The men approached the house and the dogs ventured away from them off to investigate the smells around the house. They walked some more to a bench they took a seat on.

"That is what she said about why life is the way it is in explaining the contradiction, eh?" Francis nodded. "Yep, that is what she said."

Henry thought about it some more. "You know what Francis? I've read a lot of books, but I never read this Bible, now I think I got a new read." Francis laughed at his new intent. Henry thought that was strange. "Why is that funny? It sounds interesting to me."

Francis shrugged. "I don't know that the bible is just a sit down read, Henry. Seems to me that a body could spend his whole life reading it only to re-read it and learn something new at a different point in his life. Are you sure that is what ya want to pick up for a read?"

Henry thought about the question and shrugged. "I don't guess I'll know about that until I read it."

"I guess you just suit yourself to it then." Francis looked at the morning sky. "I reckon it is about time for you to be doing that volunteering, if you'd like you can leave Adoc here and let him keep company with Old Ben."

Henry thought about Francis' suggestion and agreed.

"I guess leaving Adoc here will be alright until quitting time. I'll also try to speak to Kristina on that business of the property to see what she thinks." Henry stood up and called Adoc. "Adoc come here boy!" Adoc came running along to see what the man wanted. When they met Henry spoke to him. "Adoc, you stay here and keep company with Francis and Old Ben. I'll be back later to collect you." Adoc tilted his head. The Man made some noise to the other with the old hands then they made motions with their hands and the Man walked back to the thing that moved faster than he could run. Adoc followed him to the car and before he got in the Man made more noise.

"Adoc, you stay here." Adoc sat and the Man got into that thing that moved faster than he could run and drove away.

Old Ben remained with Francis while Adoc saw Henry off. Francis pet Old Ben while he sat next to him and it seemed to Old Ben that old hands of this man were reading his history. The old hands found scars on him and stopped at the old wound sights to feel what happened and how they resulted. Old Ben felt energy from the old hands that was uncommon from men he knew and it wasn't too much of a surprise because this place where he sat was full of strange energy. Old Ben felt that the gate between life and death was strong around the house. The energy didn't give him a reason to be unsettled, it wasn't a bad thing, nor were there bad smells. There was a need to respect the energy as it lived close by. Old Ben had experienced enough in his life to know bad things did happen even with the absence of bad smells. Old Ben knew that was a lesson the pup needed and it was a priority. While Francis pet and palpitated Old Ben, Old Ben kept a focus on Adoc. He watched his manners of being a puppy knowing that they were always capable of unwittingly finding trouble. As Adoc sniffed around Old Ben's guard began to increase. Adoc was sniffing aimlessly and that was when a puppy's focus could shift instantly and once it shifted it was very difficult to stop their desire to investigate. Francis seemed to feel to change in Old Ben's energy and he reduced his petting and palpitating.

"Go get that puppy Old Ben he looks like he is about to discover trouble." Old Ben rose from sitting and loosed a low growl. He left Francis' reach moving towards Adoc. Adoc's nose began to follow the wind. Old Ben saw that his legs were getting ready to spring and he didn't want to run after him. Old Ben growled louder and let a thunderous bark go forth.

Adoc had forgotten that the Man left and he knew that Old Ben and the other with old hands were very close, but the scent in the air was a scent he didn't know and that alone was enough to set him on a course of investigation unbounded. He was just getting ready to leap towards a blast of running to find the source of the scent. Before he could release the explosive energy required to lunge Old Ben's bark paralyzed him. The scent evaporated and his focus went immediately to Old Ben. Adoc's lunge became a dip low with a responding bark repeated a couple of more times.

Old Ben was satisfied with Adoc's response to his calling and after Adoc offered his barks of affirmation he gave a different bark meant for Adoc to come to him. It was a quiet bark with less intensity, but it carried the same authority. Adoc lunged toward Old Ben's guard and ran to him figuring to play. Instead of removing himself from the trajectory of Adoc's leap he simply turned quarter to the leap and Adoc's flight stopped as Old Ben remained standing for the collision. Old Ben looked at Adoc sprawled on the ground and offered a lick on his head. Both dogs lost their attention to each when they heard laughter from Francis. Old Ben started walking towards Francis while it took Adoc a second or two to get up and go to Francis. Adoc reached Francis first because of his explosive speed. Old Ben joined them. The man with old hands petted both dogs and laughed for the petting. Old Ben and Adoc sucked up the praise. Adoc's excitement gave him reason to leave the petting and run in circles around the yard close to the other with old hands. Every once in a loop Adoc would go after Old Ben with a bite at his neck that always came with a growl and a bark, then he darted away. It was a few short moments when Old Ben realized that the gate between life and death was very close and he paid attention to where it might be. Adoc wasn't aware of the closeness of the gate and kept after his antics. Francis read Old Ben and knew something was up.

"Is that you, Mildred? Have you blessed us all with your morning grace?" When Francis spoke both dogs got quiet and Adoc stopped his running about. They focused on Francis expecting to hear more.

Yes it is me, Francis, and I'm not here to bless you with my grace, why do you and those dogs have to disturb my morning here around the house? It is a terrible racket.

"Mildred, a terrible racket would be to hear sirens or your favorite black birds' squawking about God knows what, this is some cheerful play time with Adam's best friends."

When Old Ben and Adoc heard the beginning of the conversation between Francis and the other unseen Old Ben rose with his tail curled up under him and slinked away. He didn't like the way the words flowed and as he slinked he walked right into Adoc to push him along. As the dogs removed themselves from the area they could hear Francis talking again.

"Ah, see, there ya go, Mildred, driving Adam's best friends from a place to play, now they might have hurt feelings just look at poor Old Ben slinking away tail between his legs. You are a disagreeable fun killer Mildred."

Well you know how I get when I step in, or find one of their presents in my gardens; besides it isn't like there aren't 1000 acres here for them to have a place to ruff house and you can go with them if it amuses you, I can see to myself here alone fine without any of your aggravating ways.

Old Ben took a steady pace away from where that gate was, his time wasn't yet there to pass through it so he figured he would just avoid it when it presented itself. Adoc kept stride with him until he slowed down. Once the gate wasn't close by he took a seat in the sun allowing Adoc time to learn how to play some more. In between the bites and the growls he would share history the pup needed to know as dogs communicate.

Œ

Henry drove to the shelter trying to focus on driving. He was still rusty on the rules of the road and he didn't want to get distracted too much about the enormity of the conversation he and Francis had that morning. He figured through doing the chores at the shelter he'd organize the conversation to be had with Kristina. It wasn't long before he got there. When he entered the shelter there seemed to be a pleasant attitude abiding the structure. He gave that up to the fact that Old Ben had been homed to Francis' place instead of being put down. William greeted him enthusiastically for his arrival. The two shared a brief exchange before Henry reported to Kristina.

He wanted to make sure that his time was spent efficiently according to her needs. As Henry walked into the room he didn't like Kristina was busy with the vet examining paperwork. They greeted Henry favorably and Kristina mentioned to him that the pens would be his first task. He acknowledged her conveyance and saw to his chores. As he walked down the corridor he took notice of the residents he met yesterday. He saw that Old Ben's pen had a new occupant. In his greetings Henry experienced something he didn't expect. He didn't know that it was good or bad, but it came with a firm sense of gravity. This place was dedicated to caring for animals that much he was sure about. He realized though that for some residents it was a way station until they were homed. For others it was a last stop. Henry began the work of his chores with a melancholy nature.

He began to understand some of what he thought Kristina meant when she told him of the bad days here. While he did his work he also understood how it was that he knew discomfort of the procedure room. That was the place where the unwanted animals were put down. Henry thought about the dichotomy of this place and its function. He wondered if this was as good as it got for the care of animals or if it could be improved.

The simplistic nature of the cleaning of the pens only required repetition. Henry's mind didn't need to focus on the chores so the gravity of the place became as though it were a tale being told at a campfire on a dark night. Henry was so invested with his considerations he didn't notice that Kristina had entered the corridor. When she presented herself as there, Henry had a bit of a startle. He laughed at himself for being surprised.

"Hi there, Kristina. The place seemed to be uplifted this morning when I came in and that was nice."

Kristina nodded. "Yes indeed, anytime we can avoid a put-down it is welcome. There are not enough generous acts such as Francis'. By the way how is Old Ben getting on?"

Henry continued his work while he answered. "He and Francis seemed to know each for their lifetimes; I think it will be fine." Henry remembered what he wanted to think on to mention regarding Francis' offer. The trouble with his remembering was that he didn't organize it. He kept after his chores and recalled the conversation he and Kristina had the night before they picked up Old Ben at Francis' place having wine and cigars.

"Kristina, do you remember when Francis was discussing that you were on the right path and that he had a gift Mildred wanted him to give?" Kristina paused and thought back to the conversation. She remembered that Francis said that she was on the right path and that it came from Mildred, but she didn't remember any mention of a gift.

"No, I can't say I recall an unmentioned gift."

Henry stuck to his chores. The details of repetitive motion kept him thinking. He wanted to present her with a reference of Francis' gift so it was presently logically. "Okay, do you recall the partnership he discussed?"

She responded affirmatively. "Yes I do."

Henry ceased the chores for the moment. He wanted to word this correctly for Kristina because of the unusual nature of Francis' generosity. "After I brought Old Ben back to the property Francis and I had a stroll. Turns out the stroll was taken so as to avoid an eavesdropping of Mildred. She never ventured into the fields much as Francis said." Kristina was listening intently. Henry took notice of her awareness by her manner of facial gesture of his anecdote. "Well anyways Francis told me that Mildred wanted him to give over the property to us after his passing." The news gave Kristina a mild shock, Henry could see it in the way her eyes opened up hearing the news. He waited to see if she had more to say.

"Are you kidding me, Henry?"

Henry shook his head. Kristina processed what she heard by getting the next pen emptied so Henry could continue his cleaning. The tandem work wasn't anything they discussed it was more of an impulsive reaction to working out the offer of Francis so they could understand the motivation. While they worked they continued to discuss the offer.

"Henry, that property is huge, I wouldn't even want to think about the taxes required to keep that place, I mean I could work here 24/7 and put all my pay to that bill and it would be under funded." Henry kept after the cleaning and picked up the conversation.

"Well, you wouldn't have to worry about that at all, I can pay the taxes and more than that the property has potential to be worked to perpetually pay the expenses, that isn't really an issue to consider."

They worked together for a time without saying more. Before Henry knew it they were on the second side of the cleaning. That was when Kristina mentioned another concern. "Okay, so you can manage the expense to maintain the property; what then?"

Henry was wondering the same thing. "I am not too sure of that myself, but one thing I do know is that a whole lot of potential and responsibility go with ownership of such a property." He paused speaking to work through his thinking so as to provide more of an answer to Kristina's question. "I suppose that we could do what you want without the limitations of this place to start with and certainly some other things as well." Kristina pondered his words as they finished up the cleaning of the pens. When they were done with that she looked at Henry and asked if he was ready to know more of what she did there.

He nodded and they moved to the area that managed the cats. For the question Henry realized she was considering the offer he told her of that Francis made. He wanted to reinforce the point of the partnership aspect Francis mentioned.

"Kristina, in my experience I have come to find out that partnerships fail because those entering the partnerships make priority of all the wrong things they want to participate in mutually. Some put a different value on contribution as a priority for the success or failure for the concern and that is usually where the partnership unravels. Now if you could do what you do here without the limitation of the town's budgetary contribution do you think that you might be better fulfilled?"

She turned to Henry before she entered the cat area. "If I didn't have to do this job as an employee of the town I could run this operation as a model for animal care that zoo's would have to take notice of, but that is how it goes when the business is paid out as a community service. I'd much rather provide a service to the communities of local concern if I had my druthers."

Henry accepted her candor and asked her, "Shall we take care of this next business?" He opened the door to the cat facility. They entered and she began explaining the duties of seeing to the cats. She explained to him that working with cats could be trickier than working with dogs. Cats don't have the same affability towards handlers as dogs did. She told him that an inexperienced handler might not feel the energy of the cat before working with them and when a cat struck for unwillingness, wounds could be very disastrous. Henry paid close attention as he didn't want to be opened up by a cat. His knowledge of cats came from reading and he was well aware that size with cats meant little as compared to a dog's size. He understood that cats were capable of taking down prey much larger than their own size because of their slinky prowess and incredible speed and strength. He also was aware of the old adage of cats having 9 lives. He watched her work with two cats before he began. Much of the work was quite similar to what the dogs needed even if the process was different. When one of the cat pens was cleaned the cats were transferred from the pen they occupied to a temporary pen instead of free roaming. Cats were very difficult to contain if they didn't want to be caught. Here Henry realized that one must greet the cat differently than as with the dogs. He also realized that cats in captivity didn't get along well as the dogs generally did. Hence, another reason to use the temporary pen while cleaning out the pen. After Henry began to own the details of the duty he continued on the conversation of partnerships.

"I think it is important when discussing partnerships where the partners start from. My need here is to improve the relationship I have with Adoc. Now I know that sounds simple, but at this point in time that is my priority. As things have developed, knowing you has made that a plausible reality and through knowing you Francis has become part of the equation in seeing to my priority." Kristina listened as he went on in his explanation. "Since knowing Francis a working relationship with you has been presented as a partnership of sorts by his experience and observation. Not only did he mention the partnership but he also provided the vehicle to that partnership if that is in fact what we chose to move towards." Kristina followed along without knowing what her contribution to the partnership would be, but she had a hunch Henry would tell her.

"Now earlier you mentioned his offer to be impossible in accepting because of the required money needed to maintain the property and that is valid. As I have told you the money isn't an issue because I have plenty. So it is my proposal that any partnership we arrive on be a sort of arrangement that considers your expertise of the wellness of animals your contribution, while my volunteering and money is my half of the concern. How does that sound to you?" Kristina had to think about her response; just as Henry indicated before such a thing had great responsibility. Henry kept to his duties while she thought about his idea working on the daily documentation. She stole glances of Henry working with the cats. She had to agree with the earlier assessment of Francis that Henry was in fact a quick study. Everything he said to her made sense. It had been since forever that she considered a possibility with such a grateful confidence. It was difficult for her to understand why or how this happened. She thought of how disappointing life had been for her and wondered if she was worthy of even dreaming of such a reality as the one she was considering that moment. She realized that there was a lot to be talked about before hands could be shaken on any partnership and she felt as though no time like the present would be better for such a conversation.

"Henry the thing I am coming to know and like about you is how you say things that make sense, more sense than I could ever find with a map and two flashlights." Henry chuckled at her comment. She tilted her head and gave him a bit of a frown. After he saw it for her pause he apologized.

"I'm sorry I didn't laugh at you, but I laughed at your description of inability. You do have a great self demeaning sense of humor and I kinda like that about you. You don't take yourself so seriously and that is a rare quality." Without offering him satisfaction she continued.

"As you make sense it occurs to me that there are a great many things that would have to be seen to for making this partnership work. In as much as I think it's a good idea and even a dream come true there are practical details to be discussed." Henry nodded while he continued his work. Kristina continued, "What of those folks I work with? I'm sure the town will want an appointee for the vacancy and as good as these folks are at their jobs, none of them could run this place without a lot of work and instruction. I'd hate to leave thinking the wrong person was doing the job."

Henry finished the work on the cat pen he focused on and before he started the next he turned with her and gave his response. "To be honest with you Kristina I was thinking that for our new partnership we could approach the town with an offer to liberate them for the duty and expense. I'm sure they could use the money elsewhere." Kristina didn't expect the totality of what he said, but she sure did see the wisdom of it.

"Can that be done?"

Henry laughed once again, and did so to her delight for a smile. "It can absolutely be done, and better it can be facilitated with more ease by the politicians' greed of maintaining power or assuming power."

He smiled for his answer because he saw in her face a type of *the light bulb just went on look*. She was no slow study herself. He figured that the discussion at hand called for more discernment of their motivations.

"Let me ask you a question. Why do folks get jobs?"

She looked at him, wondering if it was a trick question. "For a paycheck?"

He nodded. "That's right, they trade their time for a compensation based upon willingness or a liking of a type of work. For that trade they get a paycheck. Now why do you think people invest in risk or a business?"

Once again she wondered where he was going with his questions but she played along. "To make a lot of money?"

He smiled and nodded. "That's also right! People invest in a business or take risk for profit." He waited to see how that sat with her.

This time her look showed him a type of *No Duh?* Look. Before he lost her interest he made another comment he hoped would hit her square between the eyes for revelation.

"Kristina, you have already indicated that your need isn't based upon whether or not you can maintain a paycheck, but rather your need is exclusive of profit which means that even though you do your job for a paycheck, the doing of your job is more important than the paycheck or the profit. So if the paycheck wasn't your priority and you had unlimited ability without profit as a consideration, you'd be fulfilled. Am I right?" Henry waited on her response. He could see her working through the logic.

"It seems to me that you have defined a charity. Am I right?"

Henry smiled and turned to his work once again. Much like he was thankful for Adoc finding him and stopping him from the unthinkable, he was thankful for establishing a partnership with Kristina. He answered her but he gave her an answer much like he asked the question. "I guess you could call this a charity simplistically, but purposes of taxation and insurance we'll want to call it an employee own community cooperative, but you don't need to worry yourself about those details." She looked at him with a positive skepticism.

"Okay fair enough. But seeing as you are going to manage the details of this business I'll leave you to seeing towards designing this thing so as the people here keep their jobs and benefits when this process happens. By the Way Mister Suit... what kind of time frame are we talking about concerning this grand transition?" Henry was amazed at Kristina's instinctual ability to process his questions and answers. He imagined she'd be quite the chess player. Henry gave her a glance for the question.

"Mr. Suit, eh?" He continued doing his job and spoke through the work. "I can imagine the legal paper work could be accomplished within a month. The variances from the town and acceptance of our proposal may come through by May's town meeting. They take forever to decide if not properly motivated. We could begin the surveying and engineering for the facility at Francis' place immediately putting us at breaking ground by June first, giving us an occupancy code and license for operation by the end of September for worse case scenario." He continued his work as though mentioning it was nothing more than simple process, but the whole description of it took the breath away from Kristina. She could do little in the way of processing documents of a daily nature for his telling.

"Henry, will you be okay here for a few minutes, there are a few things I have to see to right now?" Henry nodded, "Sure I think I can manage the rest of this at least as far as the cleaning goes. Not sure about the paperwork though."

"Don't worry about that, if you can manage the rest of the cleaning you'll claim *best volunteer* since I don't know when. We may even put you on the payroll. I won't be but a few moments, maybe quarter of an hour." Henry nodded and Kristina left. Once away from the room she literally had to focus on the steps leading her out to have a breath of fresh air. She passed William at the front desk without stopping for one of his nonsensical questions. She didn't have the time for any of his chat right then and he could waste the day in meaningless talk. She needed some time alone and away. Her conversation with Henry left her in a place that she never knew. She didn't know if she was frightened, she didn't think she was afraid, but what she felt tasted of fear.

Once she made it outdoors her feet led her to a place close by that she frequented during times of doubt. When she arrived there was no dread, there was no worry, she felt liberated and that notion occupied her thinking. She usually sat on a stump that was cut years ago. There she allowed the earth to consume her anguish when she visited previously. This time however she avoided the stump. She made her way down to a wasted creek bed. The expense of sand and rocks was evidence that the water once raged for seasonal flow of thaw. Construction elsewhere required water diversion. All that remained was a creek trickling to the lowest part of the apparent stone bed that contained various rocks of size and composition. When she panned the riverbed's exposed bottom there was a rock that some may have considered a bolder, but it certainly wasn't the largest rock in the proximity. Something about the rock drew her to it. She couldn't guess why she had the curiosity, she only served the interest. After she came to the rock she decided that sitting on it would be appropriate.

Kristina realized that she could breathe easier for her choice. She always seemed to find a place to soothe her within nature. She considered the short time she spoke with Henry and then she considered the impact of what he said concerning her life. Till now her life was simple although problematic. The choices she made were based upon necessity. She was fortunate to find a path through necessity that she could be satisfied by. Sitting upon that stone in that creek bed she had never visited before she calculated that it was an even bet to believe all Henry said. So many times in her life before she heard about grand tales based on deceptions motivated by an untold truth. Nothing Henry spoke to sounded as though it was anything but truthful. Once Kristina qualified his ideas as honest she began to wonder about a cosmic intention of the circumstance's visitation to her. After thinking about her history with Mildred and how Francis and Henry seemed to be getting on she determined that whether it be cosmic or something else, intention had to be a part of it.

Henry was honest and there seemed to be a reason for all of it. Her reasoning gave her reason to relax, her breathing became easier and she felt more like herself. She rose up off the rock and knelt beside it. Kristina always offered gratefulness to inanimate aspects of nature when she discovered the calming effects in her joining with them. She understood the possibility in front of her. Henry seemed to have an idea and all he was asking her for was her love of duty to animals and it was all because of his dog Adoc. Adoc the dog and Henry also provided Old Ben an option she couldn't offer to him. Henry seemed to be a man that was worthy of sharing at the least a business relationship with and all things in her mind had to withstand her process of considered scrutiny. The magnitude of his proposal demanded her contemplation and in those moments she stole away along the exposed creek bed Henry passed her smell test. She was okay with the fact that he passed both Adoc's and Old Ben's smell tests too. She couldn't believe that Francis found it appropriate to make such an offer. Never in her wildest dreams would she have guessed the offer was given of his accord. She was certain that Mildred may have passed on from this plain of living, but it was completely evident she waited on him in the next plain. Kristina knew that Mildred was a stubborn woman and the intention of this offer of Francis was at least part of her design. She walked back into the shelter reassuming her duties feeling much better for her walk.

It was a long time since she anticipated a summer coming. This summer coming was unlike any anticipation she allowed herself in considering. When she returned to Henry in the cat room he was just finishing up the last pen. Once he was settled he asked her what came next. She invited him to the food storage area as the inventory needed rotating and making ready for receiving an order coming later that week. After she explained to Henry what she wanted he took the chore up and managed the sacks of food as she told him, then he did the same with canned goods. The work wasn't going to take Henry long to finish. His productivity rate had no waste to be observed. After his completion of that chore he inquired about the next. Kristina took some time thinking about what might be left for Henry to do.

"Henry, most everything else that needs doing is done by others during their allotted time." She paused, trying to think of another way to exploit his being there but no other duty came to mind.

Henry understood her difficulty in finding work for him. He didn't want to eliminate the work of others or their purpose for being there. "That's fine, I'm just glad I could help as I have."

Henry's comment surprised Kristina and left her astonished. "I know this is going to seem foreign to you, but the work you just completed usually takes up to six hours by those who normally do it and what is even more incredible is that your contribution of food coming later this week has been facilitated by your diligence of very deliberate inventory management; it seems to be like that is rubbing salt into the wound."

Henry looked at her with confusion to her comments. He thought about what he could say to make her feel less desperate about working within the reality of this place. "While we consider a partnership it is going to be important for you to realize a few things about me. What I am going to say to you is what you should consider as the foundation of our relations in a partnership." She nodded and listened. "The first thing is how I do my work. It doesn't matter what the work is I only have one pace and it is likely to be very unique. The second thing to consider is how I utilize money. You see, unlike others money has never been a priority to me, rather it is more of a tool used for facilitating projects."

She looked at Henry and told him she'd be mindful of his explanation. Kristina had yet one more consideration for contemplating the summer coming. It would be an adjustment to be sure, but she felt as those it wouldn't require too much effort for the incorporation of the adjustment. As she understood it she'd make no more comments about money as contribution or efforts applied to volunteering from that moment forward. Since Henry had directed the conversation to the partnership Kristina thought it might be a good time to expand on her realizations for her walk.

"Speaking of this partnership, I have come to a conclusion."

Henry's curiosity returned his focus to what her thinking was about to reveal. "Is that right?"

She nodded. "I heard what you said and offered and I understand all of it as truthful, so I'm inclined to enter this partnership with you." She held her hand out as an acceptance of the offer.

Henry took her hand in his grasp and shook her hand. "Okay, partner!"

She smiled knowing that her investment was dependent on his. "So, partner, what comes next?"

Henry released her hand and verbalized the agenda. "First we'll have to inform Francis that we'll accept his offer and request that the paperwork be completed for the transference of the deed. Then we'll work on the articles of partnership for legal definition. Once we have that behind us, I'll begin a process to commission plans for a facility we'll want built on the property as well as surveying that will need to be done and in between I'll talk to those on the town council letting them know of our intentions."

Kristina heard the agenda and shook her head. "I'm glad that's your end of the business. I don't think I'd have the patience to manage all that. I have enough trouble submitting a budget to the town."

Henry informed her that indeed some of that was going to be her business. He could see her immediate fear of whatever aspect he had on his mind of her concerning the agenda. "Don't worry about any of what you need to do. As a matter of fact I am certain you'll be enjoying it greatly." His last comments changed her apprehension, as he'd intended.

"You think I'll have a great time in the sea of bureaucracy? Call me simple-minded, but I am not following you."

He smiled and began walking out of the inventory area. As she followed him along he clarified her part of the agenda. "In all my days and projects, I have never seen a woman who doesn't get excited at the prospect of designing their home's design, or in this case the floor work of a type of animal shelter or hospital. Those are the joys of this agenda I thought you might have a great time of, participating in the process. But I might be wrong about that and if you are the type of woman who wouldn't enjoy that part of involvement I understand." He kept walking towards the lobby knowing that his revelation couldn't be resisted. He heard her stepping more quickly in catching up to him. When she did he felt her energy and looked at her with an indifference to her new wisdom of agenda participation.

"Maybe I was inaccurate about being simple-minded earlier?"

Henry took notice of the expected twinkle in her eye. "So you are retracting your position as to swim in the sea of bureaucracy?"

She nodded enthusiastically. Henry and Kristina stopped at the desk William occupied.

"Kristina, I think we should go see a man about dog food, what do you say?"

Kristina turned to William. "Hold down the fort. I have an errand to run concerning the next food shipment. I'll have my radio and I'll be mobile so you can let me know of any calls coming in, and the pens and cages are cleaned out as well as the rotation of food inventory."

William was certainly surprised as Kristina was ordering the food unlike she normally did by phone, but his natural inclination of wondering as to the change was undone by the completion of the tasks in such short order. William nodded as to her instructions. They left William in a frustrated curiosity because of his tendency to gossip. All he could do from that point was his job.

As Henry and Kristina made their way out to the vehicles he shared a word with her. "Okay partner, it is probably a good idea to keep the wraps on letting any of your folks know what we are planning. You don't want to invite unnecessary drama before you have to do so. That kind of upheaval is nothing more than wasted breath and energy."

Kristina agreed and they both entered their vehicles making their way to go see Francis.

After they left the parking lot of the shelter Kristina realized that this old truck of hers wasn't going to be hers much longer. There were aspects about the truck she would miss and then there were others she'd have no love loss. Kristina began to realize her future and all the new changes coming. She also realized that even as those changes were coming there would still be the same issues to deal with regarding the animals and the people. What gave her comfort was the fact that she'd be seeing to the care of those animals without the limitation or authority of the town.

Henry's focus on the way to Francis' house didn't run loose like Kristina's; he remained dedicated to the fundamentals of driving. His spirits were good, but his lack of familiarity driving was more than enough to maintain the focus. The drive didn't take long and they arrived to find Adoc and Old Ben in the field playing while Francis was puttering around in the shop. Adoc was the first to run to them. Henry got out of the car while Kristina got out of the truck. Adoc was in a full dash towards them. Old Ben came much slower. Adoc's barking gave Francis a reason to forget what he was doing if only momentarily. It wasn't long before they all congregated at the back porch to discuss the business at hand. Francis didn't expect to see either of them as soon as then. He thought that Henry might be by earlier than both of them together.

"I didn't expect to see both of you here at such an early hour. What do I owe the pleasure of both your company?"

Henry was petting Adoc while Francis asked the question and Kristina seemed to be excited, more so than Henry as Francis took notice. Kristina replied to Francis with a plain response. "Henry and I have decided to take you up on the offer you made to Henry earlier."

For hearing her response Francis smiled with raised eyes brows. His surprise for hearing the answer was something Henry took notice of immediately. "Why, that is fine! I'm glad to hear it. So I suppose we are getting down to business then that would be the reason for your early arrival, right?"

Henry nodded. "Indeed I wanted to inquire as to when you think we could see to the paperwork transference. That would be the first order of business."

Francis produced a big smile. He rose up from his chair and excused himself. Henry went into the house for a moment while Henry continued petting Adoc. Kristina gazed upon the fields where she figured the new structure to be and let her imagination loose for a short time.

Henry's agenda was becoming a stronger curiosity for her. She sat silently while Henry and Adoc appreciated one another. Old Ben sat apart seemingly uninterested, but easy. Francis returned to the porch with a file and when he arrived Old Ben came out of his perched and moved towards Francis. He looked to be expecting similar attention Adoc was getting from Henry. Francis put the file in front of Henry.

"I'm sure those are in order, I'd spoken to my lawyer months ago." Francis shook his head and reached down for Old Ben. "That lawyer thought I was crazy when I requested the paperwork. I told him that he must be insane for taking retainers from crazy people."

Kristina giggled at Francis' remark. Henry stopped petting Adoc to review the file. Francis excused himself again. He muttered some words moving inside the house again. This time Old Ben followed him. It sounded to both Kristina and Henry that he was muttering to Old Ben.

"You know, boy, how it is to get old. We always seem to be absent minded about things, forgetting the politeness of a greeting." Old Ben's tail wagged as Francis talked to him. The two seemed to make a great pair.

Kristina looked at Henry reviewing the files. She thought he must have been a student of the speed reading courses they heard about when they were kids. When Francis returned with the jug and three glasses Henry had flipped through four pages of the file. Adoc took his own leave only to return with a stick. He sat next to Henry patiently expecting a stick throw shortly. Francis placed the three glasses on the table and poured wine in each. He took notice of the stick Adoc brought and began espousing his intention of the papers Henry was examining.

"There are specific instructions listed in those pages. Of course I will live out my days here and after my days both Mildred and I will be buried in a plot I have already had delineated here on the property. That is, Mildred's ashes will be buried with me." He looked towards Kristina and laughed. "Mildred never wanted to be worm food." Kristina smiled over his last comment.

Henry finished up the file he was perusing and left it open. He hadn't noticed that Francis brought out the wine. "Everything seems to be in order here and I imagine that what we have here is a celebration offering."

Francis nodded, "Of course it is a celebration offering." He passed a glass to each. They held up their glasses waiting on Francis.

"Transfer of the responsibility to owning a thing is a rarity in the day of a man and it mostly never gets celebrated during the time of living, but here as we are doing an even more infrequent transition all I can say is Mildred must be happy because I ain't hearing a single word, so thank you to both and best of luck to both of you!"

All toasted the drink and honored the toast with sips. Henry began telling Kristina that the paperwork Francis gave them minimized work which would free up time on the agenda. He was going to continue, but Old Ben did a very strange thing. He walked straight up to Adoc and sat before the stick Adoc brought for throwing. Adoc became a tad excited for Old Ben's curiosity at the stick he wanted to chase and Old Ben let a low sounding groan out for looking at it. Francis let a laugh out for the groan and Adoc tilted his head towards Francis.

Henry and Kristina were mesmerized by the interaction. They looked like children watching an unrealized favorite cartoon. Francis finished off his wine and poured another leaving the jug on the table. Adoc's focus returned to Old Ben's disapproval of the stick. He began to bark at Old Ben after he lay down on the stick. It was all noise to Old Ben and he didn't care one bit. Adoc began lunging towards Old Ben demanding that he get up off his stick. The bark sounded as though it were a supplication rather than a demand. Francis continued to laugh between sips on his wine.

Henry tried to get Adoc to calm down. Kristina watched Adoc with delight. In her mind he was communicating properly to an older dog that he was unhappy about the older dog's behavior. All too often she saw young dogs invite trouble from older dogs who thought that the older dog's behavior was unfair. When that happened it wasn't long before the younger dog went too far and invited injury.

Francis had another sip of his wine and then interrupted Henry in his need to stop Adoc.

"Henry, finish the wine and learn something." He giggled and looked at Kristina. "I think Henry may have to have another glass before he sees what is going on."

Henry was reluctant to give up his focus, but he yielded. He took a sip of his wine finishing the last of it and then poured himself another. Once he put the jug down Kristina decided to help herself to another. After she poured her own she noticed Henry's energy seemed to change. He went from reading the file and feeling good about what he read to a type of concern.

"Henry, Old Ben is doing something that goes on between old dogs and young dogs all the time. He is claiming his authority as the alpha dog over the youth of Adoc. There is no need to intervene, it is a natural thing."

Henry listened to her and accepted the fact that he might not know as much about how dogs interact. He just didn't like being so unaware of something he couldn't possibly know. Francis sipped on his wine and then took a moment to give both of them some insight. "So you two have decided to be partners, eh?" He sipped on his wine and toasted again, "Partnership!" After all took a sip he continued. "Well I am glad that you did because Mildred would have never tolerated two dogs having an argument on her porch. But she never understood dogs much, nor did she want to know their ways." Francis sipped on his drink and continued. "In as much as Kristina is right about the purpose of Old Ben's manners she isn't completely right." The comment fell on both of their listening and gave them reason to listen even more. Adoc was now on his belly trying to get the stick away from Old Ben. He nipped at Old Ben's paws and whined. When Old Ben grew tired of Adoc's nipping he showed his teeth with a silent growl. That caused the whining.

"Old Ben is telling Adoc that his need to get the stick back for what he wants is stupid, but as Adoc is young he can't figure it." The comment seemed strange to both Henry and Kristina. Neither could figure that in a dogs behavior there was a complex vocabulary. Francis sipped on his wine knowing they were baited. When he was done he elaborated.

"If Old Ben wanted the stick, he'd take possession of it and chew it into bits of wood that Adoc would continue to seek. But as he is lying upon it he is trying to tell him the stick isn't the proper thing for his want." Francis saw that the skepticism was growing from both Henry and Kristina. Francis expected it and gave them a second to respond. In considering what Francis said neither thought to respond, and he decided to offer them evidence of his point.

Francis looked at Old Ben. He made a clicking noise with his tongue to which Old Ben took focus upon Francis. "Go get it!" Old Ben took a deep breath and began standing. He was a large dog so it did take him effort. After he was up he turned and went towards the shop leaving the stick. His pace was slow, but he clearly knew where he was going. Adoc's interest went from the stick to where Old Ben was going and he decided his stick was the treasure.

"The stick meant nothing; if it did Old Ben would have taken it with him. Adoc still has his focus on the stick and as Old Ben relinquished it back to him; he'll now show him what it was that would be better for what he wanted."

Henry and Kristina's interest in the return of Old Ben became like the focus parents have watching a child trying to tie a shoe lace. Old Ben disappeared into the store and after a few seconds reappeared with a tennis ball in his mouth. Henry's face showed an abundant shock in understanding what Francis was telling him. Kristina laughed and sipped on her wine. Old Ben walked straight past Adoc with the tennis ball in his mouth and held it above his ability to sniff it. He approached Francis and sat with the ball in his mouth raising it up to Francis' grasp. Francis looked at Old Ben holding the ball for him to take.

"Good dog, good dog!" Francis reached to Old Ben's mouth and Old Ben let the ball loose gently into Francis' hand. He put the glass down with his other hand and pet Old Ben for his duty. When he was done Old Ben went back to the stick and lay upon it once again. Francis looked at Henry and asked him, "Are you tired of cleaning up splinters of old sticks or finding new ones after Adoc has torn them to shreds?"

Henry shook his head and laughed. He saw the light immediately. Francis smiled and handed the ball to Henry. Henry took the ball from Francis' hand extension and looked at both Old Ben and Francis. Henry held the ball in his hand and looked at Adoc. "Adoc, do you want to chase the ball?" Adoc heard the Man say *chase* and whined. Old Ben was still on his stick. "Adoc! Chase the ball!"

Adoc heard the enthusiasm in the Man's voice and lost his focus on the stick. He saw the ball the Man was holding and decided to see about the ball. Adoc approached the Man sniffing at his hand. He could smell the old dog's saliva on it and wanted to taste it for himself. Adoc sat in front of the Man as he lowered it for him to sniff.

Francis watched the interaction of both and when it was time to give Henry direction he did. "Henry, let him sniff it for a second or two and then let him take it in his mouth." Henry did so and once Adoc had the ball in his mouth he began to run with it. Francis laughed out loud upon Adoc's discovery.

After Adoc began running Henry looked at Kristina to see what she was thinking. She had a look of disbelief on her face, with miraculous understanding. Henry watched Adoc run around with the ball in his mouth. He chewed on it feverishly when he wasn't dropping it to pick it back up again. Henry's delight was much like a father's delight in seeing his first born son receiving a gift he hadn't expected but always wanted. The happiness Adoc expressed in his romping would stay with Henry for the rest of his days. And then Henry became the surprised proud Dad. Adoc brought the ball back to him just as he would have done so with the stick. Henry stood up and took the ball from where Adoc left it just at his feet. "Chase the ball?!"

Adoc barked and lowered himself ready to spring after the toss. Henry launched the ball and for the next fifteen minutes the world centered on the Man, the dog and a Ball. While Henry tossed the Ball with Adoc, Francis and Kristina shared words unheard by Henry or Adoc.

It was kept in the hearing of Francis and Kristina along with Old Ben. Kristina felt as though what she had seen was the most wonderful thing she ever witnessed and for the first time since Mildred had passed she knew a different happiness while visiting there. Kristina adored Mildred. The relationship between both was like an Aunt-Niece type of arrangement. Francis on the other hand was a kind but cold man. She knew plenty of those types, but Francis' kindness went further than other cold men she knew. Still she would never have visited here after Mildred's passing. When she did come here and that was a rarity, it would be for business and nothing else. Now she was thinking about setting up shop there. More than that her partner had found a reason to be a child again as a serious and contemplative man and it was all because of a dog and a ball. Before Henry finished throwing the Ball for Adoc Old Ben decided to pay a visit to Kristina. He had been sitting with Francis, but he moved towards her. Old Ben snugged up right against her chair and laid his head on her knee. He looked at her with satisfied thanks. After he set his head upon her leg he sighed a long sigh. The mystery of his actions before became revealed to Kristina while she gazed into his eyes for the sigh. She knew that all that was happening for the time was what she was supposed to be doing. She felt as though she was one with perfection it really didn't get better than that moment. A tear escaped her eye from her elation. She reached her face down to Old Ben's and gave him a kiss on the nose, and then she began scratching him. To her surprise Francis became a bit preoccupied in his person.

"Of course I'll tell her." He looked to Kristina with a feigned aggravation on his face. "Mildred says that you don't need to worry about anything anymore... she also says time for worry will arrive, but when it does don't get preoccupied or distracted in the worry, she says remember your happiness right now for when that time comes." Francis downed the last of his wine and grumbled. Then he just poured himself another and sipped.

Kristina took notice of Francis figuring he was listening to Mildred and conveying her thoughts. She felt a bittersweet sensation for what she heard. Then she rationalized that what Francis said would be much like a Carney psychic teller would say so you'd return to spend more through their availability. The upstroke of this was *Don't worry.* Kristina decided that staying here was something she wanted to do so she decided to activate her second. She gave Old Ben another kiss and a hug and went to her truck. During her absence from the porch she got on the radio and told William to go through the call system to have Jason act as the ACO in her place. She mentioned that he should come by and get the truck at Francis' place. She explained that she was dealing with a situation that would not allow her to act as her office required. When she got off the radio she returned to the porch where Adoc and Henry were taking a break from the ball tossing. Adoc was lapping on a bowl of water and Henry and Francis were looking at him with holiday jubilation. Old Ben was waiting on her. When she sat he took his place up by her again. Her hand found the back of Old Ben's neck and she began stroking him. Adoc was in a triangular motion mode. He lapped at the water in the bowl, made sure of where he left the ball and then sniffed at Henry in thankful gesture. When Adoc was done quenching his thirst and thanking Henry he laid down with his head on the ball. Old Ben had taught him something and it would be anytime soon that Adoc forgot the importance of his ball.

The sun had past noon time and they all sat in the lengthening shadows that came before day's end. Francis decided that some food would be a good idea as the celebration seemed like a notion of continuation.

"I'm going to prepare some vittles before we all think that we can live off the grape without consequence. Why don't you both relax for a time while I get some eating prepared?" Henry nodded at Francis understanding his intention. Francis left and noises from the kitchen were only interrupted by Francis speaking to an empty room. A room that wasn't empty. Henry decided to walk into the field and continue the formation of the agenda.

"Why don't we go figure a place out for the new structure?" Kristina filled her cup and then filled Henry's. It was his invitation and his invitation included her newly realized reality of freedom.

Once the glasses were full they rose up and began walking into the fields. Both Old Ben and Adoc followed them. Adoc decided to be a nudge on Old Ben while they walked. He nibbled at Old Ben's neck, ears and jowls. Old Ben kept his pace while Adoc's antics seemed to afflict nothing more than a moving puppet dog. Then something strange happened. Both dogs took an immediate interest in an area further ahead. Both broke towards it and even as Old Ben took time to gain his full speed Adoc kept a half a link behind him. The dogs ran about 400 yards in front of them and sat when they arrived to their focus. Henry and Kristina looked at each without a clue as to what happened with both dogs. They continued their walk silently to where the dogs sat enjoying the stroll through the knee high grass. When they got closer to the dogs they found Old Ben sitting, while Adoc was pawing at the ground surface. He was tearing through the deep root system of the grass with his paws. They both shared curiosity for the choice of interest but did not take much notice for it. They stopped about ten feet from where the dogs had their focus. Then they both turned to look at the house and shop Francis and Mildred had built and lived in. There was a moment of silence that neither could resist. The only noise was Adoc digging his hole. Old Ben sat in the purpose of Silence because when he decided to sit Adoc smelled around for a place to dig and they both saw it happen.

"I guess this is going to be the cornerstone." He looked around from the place only to end up watching Kristina feeling as though she knew creation. At least that is what he thought he saw. He turned to look at the dogs and Adoc ceased his digging. Kristina had given up on revelation after she informed William to call Jason. She basically thought that she'd be unprepared for anything in her responsibility for the rest of her day. Henry might have guessed that she was behind his thinking, but that was nothing new to him. Most of those he helped out before were galaxies behind his thinking. He didn't worry too much about it; he just kept his faith on what he already knew.

"Let me ask this you Kristina if you were part of the agenda I spoke to before, what would you think about Adoc's breaking ground here?" The question gave Kristina a reason to interact and answer with a question.

"I'm not sure, but I can tell you this: Starting here for construction seems to be fine, but that wood line is a concern." Henry heard her response and seemed satisfied. He looked at the wood line and told her what part of his agenda as for what he read in the file.

"Most of what you see can be used in the building of what we want to build or be something of revenue later." She looked at him and responded directly.

"Henry if you think this is where we should build the new place I am all for it as a start. What I am trying to say is that once we are in operation that wood line is going to be something we'll have to cut off." Henry heard the same thing in her response without hearing the difference. Henry knew that if they wanted to utilize the resource of that forest they could but he wasn't aware that she meant it had to be raised. He tried to ask her again.

"Do you think that where Adoc is digging amounts to the cornerstone of our effort?" Kristina knew what Henry was asking, but she didn't think he took the whole picture into his process of thinking. Adoc began digging after Old Ben sat himself down. She wondered if Old Ben sat on the source or if he was just taking a rest. She flashed back to Adoc taking up on the ball Francis gave to Henry for an offering wondering if he was still in that euphoria.

"Henry we took a walk with the dogs in between Francis making us food. Now if you think Adoc has prescience as to where we need to build based upon Old Ben deciding to have a seat I am willing to consider that reality." She thought to try a different approach. She walked beyond where the dogs took up lounging and digging and decided to give up on her approach she left all three of them walking ahead. Somehow she thought the decision to break ground happened too quickly. She thought that Henry's assumption that Adoc's particular digging spot meant little even as Old Ben sat comfortably... her walk away from the boys was abrupt, but only so to Henry.

Henry watched her walking away without commentary. Each step she took brought back memories of those he helped before. He relived the horror of giving them his advice. He felt their frustration in realizing what they heard as his consultation. In that second Henry began to realize that sometimes the truth was cold and hard. Then he realized that his essence to all those who sought him for his wisdom might have known him for a cold and hard manner.

Henry didn't have the courage to chase her down. He stood with the dogs unable to focus on much of anything. It seemed to him that his focus left with Kristina and that in itself was something he couldn't avoid pondering. Adoc was terrorizing the grass and Old Ben kept looking at the tree line and he wondered why she left. Henry turned and looked to the tree line to his right.

He felt a need to walk there. He found himself stepping towards his desire but the silent gazing from the dogs watching him fell heavy upon his shoulders. He stopped following his desired destination. He turned and looked at the house and saw Francis bringing out food while Kristina was halfway back. He turned to the dogs that already seemed focused on him wondering why he moved away. Henry began walking towards the house and they followed. Henry could hear Adoc jumping up on Old Ben in a playful manner; it seemed to him neither of them knew his troubles. They followed along as Henry watched Kristina speak to Francis and then go into the house. It wasn't long before he and the dogs returned for Francis' food preparation. Francis noticed that Henry seemed to have a troubled reality.

"How was the stroll, seems like ya lost Kristina's interest." Francis looked concerned at Henry. Henry shrugged. "I'm clueless, heck I thought I was being straightforward and I thought we were getting along fine. I figured Adoc might have decided on a place to break ground and all of a sudden the place was fine but the tree line needed cutting off." Henry shrugged. Francis raised his eye brows at his shrug.

"Henry, sometimes there are no explanations to be heard and most of the time women are the experts and they don't offer explanations. I wouldn't think on it too much, I'm sure when she figures out how she wants to tell you what is on her mind she will." Henry listened to Francis' comment as though he was a sage.

"I suppose you are right. It is just something I never experienced from someone so close."

"Well you need to have faith in that familiarity. And now it is time to have a bite to eat, so why don't you take a seat Kristina is just having a moment in the powder room. She'll be here directly." Francis had already placed some tableware on the table. He returned into the kitchen to bring out what he prepared to eat. Just after he walked in Kristina came out he heard Francis give her the same directions he just heard. Henry waited on Kristina to have a seat then he took his. Henry felt a need to speak to her, but he followed the advice Francis gave to him. The silence was brief and Francis returned with plates of sandwiches and cups of soup.

"I hope you'll like the fixings but either way it is meant to keep us level headed for the celebratory hoisting." After they began eating Francis thought to offer both Henry and Kristina some historical context about the property. It ended up being a one way conversation for the most part and that was fine with Francis. These two would need to know the details for their future in managing the property.

Adoc and Old Ben sat patiently while the older handed person spoke. Adoc might not have been so patient but he studied how Old Ben behaved and followed his lead. Old Ben knew that the Gate was close by. He stayed low when he was so close to it. For the staying low he helped the pup begin to feel what they couldn't hear. It was like the bad things happening without bad smells.

Not being able to hear something didn't mean it wasn't close by and when it was close by it was best to stay low and be unnoticed. Old Ben knew the pup had urges and he knew his place was to help the pup avoid urges that would deliver him to trouble. Old Ben felt the pup's energy and knew for all of his efforts at a time coming the pup would face serious trouble. It was the kind of trouble that might mean his end and the only way to avoid that would be to make sure that the pup realized the trouble could be his end. Old Ben knew his purpose here and he knew how important the pup was to whatever the Man and the Woman would be doing.

Francis left a portion of his sandwich on the plate and when he was done eating and giving his report to Henry and Kristina he called both dogs to his side. Of course Adoc went first to the calling; Old Ben came slowly along but stayed on the other side of where the gate was in proximity to his Man. Francis split the remainder of the tuna sandwich on his plate and held each piece to either dog. Adoc reached for the hand quickly without snapping and took the food from the other with old hands. Old Ben moved slowly towards his Man's extended hand and stole it gently from Francis' fingers. Once he had it in his mouth he backed away to where he was before and laid down to eat his share. The Gate made its noise and Adoc was frightened for a surprise. He made his way quickly to where Old Ben lay down with his tail between his legs. Henry noticed that he moved like he was scolded. Francis laughed and revealed his humor.

"Mildred always thought it to be barbaric to feed a dog at the table and it happened once. She chased a dog with a broom to the limit of her comfort outside. Needless to say she doesn't have a broom these days. That is why Adoc skedaddled away just now." Henry looked to Adoc lying on the floor. Then he looked at Kristina with a smile.

She took notice of his smile and wondered what he was thinking. She didn't ask. She had an idea that he wasn't gloating as he was the one in trouble. He wasn't really in any trouble, but she liked the idea that he might think he was. She was aggravated with herself because she didn't know how to tell him something that may have contradicted his surety and confidence. His surety and confidence was more than her unwillingness to make such a decision without thinking about it, he may have been right about knowing that is where they should break ground, but she wasn't sure and in not being able to express her doubt to his surety, she was fine with having him think he was in trouble.

Francis was a man who observed realities that nobody knew existed. He saw things happening between people that they didn't even know they were conveying. He knew that Henry and Kristina had a difference of opinion and he figured to allow them the sorting out of the difference on their own, but that would happen when they figured it out. He thought that getting them back on focusing is what needed to be done now as opposed to what would come.

"So what is your plan for the immediate future?" Henry gulped the last of the soup from his cup. Then he began an answer.

"Basically I'll be doing some convincing with the town as to our intentions. Of course there will be an offer to privately do the business of Animal Control and we'll have to see how that goes, but I am certain that they'll go with losing the liability. Secondly, I'll get surveyors up here to work with architects I still have to speak with. That is about it for now." Francis looked towards Kristina.

"Is that about it with you or does your partnership remain uninvolved during this aspect of the project?" Kristina was considering his question.

"There is something that I'll be doing during this phase of the project Francis. Henry says that the agenda we'll be undertaking needs my particular wisdom. I may not be the face on this part of the project but I'll certainly be behind the scenes." Francis listened to her response and considered it. He rose up from his chair and gathered up the plates. "I'll be back and we'll discuss more of behind the scenes; Henry why don't you pour some more of that wine?" Both dogs sat up watching Francis go into the house with the table ware. Henry poured the wine as asked. Kristina was looking at both dogs. As Henry looked upon her he took notice of the calm pleasure on her face. She looked upon Adoc and Old Ben in a way that haunted him. He wished he understood whatever it was she was feeling because he wanted to know what could motivate such a gaze.

He set the jug down after filling the glasses. He turned his focus to the dogs and saw how beautiful they looked waiting on Francis' return. It seemed as though they knew he'd have something for them, or that they just expected something. He also wanted to know what those dogs knew about Francis and how it was that they could expect something for his return.

Francis exited the kitchen through the porch door and as soon as he saw the dogs sitting for his return he began praising them.

"Look at you two dogs; sitting so handsomely!" He moved to them holding beef jerk. He held the treats just above their noses and then rewarded them. Both dogs took their portions and lay down where they were before the wait. The chewing began and Francis smiled for their manner walking back to his seat. He took his place at the table and took up his glass holding it for a toast.

Henry and Kristina did the same. Francis looked to both of them and gave his toast.

"On any endeavor of greatness there must a face of the thing and there must be the unseen body for the face. This is to both; one right up front and the second behind the scenes." He sipped his wine and set his glass down. Henry and Kristina took sips and did the same.

"So behind the scenes that is when I left." He had another sip of his wine. "After Henry is done with his work in lining this dream up the roles will switch and you, Kristina will be the face and Henry will be behind the scenes. So what you both have to realize as partners is that your roles will change by necessity of the dream." Henry followed along with Francis as did Kristina; they both sipped on the wine and continued to listen.

"We talked about partnership before and you already know the things I told you then, but The thing about partnership no partner ever knows is just how important it is to be true to oneself so that the partnership can remain intact." He sipped on his wine again and finished his glass. He poured more while both Henry and Kristina digested his wisdom. Francis looked at both of them and it seemed to him they weren't getting their heads around his thinking.

"Okay let's try this: Do either of you think that either of you could make another happy while you were unhappy?" Henry had a sip of his wine while Kristina thought about the questions.

Then she spoke. "You are talking about dichotomy, like if there is a black there must be a white, right?"

Francis heard what she said and answered her, "Sort of. But you are thinking in terms not of yourself and that is what I mean. It is more of a personal commitment to whatever the partnership demands." Francis sipped more on his wine he finished the glass and put it down on the table. "Let's have a walk, sometimes it is easier to think through things when you have distractions such as not falling down."

He rose up from the table as did Henry and Kristina. They walked towards where both were before. The dogs followed until Adoc realized the place he was digging was just ahead. He bolted to his former excavation area and begun again. Old Ben would have rather followed, but because Adoc bolted he followed him to take up his watch like before.

"This is what I love about a stroll, here I am trying to convey that hinge pin of a partnership and two dogs show it. They don't even know to call it a partnership, they just know, and they know without knowing each other's purpose. What they do know is the partnership."

Henry was having a time trying to figure out what Francis was getting after. He thought he knew what a partnership demanded. He'd seen partnerships live and die based on advice he had given. "Why do you say they know what a partnership is without knowing each other's purpose?"

Francis let out a loud laugh. "Well, they don't need to know what the purpose is, Adoc is your dog by his choice and Old Ben is your Dog by your choice that is all they need to know. They are your dogs, Henry! That is their life and their partnership is all about doing what each other needs. Old Ben sees himself as a mentor or a big brother, Adoc is just a pup doing what pups do, but he is doing what a pup does naming you the Alpha."

The conversation ended, but the walk lingered a bit. After Francis took notice of Adoc's excavation he said it might be a good place to start. After that comment Francis decided it was time to head back. Kristina and Henry stayed again at the house. The celebrating of the partnership made driving a bad decision. Before going to sleep, both said good night to each other. Kristina wasn't too eager to let Henry off the hook. There was plenty of time for that in the next day or so. Henry considered Francis' remarks as he said them and over the coming days he'd be seeing to the details and working out the possibilities of the future.

Œ

It was the end of April when Henry had concluded the last bit of business that bound him to his old life. The negotiations with the town had been concluded and after some very cool poker playing Henry closed the deal to assume the Animal Control duties of the town. It took heated debate at two council meetings but because Henry was the Town Son the opposition was dismantled by public opinion. The surveying was done at Francis' property and the site where Adoc dug the grass up didn't end up being the cornerstone site Henry thought it would become. Henry didn't care one way for another, he was just glad that the site had been picked. Kristina was happy by the fact that Francis had hinted at another place further away from the tree line area. The water level tests as well as the sewage tests supported the different location. Kristina's need to have authority was supported for the placement of the survey area and thusly she became more involved in the behind the scenes work. She became so involved that she gave up her place and moved into Francis' house as a temporary measure. Now that Henry had secured a transfer of his house to another he too would move into Francis' house so he wouldn't be split between places. In the contract with the builders Henry would be involved in the construction from start to finish. Henry had ideas about the structure that nobody was implementing in typical construction; it was his vision that would create a self sustained structure that would be capable of selling back power to the local grid.

Adoc had grown substantially adding some fifteen pounds. The skin on him still sagged which indicated he still had a great amount of growing to do. Adoc had a better awareness and minded verbal commands so well that Kristina felt as though Adoc was a dog that minimized her experience in taking care of dogs for so many years. He gave her hope as to the potential of the shelter they were determined to build. She was amazed in the fact that Henry spoke with the architect and builders and that the new facility would have a state of the art vet facility. Henry indicated to Kristina her priority would be to start picking vet students that would be able to work on the premises in a full time capacity. Henry was determined to get any tax advantage he could and he still needed to work out the details of a partnership with the Universities. Henry didn't mind giving, he just thought his choice for giving was better than any government agency could be responsible to similar generosity.

The transfer of his house wasn't profitable; he took a liability in matching the purchase price for a family in need that could only manage 60% of the cost. The profit didn't matter to Henry; money was only a tool. For that family though money did matter. It was Henry's belief that given a chance they could become a value to the community. Henry was literally making his banker crazy with all of his plans, but because the banker worked with him he might even turn enough profit over at the bank for early retirement.

The community was well aware of the plans Henry, Kristina and Francis were undertaking. Everyone seemed to know Adoc and Henry were thick as thieves. Generally speaking folks were glad of the situation even as there were some folks gossiping as there would be in any community.

A Man, a Dog and a Ball

The old ladies spoke of Henry and Kristina and the old men wishing to buy off Francis' property hoped they ran into trouble. They were the minority of the community but as always the humanity of a society always has misery as a part of the whole.   None of it bothered any of the three. They just kept focused to the plan. Over the few weeks that it took Henry to see to the business at hand Francis continued to reveal wisdom they would need to know for what lie ahead.

Old Ben remained ever patient with Adoc. They were both free to roam the property when Adoc was available. Meetings and business couldn't be facilitated with Adoc in Henry's company.

Much of the time was spent with Adoc playing and biting along with taunting Old Ben. Old Ben was a gentle giant where Adoc was concerned. Adoc would parade around Old Ben lunging and jumping after him, always displaying fearsome battle techniques. Both dogs provided a show that was better than any TV or radio watching or listening. Old Ben and Adoc would be out of sight for long periods of time as they roamed the property. Never once did Old Ben loose into the tree line. Adoc would have loved to venture into that place but Old Ben wouldn't have it. The very first time Adoc wanted to go Old Ben showed his authority by grabbing Adoc by the scruff of his neck, pinning him down into submission. Later even as Adoc understood Old Ben wouldn't allow it, he never gave up trying. There would be no biting or lunging or fearsome battle display. They would communicate as dogs do with growls and whimpers, low barks and loud barks. In all of that commotion Old Ben let Adoc know that even as he survived as a pup for his own wits, he wasn't ready to go into the woods.

Old Ben told him about packs of dogs that hunted without compassion; they hunted for food as there were no people to feed them. Old Ben told Adoc of larger type dogs that were impossible to imagine. He told them that the pack dogs would go after the larger type dogs if they were hungry enough. He told him of the hellacious noises that would come from the tearing of fur and breaking of bones. Just about every time the pack would remain hungry and weaker or less in numbers for the attempt at easing of hunger.   Even as Old Ben could hold the attention of Adoc for the telling of terrors; a butterfly would glide into their focus and then flutter away into the tree line. Or it might just be a chipmunk. Adoc's attention following the distraction would only stop after Old Ben would bark loudly after him. Adoc would run to the limit and then carry on like a pup would as to why he couldn't chase the critter or bug. Old Ben would sit guard until he was done with his carrying on and when Adoc understood he wasn't going in Old Ben would return to the house. On the return trip if Adoc wanted to carry on Old Ben would discipline him. It was a reinforcing thing the Alpha did when the pup lost focus.

Old Ben conveyed to Adoc on every trip home the importance of not being out when the light went away without the Man. It was a constant as they would head back from there jaunts, when the light began to fade in the day. Old Ben told him of other creatures that were ten times or more his size that would forage at night. If they were surprised they'd lower their great rack of thorns and charge him likely lifting him off the ground while he would be stuck on them, until they threw him off. Then they would stomp him into the soil they ran upon. He spoke of smaller dogs that traveled alone that would be tougher than any dog that lived with people. Adoc heard all that Old Ben said, but Old Ben knew Adoc wasn't listening. Old Ben was thankful for the return trip because when they arrived the Man would toss the ball which tired Adoc out. Old Ben saw the Ball as real growth. Before the Ball, Adoc would be stupid and chase sticks. Ever since the Man with old hands gave the Man the Ball Adoc had no want to ever chase a stick again.

Œ

Henry looked at his house for the last time. The car was filled with personal stuff that hadn't yet been moved to Francis' place. He laughed at the doggy doors he installed. He looked at Adoc and asked him if he appreciated the doors for the short time he was there. Adoc wagged his tail as he heard the Man making noise at him. Adoc had the sense that this would be the last time he'd be there. It was like the time he met the Man at the place where the flying things were.

Henry had a last look at the place, it wasn't his anymore he was leaving to meet his future. He turned to go to the car and Adoc followed. Adoc and Henry moved without many commands. For anyone who would have noticed they were lifelong friends which might have made other pet owners jealous of their relationship. When Adoc could be with Henry he was welcomed everywhere Henry went. The joke at the bank stood as to when Adoc would be doing transactions under his own name. Once in the car Henry looked at Adoc.

"Are ya ready, Adoc? Ready for the new home?"

Adoc wagged while sitting on his tail. He leaned to the Man and licked his face. Henry started the car and left his driveway for the last time. There were no pangs for the departure. The transaction of the house benefited the community; he'd be working for an even greater benefit at Francis' place. The property was better for Adoc and Old Ben would live his days out as it was meant to be. Since Henry spoke to Francis about religion a while ago, he'd been studying scripture. It was the toughest reading he ever committed himself to and he still had trouble getting his head around what it all meant, but he knew enough to begin trying to say prayers. Funny thing about the prayers was that around the time he stared saying them, he felt better all around. During the drive he gave a quick prayer of thanks for the shelter he had in his old house. He even went so far as to ask for good and bountiful times for the young family who'd be living there. During the ride... he left completely.

The town was abuzz with this day. News of Henry helping out the young couple was a type of big to do. Even bigger news was the fact that all three would be living up at Francis' home. The old ladies of the town speculated that Henry and Kristina were living sin. They'd soon realize their notions were just gossip. Most of the old money men found themselves along the route Henry would take leaving his house visiting with friends they never had occasion to visit before. Henry laughed along the way over all the voyeurs.

"See that, Adoc? You are the talk of the town, look you are a single vehicle parade. That's right, Adoc, all of these folks are lining up to see you go to your new home." Henry honked the horn at those who were sincere about his good intention and waved. As he drove the crowd of voyeurs thinned; Francis' place wasn't in the center of town it was toward the outskirts. The last few miles to his driveway there were no homes to be seen. Coming home this day was unexpectedly different for Henry. It was an adventure and his discovery was in days to come. Henry and Adoc drove up the driveway of their new home, a new adventure and more discoveries. At the end of the drive sat Old Ben waiting like an escort into an unknown destiny.

Œ

The new living arrangements for all worked out extremely well. There were no issues of personality differences in the living quarters of the house and only minor adjustments were needed that gave nobody difficulty in managing. As the days passed the housemate situation became more of a family unit setting. Differences of opinions weren't divisions but rather a curing of mortar that bound loving as the foundations for being together.

In the early phases of the construction Francis kept an eye on the work getting done and saw to the needs of the workers in giving them coffee and making lunches for them. Henry and Kristina saw to the duties of working at the animal shelter. Henry fulfilled his volunteer work and returned to the construction site as he could. The work at hand was met with an astounding rate of accomplishment towards completion and that was largely due to Henry's pre-construction negotiation. To a lesser extent Francis kept the work crews motivated for his manner in seeing to their needs at break time. It seemed like the guys would work with razor sharp diligence as though their efforts pushed the clock faster to break time so Francis' treats could be enjoyed.

There was another unexpected result for the construction. Because the project became the talk of the communities surrounding; Francis' feed shop saw a steep increase in business. Folks from all over made a point to drive out to the store for purchases to see all the activity. Francis needed to hire a full time worker to see to the business of the store. Neither Francis nor Henry was surprised, but Kristina never expected the boon of the effort. Each day she returned from her work; she took anywhere from fifteen minutes to a half an hour examining the changes for the day. The dogs would follow her through her examination and occasionally Henry and Francis would tag along. For the most part she did so only with the dogs as Francis and Henry took the time to brainstorm the next day while working in the kitchen making dinner. It was those times when Henry soaked up the details of the farm and how Francis lived each day for the year's need.

Francis taught Henry the responsibility of owning the property in all aspects. He taught Henry the things he did as Mildred's partner when she was alive. Francis understood that Henry might not keep up with all of the nuances of his doing, but he knew the value of knowing how it was done at one time and done successfully. Truth be told the relationship between Francis and Henry became the type of relationship a father and son would know.

After Kristina had her examination of the changes for the day, she'd visit the men cavorting in the kitchen. Usually the work at hand was well managed and they were able to focus on her joining the house. They'd sit down and share the day over a glass of wine and then eat dinner.

As the light of day lingered longer Henry and Kristina took more time to stroll after dinner. During the strolls their dreams expanded by the day. As they realized the growth of their efforts Adoc continued to grow himself. The walks they took were ritualistic and while Adoc grew his tendency to terrorize Old Ben lessened. If Henry and Kristina stopped to examine a specific addition of the day the dogs would continue along the walk. Sometimes they'd wander off out of site sometimes they'd stay close. The partnership of Henry and Kristina unified during these walks and the lessons Adoc received from Old Ben continued. Much like Henry's and Francis' relationship of father and son, so it was with Old Ben and Adoc. Old Ben revealed the laws of nature of this place to Adoc. Old Ben lent his wisdom of the laws of nature as nature presented the changes revealed by the lengthening days.

Each day brought new scents for Adoc and some of those new scents were more important than others. This was Adoc's first year for knowing the time of growing light. He'd been born during the time of lessening light and Old Ben knew that Adoc's desire to learn about all new things was a dangerous time. Pups usually had bitches to raise them up and teach them the ways; they usually had litter pups to grow with so as to know what they were. Adoc had neither and he was a special pup. Old Ben took on the duty of raising him up best he knew how, but his fear remained for him because he knew the pup's impulsivity. He hoped his years could keep up with Adoc's growth. Old Ben was glad that he wanted to play less, but he knew that less playing with him meant a greater desire to engage the mysteries of nature. Old Ben was always grateful for the end of the Man's walk. If they wandered off the Man would whistle and they'd both return. Then the pup would get his attention chasing the Ball and Old Ben hoped that Adoc's desire to engage the mysteries of nature never grew stronger than the want of the Ball. Old Ben enjoyed that ball-time Adoc shared with the Man because it was then that he could sit with the woman. She had a touch he longed to feel, her kindness soothed the aches in his old body. She seemed to know his worry and concerns for the pup, too. Then as the light fell out of the sky they'd all be together and the Man with older hands would bring out a treat they could chew on before the needed rest came. Old Ben began realizing that the presence of the Gate always loomed around the Man with old hands and for it he didn't mind the presence's closeness. He began to know that it wasn't waiting on him. But it was waiting or at least moving with the Man with old hands. Old Ben received the love from the woman counting down the last throws the Man would share with Adoc. Just before their return Old Ben would let out a sigh, thanking the woman for her loving. It always came to an end after the Ball throwing because then it was Adoc's turn to receive her warmth and love and she never missed a chance to give him his share.

Kristina loved the moments with Old Ben. Her strength grew for time with him. She knew he'd be spending his last days here and for that she was grateful. He'd not be put down in the coldness of the shelter. The end wouldn't be lonely for Old Ben and that is what she worked for relentlessly. Kristina knew that there was a heaven and a hell for dogs. Heaven was after they left this world. For some this world was hell. Her mission was to try and end that hell. She could only take comfort that the Hell she fought against ended humanely for her efforts. After Old Ben sighed she'd always give him a hug. It was a hug of promise and thanks, and for Old Ben it was the reason to live even as those days became less and less.

The unfinished conversation from dinner was always continued after the Ball tossing. The Man and the Man with old hands along with the Woman would sit on the porch and dote on the pup making their noise and sipping their drink. The smell of cigars burning during the coming darkness always came with the laughter the people all shared. Old Ben never knew a time like this, nor did he ever have such a purpose. He felt as though what was waiting on him would only be better than his time now, something in the Woman's touch gave him that sense his days were good.

Œ

As Henry didn't require much sleep he'd begun studying the bible before he went to bed at night. The reading was difficult but he kept after it. He'd picked up one of those bibles that contained instructions on how to read the books within the Old and New Testament. He referenced the glossary as he needed to in understanding the text. Henry kept a notepad near his reading and he penned questions about his reading that came to him during the reading. Typically he did this type of study whenever he read subject material that was confusing or difficult to comprehend. The notes he amassed weren't typical however. They were more copious than any notes he ever needed to write before.

Henry gave up two hours per night in his coming to know the words within the books. He began formulating some thoughts on his study and it led him to contemplation of the universal origin. Everything he read about science and philosophy before never really dealt with any type of religious mention. He came to understand was that he was ignorant of the abundance of philosophy within these discussions of religion. He also came to see that what he thought he knew about philosophy and science didn't amount to a totality of understanding he thought to possess.

The conversation he had with Francis that led him to wanting to know more about the bible was just as Francs told him. It was not a pick up read. The thought provoking implications he came to understand in the words he studied changed the way he looked at all things. Previously Henry thought that he was ultimately responsible for his own condition. The supernatural world was never a part of his thinking and now it was.

When Henry had enough study he put his notes away under the bible and gave Adoc attention. The attention he gave Adoc changed since the reading and study. Henry began to realize that his responsibility to the dog was more than what he figured during the time when Adoc and he first met. It wasn't merely feeding the dog or playing with the dog as a pet. Henry was beginning to see that Adoc might just be a gift that was intended from the super natural realm. He also realized that meeting Adoc wasn't just a random thing that occurred. The reality Henry faced for considering a higher power as being in charge of all things made sense in some ways, but in other ways it gave him a significant amount of confusion. Like all other times when he came to confusion he realized that clarity came through more study of the subject matter in hand. The directions within the King James Version suggested a fifty two week read to get through the entire text. It also mentioned that completely understanding the Bible was a lifelong endeavor and that at different points in life differences of understanding would come from reading and rereading the same words. Henry wasn't wrong in assuming that study of the bible was worthwhile but he was wrong in assuming that once read he'd be expert on the subject matter, as it was in other studies he engaged earlier in his life.

"Adoc, you don't know how sometimes I wish I could just chase a Ball like you do. I swear this book of God is the most difficult thing for understanding I ever came across before." He'd scratch Adoc's belly and then rub him.

"Don't worry there, buddy. I'll get through it, just like I do with all things, but it is just gonna take some time. You get your sleep now, pal. Tomorrow is another day of playing and chasing with Old Ben and doing whatever it is you enjoy doing." Henry would shut off his lights and lay his head down on the pillow. Then he would silently say words to a God he didn't know. He didn't know if he would ever know this God, but he was sure that his study would reveal clarity he sought. It had always worked that way for him before and there was no reason to not believe it wouldn't go that way for his study.

Œ

During the days Henry went about his volunteering at the shelter and when he had an opportunity to ask Kristina about his studies she answered him as best she could. She was actually very open to any discussion Henry wanted to engage and that was because Henry could converse while seeing to the jobs getting accomplished. For those times Henry asked her about the bible she really couldn't help him more than to say that her wisdom of the bible was based on what she came to know through reading the children's bible she read many years ago. Kristina didn't have the same hunger Henry had in wondering about the bible. She told Henry her idea of who God was as best she could.

"Henry, when I think of God I find him in the love animals have or want to have in being companions of responsible ownership. Think about Adoc, for instance. Think about his patience and his unconditional love. Think about his dedication to make you happy and for what, for a bowl of food? No he wants to be petted and walk along side of you. He wants to be the most important thing in your life and he'd likely die if it meant protecting you. That is how I guess I think of God."

The words Kristina used in her description struck Henry as beautiful, but simplistic. His questions about God weren't tied to the same need. Henry needed introspection and his undertaking of study was how he processed the complications of the vastness and diversity of the Bible. What he didn't know about how Kristina saw God would actually be his result of finding, or something very similar to how she understood God.

Henry didn't bring up more of his questions about the bible with Kristina; her explanation would suffice as she said it. He didn't know if she had any interest as he did in reading the books of the bible and it really didn't matter. What he came to know about Kristina was that in all things she did, her motivations never came from ungodly thinking.

Henry did take opportunities to banter his questions of the bible with Francis. For Henry's frustration, Francis would entertain the banter with him, but instead of revealing what was in his heart, Francis would tease Henry about his study from a proposition of devil's advocacy. Henry didn't realize that Francis actually enabled his study of the books in the bible immensely. He also didn't realize that Francis was ecstatic about Henry's desire to study the word of God. Francis wasn't going to reveal that to Henry though. Francis enjoyed being the devil's advocate. During the conversations before and after dinner Francis would provoke Henry in his forming understanding of what he studied. Francis was methodical at trying to disprove or debunk Henry's insights as he came to understand them. There was laughter from Kristina when the two would discuss the books from Genesis to whichever book Henry was reading. Francis would employ all of the atheist and agnostic commentary which was prevalent for the non believers.

In truth Francis was a very devout man in his worship of Jesus. But for talking to Francis one could only assume that Francis had no use for God and that the only logical result one could have about God meant that he was nothing more than a child full of practical jokes. Francis figured if he could present indignation of having faith in God, he'd motivate more folks to learn about God so as to disprove his own presentation of prophesied doubt. That is what he did with Mildred and he took great happiness in the furies of her condemning his blasphemy telling him that his end would be serving the devil's amusement in hell's eternity. In Francis' mind his gift of practical joker was the calling God wanted from him as it was an effective reverse psychology used in motivating people to know the type of faith he possessed in loving God. For Francis it was a perfect disguise.

He could live in faith of God's love by deed in all his actions and not give anything up to consideration of God until he prayed in his closet alone. By any who knew Francis they knew him as a man of integrity and proper living.

Kristina had an idea about Francis for knowing him for a time. She knew that most of what he argued with Henry about concerning his studies was all a joke. She knew of Mildred's fierce commitment to God and her reasoning didn't figure that Mildred would ever tolerate being married to a man who didn't have faith. Kristina unlike Henry had wisdom to Francis' motivation, but she enjoyed the pretense and Francis was quite humorous in frustrating Henry's study. Francis wasn't malicious and she enjoyed the back and forth. When Henry found his limit for the banter, he'd always leave the table or the conversation and invite Adoc to chase the ball. Per normal Francis always took opportunity for the departure.

"There he goes off to find the sum of creation. Man, Dog, Ball; The Holy Trinity incarnate!"

Henry muttered to Adoc about the crazy old man and both Kristina and Francis would laugh. Then Francis would say, "Yes, I can see it right from here; that is the Father tossing the Holy Spirit around to the Son just so the Son can bring it back."

Kristina would then begin clearing the table so as to avoid hysterical laughter. She thought that would put Henry over the edge. Francis would sit and watch both Henry and Adoc tossing the Ball along with Old Ben. When she returned to the sitting area she could see Francis and Old Ben as two fathers looking upon how their son's played nicely.

The image left her feeling a bit lonely as she saw it, but it was short lived. Old Ben would expect petting from her after she returned and he got it for the expectation. These were the close of days while the construction paused until the next hours of work. All involved experienced a fullness of life for being together none would have known had they not become like a family. The strength of that fullness for living was the result of an unspoken compassion. The exercise that built the strength came from the rituals they abided through the days trusting each other and loving on one another with respect and care of sincerity that was transparent. That fullness carried them closer to the goal they set for themselves and as life always provides difficulty that strength would be the unmentioned asset needed in realizing all that is required for attaining the goal.

Œ

A Man, a Dog and a Ball

The days of spring were coming to an end while the heat of the summer began strengthening the seedlings planted earlier. The colors of summer filled the fields and horizons with life while the creatures of Francis' farm thrived. No longer was the noise of nature the stark winds that buffeted dormant grasses and forests. There was a melody of nature's aliveness even in the stillness of the highest heat of the day. And during the evening when Adoc enjoyed the Ball toss with the Man, nature's evening always came with an orchestra.

The foundation of the building was complete and the framing was well under way for the structure. The construction specifications required more than the typical materials of any similar projects. Henry's intention was to have the building self sufficient. All the floors would be built with radiant heating, and the walls would be 8" construction rather than 4"-6". The roof of the structure would be built to support not only snow loads but an extensive solar panel array. The whole structure would also be utilizing a geo thermal installation dug under the foundations bottom level.

Henry also planned on installing a magnetic power generator. He was impressed by a company that ran its whole facility in Budapest Hungary using an EBM machine. It is based upon electromagnetic electricity generation. It was nothing that was known about to anyone in the area.

The distributor was located in Toronto, Canada and Henry figured the investment to be priceless. When the town folks heard about the plans Henry had there was quite the debate that ensued. Francis remained neutral in the banter. In his earlier days he was also the subject of the same type of thinking concerning the feed store. He actually thought Henry was an innovator and the world never really understood innovators, sometimes depending on the innovation the world wouldn't be so friendly for the change, but inevitably the world would have to accept the innovation as innovation was progress even if unrealized or unwanted. Henry had impressed the town for most of his days living, Francis figured he was still busy doing so and if the contraption worked Henry would be getting paid by the electric company for extra energy.

Kristina simply shrugged off the curiosity of Henry's plans by visitors at the shelter. When they asked her about his intention she simply told them that they'd have to ask him. None ever did and she was puzzled by that, but as she didn't have much use for knowing folks other than what her job required, she gave it little thought. Francis told her that most folks who had a deeply seated curiosity would do anything to satisfy that curiosity without actually going to the source. He said it was an innate self defense mechanism that prevented them from appearing as fools for their own curiosity. Obviously if they asked the person with the intention such as Henry, they'd not want to appear silly for asking stupid questions, so they danced around it. It occupied their time which was usually nothing more than gossip or just being busy-body know-it-alls. Kristina's fondness for Francis grew even though she knew his coldness. His explanations of why folks were the way they presented themselves was coldly funny as she heard them. It wasn't his coldness that changed, but it was her appreciation for him that did change. To her he seemed like a favorite uncle.

As the construction became more detailed Henry became more focused on working as a project manager overseeing the job. The crew that was doing the general contracting faced situations they weren't usually invested in performing. The crew's diligence however remained solid and Henry was happy to work with them. Some of the specialty crews were problematic in that they seemed to not share the work ethic of the general crew. Henry's cool kept things flowing, but the problems remained. As a matter of fact Henry's skills shined in keeping the peace between his crew and the specialty crews. The way he did it came by their readiness to work in the morning. Much of the work that did need doing needed required a morning meeting. Henry's ability to give the general contractor's crew a heads ups about what to expect did lots for the morale of the guys. They all bonded well over the time of work and Francis kept them motivated as well with morning coffee and his break time treats.

One thing that did change was the time Henry took in spending with Adoc. His willingness to toss the Ball for Adoc lengthened as the light grew towards the longest day of the year. Kristina noticed the increased time they spent together and thought it was good for them, but it seemed to her that Henry was spending the time for more than just bonding. Francis told her that even though Henry was a very capable man at just about anything he applied himself to, there was nothing like the pressure a man faces when building a structure. Francis told her that any man would immerse himself in the details of the thing that he builds, but their Henry did so beyond anything that the town thought to be normal. That along with the original focus was something of a pressure that Francis wanted no part of and she began to understand why there was a greater amount of time spent between Adoc and Henry. She spent her time growing closer to Francis' company and somehow she thought the time spent as more than satisfactory for difference.

She learned a lot about Henry through Francis and when she did have opportunity to be with Henry the wisdom she counted for Francis' insight seemed very worthwhile. After conversations with Henry the things that Francis gave her insight to always seemed to be validated. In that wisdom the coldness of Francis became familiar to her much like the crazy uncle appealed to her. Her relationship with Henry became more than it would have ever been if she faced off trying to understand his wisdom alone and for that she was grateful. She would have liked to spend more time with Henry, but his volunteering at the shelter and his living proximity was enough for his aloofness. It seemed that every day something else about her partner became revealed without his first person explanation. She felt in her very core that Henry was committed to what he was doing. For her desire it was enough, even though she thought she deserved more. She choked down her need to know more because it hadn't yet Become more than she could digest. The agitated reality she tried to sleep through was only neutralized by the wisdom of Francis. She decided that it would be her point of interest to corner Henry when he was doing his volunteering. In her estimation he spent well more time than necessary for how he managed the jobs given to him. She saw his diligence, but her curiosity was greater than any limit Henry could have attained. She systematically thought of how she would put him on the spot for interacting with her as a partner... she had a notion of her entitlement to see how he was thinking and that was her value of their partnership.

Francis gave her warning on her medaling, but he might have well had been trying to convince Mildred to go into where she was expected. Francis knew Henry was walking across a spider web of a woman's consideration. He also knew that there was nothing he could say to advise him or help him. Francis just stayed with Old Ben watching how Henry was going to manage it. It seemed to Francis that Old Ben saw the same thing coming. Francis didn't need to get sticky on being in the middle of what may or may not happen. Surely Henry was invested and even as Kristina was curious with the appetite of a woman involved, Francis would let it flow because he always knew when a Man was involved in his passion, whatever the curiosity presented may have been; a Man wouldn't allow it to derail him. Francis sat on his wisdom without speaking to it unless there was value to do so.

Kristina heard what he said and for it he didn't mind sharing it. For the most part Francis would just watch train wrecks happen. There was something different about these two folks though. They both always heard what he said and used his thinking to their own gain, even if it appeared that each of their own gain was a contradiction to the partnership. Francis was on a timeline. He never spoke to it because it really made no difference to him any way. Francis was coming to the end of his living days in the world he occupied. He knew it, Mildred confirmed it and these two youngsters that he developed such a fondness of were delivering it. It was clear to him that whatever it was he had to do was almost done. When the thing he needed to do was accomplished he'd pass on from this life to whatever was next. While he realized the end of his journey he took great possession of living. He entertained both Henry and Kristina along with Old Ben and the crazy pup Adoc that Henry had an ownership stake in. He figured that once he passed he'd join his Mildred and he counted as others would be counted. He had no worry for himself except for a possible guilt he'd likely not own. The thought of it was enough to give him worry and like most of the time he just figured it easier to give it up to God. Of all the material possessions in his world, none of them mattered much. They were to be given to the living. Most of them were tallied and left to beneficiaries, but it was something that would be coming from the lawyer. He didn't want to waste any time for things already mentioned and decided upon. He also didn't fear what was coming, but as he didn't fear passing on to be with Mildred he always loved the experience of living. His palette enjoyed the vintage of his years and he wasn't just ready to welcome his future. He knew there was an undefined purpose for his remaining. He knew that once he came to realize it that it would be time to leave life to the living.

Œ

A Man, a Dog and a Ball

In the darkness of night just before the coming of light Adoc lay awake on the floor of Henry's bedroom. He knew he was safe, but he also knew that outside there was something. His senses told him that whatever that thing was it was alive and it was close. He knew it wasn't likely he'd ever smell it during the day except in some ghostly vapor that slipped by along the wind. He felt as though the thing was foraging for food as he used to before he knew the Man. He knew how it moved, hiding in the shadows not making any noise just quietly loping through the softness of the waves that came from the ground. In that way he'd find something the world left behind to eat on the move, just keeping the hunger quiet until a more hopeful time of arriving upon a full belly. He decided to lay in quiet. The Man would be up soon enough so that he could go outside and get a better smell of the unknown thing that lurked in the same area that he and the Man tossed the ball.

He gave the dash outside a great anticipation as Old Ben would be able to come with him and tell him what that thing might be. If he thought that it meant harm he would have woken the Man to make him aware of the danger. But it wasn't like that; he knew the doings of the thing outside as he had done so many times himself.

The Man's breathing changed and soon he'd be getting up to meet the light. Adoc waited patiently even though he couldn't wait to investigate the smells of the visitor. Adoc silently rose from his lying position and moved to greet the Man's awakening. He didn't jump up on the bed in eager anticipation, nor did he let his impatience wake the Man. He did move closer to him in the darkness so his nose could smell the Man's breathing and feel it change for his waking. When he sat next to the Man his nose could taste the Man's breath and the only thing he could allow was his tail to sweep across the floor.

Henry's late morning dream receded by a noise that wasn't congruent to the dream. The noise was soft but rhythmic. It dulled the subconscious REM sleep and brought him through the birth canal of awakening from slumber. As he gained awareness of the morning the rhythmic noise took the form of Adoc's breath at his ear. The wagging tail along the floor below him and the moisture and noise of Adoc's breath gave him a smile for waking. Henry lowered his hand to Adoc's head and began petting him. Straight away Adoc lunged into bed and welcomed Henry to the darkness' departure. Henry accepted the licks and began calming Adoc down so he could rise from bed and meet in the kitchen with Francis and Old Ben to begin the day.

Henry arrived to a dark kitchen. Francis wasn't yet there which was unusual, but not so unusual to cause Henry concern. Henry turned on the kitchen lights while Adoc made his way to the door waiting for his morning relief and investigation of the evening's visitor. Henry hadn't taken more than two steps when Old Ben joined the crew. Henry greeted Old Ben and followed him towards the door where Adoc waited. Adoc's impatience earned him a growl from Old Ben. Henry looked towards the dog asking him, "Did you wake to a case of grumpiness Old Ben?" Henry petted him and reached for the door. The growl gave Adoc cause to back up and allow Old Ben his majesty.

After Henry opened the door Old Ben moved into the outside and stopped for a sniffing of the morning air. Adoc wanted so badly to get out but the growl Old Ben offered kept him in line. After a dedicated sniffing, Old Ben moved slowly outside. Adoc hesitated in watching Old Ben and reasoned that the thing he wanted to investigate was the reason Old Ben moved slowly. Henry needed a coffee and the dog's interactions didn't strike him as all that strange. He left the door open and began making the coffee he desired. As he filled the pot with water he heard Old Ben let another growl loose and a single bark. He shook his head figuring Adoc was stirring up trouble that Old Ben wasn't tolerating. After the preparation of the coffee as complete Henry took a seat at the table and waited on the brewing. It wasn't long before Francis joined Henry. He came to the kitchen and sat at the table with Henry.

"Good morning, young fella."

Henry replied, "Good morning, old man. Are you as grumpy as Old Ben?"

The question surprised Francis. He wondered if Old Ben was grumpy, or even how it was that he could be considered grumpy. "I can assure you that I didn't step out of bed grumpy today, albeit a later than usual start I am fine. I am not sure that dogs are grumpy either."

The coffee stopped percolating and Henry rose to pour two cups for him and Francis. As he poured the coffees he tried to articulate his conclusion of Old Ben as being grumpy. "Old Ben growled at Adoc when I opened the door this morning to let them out. Then after they got out Old Ben growled again and barked. I figured he was just a bit grumpy." Henry sat at the table giving Francis his coffee. They sipped on the coffee quietly until Francis figured Henry was awake enough to shed light on the growl.

Adoc walked with Old Ben through the fields as the light came back to the world. He wanted to run and chase the scent but Old Ben wouldn't have it. As they walked Old Ben warned Adoc of having too much interest in things he'd come to know without seeking those things out. He told Adoc that there was such a thing as a nose full of trouble and if he didn't realize that, there might be no more times to get a nose full of anything. Adoc listened to the warnings. The things coming out of the forest making noises were fearsome and looking for food. He listened to Old Ben tell him that the Man would be better able to manage those fearsome things and that it was his job to wake the Man when he knew of trouble. Adoc listened, but he wasn't hearing. It wasn't that he didn't trust Old Ben; he did. It was more like his need to know exceeded the reason of being respectful of things unknown. Old Ben knew that flaw about Adoc and he did all he could to contain Adoc's urge to find unwanted trouble. The oversight was not easy for Old Ben, but it was better than where he was just days ago. He would have much rather spent the days with the Man with Old Hands waiting on his generous gifts of things to eat, keeping his pace of life. As it was Old Ben realized that he'd meet that gate keeping a watch on Adoc. As difficult as chasing youth was, he was grateful in not spending his days alone in that cold place.

"Henry, your pet owner skills have improved greatly, but you still aren't hearing what the dogs mean." Francis sipped on his coffee as he watched Henry listen to his comments. Much like Adoc was listening so was Henry. Francis knew Henry might still not being fully functional so he tried another way. "Okay, you heard Old Ben growl. Now let me ask you this: When do you hear Old Ben make any noise?"

Henry responded truthfully, "Old Ben doesn't make much noise at all, he is a quiet type."

Francis smiled as he had Henry's attention. "That's right. Old Ben is a quiet dog. So when you do hear him growl or even bark what can it possibly mean for hearing it?"

Henry sipped on his coffee considering the question. Francis saw frustration in his pondering, but let him think it through. "I don't know, Francis. Maybe he is telling Adoc to stop being a pain."

The men sat quietly after the exchange. Francis was being very careful with his leading Henry to more insight because this is when pet owners tended to just throw up their hands and figure that knowing the dog's needs was impossible.

"That isn't a bad finding. Your conclusion suggests that Old Ben is conveying a message to Adoc. Even better is that you don't know. I guess I'd give you a 'C' for the lesson." Francis knew that Henry's sense of perfection was the avenue he could employ to motivate him so as to heed the insight he wanted to give him. Henry wasn't at all happy about hearing that he got a 'C' grade for his consideration.

"A 'C'? Are you kidding me?" Francis looked at him shaking his head.

"Nope I wouldn't kid ya about such a thing." Henry heard Francis and became indignant. Francis knew where Henry was and understood his desire which demonstrated disdain for his grade. Francis also knew that in a few seconds the sun would be peeking over the horizon and it would be instrumental in leading Henry to wisdom he hadn't expected for waking.

"When Adoc is biting and chewing on Old Ben, does Old Ben ever turn nasty towards Adoc?"

Henry thought about it. He shook his head.

"So then a growl and a bark wouldn't be an indication or warning of *stop being a pain.* So what else might the bark or growl mean?"

Henry thought about Francis' question. It almost seemed that he wanted to answer a few times, but all he could do was shrug. Francis could only laugh at Henry's shrug. For the laugh Henry's patience wore close to thin. Just as the sun broke and fell on the top of the tree line Francis had one more comment for Henry.

"Henry you never had brothers or sisters older or younger, and you were always too smart of a kid growing up to have an adult chastise you for doing something incorrectly. Now keep an eye on that tree line just towards that north corner."

Henry squinted to find his focus on the area Francis directed him to observe. Francis rose up to get the coffee pot and refilled both cups. After he did he put on a new pot of coffee as Kristina would be joining them shortly.

"That dog Adoc is still a pup and he is a lot like you were, without the support system of a town. The difference between you and Adoc is that the wilderness is what he survived to be what he is today, but without his siblings and without a bitch mother he didn't learn things that you were taught growing up. You see he has the call to investigate all things of nature without the protection of experience."

While Francis spoke Henry saw through the foggy mist on the field a herd of deer making their way back into the tree line. It was a large herd numbering eight. There were three adults and five youngsters as he could make out from size. Once Francis saw Henry's discovery he told Henry to remain focused on that area where he deer left the field. "Be sure to listen to what comes from inside the woods."

A few moments later there was a distant snorting and something that sounded like crashing along the floor of the forest. Then a type of scuffle and a screeching became audible resulting in silence. Henry looked at Francis with a surprised face. Francis sat back down with Henry.

"You counted eight in that herd. That is what ya said, right?"

Henry nodded in affirmation.

Francis sipped on his coffee. "Tomorrow you'll only count seven, maybe less."

Just as the light began dismissing the fog on that field Henry saw his own light for what the growl and bark meant for Adoc.

"Now Henry, you may realize what the bark and growl meant for result, but what Old Ben was telling Adoc was more than what you just came to realize. You see if Adoc's curiosity put that buck of the herd on the defensive, well Adoc would be laying out in the field all gored up. That wouldn't even be the worst of it. The coyote or wolf that was stalking that herd would then be having Adoc for breakfast. You see Henry that forest out yonder is teeming with life as nature intended. Where life teems, death always lurks and there are many ways to die, some are worse than others."

Henry sat in silence contemplating the first lessons of the day. Not only did he learn a truth of nature he hadn't known, he learned something even more frightening. As an adult he'd become attached to Adoc. It was the first attachment he'd known. Because he hadn't listened to the bark properly his Adoc may have been taken from him. Henry accepted the gravity of the lesson and understood the importance of his new awareness.

Francis could see that the light bulb went off above Henry's head and remained silent. Then he rose to start the cooking for the morning. Kristina would be there anytime and the crew would be looking for his motivations for the day. Francis knew that he moved closer towards being with Mildred because he felt her watching with an unspoken satisfaction. The day had begun and Francis was well satisfied in Henry's growth at the earliness of the day.

Œ

After breakfast but before Henry and Kristina gathered up stuff to leave Henry called on Kristina with a request. He wanted to know if she thought it would be alright to bring the dogs to the shelter and let them play with the other dogs. She thought about it for a few seconds and mentioned to him that the vet would be there for the morning and if an adoption or two didn't happen that they'd have to put a cat and a dog down. Henry heard what she said and figured it was not such a good day to have the dogs over there. His countenance must have showed his disappointment.

"Maybe tomorrow, I'm sure that will be easier all the way around." Henry smiled for the positive answer of a different day. His nature was impulsive that morning in realizing his misjudgment about the barking. It was no reason to make the day tougher than it was already scheduled for being. Both settled on the next day for the question he asked.

Francis wasn't so far out of earshot that he didn't hear Henry's question. When they reached the conclusion Francis waited on speaking to Henry. Kristina collected her things and made her way out to the truck, Henry would take his own car.

"Henry, you are a quick study, but I know you have heard me say that once or twice. The point is that you're a good man, better than most I reckon. You get urgency to something and you don't let it get away from your thinking; you sure don't let it become more important than what is at hand, and son... you have your hands full." Francis turned back to his doing but continued. "Old Ben and Adoc are sorting some things out the way dogs like those two do. Your relationship with Adoc will work itself out in time so don't be too anxious to make your Herculean burden more than it is."

Henry listened to Francis' wisdom and took it with him to the chores that needed doing at the shelter. When he pondered Francis' wisdom he worked through his frustrations methodically. In the past he used to manage several issues simultaneously with better than satisfactory results. Presently he put his efforts towards an implementation of a plan that was completely different than his old ways. There was less satisfaction because of the lacking turnover of results and Henry was learning to accept that. He thought that he could realize more satisfaction working with Adoc, but as Francis pointed out his expectations weren't practical for raising a dog. Henry's contemplation of his frustration didn't prohibit his cheerful manner in volunteering at the shelter. Once he was invested in his work he went about his duties like any other time he was there. Kristina was busy with the vet so there were only brief interactions with her until he was done with his charge. Before he departed the vet and Kristina ran into some difficulty with one of the patient/residents. For one reason or another, the anesthesia given to the dog they worked on didn't keep the dog immobile. Kristina had asked him to help restrain the dog while they could administer more sedative. Henry lent his efforts to their trouble and took hold of the dog's legs. He avoided looking at the area of work as best he could, but the dog's excitement required focus that made examination of the internal gut of the dog unavoidable. Henry hadn't been an operating assistant before and the view of the inside of the dog wasn't a pleasurable experience for him. He stood strong even though his own gut weakened. Moisture gathered on his brow but it wasn't from exertion. It was rather the type of moisture that accompanied acrid salvation build up in the back of his throat. The kind that followed with inevitable regurgitation reflex, he swallowed more as the moisture on his head increased.

Kristina saw the discomfort Henry was experiencing and told him it wouldn't be much longer. As she applied the sedative the dog became relaxed which lessened the need for Henry's assistance. She told him shortly after that that he could be excused. As Henry turned away his limit of restraining a vomit reflex seemed to have been crossed and he fought the urge with great diligence. Ultimately he got to the sink and began to consume cooling water that settled his stomach. The water he splashed on his face rinsed away the slime of sick sweat that had just started to sting his eyes from the tiny droplets that ran into his vision. His breathing also abated the reflex of upchucking and in a few moments he enjoyed a better composure for the assistance he gave. Kristina and the vet continued at their work while Henry took his leave from the procedure room. He wanted to leave the facility, but his need to return to the construction would have to wait until Kristina was available to speak to, he had a few things he needed to run by her before he could leave.

Henry walked through the pen area that he previously cleaned while he waited on Kristina. Each of the dogs was given focus as he passed them. While he pet them he thought about his squeamishness and wondered if it was something he could overcome. He laughed at himself considering that the future would require much more of that type of thing. Once the facility was built at Francis' property and they moved the operations of the facility, Henry could envision himself in more frequent and similar capacities. As he offered the dogs attention, he wondered what it would be like after the construction was completed. In the plans they included a state of the art operation room that would be able to see to the needs of all animals in the area. He thought of larger animal surgeries such as cows and horses and ended that line of thinking as the queasiness returned. Henry supposed that he'd engage in the help he could and avoid the procedures as he could. It had been a long while since he tasted the acrid salvation in his mouth and he wasn't a fan of the sensation.

Ultimately Henry's progress in giving attention to the dogs led him to an older female that was in their care. Her disposition wasn't one that matched up with recent adopters. She was one of the dogs that might be getting put down later that day. As he greeted her he experienced a helpless sense of pain and despair. As he pet her he wondered about her years and if she in fact had any pups. She received his attention without any disagreeable displays. She seemed to appreciate Henry's touch, but he could feel her willingness to surrender. The despondence he encountered for the interaction overwhelmed him more than the earlier need to vomit. His new urgency was to depart from the shelter as soon as possible. Henry was caught in a futility. If the facility they were building was complete this poor dog wouldn't have to accept the fate coming later. Henry wondered if Francis would have a problem with accepting another dog. He'd wait till he got with Kristina to see what she thought regarding his thinking. If she thought it to be a good idea, he'd discuss it with Francis. They may stay the dog's execution If Francis was okay with the invitation. He left the futility with the dog and moved along the line. It wasn't much longer that he spent with the dogs before Kristina joined him.

She asked him if he was okay and he responded positively. As he planned he asked her about adopting the female dog and what she thought. She didn't say much for her own thinking about his inquiry except to say that Francis was the man to ask. He understood her rationale. He asked her if she thought she'd need any more of his time and she didn't think that would be necessary. Henry walked out of the pen area with her towards his car. He told her before leaving that after he discussed the thinking with Francis that he'd call her to let her know one way or the other and then drove back to the ongoing construction.

After Henry departed Kristina took a moment to think on Henry's question. She wondered why he'd choose to make a point of asking her about bringing the older bitch home. The dog didn't seem to have any characteristics that anyone appreciated and as far as she was concerned the euthanizing of the dog was one of those duties of the job. She didn't feel any type of particular fondness to the dog and that was validated towards the adopter's unwillingness to see any worth for taking in the old bitch. She wrote the dog off as a goner the minute they captured her. Kristina's curiosity of Henry's desire stuck with her all day long. She was hopeful that Francis would be willing to agree, but she still kept the procedure on the schedule. She wondered what Henry saw in the dog that she may have not seen.

Henry returned to the construction site just as the morning was ending. The progress the crew made was evident for examination and that gave him an appreciation for returning home. After he got out of his car he anticipated the dogs to greet him, but the anticipation became a thought of where they might be, or what they might be doing. He walked through the kitchen door as Francis was preparing the afternoon goodies for the crew. Francis took notice of his entry with an animated smile. "Back from your usefulness in God's delivered reality?"

Henry thought the question was asked weirdly. "Indeed, I am back. Now I return to strange doings."

Francis chuckled for his response. He returned to his preparation as the time for the crew's desire grew closer. Henry had a need to use the bathroom, he didn't know if he'd do anything more than wash up, but he made his way there thinking on his supplication to Francis about the dog. After he closed the door he sat on the commode. He decided he didn't need relief. But he did look into the mirror over the basin as he turned on the water. Splashing the coolness upon his face he decided upon his return to the kitchen he'd ask Francis straight away about the dog. Henry figured that he'd get that out of the way. He didn't want to have it in front of him while he engaged speaking and interacting with the crew. Henry turned off the water and dried his face. His need to ask Francis about taking the dog gave him hesitance he noticed while peering into the mirror looking at his countenance. He left it behind as he opened the bathroom door walking back into the kitchen. Francis was deliberate in his detail to his preparation. Henry saw that there was a few moments before all he prepared would be delivered outside.

"Francis, I wanted to ask you if it would be trouble to take in another dog, she's an older bitch and it seems that nobody wants her."

Francis heard his request and smiled while he continued in his finishing off the last bit of preparation. Once he did he turned to Henry. "Are you able to lend a couple of hands to feed the hoodlums busy at seeing to your insanity?"

Henry stepped up to Francis' direction taking up plates he could manage with both hands. After Henry took up the goodies Francis grabbed the remainder.

"Let's go keep the riff raff motivated properly." When the men exited the house they were met by none other than Old Ben and Adoc. Francis greeted both of them with soothing words. "Oh, you two adoptees are about to get an older sister. How is that gonna change your food interest and worse, who is gonna get the favor of the lunatics you already know?" The men walked to the gathering crew. The dogs followed with great interest.

"Henry, I don't care if you want to bring another dog home. Soon this place will be yours to manage. I am here to assist you in coming to realize that. I said my goodbyes a long time ago and I am just waiting until Mildred works it out. For all I care set up dog condos with chain link fence."

After Francis said his piece he stopped in his stride. He looked at Henry and suggested that with the new need of a new dog placement. He might just want to have some fun with the crew to crack the whip of motivational production. Henry heard the suggestion and gave it some thought. Francis saw that Henry was uncomfortable with the advice and smiled about Henry's ambivalence. "Don't worry, Henry, leave it to me."

The men walked to the summoned crew and presented what Francis prepared. As the men participated in the receiving the offering Francis made his announcement. "Okay, you rapscallions, there is a concern that puts itself right under your backside and it is the concern of the materials manager. Later today we will be adopting yet another mooch that will nag you for the beneficent offerings I provide. That means you lowly scallywags are either moving too slowly in accomplishing your duties or you just enjoy teasing the four-legged royalty that will soon abide here rather than be made dust into the wind. Now, I am available to prepare the needed morsels of the material manager's generosity, but if you ask me…. I think you are just having a vacation at employment here, and if it were me… Well, I wouldn't stand for any of it."

The foreman laughed out loud. "Francis, you are one mean old codger. You have men working like dogs and dogs stealing the earnings of men. I think ya need a visit to the spectacle doc, so you can begin seeing just what it is that is happening around you."

The men laughed while they consumed Francis' offerings. Francis turned to Henry and gave him a peevish look. "Do you hear the disrespect for the cook, Henry? Do you hear it?"

Henry just shook his head. The interaction between Francis and the crew was absolutely perfect. Francis had responded to his question and gave the crew a reason to be refocused to what was at hand in a foolish manner of welcome. Each of the men took turns offering bits of the goodies to both Adoc and Old Ben while they ate. Henry decided that as a materials manager he'd make a supplication to the crew in the vain that Francis spoke to in admonishment. Henry waited until the men on the crew settled into serious consumption and then fulfilled the preparation of Francis' rebuke.

"Guys, when I was at the shelter doing the volunteering today I almost lost my stomach in assisting on a surgical procedure… I am a bit squeamish." The men laughed, but none interjected. Henry continued after the collective chuckles. "After the duty of almost losing my breakfast I went out to visit the penned dogs and came to an old girl that made it clear she was ready for the END of the day." Henry looked at the ground and for what he said there wasn't a noise from the group. No chewing, no breathing, no offering food to the dogs.

"I want you all to know I see the dedication you have at getting this project done and it is remarkable. The thing is this old bitch I'm bringing home tomorrow will be here because of your dedication to the end result. But she won't be the last. So while I sit here and explain my motivations to you, I hope you understand why it is that you are all busy. This isn't an exchange of money for services rendered; this is a battle against the inability of former owners to take care of dogs that'd otherwise be put down for a willful negligence of our collective charges as being human." Henry quit his talk, feeling like he could say nothing more as the dog's advocate. The foreman walked up to Henry and took him aside.

"Hey, bossman, I heard your compassion. Don't you worry about a thing. You bring that old bitch here and she'll be fine. We'll also be mindful of your intention in all phases of this project. I already know one aspect we can pick up production in dealing with the specialists." He winked and looked at his watch. Then he returned to the group and allowed them the average of time for the break. Each of the crew shared less exuberance for the remainder of the break. It wasn't a limiting type of display, but rather it was a type of considered departing of frivolity. They really heard what Henry said and responded in their own contemplative manners. It was clear to Francis that these guys would work like they were earning overtime. They would do so even if the reality was a pay cut because Henry had transformed their collective motivation. They weren't there for a paycheck anymore… they were there because of need they could respond to and it was a righteous need.

Francis saw the dynamic that was occurring. In seeing it he loosed up the tension.

"Ah, Lord have mercy that is what you get for pointing out the obvious… Who'd think a bunch of roustabouts could find an inch of compassion in motivation for an unwanted dog? Why, oh why didn't I just make shinola on a shingle and toss it away?"

The comment gave the crew a great measure of laughter. And as the laughter ended the men returned to the work at hand with a new passion. Henry took up with the foreman on the side before he left.

"Whatever we can do to get this project in ahead of any more killings at the shelter will be rewarded to each of you on top of the compensation we agreed upon. Do you understand me?"

The foreman smiled at Henry. "There is no need to give them any more distraction for the moment. What I can tell you is this: the next time I need a motivator on a project deadline I'm coming for you, Henry. Whatever you see fit as extra is your reward to each one. I am not even gonna bring it up. To do so would make the inspiration you just seeded them seeds that never took root." He smiled at Henry and turned back at the crew. "What the heck are ya doing? Do you want to tell your kids why it is there are no pups at the shelter when they want puppies or are ya gonna see to the new farm's construction so that any of your troubled offspring can go ahead and torment a dog who'd otherwise be kilt? Get to work, ya silly ladies!"

The crew offered up a disapproving grown without saying anything. The construction began and the pace was a new sound to the environs. It seemed that the entire wilderness paid attention in quiet silence. After Francis and Henry cleaned up the breaks remains Henry thought a stretch with the dogs might be a good idea.

"Interested in taking a walk with the dogs, Francis?"

Francis stayed after to cleaning up of the dishware. "I'd love to but the food store needs some oversight. Why don't you give Kristina a call and let her know that she can avoid that nasty business and bring the new four-legged royalty home tonight? Then enjoy a stretch with the dogs."

Henry listened to Francis and did as he suggested. As Henry hung up the phone he realized that the directions to bring the old bitch home gave Kristina a sense of relief and ease. He heard it in the way she spoke to him after the directions. That gave him a reason to be happy. He enjoyed it briefly as he walked outside to call on the dogs. They joined him as he paced past the work area towards the fields in the back. As he walked he lost himself to gazing at Adoc harassing Old Ben. He wondered how they would be with the new addition coming. He didn't give it too much thought, the dog's antics kept him amused. Henry walked in the fields before, but this time he wanted to do a more extensive survey of the property. While Henry approached the tree line he took notice of a change in Old Ben's manner. The dog seemed to become more aware of his surroundings and even more watchful of Adoc's curiosity.

Henry recalled the words Francis mentioned about how dogs get to doing dog things. He figured that Old Ben's change of manner was a way dogs communicated without speaking. Adoc seemed to be mindful of Old Ben as they proceeded. When Adoc got too interested in one thing or another Old Ben put himself between Adoc and the tree line. Once or twice he snarled at Adoc for getting out of line.

Henry studied Old Ben's guard. He saw the hackles on his back rise and remain that way for the entire walk along the tree line. Old Ben's authority kept Adoc from investigating his curiosity. Henry gave thought to what Adoc was so focused on as he avoided scolding from Old Ben. Henry saw the trails of herd traffic and if there was deer coming through these trails it might also be likely that predators also moved stealthily along the trails. Henry sensed Old Ben becoming stressed in his deliberate vigilance. He began walking away from the tree line which seemed to relax Old Ben. The further away from the tree line they walked went to soothing Old

Ben. His hackles receded and he became less interested in Adoc's doings. As the dogs went back to the companionship gate they paced normally. Henry figured he'd set down with Francis and pick his mind on these back woods of the property. Henry knew Francis wouldn't offer up information if there were no purpose for the revealing, but in this instance, Henry's curiosity of the woods and tree line served a purpose. The mentioning of Old Ben's behavior and Adoc's desire to investigate past Old Ben's guard made it a worthwhile conversation as Henry would be overseeing the Property. When Henry returned to the work sight and house both dogs kept each other busy romping as they did. The conversation with Francis would have to wait as Francis was seeing to business of the feed store. Henry also responded to some more questions the fore man of the project had concerning issues of the new technological inclusions of the work. Henry wasn't troubled by the assistance required even though he wanted to have that conversation with Francis. The guys never did installations required by Henry's design. He expected to be involved and his frustrations never came before the work.

Œ

In the middle of Francis' mentoring his new employee he experienced a strange sensation. In all of his years he never encountered such awareness of a daydream. A daydream was what he called it, but he was sure it was more than that; he just couldn't know the word to name it. The awareness wasn't frightening to him. It was more of an easiness that flowed through him. It seemed nothing more than the coming to the end of a very difficult day. Almost as though the pains of going beyond a need; seeing to an end meant all the sense in the world. It was almost a supernatural motivation. The sensation Francis experienced gave his employee a need to ask if he was alright. It was plainly observable.

Once Francis found his gravity he assured his charge that he was okay. He said, "It is probably just one of those senior moments and it was nothing to worry about." He said so with an authority so as to maintain the airs of an unneeded concern even though it was appreciated. When Francis was through with the mentoring he took his leave by mentioning he'd be up at the house. For his mention all seemed to be fine and business at hand was resumed. As Francis took the steps he'd known through the paces of the years; he couldn't remember any time in which so much energy was dedicated to getting to his porch. He would have rather been climbing his way through the worst and coldest of blizzards he knew throughout his life.

His legs and feet worked against no prohibition or obstacle; rather it was a mind over matter type of difficulty he faced. Summoning his legs to move seemed impossible and for the effort of the summer beginning he began to sweat profusely. He had no pain in his chest, nor was he dizzy, he just felt as though each step was an escape from sucking mud of a swamp as he stepped forward. It seemed to Francis as though the land was holding him. When he arrived at the porch he was grateful that both dogs were playing about in the yard. Seemingly, they were unaware of his arrival. He couldn't figure why that was because the dogs had always greeted him previously. Truthfully he didn't care. He was glad to have found his favorite rocking chair for reclining. His breath was labored, but he couldn't feel an explosive pulse as he expected. After a few moments Henry took notice of his presence and Henry seemed to have a desire to include himself in his company. Francis watched him work through his departure from the crew by following up on directives. When Henry had conveyed an understanding between with the foreman; he began walking towards him sitting in his rocking chair. Francis noticed that the dogs paid immediate attention to Henry moving towards him and took a moment to think of that as strange. *Why was it that the dogs didn't notice him as Henry did?*

As Henry approached Francis he experienced an angst he never knew. It was wrapped in unimagined loss for something he couldn't place losing. It smelled of doubt and the distance past seeing Francis felt like doom. Henry kept walking and he figured his legs were being pushed ahead by the dog's who chased after him, otherwise he might have just stood still in the newness of this new sensation analyzing what it was he faced. His pace didn't change moving towards Francis, but his legs felt as though they became heavier for the stepping. His focus sharpened as he walked closer towards Francis. He noticed Francis' perspiration and fatigued look and figured that maybe Francis had exceeded his ability in working at the feed store. As he moved towards Francis with dogs in his pursuit he took notice of Francis' countenance and began feeling relieved. The old man was alright and his new sensation was probably just nerves for the construction… That was his reflection in avoiding a childish concern that Francis may have noticed on his approach.

"What did you end up doing, Francis? Some real work? Something like tossing around feed sacks?"

Francis smiled in a vague sort of way. "Nope, nothing like that. My work is just a bit heavier than tossing product… I have to consider just how youngsters are going to carry on in the good will of a stubborn old man… Such a thing isn't what a pup has to think about." Henry knew Francis was lying through his teeth, but as a stubborn old man he placated him.

"Yep, one thing I've noticed about stubborn old men is their greed for nostalgic youth." Francis smiled in the retort of his wished to be son. Before Henry could take a seat Francis asked, "Be a dear and fetch us some wine, will ya?"

Henry didn't expect the request, but affirmatively responded. He went into the house while the dogs sat at Francis' feet gathering up Francis' request. It seemed a bit unusual to Henry that they'd be sitting at that hour of the afternoon having some wine, but it felt right. When he returned Francis waited on the pouring of the beverage. Henry saw to the duty at hand and took notice of Francis and the way he sat.

"Are you feeling okay, Francis? You seem a bit off."

After Henry poured the wine he sat before Francis could respond. Both men sat looking beyond the dogs and through the construction. Francis told Henry his capacity of the past few minutes. He held his wine in the glass much like a toast and began. "When you are my age very little is a surprise and sometimes when things come to you they seem more like a relief than a fright." He took a sip of his wine and continued. "I no longer have purpose in this realm I can count of my own... my experiences are more than a lucky man could ever claim and all I can do is wait on when God Almighty figures my work is done."

Henry heard his piece and sipped as he could to keep measure with Francis.

Francis continued while gazing at the dogs. "There are things that you'll need to know and I will tell you of them. My time is growing short for being here and quite honestly the time is way too late for my liking."

Henry wasn't happy about his current disposition, but he was relieved that inquiries of his immediate curiosity wouldn't need any extraordinary prying. For the realization Henry needed another wine and Francis was waiting on a refill. While Henry poured another he mentioned that he wanted to know more about the tree line. He mentioned to Francis just how old Ben was uneasy about Adoc's curiosity concerning the tree line. Henry figured that there was something Francs could offer him to explain the circumstance.

Francis pulled on his wine with delightful recollection. It was a time of living in mystery for Francis; he was a young man when he came to know the secrets of the forest. The delight in mystery was built upon of foundation of tremendous toil and labored futility at the time, but for all the sweat and disappointment Francis was definitely alive. Francis looked to Henry with a wickedly youthful smile. For Henry's witness it seemed as though Francis's appearance transformed itself in front of his very eyes. He looked as though he was a young man with a boyish secret of revelation into manhood. Francis sat back closing his eyes recalling Henry's inquiry as though it was a required confession of yesterday's doings.

"After the war and after I returned home the economic need in these parts was all but forgotten about. There was no work and it seemed like all that had been going on before the war found itself a new home for business or commerce. We literally had nothing going on, but many of us had our entire life's investments here. In other parts of the state there was a need for timber and all sorts of material for construction. My pappy talked it over with me and figured we could make something out of nothing by cutting off wood on the property. As far as anyone knew his idea was one of the better ideas in these parts. I gave it consideration and decided we were gonna be wood cutters. Now mind you, I never wanted to be a part of any of that type of work, but when nothing else was gainful, we had to settle for what was available." Francis sipped more on his wine to empty it; Henry poured once again supplying lubrication for Francis' telling.

Henry watched Francis as he told the story of his past and became immersed in the facial mannerisms of Francis' story telling. He could see the tight frustration in Francis' lips as he described the beginning of timbering without a clue. Then he could see the satisfaction of watching Francis speak to the wisdom of hiring Canadian carpenters looking for work only to take up timber cutting.

"When we decided we didn't have a clue as to how to cut off timber for profit we found ourselves in town wasting money for our effort only to see a bunch of hard drinking Canadians asking about carpentry opportunities while they spent their savings. My father being a shrewd sober man approached the seeming to be foreman of the group and said he had some work that wasn't carpentry. And after my father had a second beer with the Canuck they shook hands on a crew of timber jacks that would show up the following morning."

Henry felt at ease with Francis revealing his youth. He felt at ease because Francis truly seemed to enjoy savoring the moments of recollection. He felt more confidence in coming to know the history of the property he would own shortly... It was a rarity in any property transfer, attaining such a history.

Francis requested that Henry would take a moment and get two cigars for the afternoon relaxation and Henry did so. After he returned and both men had ignited the smoking distractions with refilled beverage vessels, Francis continued.

"The next morning before our time of waking we were abruptly woken up by a drunken band of wild eyed Canucks hollering at the moon getting into fist-a-cuffs with each other as though it was an offering of first serve coffee and each man standing to the compass of the fire was first in line. The noise and racket these fellows made woke the livestock and all heck broke loose when mother woke suddenly. My gosh, it didn't seem as though my old man could escape her wrath fast enough. It seemed like he was running by my bedroom door fetching a bucket of water to put out a fire on the barn hollering to me to get out of bed." Henry noticed something about Francis' recanting that seemed to give him an absolute gratitude for the memory. The gratitude he embraced lent him to reliving the hysteria both his parents obliged for the day. Henry couldn't imagine knowing such a deep recollection. He almost felt jealous of how Francis relived it. He knew the cigar and the wine were appropriate for such a conversation. He knew so because he'd never heard or seen such animation of the past before. Francis continued.

"By the time I had followed pappy out to meet the crew it was clear to me when I saw them that they had fun in beating the heck out of each other probably more so than they did taking up the work of the day and by that day's end I had realized that as tough as I imagined myself to be for being in the war, I was sure glad I wasn't battling these fellas. I swear Henry they were the toughest bunch of men I ever saw in any of my days. They were also the straightest drunken men I ever knew to pick up a drink. Those fellas drank all day save a cup of coffee with lunch that mother brought out defiantly." Francis looked at Henry. "Mother never like Canadians, she always said they were heathens, or cowardly patriots who knew no better as they lived under the British Empire." Francis finished off his wine. His perspiration had abated since sitting down and some of his color was back. He shook his head thinking on what his mother said about the Canadians. "Mother said to old pappy he'd be the biggest fool in town for hiring such hooligans and that she'd be the one regretting it. She was infuriated!" Henry saw the delight of a young man taking aim at launching a torpedo at pappy. Francis broke through the pause of expectation for his mother's attitude in telling of his father's counting of the day's work.

"At the end of that day Henry, my pappy took it upon himself to be a humble genius in mentioning it would take six men from town to move the landing of wood those drunken Canucks built up on a day of cutting." He smiled with the self satisfaction his pappy would never reveal. "Henry I swear my mother was so full of disgust for being wrong about those hooligans that she didn't say a word I heard for a week to my pappy." Francis laughed to himself. Mother always hated when pappy spoke to the defense of our northerly neighbors." He looked to Henry with a wink. "It was one of those types of priceless jabs pappy took at mother in a loving fun manner that absolutely made her insane." He shook his head. "I guess old Pappy knew in bringing it up he'd be in the dog house for doing so. Poor Mother couldn't resist the desire to be like a dog getting a nose on a bone." He smiled and laughed in his recollection. "Mother used to squat on an egg bringing it to hatch long after the hen gave up on it for rotten." About that time Francis figured to be feeling fit and he stood up and went into the house. He took a usual pace and the dogs became aware of him for his motion. He returned with a few hunks of beef jerk and put them on the table. After he did the dogs took an interest and moved towards the sitting area. As Francis put the jerk on the table it meant it was for communal consumption. He began chewing on his it looking at the dogs. Henry refrained from temptation knowing he'd grab up a piece shortly. As Francis masticated some of his jerk he continued with his telling.

"By the end of the week those Canucks had cut off half of what you see cleared today. Pappy had to employ half of the town to get the wood to market and he was just making a profit on the venture. I was working with those crazy carpenters and listening to their stories about how they actually had to cut off wood before they became carpenters. I watched them deliberately cut down trees in the direction of their friends for end of the day brawling." Francis shook his head. He looked at Henry and winked at him. "Henry those were days when I thought telling the about getting shot at would earn me an after work contest of toughness." He shook his head. "I wanted no part of any of that." Henry found he was empty of drink and stood up to pour another. He felt the effects of the wine consumed and steadied himself for the pouring. He poured Francis to full and after he sat down, Francis suggested that he have a bit of jerk. Henry picked up on his forgotten temptation and began gnawing on the jerk. Francis took up a piece of jerk and broke it to two then offered a piece to each patient dog. After everyone was settled, Francis continued on the story of the wood cut. Most of his anecdotal telling was over. It came down to procedural detail of telling. What Henry learned was that in the second week and towards the limit of cutting the crew began to diminish. In fact Henry learned that the line that remained was the line that Francis himself cut off a whole year after the Canadians had departed. To Henry's dismay Francis told the end of the story without giving reason to the departure of the Canadians. When Francis had realized Henry's observation he puffed on his cigar and pulled on his wine.

"Henry, I am still not sure what those Canadians' reason was for quitting the work, but as far as I can realize they were mostly native Canadians who held to a history and lore of the folks who were here before the white settlers. They say it was something about the forest of lost purpose. That is the best translation they could offer."

Henry looked at Francis with a profound disbelief. "The forest of lost purpose?"

Francis nodded in serious response. Henry couldn't believe his ears or the explanation Francis gave. Henry contemplated the name Francis had told him. He couldn't get past the notion of a forest having a design on purpose. He wondered more about it and finally had to ask Francis if he wasn't joking.

"Francis, I'm having a hard time getting my head around a forest with an intention. Is the forest of lost purpose real, or are you pulling my leg?"

Francis looked at Henry. His gaze was steely. "The forest of lost purpose is as real as the cigar you are smoking." Francis gave some thought to how he'd convince Henry that it was real. He realized he was wasting his time for considering an argument that would be convincing. He never spoke to anything but the plain truth and he wasn't going to start now.

"After that crew of drunken Canucks left I thought their superstitions were gone with them. But to be honest with you finishing off that existing tree line stymied me. And I never once before came to such a result in my life. My Pappy thought I went crazy for continuing on the intention of selling wood. He said, Son you have no idea how to cut wood off even as those Canucks showed you the business." Francis shook his head in reflection. Henry listened as he went on with his telling.

"The forest of lost purpose consumed me. I thought I'd keep the wood coming because I convinced myself I could. The lure of profit became my motivation and it was all in front of me. Each time I planned on bringing the wood out something didn't seem to go right. Either a tree fell wrong which put the production in reverse, or a tool broke or failed. It seemed as though I could realize all my efforts resulted in disaster." Francis laughed at himself and smoked more of his cigar. "It seemed that the only luck I knew was bad luck. It kept going on like that until I looked at the cut area from inside the woods. I couldn't figure out what it was that was going to happen with all that cleared area. When I walked to the clearing there were only a handful of trees left to cut which would make a fine straight line and that is when I knew making that line was going to be the end of it. We worked on those trees and they fell perfectly, for the first time in all that work something finally went right, but it wasn't until my purpose of making money for harvesting timber was lost." He sipped on the last of his wine and waited on Henry to pour another for him. After both men sat and sipped on the wine Henry knew that Francis' testimony was his reality of the past. He was convinced that Francis believed it to be true. Henry wasn't so sure that he'd believe the notion of superstitious tendency and Francis saw it as soon as he thought it.

"I understand your skepticism and I am fine with it. Here is another thing you might want to consider. I gave thought to what to do with that field and I tried several different crop sowings. I say tried because I never saw one intended harvest. After some years beyond my Pappy's passing I came to realize that his last words to me would haunt me as long as I designed a profit from that land. Eventually I gave up on the notions I had for the next year and let me tell ya, the town folks had quite a laugh at my doings." He smoked more of his cigar in silence Henry did the same. Henry looked at the tree line thinking about Francis' conclusions. He wondered whether or not his feed store was a concern before or after the cutting off.

"Francis, let me ask you about the feed store, was it a concern you built before the cutting or after the cutting?"

Francis turned to Henry and simply answered, "After."

Once Henry heard him he asked Francis another question that followed logical progression. "Why do you think the feed store worked when other enterprises yielded nothing?" Henry thought the question might have stumped Francis, but it didn't.

"Do you remember that I said those Canadians were natives?" Henry nodded and Francis continued. "Well the natives of these parts embraced what they called magic with the land, meaning that they were very in tune with natural law. They claimed they could ultimately conjure the spirit and energy of the land for purposes of their own, and one of those drunken Canadians who held out to the end revealed the intricacies of the magic utilized by the elder natives. He told me that when they saw the round eye pale faces exploding upon the land the elders of the tribe knew that the round eye pale faces could only be stopped by what mystified them or what they didn't understand. So knowing that their fate would come to an end they summoned magic from the land and told it to never allow the one thing that the round eye pale faces wanted from the land. He said, they commanded the spirits to confound the invaders by making them forget their purpose for everything they wanted that the land could offer. That way, the thing they loved and called home would always be there even after the round eye pale faces lost their reign of the land. Then it could be returned to the native generations yet to come." Francis looked at Henry fully expecting him to tell him that he was pulling Henry's leg, but hoped that he would see beyond that. Henry in turn didn't really speak too much unless he was sure about anything he processed.

"Well Francis that is one remarkable story if I ever heard one and I believe you to be sincere in what it is that you believe, but I don't have belief one way or another. Also I can't speak to something such as native mysticism. I don't know it to be true or whether it can be disproved. This is one topic I remain ignorant about and I won't formulate any thoughts on things I don't know about, that is just one of my rules." As Henry finished up he took notice of Adoc and Old Ben fixating on Francis. Their focus was sudden and simultaneous and as Francis saw them take notice in his direction he also heard his Mildred mention to him to make Henry known of her feelings when she was part of the process. Henry's focus went from watching the dog's curiosity to the smile developing on Francis' face.

Henry felt as though he was at a loss. Something was happening he wasn't privy to and he wasn't sure if the remarkable story Francis told him short circuited his ability to perceive or whether it was the wine consumed or both together. He was sure that for Francis' smile more explanation was about to be heard and his surety of more explanation was delivered.

"Henry, Mildred just told me to tell you what her reaction was when I was coming to know that the forest of lost purpose was real and I think it may be what you need so as to avoid studying native mysticism." Upon hearing what Francis told him he held his head in his hands shaking his head. He couldn't believe that Mildred was there offering more testimony in helping him see the truth of the forest of lost purpose. Henry felt as though he was in the land of lost sanity.

"Yes, Mildred. I am going to tell him, just you keep a tight lip. Can't you see the man is holding onto the last of his wits?" Francis smoked on his cigar waiting on Henry's attention. After Henry looked up to meet Francis' focus Francis began. "Back in the early days when Mildred and I were coming to know each other as man and wife things were different than they are today. Now I told you that Mildred and I never knew anything other than to be with each other, but it took some time to get there and that was due to the way things happened back then. So Mildred and I had a time of courting as it were and I was fully invested in earning a profit in bringing that wood to market when everyone else had given up. Even my Pappy thought Mildred to be touched for still wanting my hand in marriage. As it was she was more determined than I was to being my wife than I was determined to make money rather than be a husband. All the while I was focused at the business of making money she'd come on over here from town after her bit of work to come let me know that the town's betting folks were making odds on a day that I might have a wagon load of wood. She gave me the odds everyday as she heard them from the town folk and she began to get steadily upset at her being made fun of for wanting to be my wife. After a while she told be in a furious dressing down that the town folks were now giving odds on the likelihood that she'd give up on being my wife." Francis filled another cup of wine and offered more up to Henry. He declined as he hadn't yet finished his. Francis returned the jug to the table and sipped on his cup.

"Mildred was about as mad as I ever saw her and she finally came to give me her ultimatum. She said to me, *Now you listen to me Francis, we have always known we were meant to be, but if you don't quit this foolish notion of yours you are gonna give the agents of usury an ability to profit on my condition of patience and then those old hens looking down their nose at church will have reason to name me a woman of less than flattering status within our community. As I haven't yet consummated a marriage betrothal to you I will not stand to be associated to scurrilous lies because you are too stubborn or just plain stupid to realize what even the local idiot knows about this cursed property. I'll give you to the end of this week to collect any wits you have left in that so-called head of yours to finish up this nonsensical thinking before I refuse to return here anymore!* She stomped her feet and turned right around marching herself back to her parents house leaving me about as blindsided as one might be for getting kicked in the head by a disagreeable horse wanting to avoid a day's work in the field. That was the first time I heard my Pappy say that he thought Mildred finally arrived at a sensible thought in a very long time." Francis finished his detail of impersonating Mildred's dissatisfaction. That is when both dogs cowered down and turned away from the focus they had on Francis. When Francis saw Henry wonder about their shying away he chimed in once again.

"Oh don't worry about them, Henry. They're fine. Mildred is arguing with me rather fervently I might add, she is telling me that my version of what she said is wrong and that my consumption of wine makes me just as I was trying to figure out whether or not the forest of lost purpose was real or not. She says the wine makes me senseless and she can't understand why I have such an affinity for the libation." He giggled to himself as he sipped on the wine. Henry figured he was enjoying aggravating Mildred while she was visiting. Henry had heard all he could stand to hear. His doubt before hearing what Mildred had to say was greater than any that may have remained, but he heard enough of the forest of lost purpose.

"Francis, since you started that feed store business after the cutting off and subsequent periods of non growth sowing I'm assuming that running a business from the property isn't part of the lost purpose curse; would you agree?" Francis laughed at the question. It wasn't a ridiculing laugh or any type of responsive laugh other than a laugh of something he thought to be humorous. Henry was glad that Francis thought his question to be funny he asked it seriously.

"Henry, I still don't know if there is anything to those superstitions the natives were said to have made a curse on the property. I can't say I believe or don't believe. I had a better reason to give up that work than to worry about such things and I took Mildred's ultimatum to heart. I wasn't making money and I was about to lose what I took for granted for being stubborn and greedy. It wasn't a choice I had thought to make, but it sure was the easiest choice I decided upon. I guess sowing those crops was a second and third crack at proving to my worth at being able to earn a living off the land. It was something that always kept in my gut, because I always heard my Pappy say the only sense I had was the sense God gave to men in knowing four-legged wisdom." Francis smoked more on his cigar. It was burning down to being extinguished. "I guess you wouldn't recall much of what your father said to you, but even as you love your father growing up, when your Pappy says it about you, there is always a tendency to prove the old man wrong." Francis looked at Henry and finally answered his question.

"I'd agree that the curse of the lost purpose doesn't apply to running a business, but I sure was the dope whose efforts proved any validity of the curse of the forest of lost purpose, and that was on account of my tendency to know animals more than I knew about the earth or its bounties." Francis stabbed out the cigar and finished off his wine. He sat up in his chair and told Henry that he was off to lay down for a bit. He said he felt like a bit of rest before dinner. Then he was gone into the house. Old Ben followed Francis inside. Henry sat with Adoc for a bit finishing his wine. When he was done with his drink and after he finished his cigar, he told Adoc to get his ball. Adoc heard the command and his tail began wagging. It was getting near quitting time and the guys were winding down the work. When Adoc returned with the ball he dropped it at Henry's feet. The two began the ritual they were fond of in doing. It was time for Man, Dog and a Ball. The foreman had some things he wanted to run by Henry and when he saw him tossing the ball with the dog he figured he'd wait till the next day of work. It was nothing pressing and it could wait. He turned back got in his truck and left the work sight. Tomorrow was coming soon enough.

Œ

Henry and Adoc threw the ball until Adoc began sniffing for a bowl of water. Both walked back over to the porch where he and Francis sat talking and consuming wine. Henry saw to filling Adoc's bowl with cold water. Adoc waited patiently and lapped away his thirst after Henry placed the bowl for him. The ball toss with Adoc gave Henry a simple function which required very little thinking and contemplation. After hearing all that Francis said Henry was thankful for the simplicity in the toss.

Francis told him many things and some of them he could have gone without hearing about. The willingness of Francis to mention that his time was short was exactly what Henry didn't want to think about. The effects of the wine they consumed also helped Henry avoid any more consideration of what Francis told him, but as he watched Adoc lap his thirst away the spoken word loomed in his head. He knew that in a time coming he'd have to figure on it all and there was too much to the figuring for Henry's liking.

Henry was glad that Kristina was pulling up the driveway. He figured any discussion on her mind would advance distraction from the inevitable consideration he faced. At least he thought that is how it would work out. When he and Adoc greeted Kristina for her arrival she took notice of Francis' absence. When she asked Henry where Francis was she listened to his explanation and once Henry was done with his answer Kristina frowned and went directly inside to check on Francis.

Henry remained on the porch alone... Adoc joined her in seeing to Francis' condition. Henry felt as though he was missing something. The doubt that came with his wonder wasn't pleasant. Henry never liked surprises and he figured surprise was on its way. His instincts weren't wrong and when Kristina returned it was clear to Henry that she wasn't happy about something. Henry wasn't happy that Adoc wasn't following her either. Kristina took a seat where Francis sat just a while ago and waited on Henry to join her. After Henry sat as he did when Francis was there he saw Kristina had something on her mind and she was trying to figure the best way to bring it up. After waiting on her to figure out what she wanted to mention, Henry broke the ice. "Seems like you didn't have such a good day. What's the problem?"

Kristina gave a simple reply. "Oh, it was the usual day of realizing that no matter how much I work at something like trying to save animals, I only realize that for all of them I can't. Euthanizing them is just an uncomfortable part of the job." She stared at the job sight and Henry knew that she hadn't yet come to the source of all that she had a concern for. He thought about what else he might ask or say to lure her to speaking her mind. Before he could she asked him a question. "Tell me something, Henry, did you find Francis' morbid nature unsettling?"

Henry sat shocked. He couldn't understand how it was that she would have knowledge of what Francis discussed earlier. He gave up wondering how it was that she knew, there was no point in it. He gave her an answer. "I don't know that I would call it unsettling, to be honest I avoided thinking about it while Adoc and I tossed the ball." He shrugged for the telling.

His response gave Kristina a reason to consider another manner in which to convey her worrisome dissatisfaction. "How do you suppose that I knew to ask you about Francis' propensity to be morbid?"

Henry realized that responding to her question with a smart or a cute retort wouldn't be helpful. He caught himself before a flippant answer passed his lips. "I imagine that for knowing him before I did and while Mildred was alive might have something to do with that prescience." He hoped that his answer wasn't something she'd consider as being a point of contention. He studied her and it seemed as though her attitude changed for the better.

Kristina was aware that both men had consumed wine and probably a good amount of it. She saw how Mildred and Francis interacted when he drank his wine before and she never liked the interactions when they happened. She wanted to avoid arriving at a similar condition with Henry. It wasn't as though they were married, but they were invested in a business as partners so she felt obligated to mention her concerns because partnerships depended on honesty.

Moreover Henry responded to her inquiries with a rationality she didn't expect. Her assumption was that he'd be less thoughtful for an afternoon of drinking with Francis. She proceeded with her concerns.

"Henry, when Mildred was alive both Francis and she had issues with his drinking his wine and the morbid nature he experienced was associated to his drinking. It wasn't any type of impossible condition for them, but Mildred seemed to be extremely concerned with it." She looked to the fields and thought about why it was important to make Henry aware of this aspect of history. Henry waited because he in fact avoided considering Francis' troubling comments about an end coming soon. For a moment he thought she would continue, but it became clear that her interest in discussing history that he didn't know lost importance. When she was done scanning the fields she looked at Henry and said, "Let's forget about it, none of it matters all that much I suppose. I guess the day was tougher than I thought after all." She lowered heard head shaking it. "I hate putting animals down."

Henry was short on any comments that he thought would comfort her immediately. He thought about what he could say to comfort her. He figured that the old bitch that was supposed to be coming home with her was included in her last statement. He considered asking her about it, but held his question. It appeared to him that she was moving in the right direction and he didn't want to give her any more reason to think of the day or any part of the day. He was sure that such an inquiry would deliver moroseness to a day of hope and expectation that would be inescapable. He would know tomorrow during his chores if he was right about it or not. He let it be.

"Yes, I recall you saying that it wasn't your favorite part of the job." He gave more thought to her mood and then he had a moment of brilliance. He'd get her to focus on the job sight and speak to her about days when the only time they'd have to put down an animal would be when it was the humane thing to do.

"Kristina, why don't we go look at the work done on the property? I usually find that when I experience a condition I can't change, it is always better to imagine a time when change would be possible." He stood up and waited on her to rise from the chair. After she did he turned and walked towards the construction area. They stopped a few yards away from the already poured foundation.

"This is going to be a place where you'll never have to kill animals because of space." He looked at her as she gazed over the job in progress.

"Henry, when this is done it will be a fine time, but until then I have to deal with doing what goes against my moral code." She frowned for the time between standing there and its completion. "How many more will have to go down before all of this is done?"

Henry considered her question. "Well one thing is sure; the number will be less for our efforts here."

Kristina looked towards Henry. "I guess that is one way to look at it." After she spoke she turned to him and asked if they had eaten, Henry shook his head. They stood a while more looking at a future long overdue, at least for Kristina. Henry thought about the question of dinner and indicated that food was a good idea. They headed back to the rear entry moving into the kitchen.

"Kristina, why don't you go get cleaned up, I'll start on dinner. Besides I am sure Adoc and Old Ben will likely keep a supervisory eye on the process."

"Okay. After today I feel like a good washing off, I'll leave you and the lads to sort out the cuisine." She turned and made her way upstairs.

Henry began retrieving food that he'd be preparing and when the dogs heard the noise they decided to take their places as supervision taste testers for Henry's cooking. She began her walk up to the bath listening to Henry cajole the dogs about making dinner. The darkness of her day began to release its grip on her focus. In the loosening she thought about the construction and just how it would change so much more than the heartbreaking euthanizing of neglected animals.

As the warm water flowed on her body, she lathered up the list of other things which bothered her considering animals. There was such a need for rescues. Human advocacy for animals was now seeking out the horrors of puppy mills in the south. With this facility they might be able to ease the load of finding homes for those rescues as the public scrutinized irresponsible breeders. Her mind considered many other sources of cruelty to animals as she knew them and by the time the filth of the day was rinsed away her emotional condition had greatly improved. She was disappointed with herself just a bit for letting her duties command such an off-setting attitude.

As she dressed for dinner she embraced a gratefulness she wasn't sure she knew ever before. She thought on her way down to join the guys that she'd be more mindful of that gratefulness.

The dogs took notice of her rejoining them and it was plain to see that they were happy for her return by their tail wagging. It was a change from the way they sat watching Henry as he worked at dinner prep, they weren't showing much more appreciation than staring at him in pathetic anticipation. A dropped morsel of food was what they hoped and counted on. Kristina noticed the plates on the table needed setting and she decided to see if Francis would be joining them. She peered into his room and found him lying is his bed on his side. She moved closer to him and heard his breathing. She tapped lightly on his shoulder. After a second or two he woke and turned his head. His eyes were glassy and Kristina figured an afternoon of wine might have something to do with that.

"Francis, I am setting flatware at the table for dinner, will you be joining us?"

It took Francis a moment to consider the question. "I suppose I ought to eat something tonight. It will save me aggravation later on this evening. Yes, I'll join you in a bit."

Kristina nodded and left him to join them when he was ready. When she returned to the kitchen she began setting the table. She let her heart grow towards the loving way Henry made dinner with an audience of her favorite animals in this world. When the table was done being set Henry took notice of the seating. He frowned and looked to the dogs.

"Oh no, nobody told me Francis was going to be eating... looks like you guys are gonna have to beg off Kristina to get his portion in kibble."

Both dogs lay down with saddened looks. She took the lead and called the dogs to bowls where they ate; she began filling them with kibble and looked in the fridge for additional bits to toss in the bowls. When she finished up she teased the dogs for a bit before she lowered the bowls for them. They began eating the food with tails wagging. Adoc was done before Old Ben and as soon as he was done he found his spot away from Henry's work space. He waited patiently. Old Ben was more of a slow eater. He had a manner about him that worked well in the scheme of things. Adoc's puppy hood was tempered by Old Ben's mentoring if such a thing could be said about dogs. After a while Old Ben resumed sitting at his vacated place before the offering of kibble.

After Henry took notice of the dogs resuming their spots he shook his head and glanced at Kristina. "Thankless bums they are, not even a thank you lick."

Kristina smiled for his joking of the dogs. She was never happier than when dogs of a good nature were part of her life, and she hadn't had any pets recently. The work was just too much for such a dedication of time for pet ownership. It had been a while since she could just enjoy having the company of two good dogs. Henry saw the radiance in her face. It was a change from when she got home.

"Apparently the washing for the day away agreed with you."

She smiled at his mention. "Well, I took some time to consider what my partner told me about the future and I came to find a reason to be happier thinking on that future."

Henry listened as though she were revealing an unknown bit of info for the sake of his observation. "Wow, that sounds like one heck of a partner you have there."

She giggled. "Well it is a new enterprise and as it is such I am learning about all of his good qualities, it takes some time you know?"

Henry turned and then shrugged. "I guess. I never had a partner before so I'll have to take your word for it." He turned to finish up the food prep. The food smelled good and once again Kristina felt good about eating a home cooked meal. She decided to keep the banter going.

"Well, it isn't an easy thing to come to such a decision as to enter a partnership, but sometimes in this life you just have to ask yourself if what you have going on is how you want it to be. For me I was tired of working at a job where I couldn't fulfill myself for the doing. I had to ask myself if partnering up with another I didn't know would allow me to find fulfillment in what I did. That is another thing... he sure is a good salesman and he has a vision." Henry finished up his prep work and began turning off heat where it was no longer needed. He turned and said,

"Now that sounds like sounds like pretty good thinking. I guess I never heard a better motivation to take on a partner. You must be pretty good at what you do if you partnered up with a visionary."

Both were surprised by Francis joining them. He walked slowly with a stupid grin on his face. He smelled the aroma of food and then made a comment. "Usually when I hear banter as I heard, I'd feel as though I was a fifth wheel on the wagon, but that food has a powerful draw and I'll just be an intruder I suppose. Don't you mind me. You just carry on with that sophomoric wooing, I'll feed my face and entertain the dogs." Francis grabbed up a plate and made his way over to the newly cooked food. While he loaded his plate he looked at the dogs scooping extra food on the plate. "You boys better stick to my side of the table, I ain't sure that either of them will have any time to notice your ravenous hunger while they are making googly eyes at each other." Francis made his way back to the table and took his seat. The dogs followed him to the side as though they understood his specific directions.

Both Henry and Kristina were used to Francis joking with them. Even as he did joke Kristina delighted in the humor, but felt an awkward truthfulness to his humor. She hadn't much thought about anything but having a business partnership with Henry, but as it was growing she did have to admit, she was very fond of Henry and just as being grateful was new, so was this fondness she felt more and more by the days.

Henry was curious as to why Francis kept harping on the romance thing. For Henry the presentment seemed like a nagging that was unneeded. Henry's plate was full with all he had going on and he had no idea what romance meant. He understood what marriage meant for other folks. Much of his former business dealt with married people. The knowledge he captured about marriage was that most folks found the marriage to be problematic. It struck Henry that folks may not have thought things through before they engaged in such a relationship. Sure it all sounded good at the first consideration, but at least to Henry's observation, what sounded good in the beginning became very difficult as time went on and usually the result was devastating. Henry followed suit for getting his portion of food and waited for Kristina to seat himself at the table. When all were seated Francis offered up his usual prayer. Henry became more comfortable with the praying as his reading of scripture continued. Kristina didn't have any problem with waiting on a prayer to eat. She wasn't invested in prayer at any time in her life and she welcomed the change. As far as she knew life was getting better and prayer was new. Francis' prayer was always short, so it never became a grind. Once he finished all said, "Amen."

Francis knew that both Henry and Kristina never considered praying in their lives and he knew why. Neither was ever introduced into the world of worshipping God and that was fine. As far as Francis was concerned ignorance of anything wasn't good for a reasoning being. As he realized for the void he'd do his part of evangelism. He always figured making a decision about thinking was best done for knowing the thinking.

As they began eating Henry and Kristina ate silently. They also paid attention to Francis' antics with the dogs. Both realized that Francis' wisdom with dogs was unique. Henry was always a student of things he didn't understand. He studied with diligence that rewarded him. He was becoming an owner unlike other owners of dogs who might have taken offense towards Francis' ability to get dogs to behave as he did. Kristina had no lack to Francis' abilities, nor was she an owner of either dog. She was a keeper of dogs and anytime dogs were well cared for she remained euphoric for being a witness. If Kristina was in charge of the worlds' interactions with dogs, Francis would be the Czar overseeing the absolute way life was lived concerning care of dogs. Henry paid close attention to Francis' subtleties in the way Francis talked to the dogs. What amazed Henry was the link between Francis and each dog on a one-to-one interaction all while Francis balanced the audience. Both dogs must have felt as though they had Francis' undivided attention. As Henry watched he gleaned slightness of voice inflection, gentleness of gesture and most of all retaining the dog's focus in a mesmerizing way. Henry wanted to know how to apply such wisdom and by the day, he grew in understanding how to act with dogs, much like he understood more about scriptures as he read them.

There wasn't much conversation during dinner. Francis lived up to his promise while Henry studied Francis' methods with the dogs. Every once in a while Henry would look to Kristina with an awe that suggested asking a question, *Did you see that?*

Kristina gave nods when he did letting him know that she did witness what Francis was doing with the dogs. She also stole glances of Henry while he was watching Francs and the dogs and came to understand that her fondness about him was largely due to how Henry became excited about learning and how quickly he applied what he learned to his immediate behavioral patterns. Her experience left her having interactions with a lot of folks who possessed genuine love for what they did, but incorporating new skill sets for that loving sincerity wasn't an abundant asset of most. What she was coming to know about Henry was that he consistently broke down problems, needs or impossible situations to their lowest common denominator. Once he peeled away all of the layers of the issue he implemented actions and thoughts that made problems or difficulties nothing less than strengths or assets. The other thing she marveled at thinking on was Henry's ability of owning those strengths and assets so that they were like a tool collection he regularly used and applied to similar circumstances he already mastered before.

Neither Henry nor Kristina grasped what Francis saw in their future. He had offered hints to what the inevitability was, but that was all he could do. He knew they would have to grow towards their ultimate partnership and he figured that at some point Henry's study of Scripture would point him to what was yet to come. Mildred was insistent on more explanation of the ultimate marriage of the two, but Francis denied her supplications. He knew of Henry's upbringing. He understood that Henry had good support from stand-in parents. He knew Henry earned unconditional love, but he also knew Henry had very little knowledge with intimacy of Love. Francis understood implicitly that Henry's strength came from the pragmatism of men's logic. He was graced by man's generosity, but he hadn't grasped the source of that generosity. He was sure Henry had a capacity to learn such a capacity from study. He would come to see how all the evidence within scripture would leave him as a believer. Once that happened there would be no need to point him towards God's notion of Man and Woman's purpose. One thing Francis did know about was contaminating process through forced thought. He had no intention of any such meddling concerning either Henry or Kristina.

When dinner was done Francis began cleaning up the table and the dishes. Scrapings of leftovers were consumed by the dogs and once certain of them as last offerings they turned attention to Henry and Kristina. Adoc had been well exercised so his contentment was as observable as Old Ben's. Kristina, being well fed and cleaned up for the day was yielding to the toll of the working day. Henry could see that exhaustion was creeping into her consciousness. He invited her to sit on the back porch and she agreed even through a yawn. She mentioned it would be a nice way to finish the day. Both sat facing the twilight fading. The coolness of the night returned from the absence of sunlight while nocturnal orchestra's silenced the clamor of the day. Stars were presenting themselves in abundance offering untaken wishes of the two watching. Both were silently content with dogs at their sides watching darkness conjure the need to sleep. Kristina finally succumbed to the exhaustion as Francis had finished his cleaning and joined them on the porch.

Henry wasn't long to follow Kristina, but he did have a few questions for Francis. He figured sleeping on the answers would serve him well. After Kristina said her goodnights Francis asked if Henry wanted to participate in another glass of wine or another cigar. Henry declined and Francis helped himself to his own inclination. After he returned he asked Henry what his interest was.

"Well I had some questions about the study of the scripture I'm reading. I thought I'd ask you about some type of clarification if you don't mind." Francis heard his question and gave great thought as to how to respond.

"Henry, all I can do is listen to your concerns. I'm not sure I can offer any wisdom on what it is you seek, but I may give you alternative ways to find resolve in scripture as I understand it. You see Henry what all men must realize in study of scripture is the notion that it was told by brilliance of absolute knowledge. How we reason that knowledge is the mortar and bricks of faith we hold, or it is the wind and sand of doubt and skepticism we subscribe to concerning our need for faith."

Henry appreciated conversations with Francis; it was hard not to understand his meaning when he presented an answer and Henry wished it always went like that.

"When I read the scriptures I wonder how it is that there are so many different interpretations of the books in the bible concerning the followers of Christ. I can't get my head around how many denominations there are that all espouse they have the only version of the word. On top of that how it is that Catholics or Mormons can also claim authority of what the word is exclusively? Does this make any sense?" Francis laughed aloud. Henry was patient for the laughter, but Francis realized that Henry's politeness wasn't something to be taken for granted. Francis finished his wine and put the glass on the table.

"Humor and old fool and fill us again would ya?" After Henry returned with Francis' drink including one for himself both men toasted. After the toast Francis gave his answer.

"Henry, there is a trinity of the God Head regarding Christians, are you familiar with this concept?" Henry nodded, "Yes that is the Father, The Son and The Holy Ghost." Francis smiled for the affirmation.

"Okay we are presently in the Church of the Holy Ghost, God's church existed as the Old Testament, and The Son's Church existed while Jesus lived. So that leaves us with the last." Henry followed Francis's line of explanation.

"Now as told in the Church of the Holy Ghost in the first letter of Paul to Corinthians Chapter two Paul speaks to the inability of man to know the wisdom of God. When you study those scriptures you will have a better understanding of what you can't get your head around. It will also explain to you the diversity of churches claiming to know the word. Here is something else to consider when you think about Catholics and Mormons and Jews for that matter. There is no wrong way to come to know God as long as you understand the implication and reason for Jesus' resurrection and in all cases of dogma you will find those who know that faith through Jesus and those that claim to know faith through the dogma serving Jesus. There is a huge difference. Remember Jesus said, *One will not know the father except through me.* Now in the history of the Catholic Church and the Mormon Church greatness of generosity is known to Man by those who know Jesus in each Dogma. There is also great wickedness of the two for those who serve the dogma following Jesus. Now as Mormons are largely a product of recent times they haven't risen to the evils of say the Catholic Church. As a matter of fact there is a misconception of Mormons as the occult for the dogma which embraces polygamy by one faction of Mormons. That is a mistake of observation. What many don't know about Mormons is their very quiet response to natural disaster. They respond with an army to many of these difficult times with a body of do-gooders that is very well supplied and very organized and they do so without bringing attention to the generosity. So they may even be closer to Divine wisdom for not letting know the left hand know the business of the right hand." Henry heard Francis' explanation and filed it for consideration. Francis watched Henry and could see that he was formulating another question. He waited while sipping on his wine.

"What about the Jews?"

Francis turned his head and shrugged his shoulders.

"What about the Jews?!" Henry seemed confused and reminded Francis of his inclusion of Jews while speaking to the Catholics and the Mormons. Francis laughed heartily.

"I guess then I'd be one of those that Paul spoke to in Corinthians. You see the church of God was the authority before Christ and His people were the Jews…. Even as the Jews killed Christ, Christ forgave them, so that goes back to what Jesus said about getting to the Father. Are there Jews that believe Jesus was the Messiah? I'm sure there are those Jews who in their own hearts think of Christ as God, but the orthodoxy of Judaism doesn't believe that Christ was God… I guess that will have to wait on the days of judgment." Henry considered what Francis said and sipped on his drink.

Francis saw Henry's confusion. "Think on it this way Henry those who claim to be believers who serve the dogma's of faith are usually the ones who make the faiths exclusive. Those who serve Christ within the dogmas are the believers that make the dogma's valuable in God's word." He giggled to himself. "Those dogs at your side who worship you have none of the questions you have; they accept you as the authority like a child takes to a parent's love." Henry thought that Francis's cleverness deserved a toast because for all Francis imparted to the question previously asked the reference to the dogs made the most sense to him. After the toast Francis asked Henry a question.

"Henry, tell me what part of the Bible are you reading and tell me what part of it you haven't read."

"I'm finishing up the Old Testament." Francis made another inquiry. "So I take it you have not read any of the New Testament?" Henry shook his head to indicate that he hadn't. Francis looked upon the stars and breathed deeply inhaling the night air.

"If I were you Henry, I'd put the Old Testament down for now and read the Gospels of the New Testament." Henry was surprised and asked Francis why he offered him that advice. Francis looked at Henry with a face that was void of emotion he previously displayed. Francis' face became almost unrecognizable to Henry. The words that flowed from his lips even had a different sound than Henry expected to hear.

"You must know the words of Jesus, who defeated death in resurrection and realize that you know Jesus as God by the Church of the Holy Ghost." As soon as the words ended Francis' appearance that Henry knew returned to him. Francis was thinking to say more on something they just talked about. "It seems to me Henry I recall in scripture reading from the Gospel of Matthew that Jesus may have hinted on how the Jews would be dealt with. Let me think... Matthew 12: 30-32 Jesus speaks to blasphemy. That is why you should read the New Tesament. Study on what Jesus said." Francis lifted his wine and winked at Henry before he finished the last of it. "Now maybe you'll want to sleep on all you've heard." Henry was a bit taken back for his perception of Francis, but did agree to the suggestion.

"Yep I think that is just what I'll do. I'll sleep on it. Goodnight Francis." Adoc stood up with Henry as he made his way upstairs. Both retired to Henry's room leaving Francis and Old Ben sitting on the porch. Old Ben took a seat next to Francis which earned him gentle handed petting. They sat for a time as the constellations of the heavens kept watch on nocturnal activities of earth in darkness.

Œ

Henry and Adoc made ready for bed. Henry looked at Adoc thinking about what Francis said as to Adoc and Old Ben's simple desire to please him. He stroked Adoc for quite sometime. Henry thought about life before Adoc, he wondered how he ever made it through the living. Just as he saw transformation in Francis' face he relived the moment he met Adoc. He felt a vast sorrow in realizing that he was seconds away from nothing, from the end of living. He wasn't even sure if what he felt was sorrow, it almost felt like regret. He thought about the coldness in Francis' face when he spoke the words of why he told him to read the New Testament. Henry decided that he was very uncomfortable for seeing that face and as it came upon the moment he met Adoc his regret turned to shame. The memory came from his childhood when he had an accident in his pants. He was unable to make it to a bathroom and the embarrassment that followed was what he remembered as impossible to face. He remembered crying over the incident and before he knew it, he realized his eyes filled with tears stroking his friend Adoc. Adoc must have sensed the change in the Man's reality because he rose up from the floor and began licking on the tears coming from Henry's eyes.

Adoc licked away with gentle deliberation. Henry felt compassion and worry coming from Adoc. As crazy as it seemed for him to give Adoc human characteristics, he was certain that those attributes he gave to the dog were as profound as natural laws applied to weather fronts colliding and producing rain or electrical discharge. Henry began hugging on Adoc. Adoc's tail began wagging while he continued to lap up Henry's tears. Henry realized that he was tired and that any reading tonight would be better left to tomorrow. He broke away from Adoc as his tears stopped and got ready for bed. Once ready he decided Adoc would sleep with him that night. Henry realized relief from the shame and regret and it came through the value he found in this dog of his that interrupted what Henry knew as a bad choice to even consider. Adoc's presence even helped him to avoid thinking about Francis' lack of emotion for his advice. As he fell off to sleep his curiosity drew him to a desire of the words of Jesus. His sleep was sound and renewing.

Œ

    Adoc shared a bed, as a matter of fact this was the first time the Man made a bed his place to sleep. Adoc had always been very comfortable on the cedar chip pillow and he wouldn't have thought to sleep anywhere else, but the Man acted strangely. He didn't know why the salty water came from his face and it gave him some unease. He hated to think that the Man might have something wrong. If the Man wanted him to sleep on the bed with him Adoc could ignore the comfort of his pillow. As Adoc lay on the bed with the Man it became clear to him that the bed was as nice as his pillow if not nicer. It wasn't a commanding thought for Adoc. Adoc was listening to the Man's breathing like he did every other night. He thought that the breathing might give him an understanding of why the Man acted strangely. Adoc lie next to the Man feeling his warmth and noises the Man's body made while resting. He ignored the noises that the darkness was filled with; his job was to be with his Man. After the Man's breathing resumed a usual rhythm his attention softened while he thought of his favorite thing to do, chasing the Ball when the Man threw it. He wasn't enjoying it too much, just thinking on it. It was so much better than the almost forgotten times he survived before he knew the Man. Adoc's focus on the Man was so great that he wouldn't be able to think of Old Ben or the other Man with the old hands, nor did he think of the woman who had so many good smells. Adoc was on guard mode for his Man. He thought about the salty water coming from his face and the strong hug he got before he was invited onto the bed. So he lay next to him focusing on the Man, he figured it was what was needed for giving up his cedar chip pleasure the Man gave him. Adoc finally fell off into a light sleep while the Man rested easily. Dreaming of chasing the ball kept thinking of the grabbing thing and the pain for the time after the grabbing thing out of his mind. Both he and the Man would wake for the time when the light returned and there would be plenty of ball chasing to do then.

    Downstairs Old Ben lay on the floor by Francis's bed. He was content just as he lay sleeping only to rest from the activity of living. Old Ben's experience was vast. He long since forgot the excitement of puppyhood or the newness of setting. He had known many people in his days, some were cruel, and some were erratic. If they weren't mean they were overly abundant in focus of his condition. He saw most than other dogs he knew he was wise in his last years. Old Ben was grateful for this place to wander. The living was good and better, the people here were better than he ever knew at any other time. Old Ben knew his purpose even if others didn't. The puppy was the prince or the first dog. He was fine with that too. This place beat the last place he was in, here he had purpose. In the other place it was just a tomb before he required one. Old Ben knew that his last days would be spent here. This was a special place with special folks. His wisdom demanded that he know his purpose and that was to see to the proper raising of that pup. Wisdom told him that the pup was curious enough to not know better for his own well being. He sure didn't have the respect for the ancient woods he so wanted to investigate. He may have seen his way through these parts from the bitch's teat, but he didn't have any sense as to what waited in the ancient woods. Old Ben's wisdom told him there was real danger for that pup and it was his job to get him through it. There was something else Old Ben waited on for understanding. It had something to do with the Man he slept next to and he wasn't sure just what it was. He knew that the other who came along with him didn't like him too much; he also knew it didn't hate him. He thought that because the other came bringing the gate to the Man with the gentle and old hands that he might also need his wisdom of attentiveness. It wasn't like the duty of the pup, nor was it clear, but it seemed to be the same as watching out for the pup. What also became clear to Old Ben was a very simple need for the pup.

The pup was so anxious that even when his days were over, the pup would need a reminder of what Old Ben meant. Old Ben would need to join with a bitch so that the pup would carry on a responsibility he didn't yet know. It was certain to Old Ben that would be the only way to insure he pup's safety. He'd be forced to deal with the puppies Old Ben would leave behind and that would change his reckless ways.

Old Ben knew of the end coming just as the Man with gentle hands knew, but before that time came there was plenty to do. While he lay there resting from the activity of living he listened to the life of the night, full of things the pup wasn't ready for, but wanted to know. He rested by the Man that knew as many things as he knew while he waited on the inevitable knowing that work was yet to be done.

Œ

The days grew longer and warmer as the construction on Francis' property began to take shape of the finality they desired. Henry was lost to his chores at the shelter and duties of overseeing the construction. Adoc was gaining size and weight as he learned his purpose besides chasing the Ball with the Man. On as many occasions as he could Henry included bringing both Adoc and Old Ben to the shelter. He and Kristina had discussed the continuing socialization of Adoc with other dogs. That is something they'd want from Adoc in the days of running the shelter they were building. For the most part Adoc was doing well with the socialization to other dogs.

A Man, a Dog and a Ball

Old Ben didn't have the need to socializing that Adoc did, but both Henry and Kristina thought Old Ben might be a great role model for Adoc while developing the skill set they wanted for Adoc. Most of the time, Henry would only have to keep an eye on Adoc's behavior with the dogs as they were turned out of their pens for cleaning. Adoc's infractions with other dogs always came from his exuberance to play. They were minor when all was considered. Old Ben's doings with the other dogs amounted to laying in the shade and letting the younger dogs chew on him. It was very unusual to see Old Ben doing more than that. He had a tendency to walk the perimeter of the fenced in area sniffing the edges of the property and usually there was a following of little paws covering his tracks as he had his patrols.

One afternoon while Henry was away from the back pen giving Kristina assistance inside the shelter structure Old Ben's behavior revealed an action nobody at the shelter would ever have guessed as a possibility. On that particular day William couldn't be at the reception desk as scheduled. There was some type of family emergency he had to see to, so the staff was light handed. Henry could wear different hats as a volunteer so in the middle of cleaning out the pens he had left the dogs to play while he helped out inside to cover during William's absence. The duties inside required about twenty minutes of assistance and when he was finished he made his way back out to the duty of cleaning the pens. As he was picking up the implements for the chore at hand, he became aware of something that wasn't right. Something seemed to be too quiet, out of sorts.

Henry looked at the pens that still held dogs; nothing was out of the ordinary. He then began to peer past the pen area looking into the community fencing and he saw a group of dogs all focusing on something he couldn't make out. Once he moved to where he could see their focus he was utterly surprised. Old Ben was joined with a bitch and both were stuck together. He didn't know what to do. He thought about going out to break them up but decided that more experience was needed. He made his way into the shelter and informed Kristina of what he had observed.

She was quite busy at the time and couldn't manage to depart from her duties at hand.

"Henry, get a cold bucket of water on them and get them separated." Henry didn't know why he didn't think of the idea, but he wasted no time in seeing to her instructions. Once he had the bucket filled he made his way out to where he'd seen the dogs. Old Ben took notice of his approach and continued his efforts. Henry couldn't believe that Old Ben had come to this. It was surprising and confusing, but Henry was determined to do as Kristina decided. Old Ben didn't seem alarmed for Henry's approach and that left Henry feeling as though tossing the water on the two would be nothing more than pitching the bucket at them.

After Henry arrived at a distance he thought would facilitate the toss he let the pitch fly and Old Ben pushed against the bitch forward avoiding the cold interruption of Henry's intention. Henry was dumbfounded. Just as he felt for not having Kristina's idea as his own, missing his target left him feeling as inept. He turned back to fill the bucket again thinking about how foolish he felt. By the time he filled the bucket and went back to the place to pitch the water from, Old

Ben's business was done. The joining separated and Henry's efforts ended up pitching the water at the two dogs just to release frustration of his incompetence. Once again Old Ben avoided the toss of water while Henry had only hit the bitch with the bucket's contents.

Henry stood there watching Old Ben lope away from the scene. The bitch had been surprised by the water dousing and for it became weary of Henry's proximity. Henry didn't know how to react. The emotions he was feeling along with the failure of his intent gave his quiet a few moments of confusion. So much so that he was unaware of Kristina approaching him from behind. When she saw Henry standing there she made an assumption that Henry didn't have such good luck with separating the dogs.

"It isn't as easy as it sounds, is it?" Henry was startled for her question. He looked at her for her arriving question and saw her focus on Old Ben. "Seems as though you gave the bitch a cooling off, but Old Ben proved to be a bit more clever than you thought." Henry was guilty as charged. There was little he could say.

"Well, I guess Old Ben is more clever than I thought, and I'm sure sorry about letting this happen." Kristina would have liked to prevent the joining of the two dogs, but there was no blame to be laid at anyone's negligence for the coupling.

"Henry, don't worry too much about it. Old Ben never acted in such a way before so nobody could see it coming; besides stopping nature is pretty much a waste of time." Henry was relieved for her understanding, but his failure wasn't something he was too used to digesting. He laughed to himself in a nervous kind of way.

"Well I guess I won't be living this down with Francis anytime soon." Kristina laughed at his remark.

"Well that is up to you for the mentioning, personally I don't think it is worth a mention, but I'll leave that to you." She continued her focus on Old Ben and shifted her glance to the bitch. After some consideration she offered up an observation.

"Old Ben and that bitch may just make one very good natured litter of pups. Both of them are good looking dogs and they are about similar in size for purposes of mating, so it may very well be a fortunate pairing."

She paused and turned to Henry. "Why don't you put this behind you and finish up the pen cleanout, daylight is waning and I know you got work to see to back at Francis'. I'll have the vet check out the bitch to see if she can manage the litter and I guess we'll look after her until she finally does bring them into this world."

Henry followed her instructions thinking on how she thought through the result of what just happened. He was soothed by her ability to look at a circumstance and become proactive for the occurrence rather than to assume negativity for the condition. He saw to his duties thinking on her subtleties as he came to know them. He found that the more he knew about her, the more curious he became. Henry wasn't one to avoid study at all. As a matter of fact, his willingness to study about things made him what he was. Most of what he studied for learning had a finite wisdom to it. What he faced now was something unfamiliar. Henry was learning about a woman he had a great interest in while he was reading a timeless book concerning a man he never knew. Jesus as a historical figure was obviously a man he wasn't going to meet for a hand shake, but it seemed to Henry Jesus was never too far away. After the chores at the shelter were done and on the ride home with the dogs in the car Henry considered his life as it was. On one hand, he was fully engaged with building something that required his experiential wisdom. That was a full time job for anyone. On the other hand he sought wisdom from two things that were foreign to him. Even as he knew his experiential wisdom would result in a positive outcome for building the new shelter, he wondered how his two new curiosities would facilitate what his experience was sure to deliver. That was the unusual thing in Henry's life at the time. The curiosity was becoming his addiction.

He didn't say anything to the dogs on the ride home, his contemplations of his addiction along with the function of driving took most of his focus for the time. When he did arrive at Francis' place he saw that Francis was doing his business at the store. Henry was surprised at how much business was going on, he figured there would be more as the project came closer to completion, but he hadn't expected the volume of traffic he observed. It was the talk of the town. After he parked his car he got out and opened the doors for the dogs to run about as they would. Adoc didn't have the propensity to visit with folks that Old Ben did. He was still working on the dog socialization skills. Obviously Adoc's trust of folks wasn't as extroverted as Old Ben's was. Henry watched Old Ben pad up to those folks milling about the store while Adoc hung with him. Adoc let some whimpers go as he wasn't thrilled that Old Ben was having fun he couldn't bring himself to know. Henry calmed him as he could. He asked Adoc if he wanted a bowl of water as they walked towards the back porch. Along the way he heard Francis make a comment to Old Ben for his padding around the folks.

"Well there, Old Ben, looks like you have a prideful pickup in your padding around; you must be one lucky dog!" Henry stopped dead still when he heard Francis. He stood there and shook his head wondering just how it was that Francis could know such a thing. He didn't figure that Kristina would call him after she said she'd leave it up to him. So how did he know? The question Henry asked himself was one he wouldn't be able to answer until he spoke to Francis. Worse it was a question he couldn't forget. He got Adoc a bowl of water and had himself a smoke. After he lit the cigar he made his way over to the work sight. Henry tried to focus on the work as it happened. He even took time to go over concerns the foreman might have had. Adding to his frustration there were no immediate issues to be discussed. Everything was going as planned according to schedule. Henry was at a loss for what to do with himself. He thought about wanting to be at the shelter again, but that seemed like wishful thinking. Henry despised wishful thinking and then he thought about tossing the Ball with Adoc. When he looked to where Adoc was he came up empty once again. Adoc had decided to put some of his shyness away and visit with Old Ben and the visitors at the feed store.

Henry laughed at himself. He looked at Francis hamming it up with his customers and keeping an eye on the dogs considering just what he would do. While he watched Francis living life carefree. It was then something Francis mentioned to him fell upon his considerations of what to do. Henry thought it would be a great time to do some reading. He made his way to the house to collect his bible. After he brought it back to the porch he took a seat at the table and opened to the New Testament. He began reading it since Francis told him to do so one evening in the past. Henry had made it through the books of Matthew and Mark. He opened it up to the book of Luke and began reading. What was becoming clear to Henry was that the first four books of the New Testament were first-hand accounts of those who knew Jesus. He was quite impressed with the different perspectives of the same Man through different perceptions. He thought the telling of Jesus' life was quite consistent and that gave him historical evidence to make conclusions about Jesus. He eased into his reading and all that plagued him before was no longer presenting immediacy of issue.

Œ

Back at the shelter Kristina was managing the day. It was busy to be sure without William but nothing in the day required her attention elsewhere other than at the shelter. She was waiting on the vet to finish up procedures that were scheduled. She had already asked him to check on the bitch that was joined with Old Ben earlier. It was something she wasn't happy about, but there was no point in letting it ruin her day. The vet didn't charge by the patient, he gave her a rate for the week. So there was no impact on her budget. As the vet finished up the scheduled work he asked that the hopeful mother to be, be brought in. Kristina saw to it and before long the vet was completing his examination. He had a few things he wanted to know during the work and Kristina responded to each inquiry. After he was done he told her the obvious condition the dog was in presented no prohibitions to her having a litter. He did also mention that his final determination would be after lab results, but he didn't think she was anything else than a capable dog, even if she was thin. He mentioned that she should try and see to some weight gain for the dog and he'd provide her with supplements that would be beneficial to her carrying a litter. Kristina heard all the vet said and then she thanked him. She took the bitch back to her pen and walked the vet out to his vehicle. While he was in his car he asked her a question that took her surprise. "I haven't been up around Francis' place lately, how is that project going along, are you still on target for completion?"

Kristina hadn't heard anything from Henry that suggested they were behind, "As far as I know it is still on schedule."

The vet nodded. "Okay, I'll make my way up there some time to check it out. You know the whole town can't stop talking on it... well more than the town, too."

Kristina shrugged for his comment. He nodded and departed. As Kristina made her way into the shelter she thought about what the vet said. It occurred to her that the place would be open before or just about the time the bitch would be having her litter. She wondered if that was coincidence or something more…. She couldn't wonder too long the day wasn't done and the phone was ringing. She looked at the message machine before she answered and realized that she was going to be reviewing calls, she decided to begin by answering the ringing phone and minimize the list she'd have to listen through.

Œ

As the day drew on the crowd thinned at the feed store. Francis had had his hands full for the afternoon. He gave Henry a few looks while he sat and read at the back porch. Francis was happy to see Henry reading scripture. He might have been happier if Henry offered him some help, but as he thought on it, Henry was right where he needed to be. He knew Henry's day at the shelter was likely a surprise. When he saw Old Ben padding along it didn't take him but a second to realize what Old Ben got up to for the visit at the shelter. He also hoped that Old Ben's need to procreate wasn't going to put Kristina in a bad way, but as he thought on that, he also considered it likely that she wouldn't have a problem with any of it. He thought about Kristina and how he knew her. He always thought the way she acted towards animals was something God approved of and having puppies was life moving forward and that was God's gift to all living things. He looked back at Henry and smiled… Henry was coming to know just what that gift was and he thought of his guidance for Henry as part of God's plan. Francis went through the last of his day after he said a prayer for the wisdom behind everything going on; he did so knowing Mildred was pleased. He could feel her watching, but she had nothing to say and for Francis that in itself was heaven.

Henry read more slowly than his normal reading pace. Even though the style of writing was consistent he found that getting through the scriptures took more concentration that he usually applied to reading other material. The afternoon passed calmly in the gentle nature of the day. The bustling at the store was calming down and the pace of work on the project remained steady even as it was winding up for the day. Henry's focus on the reading removed his angst from earlier and the actual reading seemed to offer him hypnosis of study he always welcomed. As he read the last pages of the book of Luke he decided that it would be a good time to set the book down. He took a couple of minutes to organize his thoughts for the reading and took notice of the property. He was shocked to become aware of the lateness of the day. He noticed that most of the work crew had already left. The foreman was having a post work day meeting with the lead crew members and one of the vending consultants had arrived to discuss some aspect of the geo-thermal unit. Francis was seeing to the last details of his day over at the feed shop. He looked a bit tired for his busy day.

He didn't see the dogs right away even as he scanned the property within his field of view. He didn't have urgency to know where they were, but he was curious. After he rose from the chair on the porch and made his way towards the feed store. As he passed the corner of the house and his field of view opened his curiosity wanting to know where the dogs were ceased. He found that both Old Ben and Adoc were napping in the shade of the house. Something about what he saw looking at the dogs struck him deeply. It wasn't that he hadn't seen the dogs napping together before; he'd seen both napping as they were many times. He stood silently trying to figure out what gave him intrigue about this particular occasion. The dogs slept similarly to other times he had seen them doing so. There was no unusual arrangement of the way they slept. Henry was stumped. In his study and reflection Henry was interrupted by the general foreman of the project.

A Man, a Dog and a Ball

The conversation held was informative rather than problematic. The general foreman was reviewing the details of the week to follow. Henry turned his focus to the discussions of topics regarding the last installation procedures for the geo-thermal unit meant for maintaining the climate of the structure. The result of the meeting primed Henry with a need for him to be present over the next few days in order to oversee the procedure of installation. That is what Henry wanted and the general foreman simply seeing to facilitating the scheduling. After the details were agreed upon the general foreman took his leave while Henry turned to his former focus.

The dogs remained as they were. Obviously the conversation wasn't intriguing enough to disrupt their napping. Henry continued to wonder what it was about the dogs napping that struck him as he made his way towards Francis. Francis took notice of Henry's approach. As Henry moved towards Francis he could see that Henry didn't step lightly. As busy as Francis had been for the day he realized that his day was nowhere near over. Henry's consideration was for his own figuring, but Francis knew that Henry needed subtle nudging towards his needed conclusions. Francis would exploit Henry's accompanying him to wrap up the day using his young back for work that needed doing. He knew that getting Henry through his concerns wouldn't be the last of his day; Kristina would also have a few pieces of luggage to bring home for the day. Just as Francis always did, he managed one thing at a time.

"Finally arriving to earn your keep, young fella? I'd say it was about time. Heck if I wasn't so busy with all the folks trying to find a line to stand in I would have told ya to put the studying down and see to earning some sweat equity." Henry's pace slowed as he heard Francis' greeting. His first thought of rebuttal was priceless, but he let it be. Henry decided to humor Francis.

"Okay, old man, what is your need for the day? The more I get to know you the greater the need becomes; guess that is how it goes with old age." Francis smiled and spoke to advantage.

"Isn't that just like a whipper snapper always fulfilling a need to speak to his own unrealized inevitability?" When the two met just feet away they stopped comfortably in proximity and shared the fleeting moments of the afternoon gazing on the dogs.

"I guess Old Ben had himself a time over at the shelter for his visit." Henry heard Francis and kept to a focus on the dogs.

"Yeah I'm still wondering how it was that you knew he got connected." Francis gave a shallow belly laugh and spoke to Henry with a hope to reseat a lesson he tried to offer before.

"I spoke to you about understanding dogs before. And now I can see that even though my words were seeded the harvest of wisdom isn't yet reaped." Both men kept gazing at the dogs.

"Tell me Henry where are you at reading in the scriptures?" Henry didn't drop his gaze or even turn to Francis to answer. He was still trying to figure out what was different about seeing the dogs napping on each other.

"Well Francis I finished up the book of Luke." As Francis heard Henry's response he turned away heading into the feed shop to close down the day's efforts and rewards.

"Come along, young fella and I'll tender you wisdom." Henry turned and followed Francis into the shop. Henry restocked feed bags and sundries as Francis directed. During the effort Francis revealed his thinking.

" Old Ben had a step in his padding along that could only mean one thing... His stride indicated that he might be the greatest painter that ever lived who had just offered his last brush stroke for the enjoyment and worship of creation... and you didn't take notice. Now in a dog's life the only ability of such confidence is reseeding his line before his last day alive. His pride was so great that even if he never saw his pups he knew his legacy would be fulfilled and that sonny boy is why you are lumping those sacks of feed." Henry heard Francis' words and he hated the conclusion for each syllable delivered. He hated that he didn't have the wisdom Francis possessed.

Henry continued with the work at hand silently while Francis did the paperwork for inventory rotation. The two worked to minimize the efforts of one and that was what both of them desired. The day was running out of sunlight. After Henry saw to the last of the sack shuffling he turned to Francis and waited further directions. Francis heard the end of effort while he continued with his inventory accounting...

"Seems to me that you'd know how to drive a broom around; a place of business has to have a cleanly decorum does it not?" Once again Henry did as Francis mentioned. He didn't take offense to the suggestion; he just wished he'd seen to it before the need to speak it. He knew Francis was helping himself to help his difficulties and because he needed to be directed in his impatience for wisdom he fulfilled the humbling of the wait by driving the broom. Henry wasn't one to throw the baby out with the bath water. Henry finished sweeping up about the time Francis was counting off the till. As Henry put the broom up Francs carried the revenues of the day after he shut off the light. Both men walked towards the house looking upon the dogs in their folly.

"Okay, Henry. I know you have been biting at the bit; let's get to it before you need to toss the ball with that silly dope Adoc and surely before the Woman gets home." As soon as Francis referred to Adoc the peaceful rest both dogs knew ended. Adoc's eyes opened and his head rose up off the comfort of Old Ben's belly. Henry was waiting for this and he let Francis have it right between his wisdom and elderly station.

"Yeah I can see you are invested in hearing about my concerns while addressing Adoc's need to toss a ball. Way to go, old man!" Francis laughed. They stepped towards Adoc coming out of his pleasurable respite on Old Ben. Once Adoc stood up Old Ben's eyes opened and in a few seconds both dogs were on their way to meet both men's approach.

"Don't worry Henry we can kill two birds with a single stone. I have a feeling by the time we finish up with Adoc's ball tossing and Old Ben's lounging we'll have gotten to the meat of your troubles. We may be a bit late with dinner preparation though so make sure we can bail ourselves out of that when Kristina shows up." The dogs joined them with tails wagging; Adoc was busy trying to meet the higher level of greeting Henry without effective result. Henry posted his knee before Adoc's desired notion. When Henry reached the Ball stash Adoc's excitement demanded launching the Ball. The men and Old Ben moved away from the porch and took a perch to toss the Ball to Adoc. While the back and forth continued Old Ben took up residence laying his head on Francis' foot. Francis engaged Henry while he had distraction of the tossing of the Ball with Adoc.

"So, what is on you mind, young fella? The concern you're carrying makes you look like ya got the weight of the world on your back."

Henry grimaced for the directness of the question. Francis put him into a whirlwind of thought. He tried desperately to grasp what it was that gave him concern before he returned to the house. "Well the whole thing with seeing Old Ben attached to the bitch at the shelter was something I thought would give Kristina a reason to be upset. I didn't expect it. Then when I finally got home you seemed to know what happened so that I thought you knew because Kristina may have called you.... That was just my irrational thinking." Henry tossed the ball seeming like he wanted to be doing it forever.

Francis saw and felt his doubt and steered him back to what he might have gained for the reading. "Tell me, what do you think of the scripture you have been reading?"

The question shook Henry's conversational tone. When Adoc returned the Ball Henry paused the tossing and lowered his hand to claim Adoc's love and admiration. Once the dog accepted his hand's gentle grace he responded to Francis.

"I'm finished with the book of Luke." Francis heard Henry's response and nodded.

"That is a bit of reading isn't it?" Henry tossed the ball, watching Adoc tear away grass in his grousing to fetch the ball.

"It sure is a bit of reading, I have to force myself to figure the common speak of the day. Then I have to figure all that is being revealed. Yep, quite a bit of reading." Francis knew what he wanted to hear and waited on Henry's realization. He watched Henry toss the Ball for Adoc's need to exercise. He also knew that Henry was contemplating his finding while enjoying time spent in the back and forth. It occurred to Francis that both Henry and Adoc were in participation of a routine that served more of a purpose than just tossing a Ball. Adoc was bonding to a relationship with Henry from repetition. Each toss fortified the consistency Adoc could count on for his need of growth and strength. Henry found that the tossing of the Ball gave him time to ponder the responsibility of unconditional love, both to Adoc and for his own purpose in this life. Francis developed a smile for his accruing of wisdom. He realized that Henry processed things much like Adoc accepted trust. He knew it was a constant but slow transformation. It surely was one that was happening. While Francis considered his revelation Henry surprised him with an almost blurted response.

"I'm not exactly sure what the scripture means to me. This Man Jesus in his short life opens my mind up to implications of a thing I never knew to exist. Let me ask you something

Francis?" Henry stopped the Ball tossing with Adoc for the question. Adoc waited patiently. "Do you believe that Jesus is the son of God?" Francis' smile grew more cheerful.

"Henry, what I think or believe is of little value while you are digesting the material. Here is why. You have to examine the evidence presented in the Gospels. Then you must determine if it is credible. And if you can't make that determination then there is more evidence to examine so as to apply to your curiosity. Of course it is prophetic evidence, but that shouldn't be difficult for you to reason through. If you need prophesy to answer the same question after you have read the New Testament, you can follow it in the book of Genesis. That is where I AM or God establishes the Blood Line that ultimately produces Christ. I'm certain it is Genesis 22: 16-18. " Henry heard what Francis mentioned and he also heard what he didn't mention. Henry began tossing the Ball again to Adoc. Francis' ability to quote scripture left Henry feeling small. Whenever he did quote it as instruction Henry studied it and then applied it to why Francis answered his question in such a direct way. The sun was getting lower on the horizon; he figured Adoc was enjoying the exercise. He let it be with asking anymore of Francis on the topic.

It was clear that Francis would remain reticent until he had more qualified questions. Francis also took notice of the sun's setting and figured that dinner was the next chore to be seen to for doing. As he walked away he left Henry with a parting thought.

"Henry, you have fun with that crazy little puppy of yours and don't make scripture more than it is… judging by the way that pup takes to you it is pretty much something you already know, just something ya didn't know what to name." Henry didn't miss any repetition of tossing the Ball for Francis' last words even as he did have a glance at the Old man walking away. Henry tossed the Ball as Adoc chased it. Henry tried to connect the dots within Francis ambiguous words along with his specific points. While he watched the Dog chasing the Ball he wondered what it was that was as the connection to the reading of Gospels and how he already knew the simplicity of it. Adoc brought the Ball back and he tossed it with an effort greater than he for the time. Once he released the Ball, something Francis mentioned came to his mind.

If you can't make that determination then there is more evidence to examine so as to apply to your curiosity. Of course it is prophetic evidence, but that shouldn't be difficult for you to reason through. Henry continued tossing the Ball. He lost himself to what he read about the doings of Jesus as written.

After the sun dropped to halfway below the tree line Kristina's truck arrived on the driveway as she found her way home. The sound of the truck took Adoc's attention from the Ball tossing. He stopped and saw the arrival of Kristina's truck and darted to the greeting of the one who smelled good. Adoc's awareness of love was the thing he couldn't resist calmly and Henry was left empty handed watching Adoc kick up grass running to her truck. She had the door open before he got there but it meant nothing to accost her as she exited the truck. Henry watched his joy in seeing her and he felt as though he was closer to understanding what Francis meant in his departing comment for seeing the greeting. Old Ben rose up slowly and made his way to say hello to Kristina as per normal. By the time he got there Adoc had gotten his demanded greeting from Kristina and his attention for her faded. While Kristina welcomed Old Ben Adoc's attention vacillated between the one with good smells and Henry. Henry watched stepping towards them as the transfer of hellos became satisfied. His smile for the scene was interrupted. In between Adoc's focus of Kristina and Old Ben Adoc took a laser beam focus on nothing apparent to either Henry or Kristina. As Henry watched Adoc he caught Old Ben hearken to the same focus as Adoc. Between a blink and a turn of Henry's head Adoc launched himself to the source. Henry was astounded at Adoc's explosive motion. As Henry was some distance from the focus of what was a perfect picture he noticed the gravity Old Ben put to Adoc's focus. Old Ben departed with effort from Kristina that left her off balance and on the ground. Both dogs now were racing to whatever gave them curiosity barking loudly. Kristina was left in the split seconds of Henry's confusion as she lay upon the ground. Henry's instinct was a tightening of his belly knowing that Kristina likely paid a cost for being in the path of Old Ben's insistence to chase down Adoc. Both dogs were gone barking fiercely as they made their presence known to the rambunctious investigation of Adoc. Henry moved quickly to Kristina, he could hear Adoc's bark of reckless curiosity. Old Ben's Bark of unheard authority faded as their distance grew from Kristina's unknown injury. Approaching Kristina Henry realized by her position that she was in trouble and in moving closer to her he also heard the fading desperation in Old Ben's barking. Arriving at the fall of Kristina he realized that even though she wasn't in a condition of imminent danger she was in trouble. Old Ben's departure from her gave her action to land on her arm that presented a costly fracture to her right arm. Her cries of displeasure couldn't be ignored, but they didn't silence the raucous that he heard from the dogs engaging their quarry. As Henry began offering her assistance there was a horrible sound in the field were the dogs ran to wildly.   She summoned Henry's attention in a plea beyond her own pain of a broken forearm.

"Go see what those dogs got their nose into, I'll be all right!"

Henry stole a second to watch on her and stood up to turn away. He hadn't taken more than a step when the kitchen door was kicked open by Henry loading up a shotgun Henry hadn't known he possessed. The sight of Francis wielding a shotgun gave Henry a sense of immediacy he couldn't have possibly imagined. While he watched Francis step in strides loading his gun cursing like a madman the final sounds came from the distance. A sharp yelp from Adoc made everything quiet. In a second of quiet after the yelp an Ungodly viciousness began. Old Ben's barking and growling were fierce for a fraction of a second then a growl straight from the depths of an unknown cave became released. Henry and Francis began sprints to the edge of the property they'd not get to in a time for salvation. While they ran they heard Kristina howling not of her own pain, but in what she knew to be disastrous for her earlier greetings. Francis howled like a cowboy on a horse trying to prevent a stampede going off a cliff firing. He fired both rounds of the shotgun towards the commotion. In the excruciating strides of a desperate run Henry saw the confrontation of Adoc's curiosity and it was terrible for the witnessing. Adoc was lying as though he was injured from a death blow and poor Old Ben was defending his younger brother in a dance with his creator. Henry saw Old Ben being tossed about by a Lone Wolf who had been out looking for dinner early. Henry was horrified running to the place of battle while Francis was stepping slowly reloading the shotgun. Before Henry could even get close enough to the viscous engagement he saw Old Ben become a brave victim to a reality of nature's wickedness.

The wolf had Old Ben in his jaws from a downward bite standing on his haunches. At the end of the attack Old Ben was pushed to the ground without effort... his last yelps were abrupt and final. Francis has reloaded the shotgun and laid the muzzle toward the offending culprit of terror and released both barrels. The first round claimed the attention of the wolf and only a partial part of the second round had found its mark which left the offender limping away in a horrific howl of pain. When Henry and Francis arrived at the dogs their discovery was grim. Henry went to Adoc impulsively as he saw Old Ben's end running to the incident. Francis stopped running and walked to where Old Ben remained. When Francis saw Old Ben's condition he made his way to Henry and Adoc hoping for a better outcome. He was relieved to see that Henry was tending to the dog. When he arrived he placed the gun down and then knelt down to offer assistance to Henry. He saw Adoc's condition and took notice of Henry's shock. He put his hand on Henry's shoulder and took control.

"Henry, take hold of my gun and see to Kristina, I'll tend to Adoc and see you back at the house." When Henry looked up at him Francis recognized that Henry had never been involved as a part of such a tragedy. He saw weakness and loss in Henry's eyes and he grabbed him up at the back of the neck. He looked into his eyes deeply.

"Henry, Adoc will be fine, but Kristina needs your help right now. Go to her and I'll bring Adoc along directly." Henry tried to look towards Old Ben and Francis held Henry's face to his kind eyes. Francis shook his head. "There is no point looking there, you need to see to living things now son. Go to Kristina and I'll be back with Adoc just as soon as I can." Henry looked into Francs' eyes wanting to deny all that had just happened. Francis put his hand on Henry's cheek. "There is nothing else to be done except to see to what is in need. Now got see to Kristina, I'll be along with Adoc directly!"

Henry's hesitance lingered as he realized Francis was right. Without turning a head Francis blurted out with strict inflection, "Leave all that is as it is and do what I said son. There ain't no need to focus anywhere else except seeing to Kristina, now move to it. I'll be along shortly." Henry's inexperience with a situation such as he faced left him to defaulting to Francis' wisdom. He forgot all he couldn't process and moved to assisting Kristina. He walked never recalling seeing such waste in his days. In a matter of seconds a perfect harmony became chaos. Henry realized he hurt. He realized his hurt was fierce. He hated the hurt he knew because in all other things he knew... he couldn't avoid this agony. Along his steps against gravity he wondered if he should have seen it coming. By the time he got to Kristina his shirt was sweat soaked and his breathing was labored. His eyes stung from tears he didn't know he shed. She saw his agony and lifted up both arms to accept him. Henry cradled her from the uninjured side and lifted her so they could move to the porch. She saw in Henry a painful fear. Kristina knew it was bad, but she didn't know the completeness of the bad. The pain in her broken forearm became the pain of Henry's disbelief. She hugged on him as she could with minor discomfort. He collapsed in her arms with a sobbing he never knew to release in his life. His condition was fragile and in the minutes of his weakness Kristina allowed herself to put her own pain off. She saw between hugs and solacing Henry that Francis was carrying Adoc to the house across the field of Henry's realized loss. She nudged him in the direction of dealing with what was coming and Henry regained some type of composure. They made their way to the house where pain killing and function of healing needed to happen. Adoc was finally laid upon the kitchen table while the dinner Francis was preparing was turned off by Henry from Francis' direction. Francis took a look at Kristina's arm and spoke firmly.

"Henry, we are in the middle of a crisis. Adoc is in trouble and Kristina is disabled, so you need to get the vet on the phone and see to immediacy." He looked at Henry in a glance and saw that Henry was still in shock. "Henry the phone is over there!" Henry responded like he was a scolded child. His steps to start came with doubt, but after a second his hurry would have knocked over anyone in his way. After the call was made, Francis instructed Henry to get ice for Kristina's arm. Then he told him to work with her to manipulate her arm to elevation so that once he was done with Adoc he could respond to Kristina. Henry was in the responder mode of a direct authority of the crisis. Francis took notice of Henry's ability to depart from shock and get to action and he was relieved. Francis understood Henry's confusion. He knew while he tended Adoc that Henry was capable of all things for a time coming. The experience of today was the last thing Henry needed to be schooled about. This experience would make him ready for the unknown future. Francis remained dedicated to applying first aide. He knew it would be the most important lesson Henry would come to know. Francis felt himself departing on the care and healing he dispensed.   His weakness was becoming a struggle he knew that would tax him mortally even if his mortality would linger, but just as Old Ben had sacrificed himself Francis was long waiting on a time to join Mildred. That single consideration gave Francis his inspiration of a greatness no emergency room doctor could even approach. Francis felt Mildred calling his home, but he was as stubborn as his dedication to making a garden grow on the edge of the forest of lost hope. Francis took his pride in being a Swamp Yankee.   His wife could wait for his departure from here even if it made her angry like she was when she was living. Francis understood the responsibility of being a man and his partner could wait. The prospect of living life was much more favorable than living in eternity with his wife as she was in life... He sure hoped it was all as God said as to folks being transformed in perfection of God's intention. Mildred might be bearable then. Francis laughed for his exhausted revelation tending to Adoc. Adoc was a wreck.

His head was like a ball the wolf didn't get a full bite on. His right eye looked as though it may not offer any more sight and his right ear was hanging onto fur. Adoc also had a laceration along his belly that wasn't a life ending wound, but it sure would take time to rehab from. Francis knew that if it were left to Henry Adoc might not make it till the Vet got there. The Vet was going to be busy. Francis figured the dog might need over a hundred stitches and maybe some staples. Adoc wasn't losing blood inordinately and for the carrying across the field Francis was sure there would be time to make him right for the Vets appearance. Francis figured for his effort Adoc might even retain sight in his right eye even if it was diminished. He looked at Henry tending to Kristina's arm and invited Henry to come over to Adoc's side. Once he did he gave Henry some comforting words.

"Henry Adoc should be fine even if he is blind in his right eye." Kristina murmured discomfort for hearing the report of Francis. Apparently she wasn't thinking much for her own condition. She was hit by the loss of Old Ben but realized Old Ben went out as a dog living... She considered Old Ben as Noble in her sense of morality, but Adoc's wounds gave her a reason to fall to sorrow. Her complaint wasn't dramatic, it was sincere. She knew what Adoc meant to Henry even if Henry didn't, and it hurt her own type of maternal instinct. Her broken arm didn't phase her yet, but Francis knew it would.

"Henry, make sure she has plenty of ice on her arm." He lent towards Henry to whisper. "She ain't feeling her arm yet... she loves the dogs more than her body can reveal its own pain." He winked at Henry after gaining his focus. Henry took Francis' directives as life saving recommendations. Henry saw to the need while Francis poured his energy into Adoc. It wasn't but a short time before the vet arrived and saw to Adoc. Once the vet was busy Francis went to Kristina.

The vet began his work as Francis put his focus to Kristina's arm. Henry watched all of what he did as though it was a narration from a book he read conveyed in 3-d dimension. Kristina welcomed Francis' attentiveness. She gave up her condition to Francis as though he delivered her into the world.

"Henry, in the dining room up in the high wall cabinet of the dining service go fetch me the drinking whiskey in the top cabinet."

Henry hadn't known of the drinking whiskey but he did as was told dutifully. When he returned with it Francis instructed him to stand behind Kristina. He was about to instruct Henry on what to do next when the vet interrupted. "I'm working here and I could use a nurse, why don't ya take her to Dr. Martin's and deal with that there?"

Francis ignored the vet and gave Henry instructions to hold Kristina in a certain way of retention. A whiskey was poured and given to Kristina. She drank it and prepared herself.

"Henry, stay steady, son. I don't want the vet to be sewing up my head...now Kristina you know what is coming and it is only gonna be a second or two." After Francis placed his hands on her arm she told Francis, "It better be only a second otherwise I'll be giving you a reason to see Dr. Martin." And as soon as she said her piece Francis set her arm. Her reaction surprised both Henry for just hanging onto her reaction impulse and to Adoc as he raised his head for her expression. Adoc's head motion gave the vet a reason to be a complaining fool and he made mention to the inconvenience of Adoc focusing on Kristina's discomfort.

"Francis, I don't know why I do house calls to this address. Every time I offer you service you make my work nothing more than a waste of time. Look at the mess I have now."

Francis looked at the vet pathetically. "Doc, I don't know why I deal with you, myself. Here I am making your job easy and doing triage on the next patient and you cry like a babe with a soiled diaper. Why can't I just get a sensible vet?"

The vet looked at Francis and told him flat out that if he had to wait for the next vet he'd be a nurse all night. Once Kristina's arm was set he instructed Henry on her comfort. He walked to the side of the vet and watched the work briefly. Adoc was looking better already for the vet's attention. Once Francis determined that all was good in the house he went back to the whiskey that Henry had brought out and picked up the bottle. He took a hit off the bottle without benefit of a glass. To all there it seemed like an extended helping. When Francis returned the bottle to the table he examined the job Henry did in applying the stint. After he approved of the job he took another hit off the bottle. He looked at the vet thinking heavily only to turn back to Kristina and Henry.

"I guess you should stay with both here, Henry. Kristina might need more pain killer and the vet might need more babysitting. I'm going to do some business otherwise."

Henry listened to Francis' mention and before he could respond Francis was gone. Henry saw Francis leave but he seemed to feel something else for his departure that remained. Adoc was losing patience on the table and he became difficult for the vet. The immediacy of the vet's need became the focus as Henry responded to the Vet's beckoning. Apparently Kristina was okay for the manipulation that Francis gave her and the whiskey and ice gave her what she needed for the moment. Henry calmed Adoc as he could, but he couldn't help to feel that some part of Francis was still there. He stood over Adoc knowing Francis was dealing with Old Ben. The difference was Adoc had life Old Ben didn't and Henry was in the middle of his most difficult moment of his life.

Kristina asked about Adoc with an apprehension. It was clear to Henry that Kristina cared very little of her own condition. He didn't know what to make of that nor did he have any thinking to know how Francis was going to deal with a dog twice the size of Adoc. Henry figured Francis would either put him in the ground where he lay or carry him elsewhere. What made Henry doubtful was the seeping of life he saw Francis enduring for the last hour. Then there was that feeling that he left half himself with them after he left to see to Old Ben. Henry was overwhelmed by all the chaos of how the past minutes uprooted his simple considerations. His partner had a broken arm and he couldn't process the implications of that for the six weeks coming or how it might affect her abilities. He saw his new best friend diminish in life force, one of his two dogs was dead and the other was in some trouble. More than that he couldn't see who he felt was looking over his shoulder, and this all came down on consideration of a new realization in his studies of the day. It was an impossible situation and somehow he knew that he'd been in the same place before. He couldn't place it and he had none of his usual dialogue faces of late to discuss any of it with. The vet seemed to be busy at the moment without any need of his help. He scanned around the room looking for the presence he couldn't see and decided that he could use a sip off the bottle that both served Francis and Kristina earlier. He moved to it and took the drink to biting it down giving him reason to forget all immediate need and focus again on his own reality of bitterness. He placed the bottle down figuring that wasn't soothing like the wine. He felt the presence he associated to half of Francis that remained left. It wasn't a warm or welcoming feeling… it was almost as though he were standing in a room waiting to see his date for a prom in front of an audience of brothers who didn't want him there, dating their sister. Kristina was focusing on the vet working on Adoc. She seemed to be managing well enough considering her injury. She kept the ice on the fracture as Francis had directed. She watched the vet complete his work on Adoc. He listened as the vet and her shared words over his prescribed care.

"I've done the best that can be done to save his eye. Whether or not he will see depends on how the injury heals up. If we can avoid infection I'd reckon he'll likely have some type of vision. His ear is stitched back up along with of belly and we'll also need to keep an eye on how they heal up. I'd advised crating the dog so as to keep him off his paws and inactive. At least for a few days; the sedative he is on now will keep him calm for a time and I'll get you an antidote prescription to supplement the injected dose he has already received. That will be a ten day cycle."

Kristina listened to his directions and nodded after he finished. The vet looked to her gave her his medical opinion for her. "If I were you, I'd see Dr. Martin for your own condition. Just my opinion."

Again she nodded. "I may just do that, but you have seen to the priority for now."

As he left he said he'd be by in a couple of days to check the dog. Henry, Kristina and Adoc remained. Henry asked about her arm and whether or not he could do anything. She thought she'd have another sip of the whiskey, he saw to it. She sipped on it as Henry stood over Adoc. He shook his head as he gazed at him. Kristina saw his anguish.

"He'll be fine, Henry. The doc is the best around and he gives a solid prognosis as I know. He'll just need TLC over the next week or so. Before you know it he'll want to be chasing his ball with you."

Henry glanced at her and nodded. "I'm sure you're right, It's just I've never had to deal with anything like this before. The more I recall it the worse it seems… Old Ben is dead and you're in a fix." He shook his head once again.

"Don't worry about me. A broken bone will heal and so will Adoc. It saddens me about Old Ben too, but he died and did so in protecting Adoc. As bad as it is, he didn't die in a pen at the shelter." She sipped some more on her whiskey. After a grimace for the sip she gave him an instruction. "Henry, why don't you go and help Francis see to Old Ben? Adoc is going to be resting for a while and I'll be fine watching over him. It may help you to be a part of working with Francis in seeing to Old Ben's care."

Henry heard what she told him and looked at her before he could raise an objection she mentioned that a flashlight might be in order. Henry did as told and for it he felt better leaving the kitchen. Stepping out of the door liberated him from the unseen presence he felt.

Œ

Henry couldn't see Francis as he walked across the field in the day's twilight. He heard a shovel working and concluded that Francis decided Old Ben should be buried where he fell. He had no problem with Francis' conclusion it seemed reasonable. As the shovel strikes became more audible he clicked on the flashlight approaching Francis. Francis paused from his duty and Henry suggested that they should trade duties. With labored breath Francis accepted the suggestion.

Henry worked steadily at continuing the hole Francis began digging. The light he worked by was sufficient to complete the job. Both men grabbed the remains of Old Ben and lowered him into the burial site. Nothing was said by either man. Henry worked dutifully in covering up Old Ben.

Francis knew instinctively that the work Henry was seeing to was therapy for him. It gave him something to focus on besides the doubt and confusion. When he was done with the grim detail Francis gave him a few thoughts to consider.

"It seems to me Henry that a suitable memorial should be made here for Old Ben. A sacrifice such as his ought to be marked honoring the battle, wouldn't you agree?"

As he listened to the suggestion and question there was a difference in the inflection of Francis' voice. While he formulated his response he tried to name that difference he heard. "I suppose that is right. To tell you the truth of it I'm a bit embarrassed feeling sorry for his loss rather than realizing his victory for the battle."

Francis wasn't surprised at the response. He let Henry mull the realization over in his thoughts. After they paced a good distance away from Old Ben's new home Francis again consoled Henry.

"Don't beat yourself up about it too much. A witnessed sacrifice is never an easy thing to see, and worse, making sense out of it in being witness to it the first or second time is even more difficult. Shame is your evidence of gaining wisdom." The words were spoken with the same inflection. Henry began to realize that the events that just unfolded took something from Francis.

They proceeded to house silently. Francis left the shovel standing on the outside wall of porch area as they entered the kitchen. He went directly to where Adoc lie and inspected the vet's work. He turned to Kristina and inquired about how she felt. It was determined some aspirin might be helpful. Henry saw to her need while Francis helped himself to pouring a couple of drinks.

After all were seated it was clear to both Henry and Kristina that Francis was depleted. Kristina knew what the appearance meant as she had seen it in so many animals in her care; she could see that it wasn't something Henry grasped. She held her thoughts knowing that discussion would have to wait. She was in no condition to begin it then, nor did she think Francis would welcome it. After Francis finished his drink he placed the glass on the table and offered some thoughts before retiring.

"Henry, as I think on it the only other time in your life you knew of death was likely a time you don't remember. It isn't an easy thing to face once you let someone or something like a pet into your heart. There is also no shame in sadness for loss." Francis stretched and yawned. He looked to Henry continuing his commentary. "While you study those scriptures Henry you'll come to know that the shortest scripture is, *Jesus wept.* He wept at the loss of his friend Lazarus. Now if the creator of all things can weep for a friend then there is no shame in having the same feeling."

After he said it he put his feet to the floor firmly stood up and excused himself for the evening.

Kristina began thinking of her own exhaustion. She repositioned herself to steady her balance before standing from her chair. Henry took notice and moved towards her. "Here let me help you up." She allowed him to help her gain her balance. "Tell me what can I do for you, are you hungry?" She shook her head in response.

"No, like Francis I am going to settle in early and get rest, tomorrow is going to be a busy day. I'll need to see Dr. Martin and have this set and make some calls as I'll be out of work for a time. I'll need all the rest I can get tonight. If there is anything I need I'll let you know." Kristina made her way to her room. Henry settled in to watch over Adoc through the night.

Henry remained with Adoc watching over him on the table. He could see his body moving as he breathed. Adoc passed air through his nose with slight whistle sounds from the exhalations. The long wound along his side looked like it hurt for the breathing. The stitch work the vet did was effective holding the skin together. Henry wondered how such a wound could be received. He imagined it came from a single fang in the wolf's mouth maybe as a missed bite. It might have happened as Adoc loosed his head from the attack leaving the wolf only biting at air. His thinking on it didn't remain his focus. He was thankful it wasn't worse. He was grateful for the intervention of Old Ben.

Intervention…. The word meant so much more to him for his realization. He couldn't figure out why it struck him as though it were a hit from a lightning bolt. He did have a strange sensation in his chest while he considered the word's new meaning for thinking about it. For all his pondering he couldn't get his mind around the obsessive curiosity he faced. He realized that fatigue and shock might be part of the problem for finding insight. He'd let it be for now.

Tomorrow might be a better day to think on it. The exhaustion he felt for digging Old Ben's Grave was taking its toll. He lowered his head on the same table Adoc laid on wondering if he'd sleep through the night there. If the Adoc woke and didn't realize where he lay he didn't want the vet's handy work to be undone.

If Adoc did wake he'd be there to remove him and lower the dog to the ground. Henry focused on Adoc's breathing as he fell off into his own sleep at the table.

Œ

Morning came early upon the property next to the Forest of Lost Purpose. Dawn arrived in the grayness of a misty morning. The usual joy of any previous day was nowhere to be found. Kristina's fractured arm gave her difficult sleeping and Henry's duty over Adoc was no better for rest. Francis woke after both were up. It was likely that his sleep was the best any rested by. His appearance certainly lacked the energy his joyous and friendly nature was accompanied by.

He looked at the trio with heavy focus. He asked Kristina of her condition and then inquired about Adoc. The anxious response he received from Kristina along with the worry he heard in Henry's voice concerning Adoc gave him motivation to make coffee and share his thoughts.

"After I make coffee and have a cup along with Henry I think both of you should go see Dr. Martin and have Kristina's arm casted properly. I'll keep close to Adoc and watch him while you are gone. That way I can close the feed shop or just open it later after you get back. I'll also see to the crew arriving to work. That will be the first order of business, unless either of you have other thoughts?" While Francis made the coffee he listened. There were no objections. He was glad for that because by the looks of things Henry was doing the best he could with Adoc, but his best was an effort he struggled with an probably not on a whole lot of rest. Continual focusing on the dog wouldn't be in anyone's best interest for the day ahead. After he prepared the coffee for brewing he moved to Kristina to examine her with more scrutiny. She had done well to keep the ice on it and the swelling for the injury was minimal. There was bruising to be sure but putting a cast on her arm wouldn't be too much trouble for Dr. Martin. He concluded she had received good first aide.

"I'll bet that is pretty sore about now." Kristina grimaced a bit while looking at Francis.

"It's tender, but not too bad." Francis gave her a wink and then moved towards Adoc. When Adoc heard Francis' approached his tail wiggle at the tip of its end. Francis placed his hand on Adoc's rear quarter gently holding it there for a moment. He stroked the pup saying no words at first. He looked at Henry and suggested he might want to use the time to clean up before his coffee. Henry rose from the seat he maintained stretching as he rose. The steps he took towards the stairs included more stretching from the sitting posture of the evening. After Henry made his way up the stairs Kristina thought to ask Francis how he was. He was going through the motions of this day, but the look in his eye gave her reason to suspect that he was still depleted.

"Francis, how are you? Are you feeling okay, you look tired." Francis turned his focus from the dog and gazed upon Kristina.

"I'm feeling okay dear. Life has been good to me and I have no regrets." He smiled at her to ease her concern. He knew how she saw him; she'd been seeing this stage of life in critters most of her time spent for caring. "There is nothing to worry about child all life has a cycle and I'm almost through mine. What you need to worry on is that man getting himself presentable so he can take you to see Dr. Martin. He still has more growing to do and I'm about done with any wisdom I have to offer him, but you'll be his strength after I'm gone." As he finished up his piece of conversation Henry's footsteps indicated he was returning for the coffee he'd be having before the trip to the Doctors could be seen to. Francis stood up from his seat and reached for mugs he'd pour into. He poured two as coffee for Kristina wasn't what she'd be wanting. When he returned to the table with the coffee he realized he hadn't asked her if she wanted something to drink. "What can I get you to sip on this morning?" Kristina didn't respond immediately the question presented her a need to swallow her next words as though they might have passed in a whimper. She wiped a tear from her eye as Henry returned to the kitchen.

"Orange Juice will be fine." She sniffled. The scene stopped Henry in his tracks. She looked at him in his confusion. "It is okay just a bit of a pinch in the arm." He returned to the table to sit and drink his coffee. He was lost between feelings for both Adoc and Kristina.

Francis returned with her orange juice and took a seat up at the table he sipped on his coffee as did Henry. He shared a thought at Henry's expense.

"What a sight! I don't know what to make of it. One with a broken wing, another torn up lying to heal and one apparent survivor guilt ridden for letting the catastrophe happen." Sipping on the coffees Henry relaxed some for the comment while Francis continued. "Ah heck that was an unfair thing to say Henry, I'm sorry about it. I just thought to lighten it up a bit around here." Henry shrugged and drank more of his. Kristina thought to give Francis a snap back, but he did apologize.

"Nobody is at fault here, it was puppy curiosity. He got into a nose-full of trouble and it almost killed him." The men listened to Kristina's comment quietly. Francis sipped on his coffee, while Henry thought on what she said. His head tilted to the ground before he spoke almost through a whisper. "He would have got killed if Old Ben hadn't intervened." Francis wanted to stop the morose direction Henry might be taking this.

"Yep, and if I had gotten off a sooner shot like the last one, Old Ben might be alive. Now tell me how any of this is useful?" Nobody answered. "That is right... it isn't useful, so let's forget the *would haves* and the *should haves*." He finished his coffee and got another one. He wasn't sorry for the chastening. In his mind there was work to do and he didn't have any time to waste.

Kristina finished her orange juice. She knew Henry felt horribly and she wished Francis was his old self, but that was the problem, his old self was older and he was grumpy. She knew he loved Old Ben and even as he did he was cold in his abrupt dismissal of the loss. She was half expecting to hear one of his war stories begin. After Francis turned back to his seat he placed the coffee on the table and stepped to the phone. He dialed the phone for Dr. Martin and while it rung he looked at both of them. "No we aren't going to let the Dr. Sleep in, he can pick up the phone and see you early." Henry shook his head and muttered something to which Kristina's focus shifted to almost instantly. Henry noticed her gaze on him.

"What I said is that I'm sure Dr. Martin is going to love a call from Mr. Congeniality so early in the morning."

Kristina smiled for his comment. She didn't risk a laugh, her arm was very sore. "Would you get me some aspirin?"

Henry nodded and proceeded seeing to her request. He opened the container dispensing two tablets bringing them back to her. After she received them her smile rewarded Henry's assistance. She popped them into her mouth and sipped on her juice. The Dr. finally answered his phone and took the call from Francis. After a persuasive discussion Francis simply said "Thanks Doc." He hung up the phone and reported that the Doc would open the office up directly. His house served as his office. Henry poured himself another cup of coffee and sipped on it looking over Adoc. Francis joined him examining the dog.

"He's gonna be fine, Henry. He'll be sore for a bit. The good thing is that he is young and growing, his healing will happen fast."

He sipped on his coffee after hearing the consoling offered by the grumpy old man. "Yeah he'll be back to chasing balls shortly." Then he had the last of his coffee and turned to Kristina. "Anytime you are ready we can be off and get that arm casted up."

She finished her juice then indicated she was ready to go by offering up her good arm. Henry went to her and gently helped her to her feet. Once she was up Henry released her. Both of them dressed for the cool morning air before they left the house. Kristina managed one arm through a jacket sleeve and carefully draped the other arm for warmth. On their way out both looked over to Adoc and Mr. Congeniality. Henry opened the door and they were on their way. Henry stole a glance towards where Old Ben was buried. The mist still lingered consuming the distance between where he lie and the exit from the kitchen. Henry promised himself to go back out the grave after Kristina had her arm properly casted. The morning horizon saluted the latest loss and welcomed the ghost of Old Ben in a properly eerie fashion.

Francis filled a pie plate with water and placed it under his nose. Adoc sniffed at it and let his long tongue begin a gentle lapping. Francis understood how raw, sore and busted up Adoc felt. He placed his hand on his rear quarter leg gently.

Adoc could smell The Man with Old Hands. He was thankful for the water; it was a long night of achy sleep. Adoc realized that there were worse hurts than when the grabbing thing hurt him. When he tried to look up at the Man with Old Hands pain seared down his side from his ear. The place from where he saw had no sight; it felt like he was stuck there by a stick he collided with in the woods. He whimpered for the flash of burning pain and lowered his head down. He lapped at the water and lie there on the table feeling the old hands. He heard the Man with Old Hands saying something, it sounded soft and kind. It wasn't the Man he knew but the Man with Old Hands soothed him.

"Yeah, Adoc, it is going to feel pretty bad for a while, but you'll feel better soon enough." Francis began making more coffee and fixing up corn muffins. The workers would be here soon enough and there was work to do. He also figured putting some broth on the stove for the dog. He'd also figure out some sort of better bedding than where he was. Francis grumbled to himself thinking on the work of the day.

Œ

Henry drove slowly and carefully to the Doctors home/office. Kristina was managing the pain and he was extremely concerned in not making it worse than it was. The lights were on inside the office and the Doctor was waiting on them in his robe. Henry expressed an appreciation to Dr. Martin that Francis may not have and Dr. Martin grumbled a bit before he responded.

"Sure, Henry, in this line of work I have gotten used to irregular hours. Now let me see that arm Kristina." He examined the injury and when the usual questions were over he made note of the splint applied. "Francis did a fine job with setting the fracture and splint. I have seen his work before. I doubt that I could have done better." After he removed the splint he examined her arm more closely. By the bruising he could see how the fracture broke. He was impressed with the lack of swelling a well.

"So, Kristina, how did you manage ending up like this?"

She responded directly and without the worse result. "I was in the path of a dog and his greeting when his focus shifted to another place."

Dr. Martin made mention that she obviously was worse off than the dog for the encounter. One of those awkward silences befell the room.

"Not really, Doc. The other focus was protecting my puppy, Adoc; he was being attacked by a wolf at the tree line of Francis' property. It was a noble sacrifice that happened before Francis could fire off a couple of shotgun discharges."

Kristina was thankful Henry made mention of it. It was short complete and an eye witness testimony. She would have fumbled through the words trying to explain it. Dr. Martin heard Henry with a sense of regret for inquiry.

"I'm sorry to hear that bit of news. I know how much the dogs mean to both of you." Dr. Martin wasted no time in immobilizing her arm. He applied the fiberglass casting as the plaster wouldn't be useful for her work. When the procedure was done he told her the usual directions in care for the injury. They didn't have any questions and in short order they departed the office and headed home. Henry didn't need to be as careful for the drive home. It was more of a casual ride to the long drive up to the feed store and house. The mist departed for the time away and after they parked Henry opened the door for Kristina.

"Kristina, what are your plans for work? Do you want to come along with me when I do my chores?" She walked towards the house thinking about what she wanted to do.

"To be honest with you, I'm awfully tired and I didn't get much sleep last night, I think I'll see if I can't catch up on some rest. They all know already I won't be in today."

Henry nodded it is almost what he expected. Kristina walked on into the house as Henry went to the work site. The workers were already at their respective work station continuing production. The foreman on the job had some discussion with Henry about concerns of the work. Henry gave him direction for the immediate concerns and made a mental list of what would be needed shortly. Overall the meetings both shared were productive. Henry was satisfied and he departed to the house to check in before going to the shelter to see to his chores.

Francis was putting together his usual goodies for the workers and Adoc was given different bedding from where Henry left him earlier. Adoc looked restful. Kristina must have gone upstairs to get her rest she wasn't to be seen.

"Dr. Martin said you did fine work setting and splinting Kristina's injury; he said he has seen that work before." Francis nodded for the report.

"It is one of the things we all had to know in earlier times Henry. The good doc wasn't here when I was a younger man. Accidents happen just as they always have and always will." He turned to Henry and looked at him with a serious intent. "Very soon you'll be the authority of the property and some of these duties will fall to you." The statement came abruptly. Henry didn't want to hear it, but he understood it.

"Yeah, but it won't be today." He took a last look at Adoc and then mentioned he was going to see to his chores. Francis let him be. Henry's response had its own curt inflection as Francis heard it. He wasn't interested in picking a fight. "You know where we'll be." Henry left and made his way to the shelter.

Henry thought about life just a day ago, it seemed like everything was going so well. He wondered just how things could end up so badly in seconds. He realized how silly it was to think like that. It was a waste of time. Not believing that times could be difficult such as they were was exactly why Francis had prompted him with the inevitable outcome for a future without the old man.

Henry realized that whatever came their way, it would be better managed without disbelief that it was happening or could happen. By the time he came to his conclusion he arrived at the shelter.

It was time to get to the chores at hand and also apply his energy to doing what he could in terms of Kristina's absence to keep the pace going. Henry decided that the plans to bring the shelter to the project they were working on meant that he needed to step up and make it his own as his partner couldn't be there. He'd seen Kristina do her work over the past weeks and he'd duplicate her duties as best he could for the day. He walked through the door assuming her daily schedule as he could and began his chores.

Œ

The next days came with adjustments and minor difficulties. Henry saw to begin the work on Old Ben's memorial and Francis oversaw Adoc's rehab and healing. Kristina managed to make it to her job at the shelter while Henry helped her out when she absolutely needed it. Henry trained another volunteer for his duties and let the trainee know that in the future it would become a paid position. Both Henry and Francis saw to hiring on a full time manager for the feed store Francis just didn't have the energy to manage it anymore. After a week or so Adoc began rising up regularly. His healing avoided getting an infection in the eye. The wound about his ear, neck and body also mended without infection.

Francis' condition declined rapidly. He tried to stay after the simple duties of preparing the work crew's goodies but even that was becoming difficult. It was clear to both Henry and Kristina that the storm cloud of this season hadn't yet departed. Dr. Martin visited and checked on Francis even when he didn't ask for the visit. It was Henry's idea and the prognosis Dr. Martin offered was what they all expected. When Henry saw the Dr. to his car Dr. Martin shared a word with him.

"Henry, quite honestly I am amazed that he is even alive. There is no scientific reason why he remains alive. I guess he is just a stubborn old cuss. Do the best you can to keep him comfortable and I'll give his lawyer a call to be expecting the end." Dr. Martin shook Henry's and told him to call him when it happened.

"Henry, I mean it. Any time it happens and I'll see to details."

Henry released his grip of the hand shake. "I'll do that Dr. Martin." Henry watched as he drove off. The inevitable was lurking. The veil between things alive and things past was parked at the edges of the Forest of lost purpose.

It waited and it was patient.

Henry turned to the house and to his delight there he saw Adoc. Obviously he was let out of the house by Kristina. Henry smiled as he walked towards his pup. Adoc was getting big even as he was healing. He seemed to grow in the week or two of healing. As he approached the dog Adoc's tail began wagging. Henry stopped just in front of Adoc.

"Look at you, good boy." He bent to pet Adoc gently. He did so as a tear fell from his eye. Both Kristina and Francis were at the door watching the greeting.

"Would you look at that young lady; that is loyalty of love if you ever saw it." The surprise of seeing Adoc was only outdone for hearing the familiar voice of his friend Francis. He looked up and seeing both of them coming through the door Francis took a seat at the table on the porch. Kristina remained where she was watching the 3 most important living things in her life shine in the glory of victory. As Henry sat Adoc perched between both, leaning towards Francis. She didn't need to be told what to do. She went to the kitchen and got the home made wine and 3 glasses along with cigars. She even got Adoc a bit of Francis' special beef jerk. She put it on a tray and carried it without difficulty through the door. She placed the tray on the table and sat with both men and the Adoc. Henry did the honors and in a short time they toasted each over Adoc's chewing on the jerk. Francis held up his glass as did both Henry and Kristina.

"Here is to loyalty of love." He sipped on his wine to start and then finished his glass. He placed it down on the table. Then he reached or his cigar. He lit it up while Henry and Kristina did the same. After they all enjoyed the afternoon in the dinge of their smoking Francis asked Henry to pour another wine. Henry heard the request and for a second he almost gave worry to it as asked. He reached and poured dismissing the worry from his mind. After the glasses were filled Francis raised his up again. Once Henry and Kristina matched his offering he mentioned another toast.

"Sacrifice of life can only come from loyalty of love. Loyalty of love can only come from family in celebration of that sacrifice. We Praise our Old Ben as the family we are and rejoice in the abundance he left us too. The Forest of Lost Purpose has been defeated as the beginning of Purpose for the Lost becomes built." He sipped on his wine greatly settled in his words.

Both Henry and Kristina did the same and in the toast they came to understand the future. The strange thing happening during the toast was Adoc's pause for it. It was though Francis' words briefly fell upon Adoc's ears so he could understand them. He left his jerk on the deck surface and put his nose as close as he could manage for a pet from Francis. Francis was lucid enough for it and gave the pup his reward. While he scratched on Adoc Henry thought about the toast they just drank to. The words fell upon him as though he'd never forget hearing them. After a bit of scratching Adoc returned to his chewing and Francis once again took focus to the gathering. He looked upon both of them knowing things yet to come that they couldn't hear for his telling, they weren't ready to hear about those things. He wished he could tell them, but it was up to them to arrive at conclusions they would come to find sensible later on.

"Henry, what I have come to know in life is pretty simple to reckon for a man seeking wisdom. I'm telling you this because you realize knowledge with an ease uncommon to most men. For all your knowledge wisdom seems to come slowly. Life is going to throw curve balls at you. All that knowledge alone will not be able to answer those difficulties. Wisdom is the key to anything and everything life will bring to you Henry. Scriptures hold wisdom. Encyclopedias hold knowledge." Francis put his glass back on the table. Kristina and Henry finished theirs and took the lead of Francis. Henry poured another. Kristina might have refused if her arm wasn't fractured. She didn't much like the pain pills so the wine was appreciated. Kristina stole the moment after the pouring.

"Here then is to wisdom!" Francs smiled and raised his glass. Henry was inclined to share in his exuberance. "To wisdom." The three sipped and listened to the business of life. The job site was progressing nicely and Adoc sat licking on his chops. While they smoked their cigars looking on the property enjoying the company of each Francis continued with his discussion.

"Henry, my boy there are 3 things you must remember while you make your way through life. Remember the two rules Jesus said to live by and don't forget that entering the kingdom comes in having the heart of a child. If you stick to that you'll enjoy your living here making your way through life. Don't succumb to disappointment. For every difficulty there is in your path ask what it is to gain for the experience." Henry considered all that Francis said. Apparently Francis was done with his offerings for the moment.

I think I have a handle on that last bit you spoke. Something like the saying, *If it doesn't kill you, it only makes you stronger?*" Francis thought on his association. Then he nodded.

"Something like that Henry. Ah don't put too much into what an old man offers as advice. Most folks around here gave up on me a long time ago and I can't say as I blame them." Kristina wasn't going to hear any more of that kind of talk.

"That is why you still have the feed store Francis, because so many gave up on you..." She shook her head and made a raspberry sound out of her mouth.

Francis' eyebrows rose looking at her. "Yes, go ahead and remind me of Mildred and her sassy ways." He smiled at her with a look nostalgic reflection.

Adoc became very curious about Francis. He had difficulty but he licked furiously at him. Both Henry and Kristina took a notice of his interaction. Francis looked at Adoc and lowered his hand to Adoc petting on him. "Yes, Adoc. I know you are a good boy... Henry you make sure and finish that monument up for Old Ben, all right?" Adoc settled down for Francis while he kept his focus to the dog.

"Yep, I'll make sure to do that, Old Man."

Francis sipped the last of his wine. He pet the dog some more with love the dog couldn't resist. He looked at Kristina and told her to keep Henry out of trouble like Mildred did for him. She grabbed Henry's hand with her good hand and promised she would. Tears came to her eyes. Francis looked upon the field he knew as his life and said, "See, Mildred? I told you that those Canadian tree cutters didn't know what they were talking about.... The forest of lost purpose is no more. Just look at what these youngsters have done..."

Francis' hand fell from Adoc and his last breath came just as a wind on a still day blew across the porch. It was extremely unusual as there had been no breezes and when it departed Francis' head fell forward just where he sat. Kristina's grip remained on Henry's hand tightening as tears fell from her eyes. Adoc began whimpering just slightly as he came to know the Man with Old Hands went to the veil between here and there along with Old Ben. He sniffed at

Francis one last time and moved closely to Henry seeking the same praise he sought from the Man with Old Hands.

Henry stood up and went to Francis. He removed the cigar from his hand and disposed it in the ash tray. He returned to Kristina and took the hand that grasped his and gently lifted her from her seat. He embraced her as she cried. She didn't ball she wept. Her demonstration may have been a bit of happiness for his joining Mildred and loss for losing a well loved uncle. She ended her weeping and picked her head up off Henry's chest.

"I'm sorry, I didn't mean to cry on you." She sought the words while she sniffled and wiped the tears from her eyes.

Henry let her to herself saying, "No need to be sorry."

She looked at him and said that she'd call Dr. Martin. She turned making her way into the house.

Henry poured himself another glass of wine and held it towards Francis. "I wish you had longer in this world, I did enjoy your company." Henry finished off the wine. He took his seat and sat down. Adoc stayed very close to him. Henry consoled the dog with petting.

"I know … first Old Ben and now the Old Man." He looked at Adoc and told him, "Life goes like that, one minute you are feasting, the next it is all famine. Ah don't worry pal, I ain't leaving anytime soon and besides that... pretty soon you'll be doing for Old Ben's litter as he did for you. Let's just hope none of them are like you." Adoc liked it when the Man talked to him. His hand's stroked him gently.

Kristina returned from the kitchen. She sat with Henry and Adoc looking over the field and the construction. "Dr. Martin says he'll make his way over here after he finishes up. He also said he'll collect the Sherriff or let him know of Francis' passing. He said not to worry about a thing."

Henry turned his focus to her. "I'm not worrying at all about any of it. In fact I'm happy for the Old Man." He looked at Francis sitting in his chair. "Can you imagine any better way to go?" He looked back at her and she just shook her head for her response. "You're probably right; maybe we'll be so lucky?" He shrugged. There was a pause.

"Whatever it is as to how we end up, I know there will be a lot of lucky animals making this place just as Francis said. *'The Forest of Lost Purpose has been defeated as the beginning of Purpose for the Lost becomes built.'*" He stood up and poured another wine for each of them. "Hey, partner, how's that sound for a business name? *Purpose for the Lost*".

She held up her wine. "I'll think on it, after we are less medicated." They sipped on the wine watching the workers. She was thinking through his question. "It might not be a bad premise for a mission statement, "Our Purpose is for the Lost".

Henry listened with usual sincerity. He thought about Francis and the way he used to look at them reflecting on himself and Mildred. He smiled finishing his wine. He put the glass down. Kristina wondered what he was smiling about.

"Is what I said something you find funny?"

He shook his head. "No not at all. I was just thinking about what Francis might say. Something like *Now see that is just like a woman for you, showing you just how your brilliant idea is almost genius.*"

Kristina giggled and looked at her glass. "Oh I can't drink anymore of this." She handed Henry the glass and he finished it off, reflecting on Francis. Just as they sat in quiet next to Adoc along with Francis recently past; a car pulled into the driveway. Neither of them knew the car, but when the door opened a funny little man got out of the car dressed in a business suit. He was carrying a brief case. He began walking to where they sat on the porch. He stopped when he realized Francis was sitting there dead.

"Hi. My name is Abraham Abrahamson. I am the attorney for Francis. I have some paperwork I need to show to a Henry and a Kristina." It was obvious that Mr. Abrahamson wasn't comfortable approaching them while Francis sat dead in close proximity. "Is there a place I can get you to examine documents and sign off as the deceased requested?"

Henry stood up along with Kristina. "Mr. Abrahamson, my name is Henry and this is Kristina." He waved as they walked towards him. "Why don't we go to the store and see to that business there?"

Abraham nodded gratefully. "That sounds acceptable." As they walked into the store Abraham mentioned the details of execution for Francis final wishes weren't complex at all. He further mentioned that it shouldn't take more than a few minutes. Henry and Kristina listened to the attorney and at the end of his presentation he asked, "Any questions?"

Neither had any it was straight forward just as he said. He moved to the form of beneficiary acceptance.

"Very well then all you'll need to do is sign here and you'll retain all possession of the deceased."

He held his pen out and Henry accepted it. His put his signature on the form and offered the pen to Kristina. She accepted it and scribbled her name. The attorney frowned a bit for her attempt to sign it with her broken hand while he examined it. He took the pen from her and made a notation on the bottom of the signature area explaining the quality of penmanship due to a broken hand. Then he signed it and left them all the paperwork.

"Of course I'll file all the transference obligations at the proper offices and mail you the return receipt of the filings." Henry nodded and offered his hand for shaking. Abraham put his hand to his chest. "My apologies, I am not in the custom of shaking hands and may I extend my condolences."

Henry saw Abraham to the door, thanking him. In short order the funny little attorney was in his car and gone.

Henry and Kristina walked back up to the house. Henry was carrying all the paper work with him. Adoc was dutifully sitting next to Francis. His tail began wagging as both approached. Kristina was the first to tell him how much of a good boy he was. He wasn't up to moving like he would regularly. His stiffness from injury prevented his wanting to demonstrate more appreciation. Henry went inside the house to place the paperwork inside and then returned after he put coffee on for all that was to come. It wasn't long after that the Dr. arrived along with the Sherriff. Shortly after that a hearse arrived. Dr. Martin made the medical ruling necessary to the laws of the Land. He pronounced Francis dead and the Sherriff reported it in his log. After the details of Francis death were recorded the gurney was brought to the chair where Francis sat. The two attendants gently removed him and placed him into the body bag on the gurney. The bag was zipped closed. The work had stopped and the zipping of the bag sounded like a jet high in the sky moving past them. Dr. Martin explained after the men wheeled him to the hearse.

"Francis as you know had made preparations to every detail. This was all put in effect for when he passed. Don't worry, now. They will take good care of him. You'll be getting a call letting you know when he will be ready to be picked up. He is to be cremated. His ashes and Mildred's will be presented to you. The rest as you know is in the details the attorney left for you." Henry and Kristina listened and just as soon as everyone showed up, they were all gone. They stood there thinking about all that happened when they were interrupted by the foreman. Henry was apologetic to him.

"Oh, jeez, I'm sorry about all of this, Jerald. Listen, why don't you fellas take the rest of the day off... We'll see you back in the morning."

Jerald nodded. "We are all sorry about Francis's passing, we're all gonna miss his goodies."

Henry agreed. "Indeed we will, and thanks."

Jerald turned around and the crew began packing it up. In fifteen minutes they too were gone.

Both sat at the table quietly. Adoc was tired from his efforts and he lay between them. "I know one sure thing about that monument in back for Old Ben." Kristina listened to Henry. "I'm going to find a headstone man and have him engrave that toast Francis made for the earlier drink."

Kristina smiled thinking on what Henry would make that monument into. "I'm sure it will be just right, after all when you put your mind to a thing it comes to being a reality."

Œ

Francis' absence after his passing loomed while Henry kept to his study of scripture. Adoc's healing was remarkable for all to see. The wounds covered up nicely due to the stitch work of a vet blessed in his vocation. Kristina worked through Francis' passing without showing much of her heartache. Life kept moving along.

Henry's focus on the construction became more of a priority as the new technology became part of the work's completion. He also kept an eye on the feed store and helped the manager Francis hired on for the job. His duty as a volunteer at the shelter lessened in frequency for his oversight at the property. Both he and Kristina did manage to get other folks to help out after promising to hire them on once their facility was operational.

While Adoc rehabbed, Kristina brought the bitch home that Old Ben had been attached to just before he sacrificed his stake at the property of lost purpose. They both felt that Adoc would enjoy the company. They also wanted to have Old Ben's line born to the legacy he protected. The bitch was swelled up, growing the litter that would be born to a life without hardship. Those pups would know love, more so than their mother had. Kristina and Henry delighted in watching Adoc offer the bitch attention to her changing he didn't yet understand. They both saw him sniffing at her, curiously padding around her as though he were trying to steal a bit of food off the counter. Adoc was many things, but sneaky wasn't his calling.

Henry waited patiently on Adoc's recovery. He enjoyed the ball tossing with Adoc, but he hadn't yet recovered to a point for such play. The long wound on his side was healing but any type of running might have opened it up. Adoc would sit near Henry while he read scriptures. The companionship between the two was a force of nature. Kristina would watch both of them and laugh at Henry when he began asking Adoc what he pondered upon for reading. What was even more captivating was the manner in which Adoc seemed to listen. She couldn't recall seeing any type of man-dog relationship the two shared. She wished all animals knew the love Henry and Adoc shared. That would be heaven to her.

The traffic flow of folks increased as the facility they were constructing became complete. Many folks from different places marveled at Henry and Kristina's dream. Town pride was abundant over the shared undertaking. They sat quietly at night conversing about the stream of folks who visited. What they conceived previously became manifest and it was delivered regularly by those drawn to the energy of the place. The reality of their dream was more than they expected and on several of those quiet evenings they discussed just what they'd need to implement for functionality of the endeavor. It was clear to them that their dream was more than a job. It would in fact be a life laboring at love.

Œ

Henry was pleasantly surprised one evening. His pal Adoc must have felt better for the healing as he came to Henry with a ball in mouth. Kristina watched Adoc bring Henry the ball and her heart swelled with delight. She knew Henry lost himself in the time spent with Adoc tossing the ball. A tear fell from her eye as she saw Henry respond to Adoc's insisting it was time to chase the ball.

Kristina knew more so than Henry did that he just didn't lose himself to the interaction with Adoc. She knew that thing between Adoc and him was where and how Henry found himself. She remembered the story he told her about meeting the dog. She often wondered if he ever considered it as he tossed the ball to Adoc. She recalled the first time she met the two. It was back at Henry's old house. Back then, Adoc chased sticks. She laughed at the recollection, thinking about how Henry was amazed at the dog's destruction of the sticks. As she looked on both sharing the ball she came to realize that the Creator blessed them both. Each was lost to uncertainty of life, until that day when Adoc interrupted Henry at the bridge. The simplicity of it struck her as miraculous.

Her life improved greatly for something as silly as the shared love between a Man, a Dog and a Ball. Kristina sat on the back porch with the fat bitch growing pups resting at her side. She thought about Old Ben defeating the property of lost purpose knowing that there would be armies of puppies running freely. Sure, she would deal with all the coldness of humans being cruel to animals; that was her work. But at this place she'd not be limited by the same human negligence of bureaucratic ineffectiveness. She was grateful in knowing that she'd never have to put an animal down again unless it was truly humane. That was the greatest agony of her old life. Her new life was all because of the Man and the Dog sharing the Ball. She knew a perfection of life even if it was just a glimpse in all the imperfection of living. Her heaven was right in front of her and she never knew such happiness before.

The ball tossing was brief. Adoc wasn't quite up to his usual speed but his desire was monumental. Henry's attitude shifted from a deliberate focus of business at hand to a boyish excitement, vibrant with youthful glory. After Adoc quit the chasing Henry took time to lower himself to the ground with him. The praise he gave the dog was a sight to see.

When Henry returned to the back porch to sit with Kristina she couldn't help but to mention her approval of the toss. "Once again all things are right in the world between you two."

Henry looked at her with a grin that stole her heart. "Adoc is getting back to himself, thank God, and there is nothing that I find more pleasing than tossing him his ball. I think if I could I'd spend the rest of my days doing just that I would have no other desire." After Adoc had water he took his seat next to Henry. Henry's hand kept praising Adoc with strokes of loving affection.

They spoke of days coming as the twilight grew to dark. When the efforts of the day delivered them to find rest they left the porch and said good night to each other. The days ahead would be full.

Œ

After the completion of the facility Henry and Kristina saw to the transferring of animals from the shelter to their new home. The day was a celebration within the town unlike any knew. Neither Henry nor Kristina had planned any celebration; it was the doing of the town folk. They were gracious for the offering. It had been decided by Kristina that the facility would be named *A Perfect Promise.* Henry liked the name as she told it and on the day of opening the sign was installed at the beginning of the driveway.

People toured *A Perfect Promise* days after its opening. Even after rescues were delivered from far off places they were never short of space. When they were fully operational *A Perfect Promise* employed fifteen people. They had a fulltime vet on site. Surgeries and treatments happened daily. The feed store now had three full time employees and business was more than it had ever been when Francis ran it. The days following fulfilled many folks. *A Perfect Promise* transformed their little town.

Shortly after opening the fattened bitch birthed her litter. Old Ben's legacy was born into the world Henry and Kristina made. Adoc became extremely protective over the pups. Five pups of six lay in the bed Kristina made for them and their mother. Unfortunately the sixth pup was stillborn. They delighted in the new arrival of the pups like parents might dote on a newborn babe. Henry watched Kristina fuss over the pups. Just as she had noticed Henry receive the ball from Adoc, he saw her in a very similar light. She glowed, and it was a first for him. All things were good as Henry saw them except one thing and the pups made that one thing heavy on his heart.

Henry thought about the monument they'd be erecting for Old Ben. He was a bit annoyed with the head stone engraver. Francis' last words haunted him a bit. He figured that he'd make another call to the engraver the following day. In his thinking, *A Perfect Promise* might have been the reality Kristina wanted and desired. It was his also, but the sanctification or blessing of it all was staked upon Old Ben's sacrifice. In the glory of welcoming Old Ben's legacy it was a detail that Henry considered silently. He saw no point in tainting the celebration that was so agreeable to Kristina. They delighted in their new family as the day moved along. Henry felt as though he was on the verge of some type of discovery. He couldn't get his head around the totality of it, but he was certain that a new enlightening would be upon him soon.

Three days after the pups were born and some discussions on the phone a truck rolled up the driveway at *A Perfect Promise*. The cargo on board was a large obelisk ten feet in length. The base of the piece contained the engraving: *Victory over Lost Purpose* On the column was an image of Old Ben and just under it was engraved the name, *Old Ben.*

Henry walked to where the battle ensued between Old Ben and the wolf. He guided the driver to a spot he marked off previously. As the driver manned the crane Henry showed him where to place the obelisk. After the piece was set to its new home the driver returned to the truck and made his way off the property. The delivery of the monument had been seen to and Henry felt closer to the enlightenment that evaded him. He looked upon the piece from different angles. Maybe he thought wisdom could be gleaned from different perspectives. He was satisfied now with the sanctification of *A Perfect Promise.*

He returned to the porch walking across the field. Kristina saw Henry's return knowing that he carried a frustration. In their growth of the months and their coming to know each other, she became more aware of Henry's need to realize something she couldn't possibly tell him. It was the sort of thing that had to be self-realized. She came to know Henry from the days when he tossed Adoc a stick. She knew his growth would bring him to the moments of trouble he wrestled with in his thinking.

When he arrived she asked, "How does the monument fit?"

He responded, "Fits just fine. I'm happy and satisfied for it having a new home."

She waited while Henry tried to conceal his frustration. "That's good that you're satisfied, but there is something else isn't there?"

He looked at her with surprise. "Yes I guess there is, I'm just not sure what it is."

Kristina nudged him to the inevitable truth awaiting him. "Why don't you and your silly dog go figure it out? Don't forget to take that ball."

Henry turned to Adoc and invited him to toss the ball. The two left to honor the placement of the monument commemorating Old Ben's intervention.

Kristina watched the Man and the Dog tossing the Ball in the field along with Old Ben's pups. They watched as Henry figured out that life wasn't free, it came from sacrifice and all debt was paid by blood of the selfless. Henry recalled the time he and Adoc met. His intention at the time was his shame. At that time, in that place; he threw away the guilt of his contemplations. He began enjoying the life he had with his savior; a dog named Adoc. He had Adoc because of the noble actions of Old Ben. That afternoon he tossed the ball to his pal Adoc. They glorified life nearly wasted, but only by the redemption of sacrifice. That is how a Man, a Dog and A Ball found perfection of heaven where lost purpose was defeated at a place know as *A Perfect Promise.*